To Mom,
To add to your
John Jakes-esque
books. ☺ I love
you _so_ so much!
Happy Mothers Day!
Love,
Elizabeth

UNFORGOTTEN

UNFORGOTTEN

A NOVEL

D. J. MEADOR

PELICAN PUBLISHING COMPANY

Gretna 1998

*The word "Pelican" and the depiction of a pelican are
trademarks of Pelican Publishing Company, Inc., and are
registered in the U.S. Patent and Trademark Office.*

Library of Congress Cataloging-in-Publication Data

Meador, Daniel John.
　Unforgotten : a novel / D. J. Meador.
　　　cm.
　ISBN 1-56554-349-1 (alk. paper)
　I. Title.
　PS3563.E1687U54　1998
　813'.54—dc21　　　　　　　　　　　　　　　　98-6070
　　　　　　　　　　　　　　　　　　　　　　　　　　　CIP

Manufactured in the United States of America

Published by Pelican Publishing Company, Inc.
1000 Burmaster Street, Gretna, Louisiana 70053

*To the memory
of those Americans who served
in Korea under the
United Nations Command,
1950-53,
and for whom
there was no homecoming:*

*54,246 dead
8,177 missing*

I call heaven and earth to witness against you this day, that I have set before you life and death, blessing and curse.

Deut. 30:19

To me the issues are clear. It is not a question of this or that Korean town or village. Real estate is here incidental. It is not restricted to the issue of freedom for our South Korean allies whose fidelity and valor under the severest stresses of battle we recognize, though that freedom is a symbol of the wider issues and included among them.

The real issues are whether the power of western civilization as God has permitted it to flower in our own beloved land shall defy and defeat communism, whether the rule of men who shoot their prisoners, enslave their citizens, and deride the dignity of men shall displace the rule of those to whom the individual and his individual rights are sacred, whether we are to survive with God's hand to guide and lead us or to perish in the dead existence of a Godless world.

Gen. Matthew B. Ridgeway
Commander in Chief
United Nations Command
Korea, 1951

Contents

Prologue

JOHN WINSTON SAT in his high-backed, upholstered chair pondering a front-page item in the morning's *Birmingham Post-Herald*. The headline read: "Former State Bar President Slated for Federal Appeals Court." He was perturbed and perplexed. How did the paper know of this?

The article reported that John Winston, well-known local lawyer and decorated Korean War veteran, long active in civic and charitable affairs, was under consideration for appointment to a seat on the U.S. Court of Appeals. According to a source who asked not to be identified, Winston was a compromise choice, the state's senators and the White House having been unable to agree on their preferred prospects.

He laid the paper on his desk, swiveled the chair around, and gazed into the distance. From his twelfth-floor office window in downtown Birmingham, he had a view of the city's southern horizon formed by the crest of Red Mountain. It was not much of a mountain at all, but a high ridge running east and west, gashed at one point by the expressway and punctuated on its western skyline by the massive iron statue of Vulcan, symbol of this city of coal, iron, and steel. The early morning haze had not yet dissipated, and rush-hour traffic was still streaming over the mountain into the city.

The call from the Justice Department had come a week earlier, catching him by surprise. It was from Associate Attorney General

Roger Evans, the department's man on judicial nominations. The two had never met. After introducing himself and exchanging a few pleasantries, Evans explained that he was calling about the vacancy on the Eleventh Circuit. "A lot of politics has gotten mixed up in this nomination. At the moment the senators and the White House are at loggerheads." He spoke with a slight air of exasperation.

"I read something about it in the paper a while back."

"Well, we think we have the ideal solution. It's you."

He was stunned. All he could say was: "Me? Are you serious?" Years ago he thought a judgeship to be the pinnacle of a legal career, and he hoped that one day he would go on the bench, the culminating step in his professional life. But as time passed he had reluctantly given up that ambition, thinking that his age and lack of active political involvement ruled him out. Now this call out of the blue instantly revived that interest, reopening a possibility he assumed lost forever.

"Absolutely. However, I have to say that this is purely an informal, preliminary inquiry to find out whether you're willing to be considered. If you understand anything about Washington, you know I can't guarantee it."

"I'm not the political type."

"That's the beauty of your case. We have reason to think that if we come up with an absolutely unimpeachable lawyer with strong professional standing, a man not tangled up in politics, we can put him over. After all, what we're mainly interested in is getting a good judge on the bench."

"Well, I certainly appreciate the compliment. Never occurred to me I'd be considered. These appointments are usually politically related."

"Usually, but not always. As I said, we think you're the man for this slot. If you give us the green light, we'll initiate the usual FBI investigation."

"I'm sixty-three. Doesn't that put me out of the running?"

"If your medical exam doesn't show any problems, there shouldn't be any difficulty."

"Can I have overnight to think about it?"

"Oh, sure. I should add that we've got to run this past the White House and the senators, but I need your consent before going forward."

He had spent a restless night, too stirred up by the call to sleep. He was a trial lawyer, with a love for the active arena. An appellate judgeship would be a different way of life—a quieter, more contemplative existence, reclusive, even monastic by comparison. But the appellate bench had its powerful attractions, especially its intellectual challenge and the opportunity it presented to help shape the law, to participate in the centuries-old common law process through which the law evolved and was adapted to the circumstances of the times. Moreover, he could see the day coming when trial work would be a chore. Many trial lawyers burned out by their mid-sixties. Then, too, with Sally gone, he was sensing the need for a change of pace and setting. He had little difficulty in deciding before the night was over that this unexpected opportunity for which he had long ago yearned could not be passed up. By the time he was in the kitchen fixing coffee, he was positively enthusiastic over the prospect.

The medical exam should give no difficulty. He was in excellent health—six feet tall, 170 pounds, kept trim by tennis twice a week.

When John called Evans back, trying not to seem too eager, and said he could proceed, Evans said, "Great. Now keep this strictly under your hat until we get all our ducks in a row. I'll be back in touch."

The more he mused about a judgeship, the more it seemed to be the thing for him to do. He was at the height of his professional and civic life, as evidenced by the documents adorning his office wall: his law school diploma and certificates of all kinds—bar admissions, memberships in numerous legal and civic groups, and plaques of appreciation from the Boy Scouts, the Red Cross, and a half-dozen other worthy organizations. Appointment to the bench began to take on the aura of a natural next step. Indeed, it now seemed to be not only a welcome opportunity but one he actually needed, something that would fill a void and inner yearning, something that he had to have.

The buzzer on his desk sounded. "Call for you from the TV station."

He hesitated. "Tell them I'm tied up. And hold all calls until after the Investors Bank deposition."

"Come in," he said, responding to a knock at the door.

A stoutly built man of medium height pushed open the door. He

was Joseph Long, who, with John and Richard Holiday, had formed
the law firm of Winston, Long, and Holiday. The three had been
together in one of the city's large firms until they left to launch their
own practice. Long, the firm's toughest litigator, had worked his way
through the state law school and was brusque in manner and
speech. Dick Holiday, the youngest, was a mild-mannered graduate
of the University of Virginia Law School, and, in contrast to his partners, rarely went into the courtroom; the library was his natural
habitat.

"I thought this judgeship business was supposed to be confidential," Long said, holding out a copy of the newspaper. He was in shirt-
sleeves with his collar unbuttoned and tie loosened, suggesting that
although the day was young, he had already been at work for some
time.

"Joe, you're right," Winston said sheepishly. "Other than the associate attorney general, you and Dick are the only human beings I've
discussed it with. I haven't the slightest idea where the paper picked
this up."

Long plopped down in a chair facing the desk. "It isn't good.
Clients get nervous. They think you're leaving, and the next thing
you know they're looking for another firm."

"I know. I know. It's just too bad. Especially since I may never be
offered the nomination. All I've had is a tentative telephone conversation."

"I have mixed feelings about it. It's a great tribute and you'll make
a fine judge. They need more like you. But it's a blow. Dick and I
can carry on, of course, and I don't think the ship would sink. But it's
going to be a big loss."

They talked on about the pros and cons of the move. He would
take a cut in income, but he had never aspired to be wealthy.

"Without Sally, things get pretty lonesome around the house,"
Winston said. "This might be a good tonic. I hate to leave you and
Dick. We've had some fine times together. But I have to say in all hon-
esty that I've decided I should take this judgeship. I've realized it's
something I really want."

"I'm sure this last year has been rough. If you were on the court,
you'd have a week every month on the road. Atlanta and Miami
could be interesting. It may be the best thing for you now, and I don't

want to throw cold water on it. But let's hope we don't get any more news coverage until it's all set."

"I'm maintaining a tight 'no comment' position. We can't do much else." Winston rose, picking up some papers on his desk. "Now I've got to get to a deposition."

Back in his office after the deposition, he was munching a sandwich when the receptionist came in. "The phone's been ringing all morning. There must be three dozen messages here. They all say about the same thing: 'Congratulations!'" She handed him a stack of pink telephone message slips.

"Thanks," he said. "From now on, I'll probably take most of the calls."

He peeled off the slips one by one, as though dealing from a deck of cards. Some calls were from old friends, some from longtime acquaintances, other lawyers he hardly knew, already currying favor with a potential judge. He was reassured that the idea of his becoming a federal appellate judge not only didn't seem ridiculous to others but was drawing a favorable response. "The court is where you belong." "At last we're getting a real judge instead of a politician." He leaned back in his chair, savoring increasingly the thought of donning the black robe and taking on a whole new line of legal work. Yes, there would be Judge Winston, sitting on the high bench, guardian of the rule of law.

The buzzer sounded. "A woman is on the line," the receptionist said. "At least I think it's a woman. She won't give her name, but says it's urgent she speak to you."

The message was not unusual. Troubled clients and potential clients were sometimes so concerned about confidentiality that they would not reveal their identity to anyone else. "All right. Put her on."

The voice was husky, slow, deliberate, almost slurred, neither young nor old. It was hard to tell whether it belonged to a male or a female. "Are you the John Winston they're talking about for the federal court?"

"Well," he said, "that's what the newspaper says."

"Then I want to ask you a question."

There was a pause. She—he now thought it was a woman—seemed to be waiting for some response.

"What is it?"

"Were you in Korea in 1951?"

He sat up straight as though an alert had been signaled to every part of his body. After a moment's hesitation, he said, "May I ask who's calling?"

"Doesn't matter. What matters is whether you were in the army in Korea in 1951."

"What difference does that make? Why do you want to know?" A touch of anxiety was in his voice.

"It's very important when you're talking about being a federal judge."

"I can't talk with someone who will not identify herself."

"Do you remember Hill 1080?"

A new surge of anxiety rose within him. His stomach tightened.

"Where are you? Are you in Birmingham?" He made an effort to keep his voice low and calm.

"I know what happened there—know what you did."

He closed his eyes, gripping the telephone, his knuckles gone white.

"I cannot continue this conversation. If you want to come to my office, I'll see you. Or we could meet somewhere else."

"If you get nominated, I'll tell people, tell the senators, tell 'em about what you did at Hill 1080." She hung up.

He slowly put down the phone, his mind in turmoil. He swiveled in his chair and looked out the window, past the distant cluster of tall buildings marking the medical center. Beyond them, lost in the urban maze, was Five Points, and beyond that, over the mountain, was Shades Valley. Between there and downtown, where he now sat, he had passed the last thirty-five years of his life. A small-town boy at heart, he had never felt altogether at home in this brash new city. But it was here that he had made his mark in the legal profession.

Through all those years, the Korean War had been a mere foot-note in his professional life, as it had been for the whole country. Occasionally when introduced at events, someone mentioned, to his embarrassment, his outstanding war record. But there had been times—long stretches of time—when the press of law practice and family life crowded out the memories. As the years passed he, like everyone else, had largely forgotten the war. But the tangible reminders were always there: the faded scar along the right side of his stomach, the ridge of scar tissue above his right ear. And Hill 1080 flickered from time to time in his consciousness, like distant lightning on a summer night. He had kept Hill 1080 an absolute secret, had tried to suppress it, had sworn to himself never to divulge what had happened there to anyone.

He tried to think calmly. This was hardly just a crank call. Her information was too specific. Who could she possibly be? She could only have learned of the possible judgeship from the newspaper. Did that mean she had to be in Birmingham? No, the same story could have run in other papers in the Eleventh Circuit. That opened up all of Alabama, Georgia, and Florida. If only he could get to her, he could find out what she knew and where she got her information. Maybe he could somehow mollify her.

"Do you remember Hill 1080?" she had asked. A sick laugh escaped his lips. Remember? How in God's name could he forget? Yes, and Hill 969 and 274 and all the other everlasting ridges and valleys along the Chongchon and stretching on forever from the Soyang northward toward the Yalu, scarred and blasted slopes that had filled his years with intermittent nightmares.

He sat for a long while, staring at the far ridge line, oblivious to his surroundings. So here it is at last, he thought. Those events from decades ago and thousands of miles away were to rise up and smite him—a postponed judgment and day of reckoning. Could the dead past now deprive him of this judgeship? Worse, he feared. He sat in agonized frustration, unable to think of any way to locate this mystery caller and unable to talk with anyone about it.

He could, of course, keep the past buried by giving up the judgeship, by issuing a public statement that he was not interested in being considered. Everyone would understand that. But he couldn't bring himself to take that step. He wanted that judgeship too much.

How could it be that those painful events on a remote Asian peninsula could now threaten his career? It was all so far in the past . . . such a very long time ago . . .

PART ONE
The Remberton Progress

Chapter 1

THE CLATTERING OF THE ANTIQUATED TYPEWRITER stopped. Herbert Winston leaned back from his vigorous two-fingered punching and reached for the pack of Camels on his desk. He examined his handiwork, rolling the paper up to get a better look at the last couple of lines, and fumbled for a kitchen match in a box nestled among an unruly pile of papers.

Herbert Winston, editor of the *Remberton Progress*, was fifty-five years old, stood just under six feet, and was slightly overweight. A shock of graying brown hair topped his large head and kindly basset-hound face. The midafternoon June heat had wilted his shirt—he had earlier hung his coat up on a rack in the corner—giving him a more disheveled appearance than usual.

"Well, son," he said in his slow, melodious voice, turning toward John Winston, who was seated at a desk some ten feet to his flank, "I think this story on the ribbon cutting at the glove factory will be our lead item next week." Fire sprang from the match as he pulled it along the side of the box. He lit a cigarette and exhaled a plume of smoke.

John looked up from the yellow legal pad on which he had been scribbling. "Yes, sir. That sounds fine. And what else did you have in mind?"

"Didn't you say you'd do a piece on the Fourth of July schedule?"

"Right. I plan to get to it on Monday. The Fourth is week after next." They both looked up at the poster-size L & N Railroad

19

calendar on the wall above them, showing all twelve months of the year 1950.

"What about that Baptist church revival?" Herbert asked.

"Dr. Revercomb said he'd have something in here by Tuesday."

It was Friday, the day on which planning for the next issue always began. Wednesday was press day, an afternoon and evening of flurried, sometimes frantic, activity. It was a point of considerable pride that for eighty-five years the *Remberton Progress* had missed its Thursday publication schedule only three times, each caused by a press breakdown.

Herbert Winston turned in his rotating captain's chair to face a woman seated across the room at a desk piled high with ledgers and papers. "Miss Effie, what about the news from the garden club and the DAR?"

Effie McCune was in her mid-forties, prim and professional looking, no beauty but not unattractive. She had gone to Birmingham after graduating from high school in Remberton, but returned a few years later, trailed by vague rumors of a short, failed marriage. Nobody ever knew exactly what had happened. For twenty years now she had been sitting at her desk here as general secretary and office manager. There had been occasional suitors—local bachelors and widowers—but nothing ever developed.

"They brought them in this morning," she said, walking over and handing several sheets of paper to the editor, who was taking a deep drag on his cigarette. "It just dawned on me," she added, smiling toward the younger Winston, "that this is John's first anniversary back here with us."

John looked at her with a pensive smile, careful not to show the doubts churning within him. He had come home a year ago, immediately after graduating from the University, to follow in the footsteps of his father and grandfather. It was preordained that he would one day succeed to the editorship. But he had long been uncertain about whether that was how he wanted to spend his life.

"I would say that it's been a mighty good year, too," Effie McCune continued. "Wouldn't you say so, Mr. Herbert?"

"I certainly would," Herbert said, in his slow-cadenced voice.

The three of them sat together in the large high-ceilinged room that housed the editorial and business office of the county's only newspaper. Filing cabinets and bookcases lined the walls between their desks. The three were separated from the small public area by only a waist-high counter running alongside Effie McCune's desk. The counter was next to the front door—a screened door this time of year—which opened directly onto the sidewalk. To this counter all manner of citizens came to report news (or gossip), place advertisements, pay subscription bills, order stationery and various printing jobs, and sometimes just to pass the time of day.

The office faced directly on Center Street, the town's main thoroughfare. On this cloudless summer afternoon, the sun beat down on the treeless sidewalk just outside the large open window and the screened door. In the far corner of the room an electric fan of airplane-propeller size droned on at full speed in a vain effort to overcome the ninety-five-degree temperature and humidity of similar magnitude. It gave a hint of a breeze to each of the occupants, but none its full effect. The saving grace was that the old building, built in the 1880s, had thick brick walls and high ceilings.

Rufus Scruggs came through a door from the rear. A wiry middle-aged man with metal-rimmed spectacles, he was the typesetter, press operator, and local sports writer. From neck to knees he was wrapped in a black, rubberlike apron. "Those A & P circulars are running now, and that's the last job for the week," he said, wiping black ink from his hands with a dirty towel.

"What about those Lions Club programs?" Herbert asked.

"They're all set up. I'll run 'em off on Monday." He probed for a moment under his apron. "Look's like I'm out of cigarettes. How about bumming a Camel?" Herbert passed him the pack.

"I declare, this is one hot day," Miss Effie exclaimed. "I'm going next door to get a Coke. Anybody else want one?" She stood and picked up her pocketbook. Perspiration glistened on her brow, and her cotton blouse was wet under the arms.

"Think I will," Rufus said, fishing out a nickel from beneath his apron.

He retreated to his domain in the rear. As he opened the door, the clanking of the press and a faint aroma of printer's ink came from the back. One of John's earliest memories was the sight and sound of the black mechanical monster. Its thin metallic claws shoved sheets of paper, one by one, into the yawning jaws. The monster brought down a great metal plate onto each sheet, then lifted it, revealing the paper covered with wet black print, then reached with its claws to remove that sheet, making way for the next, all within the blink of an eye and accompanied by awesome sounds.

Thelma Parker breezed into the office and sat down at a spare typewriter. The society page was in her hands. A gregarious, hard-drinking, heavy-smoking widow, Thelma worked part-time, but she took it to be her full-time responsibility to know what was going on among the eight thousand souls in town, or at least among the nearly two-thirds of them who were white, or, more precisely, among those few she viewed as being in her social set. John didn't particularly care for her, but she treated him as her confidant, letting him know her true feelings about the occasions she covered.

"What did you think of the Hankins wedding?" she asked him in her typically confidential tone.

"It was quite an affair," he responded, noncommittally.

She rolled her eyes. "Overdone. Lucy's usual garish effort to keep up." She lit a cigarette and began typing furiously.

John's eyes drifted above her to the large, ornately framed, turn-of-the-century photograph of his grandfather, the paper's founder, the first John Winston. All his life John had heard stories of this formidable figure who had died in 1930. He had gone to Virginia in 1862 as an officer in the Fifth Alabama Infantry, seen heavy fighting from the Seven Days onward, been wounded at Gettysburg, and emerged with the rank of major. The title stuck, and he had been known ever after as simply "the Major." Having little else to do after the war, he started the newspaper as a way to promote progress in the defeated region. The motto he bestowed on the paper—still displayed across the top of the front page—was "The progress of Remberton is the business of the *Remberton Progress*."

John had also been told much over the years about the man in the large, faded photograph hanging next to the Major. He was the district's one-time congressman, Hilary Herbert, greatly admired by the Major, former colonel, CSA, and secretary of the navy under Grover Cleveland. It was for him that John's father was named, the only child of the Major's late-life marriage.

The screened door from the sidewalk emitted its opening and closing squeaks. "Afternoon, Mr. Herbert." The speaker was a tall black man standing at the counter. He gave an appropriate nod in the editor's direction. He was well known to them, but even a stranger would have recognized from the black suit and tie that he had one of three occupations: preacher, schoolteacher, or undertaker.

"Howdy, Reverend," Herbert said, half-swiveling in his chair. "What can we do for you today?"

"The congregation at the AME Zion Church wants to have a fundraising drive." He spoke with an exaggerated emphasis, attentive to correct grammar and taking pains to enunciate every syllable properly. "They think it would be a great help if we could get a little publicity in the paper."

"What do they plan to do with the money?" Herbert asked goodnaturedly.

"They want to fix the roof. Rain is coming in. And they want to get some more pews. It's a big project, but they think they can do it with the Lord's help."

"But you think the Lord needs a little help from the *Progress*?"

"Yes, sir. Sometimes the Lord needs all the help He can get." They both chuckled.

"Let's see what you've got there." The preacher walked around the counter and handed Herbert a sheet of paper. He retreated to the public side of the counter as Herbert perused it. "Well," Herbert said after a moment, "I think we can run this."

"That would be mighty fine, Mr. Herbert, and we thank you."

John, ignoring this exchange, was immersed in the *Birmingham News*. The day's edition had just been dropped off by a frazzled youth whose job was to pick up the batch of fifty copies thrown off the afternoon Greyhound bus and distribute them by bicycle to the town's subscribers. Reading papers from elsewhere, particularly the *Washington Post*, was John's favorite part of the job. Herbert had decided to subscribe to the *Post* after his 1939 trip with a delegation of Alabama editors for a meeting with President Roosevelt, reasoning that it was increasingly important to keep up with events in the nation's capital.

During his high school years when the war was in progress, John had avidly followed the newspapers' map drawings with heavy black arrows showing the back and forth movement of armies. The disastrous American defeat on Bataan and Corregidor had left an indelible impression on him. The United States had been humiliated, a humiliation heaped upon the Pearl Harbor humiliation. He anxiously watched the newspaper arrows move back northward from Australia. Somewhere along the way Gen. Douglas MacArthur entered his pantheon of heroes. MacArthur's sonorous radio voice and his command of the English language gripped John: "I do not know the dignity of their birth, but I do know the glory of their death."

In that growing-up time, John had been left in no doubt about the expectations for his future. He would often hear family friends say to his father: "Herbert, you gonna make a newspaper man out of that boy?"

"Well, we hope so," his father would say, usually patting him fondly on the back.

Secretly, though, John was setting his mind on West Point. Tales of his grandfather's experiences and the military exploits he was reading about daily had stirred his imagination. "If only the war will last long enough for me to get in it," he told himself. But by the time he graduated from high school, the war had ended and the men were coming home; demobilization was in the air.

He had gone to see his mother's cousin, Col. Noble Shepperson, the town's only living West Point graduate, just back from the European theater and resuming his law practice. "No," said the colonel, in his parade-ground voice, "I don't see a lot of future in the military right now. The politicians are hell-bent on cutting back, and I suspect the taxpayers are too."

"But you went to West Point in peacetime," John said. "The last war was over."

"Yes, and I got out. In the twenties there didn't seem to be much future . . . same as now."

"Then look what happened."

Colonel Shepperson laughed. "You're right. If I'd stayed in, I'd probably have come home now wearing stars instead of an eagle. But I don't think we're going to see another big one in your time. Remember, we've got the atom bomb, and nobody wants to take that on."

So the West Point dream faded, and John followed his forebears to the University of Alabama. He took journalism courses, but he found himself more excited by diplomatic history and post-war international affairs. The founding of the United Nations, the Marshall Plan, the Berlin Airlift, and the darkening shadow of communism all gripped his interest. He joined the ROTC, graduating with a second lieutenant's commission in the infantry reserve.

Settled now at a desk in the *Progress* office, John often contemplated the sharp, academic visage of Woodrow Wilson, whose photograph hung above a bookcase across the office. He was one of the Major's heroes, and he had come to be one of John's. He was moved by Wilson's dream of a League of Nations. Because it failed, the Second World War came. The U.N., John thought, was a delayed fulfillment of Wilson's vision. The subject had become his chief interest in his senior year, and he had written a paper about the U.N. Charter's provisions on collective security against armed aggression.

Those interests led him into daydreaming of far-off places and exciting global adventures. He applied for a Rhodes scholarship and was selected at the state level but failed to make it in the regional competition in New Orleans. Then he thought of applying for the Foreign Service. He imagined himself in a pith helmet in Nairobi monitoring some local crisis, or, better still, as a black-suited aide to the ambassador in Bonn, sitting in on tense negotiations with the Soviets over the Berlin air corridors.

His parents were unaware of these musings, all the while assuming, as he well knew, that he would come home to take his place in the line of succession for the editorship of the *Remberton Progress*. And in the end that is what he did, partly out of a sense of obligation to family and place and partly because there was no other clear option. But inwardly he had never been satisfied.

Having come home, though, he tried to enliven the paper with fresh ideas. If I'm going to be there, he thought, I want to jazz it up a little. The idea that excited him most was the notion of beginning a regular column on Washington political news. A fellow journalism student at the University of Alabama, Jack Thompson, had just taken a staff job on a Senate committee, perfectly positioned, John thought, to report from Capitol Hill. But Herbert had been reluctant.

"We can't afford to get into controversial matters," he said. "This paper is respected and serves the community well because we report on what is going on here and avoid upsetting folks over politics."

John smiled to himself at this last statement. The most obvious thing about the *Remberton Progress* was that it did not in fact report all that was really going on in Remberton. It reported only the sunny side—business and agricultural successes, achievements of its citizens and youth, marriages, births, and uplifting activities in general. Of the darker side of life there was no hint. Business failures, wayward children, alcoholism, marital discord, adultery, and the whole range of mankind's shortcomings found no place in its pages. The one sad aspect of the human condition that was included was death—described with appropriate dignity, but the cause never mentioned. Reporting the cause might require the paper to use the dreaded word "cancer," or worse, "suicide."

Herbert finally agreed, however, to give the Washington column a try, stressing that their "Washington correspondent" be instructed to keep his articles nonpartisan and making no advance commitment to publish any piece. So John was eagerly awaiting Thompson's first column, which was to deal with the Trumans' life in Blair House, where they were living while the White House was being renovated.

On this sultry June afternoon, father and son sat at their desks, each lost in his own work and thoughts. The afternoon heat had stilled activity on Center Street. The droning electric fan in the corner had a mesmerizing effect. The clock in the courthouse tower two blocks up the street struck three.

Effie McCune, red-faced and perspiring, came in through the front door. She carried two bottles of Coca-Cola, dripping wet from the drink box in Ratcher's Grocery next door. "Mr. Will says to remind you of the VFW meeting Monday night," she told Herbert.

"I haven't forgotten it," Herbert said in a resigned tone. John had heard him remark that most veterans organizations were mainly a bunch of ex-GIs looking for a place to take a drink in a dry town. Having been no closer to the Germans in 1918 than howitzer range, he did not make much of his army days. But John had often asked him about his experiences in France, noting with a little envy the photograph from that grand adventure hanging above the desk. Standing with an artillery battalion staff at Chateau-Thierry with the River Marne in the background was the trim, young Lt. Hilary

Herbert Winston, in high-top leather boots and Sam Browne belt, contrasting sharply with the middle-aged, overweight editor now sitting here. He had occasionally reminded John, with a wry smile and twinkle in his eyes, that they'd been there to make the world safe for democracy, not the least noble of man's works on this earth.

The photograph was one of many strung along the wall above the editorial desks, constant reminders to John of his heritage. Several were shots taken at various state press association meetings. The Major and Herbert were there shaking hands with the state president at the 1923 meeting when the *Progress* won the award for best weekly in the state. In another, the governor, the chief justice, and the Major were wielding trowels at the laying of the cornerstone for the new courthouse in 1900. Then there was FDR at his desk in the Oval Office surrounded by Alabama editors. Herbert was standing just behind the president's right shoulder. One of John's favorites was a three-generation shot showing him with his father and grandfather on the latter's ninety-second birthday. John, then two years old, was perched on the counter in this very office, between Herbert and the Major.

The screened door opened and closed. "Well, Mattie, how you doing this afternoon?" Herbert was addressing a thin elderly woman who had just appeared from the street. She wore a wide-brimmed hat of uncertain material and was vigorously fanning herself with a cardboard fan bearing a funeral parlor advertisement on one side and a picture of cut flowers on the other.

"They don't get much hotter than this," she said, her nostrils dilating like the gills of a fish just pulled from the water. Her face was flushed red.

"Maybe we'll have a thunderstorm this evening to break it off," Herbert said.

"My tomatoes are coming in so fast I don't know what to do with them. I thought you all might like some for the weekend."

"You know there's nothing I like better than good, blood red tomatoes."

"That's what these are. I've got a peck out here in the car if you'd like them."

"John," Herbert said, turning to his son, who had been ignoring the conversation, "see if Booker is back there and get him to bring in the tomatoes."

A few minutes later Booker Jackson, the janitor and general utility man, heaved a large cardboard box filled with tomatoes up on the counter. They called Rufus Scruggs out of the back, and they all divided them, with profuse thanks to Mattie.

"Daddy," John said, when Mattie departed and normalcy returned to the little journalistic beehive, "you remember I mentioned I'd like to leave a little early today. A crowd's going down to the coast, and we want to get started before too late."

"I guess you did say something about that. Weren't y'all just down there?"

"Not since April. We couldn't get everybody together until now."

"Where to this time?"

"The Simmons' place at Mary Esther." John stood up, putting papers away in a drawer. The courthouse clock announced the hour of four.

"That's mighty good of Bart and Lucille to let you young folks take over their place again," Herbert said, lighting a cigarette and watching his son close up shop for the weekend.

"They might as well. They don't use it much themselves. Anyway, we clean it up for them."

"OK. Have a good time, but be careful. I'm always reading about some kind of accident down there."

"I'm going to run by the house first. Bartow is picking me up in a little bit."

"Tell your mother I'll be along around five."

John headed around the counter toward the front door. "See y'all Monday." He left Effie McCune sorting her invoices and his father looking dubious, as he always did about his son's weekend ventures.

Chapter 2

JOHN PULLED HIS CHEVROLET AROUND to the back of the house and stopped next to the garage. The house, at 53 Taylor Street and built in the 1850s by an earlier Winston, was in the oldest section of town. The streets there were named for the presidents popular in the region when the town was laid out: Jackson, Polk, Taylor, and Van Buren.

John bounded up the steps, across the back porch, and into the hall that ran through from front to rear. Despite the heat of the day, the two-story solid brick structure with twelve-foot ceilings remained cool inside. He took the main stairway two steps at a time and went along the upstairs hall to his room.

He felt a rising sense of anticipation. It had been two months since he had been away from the house, the office, and the town. All of a sudden now he felt released, a momentary freedom, something akin, he imagined, to the feeling of a prisoner being let out on parole for a few days.

From a closet he extracted a small suitcase and began throwing various items into it: bathing suit, Bermuda shorts, shirts, underwear, toilet articles, and a camera. Running his hand under pajamas in the bottom dresser drawer, he pulled out a fifth of Early Times encased in a brown paper bag. He was just closing the suitcase when he heard his mother's voice.

"John, is that you?"

"Yes'm, I'm getting ready to go."

His mother appeared in the doorway, a middle-aged woman of medium height and build, with a soft, roundish face and brown, graying hair pulled back softly into a bun.

"Are you going in your car?" she asked.

"No'm, Bartow's driving."

"Who are you taking, if I may ask?"

He broke into an embarrassed grin. "Jeanie Harris."

"Well," his mother said, feigning surprise, "that's a new direction, isn't it? I thought she and Buster were going together."

"That's all off. They haven't had a date since she was home for spring vacation."

She wanted to know who else was going. He rattled off their names, all of whom were well known to her, the whole group having grown up together in Remberton. She listened, not with an altogether disapproving look but with an air of concern about the propriety of this unchaperoned junket to the Gulf Coast. John and his friends were aware of parental suspicions about drinking on these outings and, more darkly, anxiety about the possibility of sexual activity. But the group nature of the venture gave it a cover of respectability sufficient to mollify the parents, considering that these children were, after all, college age or older and parental control had long been eroded. His mother went downstairs, and he ripped off his office clothes and slipped on a pair of khaki pants, a casual short-sleeved shirt, and a pair of loafers.

He looked around the room to see whether there was anything else he wanted to take. He had grown up in this room and had never known another until he left for the University. It was large and pleasant, with tall windows overlooking a giant magnolia and some oak trees in the backyard. The walls and mantel were adorned with evidences of all the steps in his progress from childhood to the present: Boy Scout mementos, certificates of college organizations, and photos of family and gatherings of his friends at the beach. On his dresser was a large photograph of his older sister, Becky, in her wedding dress, with new husband, Frank Brandon. Two of his favorites were his Phi Beta Kappa certificate and the shot of him with the university track team, where he excelled at the 440. A color photograph of Douglas MacArthur, with crushed cap and corncob pipe, hung nearby, something he had cut out of a magazine and framed during the war. On the mantel stood three .50-caliber machine-gun bullets, souvenirs from ROTC camp. Next to them was one of his prized possessions, a daguerreotype of his grandfather in the gray uniform of a major, CSA, taken in Richmond near the end of the war.

He had fixed up a comfortable chair in the corner by a good reading lamp, and there he spent many evenings, especially during those months when most of his friends, male and female, were away at college or graduate school. The bookcase by the chair was stuffed with works on diplomatic and military history. Stacked on the floor was the four volume *R. E. Lee* by Douglas Southall Freeman, which he was reading at the moment, having checked the entire set out of the local library.

He was coming down the stairs as a car horn sounded twice out front. "Mother, here's Bartow."

She came into the hall from the parlor. "We'll be back Sunday night, maybe late," he said, kissing her on the cheek. "Daddy said he'd be home around five."

"Now you all be careful," she said, grasping his arm just above the elbow. "Do you understand?"

"We will," he said as he went out the front door, giving his routine response to her routine admonition.

Bartow Simmons was standing at the opened trunk of his father's Oldsmobile. In contrast to John's lean six-foot build, he was heavy-set and shorter, his fleshy face surmounted by blond, semi-crew-cut hair. He was home for a short break after his first year in medical school at Vanderbilt.

"Let's put all our stuff back here so we'll have more room in the car," Bartow said. "I've got a case of Pabst cooling in the back seat."

It took them half an hour to collect their dates, Jeanie Harris and Sally Young. Neither girl had been quite ready when they arrived at each house. Finally, though, they were passing the cotton mill, the last vestige of town before hitting the highway south.

"Here's the opener," Bartow said, passing the sharp-pointed metal object back to John. "Let's crack a cool one."

"It's about that time," John said, fishing a can out of the ice chest. It gave off a slight hiss and a beery spray as the opener pierced its top. John passed it up front and proceeded to open three more.

Now they could all relax. Remberton was falling behind, and

ahead, a little over two hours away, lay Fort Walton and Mary Esther, water and sand, boat and water skis, and two long delicious summer nights of irresponsibility.

"You remember the last time. A case didn't quite get us there," Bartow said.

"Right," John said, "but we had six people. This ought to do it this time."

In the front seat beside Bartow was Sally Young. Her black, wavy hair cut short, expressive dark eyes, and sensuous mouth led John, like others in Remberton, to consider her exotic. She had an uncommonly good figure for one who was so thin. Her parents had sent her off to Sweet Briar, where she had stayed the mandatory two years before transferring to the University at Tuscaloosa. She had a sharp tongue and a reputation for being something of a hot date. She had made a play for John from time to time, giving him her special blinking-eye treatment and holding him on the dance floor more tightly than necessary. Although he considered her the brightest gal in the group—and he had to acknowledge an undeniable sexual attraction—he had been put off by her sarcastic style.

Jeanie Harris was more to his liking. She came from one of the town's oldest families, whose fortunes had been depleted but had been rejuvenated miraculously by the happenstance that her great uncle had gone west, made a huge amount of money, and then died unwed and childless. This turned out to be especially fortunate for her father, Ben Harris, who had neither talent nor inclination for business or any other gainful occupation. A Sewanee graduate with a zeal for history and literature, he had the finest private library in Remberton. Among the older generation around town, John found him to be the most interesting.

He was not sure whether it was those books and his conversations with Ben Harris that attracted him to that house or whether it was Jeanie. She sat beside him now, closer than usual because of the ice chest accompanying them on the back seat. He admired her bright, tan, boyish face, framed by short honey-blond hair. She ran a bit to the chubby side and lacked Sally's sensuality, but overall she radiated a cuddly wholesomeness that appealed to him.

As they reached the outskirts of Andalusia, John cracked another beer for himself and Bartow and Sally. Jeanie was still nursing the first.

"I'll tell you," Bartow exclaimed after taking a long swallow, "it's mighty good to get away from those cadavers."

"When do you think the others will get down?" Sally asked. She sat, as was her habit, sideways in the front seat, with her back to the car door so she could keep the backseat passengers in view.

"Skip said he couldn't leave until six, so I guess they'll be along around eight-thirty or nine," Bartow said.

In another hour Bartow pulled off at a Texaco filling station and parked to the side. The flat, uninteresting, sandy country of the Florida Panhandle, covered with scrub oak and pine, stretched out in all directions. They all got out and went to the rest rooms.

"They don't have Chesterfields," Bartow said, as he came toward the car from the station. "Lucky Strikes will have to do." He peeled away the top of the pack and shook a cigarette halfway out, extending the pack toward Sally.

She took one and said, "That's fine with me." Bartow flicked his metal lighter into flame and lit them both up. She handled her cigarette in a way John thought she had copied from movie stars.

John leaned inside the back door of the car and pulled fresh cans of Pabst from the ice chest. He opened Sally's third, Jeanie's second, and the fourth for himself and Bartow.

They stood around the car, sipping beer and talking. "John, when is the *Progress* going to start printing some real news?" Sally asked. She was good at jabs of that sort. He didn't care for them. This one was touchy because he tended to agree with it but couldn't publicly disagree with the paper's policy.

"What do you mean by real news?"

"Some of the lowdown around town that everybody knows about."

"If everybody knows about it, then there's no point in printing it."

"Don't you think it's important to give a well-rounded picture? If you give only the rosy side of life, aren't you being dishonest?"

Jeanie intervened. "Don't you think it's bad enough to have all that mess going on in the world? Do we really need to read about it?"

"Give me an example of something that should have been reported," John said.

"Oh my Lord," Sally said, waving her cigarette in a gesture of futility. "There're too many to mention. Anyway, I'd rather not get into names. We all know these folks and their problems."

"Mr. Herbert probably thinks the same way and that's why he doesn't print that stuff," Bartow said.

"John, you know I'm just pulling your leg. The *Progress* will always be the *Progress,*" Sally said.

"Let's get going," Bartow said. "I'd like to get there while it's still daylight."

Half an hour later they stopped at the pit barbecue place in Fort Walton and loaded up on barbecue, potato chips, and cole slaw for supper.

Driving westward, they reached the long strip of houses and cottages facing Santa Rosa Sound and known also by the odd name of Mary Esther. The entire strip was densely wooded with oaks draped in Spanish moss. Amidst these summer vacation places, built years earlier, John felt very much at home. He had been coming here with his family every summer since childhood. The houses were frame and rustic, some quite modest, others spacious and even imposing. Across the half-mile-wide sound was Santa Rosa Island, a shoestring of white sand beyond which was the unseen Gulf of Mexico.

They turned off the highway into a narrow dirt lane that ran for a long stretch under a canopy of moss hanging from the venerable oaks, pulled up to the back door of the Simmons' cottage, and all went in, passing by the kitchen into the large central room with a long eating table and many wicker chairs. They threw open the double doors to the screened porch. The evening breeze from the Gulf ruffled their hair. It carried a faint saltwater aroma and the far-off sound of surf breaking on the beach.

"This is worth it all," John said, as they came out onto the porch and looked out across the sound, now bathed in fading sunlight.

Finally, the rest of the crowd arrived, and they all ate barbecue, drank more beer, and sat on the porch in the dark for a long while.

"The rest of you can stay here if you want to," Bartow announced, "but I'm going to call it quits. I want to be bright-eyed and bushy-tailed for tomorrow."

"I think I'll sit here for just a little bit longer and enjoy this breeze," John said.

The group drifted off to the sleeping rooms, one for the men and one for the women. In each there were six wooden frame single beds, simple and rustic, but comfortable. Bartow's parents' bedroom was in the rear.

John and Sally Young were left alone on the porch. She lit a cigarette and moved over to a chair next to him.

"How about another beer?" he asked.

"OK."

He was back in a couple of minutes with two icy cans. He handed her one and sat down.

They rocked in silence for a few moments, listening to the distant, mournful murmuring of the Gulf surf. Then he asked, "What do you think about teaching in Montgomery?"

"It's the only place I got an offer."

"Where'd you rather be?"

"Oh, maybe Atlanta or even Birmingham." They talked on about the English courses she would teach.

"I can see Remberton is going to be mighty quiet next year. Everybody's scattering."

"Can I tell you something?"

"Sure," he said, with a slight laugh, anticipating one of her typically sarcastic remarks.

"I think you ought to get out of Remberton," she said seriously. "You're wasting yourself there. You ought to go for the big time."

She had touched his innermost thoughts, saying what he had been reluctant to admit even to himself. He didn't care to bare his soul to her, so he simply said, "I'll give it some thought."

They sipped their beer in silence for a moment. Then he said, in a lighter tone, "Well, I'm not going to worry about it now. We're here to relax. Tell me about your trip to Europe." Sally was going on a European tour with her cousin later in thesummer.

She described the itinerary—London, Paris, Frankfurt, Brussels. They talked on about what she especially wanted to see and about some of her amusing experiences at the University during the past year. She did, he had to admit, have a keen sense of humor, sarcastic though much of it was, and he found himself laughing. He drained the last swallow from the can.

"Say," she said suddenly in a low voice, "why don't we take a swim? Have you ever been swimming at night?"

"Only at Scout camp."

"I've never been, but I'd like to try it. Come on, let's get on bathing suits."

"What about everybody else?"

"They're asleep."

John thought of Jeanie. After all, she was his date, not Sally. But he found her proposition exciting. His misgivings did not linger. "OK," he said in a hushed voice, "but we've got to be very quiet."

In a few minutes they were back on the porch in bathing suits. Easing open the screened door and shutting it softly, they took the path down to the water. The night was dark and black, without moon or stars.

"Hope we don't pick up any sandspurs," she said, taking his hand as they groped their way barefooted down the sandy slope. They reached the water's edge, where a small beach marked the swimming area. A slight breeze was blowing in from the Gulf. The water lapped quietly against the beach and the nearby pilings on the pier. Otherwise, the world was without sound. They waded out until they were waist deep.

"Doesn't it feel good!" she said. "Just right."

To John the water was cool. He shivered a bit, partly from the cooling sensation but partly from his excitement of being in the night black water with Sally Young beside him, both in nothing but bathing suits and with no one else in the world knowing of their midnight escapade.

Now with the faint illumination in the east from the lights of Fort Walton, he could make out her form next to him. Some ten yards farther out was a post sticking out of the water.

"Let's swim out there," she said.

They both plunged forward into the water and within a few strokes grabbed the post.

"Watch out for barnacles," John said. "Hang on. This is over our heads." Water dripped from their hair and faces.

They were close together now. He felt her bobbling against his side, the contours of her body revealed by her bathing suit.

"This night swimming is the thing, don't you think?" she said. She ran her arm around his waist.

John's heart was thumping. Their faces were almost touching. "Say," she whispered, "I've got an idea."

"What is it?"

"Let's try skinny dipping. I've always wanted to see how it feels."

For an instant he was speechless with both embarrassment and excitement. Rallying to overcome his shyness and appear a man of the world, he said, with a nervous laugh and mock seriousness, "Out here before God and everybody?"

"Everybody's asleep, and God's got other things to worry about."

He could hardly believe what was happening. A longtime fantasy was about to become reality—the fantasy of seeing Sally Young without any clothes on. Except it was so dark that he wouldn't see her. But that mattered little in light of the prospect of being next to a naked Sally Young and coming in contact with that voluptuous body.

"All right," he said, already squirming out of his trunks. She swished around in the water, hanging on to the post with one hand as she pulled her bathing suit down, finally working it off her feet. He took it and stuck it with his on top of the post.

"This is great," she exclaimed, in a hushed voice. "I feel so free!" They had moved a little away from the post, treading water.

John swam back to the post. He wanted to grab her and hold her, but she continued to splash around. Then she swam forward and grasped the post. Impulsively, he ran both his arms around her waist and pulled her hard against him. She lost her grip on the post, and they sank beneath the water. They instantly resurfaced, gasping.

"Hey, we don't want to drown," he said, sputtering and laughing a little, as one hand regained the post.

"I thought we were out here to take a swim."

"That's what we're doing," he said. He craved to see her. But what he felt was already more than he could have imagined in his wildest dreams. Never before had he been in the presence of an undressed woman, much less in contact with one—and Sally Young at that!

They held together for a long minute, each with a hand gripping the post. Underwater, their bodies slithered against each other, their legs intertwined. The water's buoyancy added a peculiar sensation. Their mouths came together in a long kiss, only the third time in his life John had kissed a girl.

"Maybe we better go in," she whispered, without conviction.

He started to protest, but his rational faculties took hold, and he said unenthusiastically, "I guess we should."

Disengaging themselves from their watery embrace, they splashed around awkwardly, struggling to pull their bathing suits back on.

Saturday was now fading into night. The sky was red in the west over Santa Rosa Sound. The powerboats had been berthed. The heat of the day had gone, and a steady breeze was blowing in from the Gulf. Water lapped gently against the wooden pilings of the Simmons' pier and the sides of the boat tied up in its covered slot, the propellers of its monstrous outboard motor hoisted clear of the water. The serenity of a June evening was settling over Mary Esther.

It had been a good, hot Gulf Coast day. In the morning they had gone to Tower Beach, romped in the clear aqua water, and lazed on towels on the sugar-white sand, plying themselves with suntan lotion. By the time they got through a case of beer and lunch back at the house, they were ready to flop down in the deep-cushioned wicker chairs on the wide expanse of screened porch.

As the intensity of the midday heat diminished, the crowd stirred back to life and collectively and desultorily decided that water skiing was the thing to do. For the next couple of hours they had one by one mounted the skis, some plunging headlong into the water as the boat leaped forward, but most getting up and making at least one wide loop into the main channel.

Now they were all gathered on the pier in the dying light of the already-set sun. All had showered. Most of their freshly scrubbed faces were overly red, and there were many pink, almost blistered, legs protruding from shorts. The smell of Noxzema was in the air. Perched on benches or stretched out on the pier's plank floor, they all had a drink—gin and tonic, scotch and water, or bourbon and something. It was the day's finest hour.

"Baby Sister, who was that gal I saw you talking to this morning at the casino? She looked mighty familiar." Bartow was addressing a doll-like figure whose name was Sara Carpenter, but nobody called her that.

"Cammie Baker from Demopolis. Her folks have a place at Destin. She says she's down here for a whole month."

"I think I've seen her around the Tri Delt House," chimed in Scott. "Does that figure?"

"Right," said Berta.

"Wasn't she dating somebody at the SAE House?" asked Bookie.

"That was Jim Deets from . . ." Berta trailed off. "Where was he from?"

"Huntsville," said Sally, with a hint of disgust. "We had a few dates, and she's welcome to him." She rolled her eyes.

All day John had tried to avoid Sally. He felt an awkward sense of embarrassment over last night's swimming venture. But he hadn't been able to avoid all eye contact with her, and there were moments when they exchanged sheepish smiles. He felt guilty over what he considered a disloyalty to Jeanie. On a weekend date, he thought, a man should stick to his own date. Looking now at the two women, he came back to what he had long thought, that Sally was an exciting, sexy date, a great party gal and lots of fun, but Jeanie was a more solid type, with sounder values, someone who would wear better in the long run. She was the type of girl mothers wanted their sons to marry. He knew he should stick with her. But the thrill of that nude swim and the feel of Sally's soft flesh against him lingered on, both disturbing and enticing, almost irresistible. He had spent much of the night in sleepless arousal, reliving it in his mind. The best thing to do, at least for the present, he concluded, was to try as best he could to put that little escapade out of his thoughts and concentrate on Jeanie.

John was troubled by something else: Sally's comment last night about leaving Remberton. Deep down, he realized he was coming more and more to that view. If only he had gotten the Rhodes scholarship, he would have had two or three years at Oxford. Or maybe he should have gone to West Point despite Noble Shepperson's discouragement.

It was not that he disliked Remberton or these people. On the contrary, he felt a deep-rooted attachment to the place and his lifelong friends. He felt close to them, but he wondered about being with them forever. In any case, it was unclear how many would come home for the long run, especially the most interesting ones.

In the peaceful glow of the sunset, ignoring the chatter around him, John's imagination—stimulated by Early Times—wandered to distant places. The turning of the earth that was bringing darkness to Santa Rosa Sound was at the same time bringing the first pale dawn of a new day to the far Pacific. The faint lightening of the sky would be moving ever westward, touching the Japanese Islands and moving on to the immense Asian land mass, from Siberia down through Manchuria and across the almost limitless expanse of China. There, beyond the International Date Line, it would now be Sunday morning.

"Hey, John," Berta said, "are you with us?"

"Uh, yes," he said, snapping out of his reverie. "I was just thinking about something I need to write for the paper."

"I guess journalists are never off duty," she said.

Skip Johnson stood up. "I'm going up for a refill. Anybody else interested?"

"Yep, think so," Bartow said, rising from a bench set against the front railing. "How about it, Miss Sally?" He shook her shoulder playfully.

"All right, but I think I've already got a buzz on."

They all headed toward the porch, several tilting their cups upward to drain the last watery swallow.

In the kitchen there was much clattering of ice as trays were emptied. The counter was crowded with assorted fifths and bottles of tonic, soda, ginger ale, and Coca-Cola.

"What time are we going to eat?"

"I'm not hungry yet."

"About another hour, I'd say."

"Where're we going?"

"Didn't we'd talk about Staff's?"

"We did, but we don't have to go there."

"Sounds fine to me."

"Right. They have the best soft-shell crab."

"Is that still OK with everybody?"

Drinks in hand, they drifted back out to the porch. John and Jeanie walked back down to the pier, their cups brimming with Early Times.

Music swelled from the porch—"In the Mood," an old Glenn Miller tune—accompanied by the scraping of chairs being pushed back to clear the floor for dancing. The record player and some of the records had weathered many summers, and the sound was scratchy, but good enough.

Out on the pier, John and Jeanie sat with their legs dangling over the water. Dusk deepened, but a thin line of red remained in the west. Far down the way, lights on the channel markers flickered. The low white line of sand dunes on the edge of Santa Rosa Island could still be seen. Water lapped quietly against the pilings and the boat. Music wafted down from the porch: "Gonna take a sentimental journey . . . Gonna set my heart at ease . . ."

"John, how do you feel about being back in Remberton?" Jeanie asked in a soft, low voice.

"What about being back?"

"Mainly your job at the paper and living at home."

There was that question again. He did not respond immediately. From the porch the vocalist belted out words with heightened zest: ". . . to renew old memories . . . Seven, that's the time we leave, at seven . . ."

Then he said hesitantly, "That's a hard question to answer. Daddy always counted on my coming back." He paused, aware that the bourbon had taken hold.

She interrupted: "What I'm asking is how you like it now that you're back?"

She sipped from her cup, and he followed suit, taking a larger gulp than he had intended. The music stopped. "Put on something faster." It was Baby Sister's voice, followed in a few seconds by "String of Pearls." They could see jitterbugging couples on the dimly lighted porch. They all danced with each other interchangeably.

While he had not wanted to talk about this with Sally, with Jeanie it was different. It was the difference between the two girls. He felt more comfortable with Jeanie, trusted her more. Her sympathetic tone of voice and her sincerity had touched him in a way that Sally's comments had not. He had a surge of affection for her. "Well," he said slowly, "I've never really talked with anybody about this, so what I'm about to say is just between you and me. Can I count on you?"

"Absolutely. I'm good at keeping secrets."

"I'm glad to hear it, because I really would like to talk about it. The fact is I'm not sure about the long run. There's a lot of world out there I'd like to see."

She laid her hand on top of his. In the darkness her unexpected touch, soft and warm, gave him a start. He took another long swallow from his cup.

"You know better than I do," she said, "your parents would be terribly disappointed, but sometimes you have to make hard decisions about your own life. It wouldn't be good for them or the paper if you were miserable there."

"Sometimes I think that if I went away for two or three years, I could get whatever it is out of my system and be content to come on back."

"That sounds promising," she said with some enthusiasm. She removed her hand and lay back on the pier, her arms under her head. "That reminds me, there's a girl at the KD House—I don't think you know her, Peggy Butcher from Nashville—who wants to work in New York for a while. We've talked about going up together after we graduate. We'd get an apartment and find some sort of job."

The tempo of the music had changed again. Now it was "Always," the ultimate in romantic saccharin: "I'll be loving you, al-ways . . . With a love that's true, al-ways . . ."

It was fully dark now, and a scattering of stars had emerged. He could see the silhouette of her body stretched out on the pier. He was drawn to her more than ever, captivated by her warmth and understanding. He leaned down on his elbow, hesitated for a moment, then kissed her. In the dim starlight, he could now see her face. He kissed her again. She brought her arms from beneath her head and encircled his neck.

There was only the lapping of water against the pilings, the far-off mournful surf, and the distant strains of "Always . . . I'll be loving you, al-ways . . ."

A voice from the porch: "Hey, John! Jeanie! Let's go. Time to eat!"

Chapter 3

"WELL, SON," HERBERT WINSTON SAID, putting down a cup of coffee as John entered the breakfast room, "how did the weekend go?" He and Anna looked at their son quizzically, even suspiciously, as they always did on Monday mornings after these expeditions, searching for evidence of a hangover or some grievous mishap.

"Fine," John said, in the noncommittal tone he usually assumed under parental interrogation. He managed to give the impression of feeling better than he did. The homeward journey had begun with a couple of late afternoon hours in a Fort Walton bar, followed by several stops along the way for some more nipping as they progressed northward. They had not reached Remberton until after midnight.

"Looks like you got plenty of sun," his mother said. Getting no response, she continued, with a sly smile. "How was Jeanie?"

"Oh, she was OK. She's always a lot of fun."

Annie May, their cook of many years, set a plate of scrambled eggs, bacon, and grits in front of him. They had not eaten anything much the evening before, and he was hungry. He stirred butter into the grits and plunged in with his fork as Annie May filled his coffee cup.

"Have you heard the news?" Herbert said.

"No, we haven't had any. What is it?" He added a bite of bacon to his mouthful of scrambled eggs.

"The North Korean Communists have invaded South Korea," Herbert said, pushing the morning paper over toward him. "And they're taking this right seriously in Washington. Americans are being

43

evacuated from Seoul. Yesterday the U.N. Security Council passed a resolution calling on the North Koreans to pull back."

John scanned the news articles on the front page. The surprise Sunday morning attack, spearheaded by Soviet-made tanks, was clearly more than a border raid. He read on, forgetting what was left of his eggs and grits. His interest was heightened by the text of the Security Council resolution invoking for the first time the principle that armed aggression was impermissible in the post-war world of the United Nations.

Anna excused herself and left the table. Herbert leaned back in his chair with a second cup of coffee. "This is a little like Pearl Harbor: surprise attack, Sunday morning, we unprepared. But isn't this just a fuss among Koreans?"

"Ah!" John reacted with a momentary sense of superiority. "Remember Munich? They didn't stop Hitler then, and look what happened."

"But Germany crossed an international border to take over Czechoslovakia. Here we have Koreans attacking other Koreans."

"You have to view the 38th parallel as an international line. It's like the division between East and West Germany."

"My guess is that the threat of world communism is what Washington's worried about. The North Korean dictator, Kim Il-sung, is really a Soviet puppet. If it weren't for that, the Koreans would probably be left to fight it out on their own. How many Americans have even heard of Korea?"

Although he had barely heard of Korea before, the invasion now seized John's mind as nothing had in a long time. It was the U.N. involvement, the very subject of his college paper that fascinated him. All week he soaked up the AP and UP stories arriving at the office, and in the evenings he stayed by the radio listening to the news. He was engrossed by reports of the emergency meeting called by President Truman in Blair House on Sunday evening, June 25. The top national security advisors were there, all imbued with the major lesson of the thirties: Unchecked aggression leads to war. The commentators said that the group's determination to act was clear, but the situation was not, and the unknowns were large: Was the Soviet Union involved? What about China? Could the South Korean army hold the line? Above all, was this the beginning of World War III?

The news was all bad. American air and sea power and the South Korean army were not stopping the North Koreans. The capital city of Seoul had fallen, the government in flight to the south. The most dramatic news was that Gen. Douglas MacArthur had just been placed in command of all United Nations forces in Korea and had flown there from his headquarters in Tokyo to make a personal inspection on the ground. According to reports, he had found thousands of Korean refugees streaming south, clogging the roads— women in ankle-length dresses carrying babies, old men in flowing white robes and tall black birdcage hats, with heavily loaded A-frames on their backs, all pushing or pulling overloaded carts. Mixed in with them were remnants of the army of the Republic of Korea in disarrayed retreat. General MacArthur had immediately informed President Truman that American ground forces would be necessary to prevent total defeat and a North Korean occupation of the entire peninsula.

The radio, a large RCA cabinet model, surrounded by comfortable chairs, was in the room just off the parlor. John and his parents gathered there every night before supper to listen to the news. Light from the setting sun filtered through leaves of the pecan trees and filled the room with a soft evening glow. The slowly moving ceiling fan stirred the humid air.

A few days after the North Korean attack, the radio reported that President Truman had authorized the immediate dispatch of American ground forces from Japan to Korea—chiefly the Twenty-Fourth Infantry Division. The U.N. Security Council called on all member states to render assistance to the Republic of Korea. The president also authorized the call-up of reservists and National Guard units. There was no indication of how many or how soon.

Herbert said slowly, as though speaking to himself, "If this is a police action and we're not going to war, why is the president talking about a call-up?"

"Maybe they know something they're not telling us," John said.

"Aren't you a reservist?" his mother said, as though realizing it for the first time.

"I guess I am," he said slowly, "but I hadn't really thought about it."

They sat in silence for a few moments. Then Anna said, "Does this mean you'll have to go?"

"Who knows?" John paused. "Come to think of it, I doubt there's anything they need more than infantry lieutenants."

"Those North Koreans will turn tail and run as soon as they see some real American troops facing them. This should all be over pretty quickly," Herbert said.

Work went on as usual at the *Remberton Progress*, as it did everywhere else. As far as John could tell, there was little interest in remote Korea.

Two weeks passed; the *Progress* staff was in its Monday flurry of activity. "Here's the week's historical notes," John said to his father as he came through the door from the pressroom. "For 'Twenty-five Years Ago,'" he continued, "we've got the first cotton bloom of the season, a couple of golden wedding anniversaries, three lawyers back from the state bar meeting, and—here's a good one—a fifty-pound watermelon brought in to the *Progress* office."

"They sound pretty good," Herbert said with a mildly surprised look. "What about the opening of the new swimming pool?" His personal, decades-long memory was a reliable check on John's research.

"That comes up next week. But here's a biggie for fifty years ago: the laying of the cornerstone of the new courthouse. I think we ought to do a special story on that. We could run the picture hanging there." He pointed to the photograph of the Major and other dignitaries gathered for the occasion.

Herbert smiled. "Now that's sharp journalistic thinking. How about writing it up? I was a little young to remember that one, but I know the paper covered it in detail."

John found the historical columns fascinating. He was under no illusion, however, that he was getting all the news of those bygone days. He knew that then as now the darker side of the human condition was rarely reported. Indeed, he became so captivated by local history that he set out to peruse all issues of the paper since its founding, spending hours in the musty storage room where they were kept, bound into six-month bundles.

There he had come across a series of articles written by the Major entitled "Recollections of the War." His grandfather had recounted his experiences in the Army of Northern Virginia, beginning with the Seven Days before Richmond and going through Gettysburg, where he was wounded. He returned to duty in the trenches at Petersburg in the last dark days. His final article in the series was a poignant account of the army's encirclement and surrender at Appomattox Court House, describing the scene of humiliation and defeat in his florid Victorian style. As John read it, tears welled up in his eyes.

"John, it's for you," Effie McCune said, holding out the telephone receiver. A couple of years earlier, the office had acquired the latest in telephone design, what was referred to as a "French style" phone, to replace the old upright model. Now the listening and talking devices were combined into one piece.

"John, it's Jeanie," came the soft, familiar voice. "Mama and Papa are going to Destin this weekend, and Baby Sister's spending Saturday night with me. We thought it would be nice to have a little party. We hope you can come."

He had seen Jeanie only once since the coast trip. They went to the picture show with another couple and had no time alone.

"I'd love to!" he replied. "Sounds like fun. Can I help?"

"We thought we'd have everybody brown-bag it. How does that sound?"

"Fine. I guess our friend Earl E. Times will be welcome."

"Right," she giggled.

"The best I can make out of this from the papers and radio," Herbert said, "is that we plan to make a stand at the Kum River." They had just turned off the six o'clock news. Herbert had a world atlas on his lap, opened to a map of Korea.

"I don't see why they haven't been able to stop them before now," John said.

From the news accounts they had learned of the disasters that had befallen the first American army units to come in contact with the North Koreans. Far from turning and running, the North Koreans had pushed on, undeterred, with their Soviet-made T-34 tanks.

"I think I can tell you why. All we've got in there are some occupation troops from Japan—been living the good life since the war. I saw some occupation duty before I came home in 1919, and I know how fast soldiers can deteriorate."

"They say we've got marines, another army division, and some other units on the way. That ought to do it."

"I wouldn't be too sure. I'm afraid our armed forces are in pretty bad shape. It happened in the twenties and thirties, and here it is again. When a war's over, we always want to bring the boys home and disband everything."

Herbert studied the map again. "Now look at this. There's one more fallback possibility if they can't hold at the Kum River. Here you have the Naktong." He ran his finger along a river farther to the southeast.

"If we have to fall back there, there's not much room for maneuver," John observed, looking at the map over his father's shoulder and recalling some summer-camp tactical instruction. "All that's left then is Pusan, the only place we can bring in reinforcements."

"Right," Herbert mused. "If the North Koreans cross the Naktong, I'd say church is out."

"Well, let's pray the thing straightens out before long," Anna said. "Now, we need to go in to supper."

John followed his parents back to the breakfast room, contemplating his reserve commission. Up until now, it had simply been a nice, sociable thing to have, an accomplishment without consequences. But overnight, that piece of paper upstairs in his dresser drawer—his official commission as a second lieutenant, Infantry, United States Army Reserve—had taken on an unimagined significance.

In the following days, the black arrows on the newspaper maps kept pushing farther and farther south. The North Koreans overran Taejon, the key defensive point on the Kum River. The city had been defended by the U.S. Twenty-Fourth Infantry Division—the South Korean army having disintegrated—but that ill-prepared and already mauled unit now ceased to exist as an organized fighting force. Commentators were pessimistic: the United States Army was suffering a humiliating defeat, and a Communist takeover of the entire Korean peninsula was growing likelier by the day.

"Listen, we've got to get back out there," Jeanie murmured with a soft, breathy giggle. "They'll be wondering where we are." She nuzzled up against John, her arms around his neck.

The Saturday night party at her house had been under way for a couple of hours. The noise level was rising, the drinking progressing.

When the rest of the crowd drifted from the kitchen back toward the den, she and John ducked into a side hallway.

They had been there several minutes, embracing and kissing, without saying anything. Whispering in her ear, John said, "I'm sorry I haven't been around lately. This Korean thing has had me totally preoccupied."

"Let's don't talk about that now."

"You realize I'll probably have to go?" They looked each other in the eyes. He saw her soulful expression and hugged her tightly, kissing her cheek. "I'll miss you . . . miss you more than I can say."

"Not more than I'll miss you," she said. "But we can't let all that ruin tonight."

He kissed her intensely and hugged her tighter than ever. When he released his grip, she said, "We really do have to get back," pulling away and taking him by the hand to head toward the noisy group at the front of the house.

"Well, where have you two been?" chirped Sally Young, a Scotch in one hand, a cigarette in the other.

"Straightening up the kitchen," said Jeanie.

Gregory Nichols stood beside Sally. He had graduated at Princeton two years before, the only one of the crowd who had gone north to college—way north, north of Virginia. He now worked in the trust department of an Atlanta bank.

"Say, John," he said, "I hear you might have to go in the army."

"It's a possibility. How about you?" Greg had a Navy ROTC commission.

"Look's like it might happen. I just got back from two weeks training at Jacksonville. They think there'll be a call-up. The good news is I'll probably get assigned to a ship heading for the Mediterranean."

"Now that won't be a bad sightseeing trip," Sally said. "Will you have something like that, John?"

"Oh, probably much more exotic," he said. "What would you think of Korea, with an overland tour? A closer look at the country, the historic sights, and all that. None of this sleeping in bunks on mattresses with sheets every night and three hot meals a day."

"Some people do have all the luck," Greg said. He had a slight air of superiority—some said arrogance—that fit well, John thought, with Sally's sarcastic bent.

John caught her dark eyes boring in on him, and for an instant he met her gaze, his mind filled with the image of their naked bodies pressing together in the watery blackness of Santa Rosa Sound. But this, he resolved, is the forbidden fruit I must not touch. He turned and moved away with Jeanie.

The days became shorter as the summer waned. The katydids were in full voice as John and his parents gathered once more around the radio in the early evening, apprehensive the news would again be bad. And it was.

The U.N. Command had fallen back to the Naktong, the last natural defensive position before Pusan and the sea. If, as the press reported, the controlling image at that Blair House meeting on Sunday evening, June 25th, had been Munich, it was now Dunkirk. And the resolve was equally firm: There was to be no repetition of that disaster, no abandonment of Korea. For the men on the ground, there was no choice but to stand or die on that line, as Gen. Johnny Walker had ordered. The president had directed that all enlistments be extended for a year and announced that fifty thousand inductees would be the next month's quota. So it was no surprise when they heard in that summer twilight that thirty thousand reservists would be called up.

They sat without saying anything as the newscast droned on.

"Well, son," Herbert said, "looks like you might get your chance at a war after all. Remember how you used to talk about missing one?"

John looked absently through the window at the reddened western sky. When he spoke, his voice was barely audible. "Yes. Yes, I do."

Chapter 4

TEN DAYS LATER HIS ORDERS ARRIVED in the mail—multiple copies of mimeographed military jargon and abbreviations. He had to translate for his parents. "John H. Winston, 02205008, 2nd Lt, Inf, USAR," was ordered to EAD (extended active duty) for two years and directed to report to the POE (Port of Embarkation) at Camp Stoneman, California, within twenty-one days for reassignment to FECOM (Far East Command).

The next morning, as he was leaving for work, Anna said, "It's not like last time when everybody was going. Do you know anybody else going?"

"Greg says he'll probably get called up," John said. "You know that Richards fellow down at the trucking warehouse? I heard he's gotten orders."

"But it's different from Pearl Harbor. Then we had long lines at the recruiting stations."

"But Mama, the president says this is a police action, not a war," he said facetiously.

"I can't tell the difference from the pictures we've seen."

He gave her a longer and more loving than usual hug. "Now don't worry about what might not happen. Be home as usual before supper." Then he was out the back door to his car.

In the remaining days he worked feverishly to wind up all the projects he could. He sold his car. He got out the uniforms he had not expected to wear again. He came across an assortment of field

51

manuals left over from ROTC and spent odd times skimming through pages on small-unit tactics, principles of leadership, and various weapons.

He'd hunted for years with his own shotgun and rifle and felt at home with small arms. At summer camp at Fort Benning, he had stripped down the M-1, the carbine, and the .45-caliber pistol many times. He had become acquainted with the heavier stuff: the thirty-caliber machine guns—one light and air-cooled, the other heavy and water-cooled—the .50-caliber machine gun, and the Browning automatic rifle, known as the BAR.

Sweating in heavy green fatigues in the midsummer Georgia sun, he and a host of other would-be officers had been put through obstacle and infiltration courses, map-reading instruction, and field exercises. He liked the infantry school motto: "Follow me." It was the opposite of "Go ahead." The infantry officer was expected to be out in front, leading, always leading. Where he would not go, he could not expect his men to go.

But that Fort Benning experience seemed scant preparation for what might lie ahead. He doubted his ability to lead. It was not only doubt about knowing what to do but also—reluctant though he was to acknowledge it—uncertainty about how he would react under fire. Death was out there in those Korean hills and rice paddies, not an abstraction, not a hypothetical possibility. He had seen accounts of ill-equipped American units being overrun, and he had read the casualty figures. Fear—he resisted even the word—was the sensation he dreaded above all else. He viewed it as an enemy that threatened his ability to function as well as his self-respect. Yet he had read that in battle all men experience it. You somehow had to function despite it, somehow hold it at bay.

In the late hours of the passing nights he sat in his room, lost in a jumble of thoughts. He was inspired by the idea that he was to become part of the first international army ever to fight under the blue and white flag of the United Nations. Destiny would, after all, not pass him by. This was not what he had dreamed of, but a man does not pick his time and place. In any event, his uncertainty about his future in Remberton had been resolved for him by Kim Il-sung, at least for now.

"Becky and Frank are definitely coming down this weekend," his mother said at the beginning of his last week at home. His sister and her husband had been on a West Coast trip ever since his orders had arrived, but they were cutting it short to see him before he left.

"Good! I was afraid they might not make it."

"I'm worried about their situation," she said. "I'm not sure Frank likes his work."

"I have a feeling they don't care for Birmingham. Do you think there's any chance they'd want to move back here and Frank go to work at the *Progress*?" This thought had been growing in his mind in recent months.

"Your father and I have talked about that," Anna said. "Of course we'd love to see them back here. Herbert says we'd need to be sure there's room for both of you at the paper."

John said nothing, but he thought that this might be no problem—indeed, that it might solve his own problem.

In his last days in Remberton, he developed a peculiar obsession about his body—his arms, legs, eyes—morbidly fearing that he might come back without them. He engaged frenetically in physical activity, playing as much tennis as he could work in, thinking that he might never be able to play again. He was consciously aware, as he had never been, of his limbs, of how important his hands and feet were, and he imagined how things would be without them. And his eyes too. What if he lost them? He looked at people and things more closely than he ever had.

He spent odd hours driving around town and into the countryside. He saw the houses, streets, fields, and woods he had known all his life as if for the first time. They seemed to stand out more vividly in the late summer sunlight under the deep blue sky. He drank it all up, storing the images in a place where they would remain forever.

He drove slowly through the old streets of his neighborhood, then through the newer sections—Morgan Street, School Street, Jeff Davis Road—with their Victorian and turn-of-the-century houses, and the postwar ranch styles farther out. He passed the grammar school and the high school and the country club and the swimming pool in the park on the edge of town.

Driving slowly down Center Street, the town's only business section, he passed stores, the lawyers' offices, the *Progress* office, then the oldest and largest antebellum houses, the Presbyterian, Methodist, and Baptist churches, the city hall, the Confederate monument, the post office, the bank, the picture show, more stores, and finally the train station. On this milelong stretch, he knew almost everyone in every store.

"Well, John, when are you leaving?" they all asked, one after the other.

"Next Sunday."

"It's too bad we're in this messy situation. We sure hate to see you go. Maybe it'll all be over soon."

On one of his drives, late one sultry afternoon, he went by Jeanie's house and picked her up. She was good company—for him, as it had developed this summer, the best in Remberton. How much easier it would be to leave if it weren't for her.

The day was hot and humid, the air heavy and unmoving. The sky was overcast, with rain threatening. He took a little-used county road out of town, driving fast, with all windows down and ventilators turned full on themselves, to try to cool off. With reckless abandon he sped past cotton fields turning white, past cows clustered in pastures, past thick woods. He swerved abruptly to avoid slamming into the rear of a wagon he suddenly came upon over the crest of a hill; he barely missed it, startling both the somnambulant mule and aged black man perched on the plank seat. He raced on, heedless of such dangers on the narrow, curving road, exhilarated by his engine's power, the wind in his face, and Jeanie at his side. When would there be such times again?

He wound up on the road at the back side of the golf course and pulled the car off into a clearing ringed by tall pines. They had talked little about what lay ahead for him. But when he cut off the ignition, there was a momentary stillness, the only sounds being the tick-tick of the overheated engine and the cawing of crows in the field across the road, and she asked, "John, how long do you think you'll be gone?"

He still had both hands on the steering wheel, looking straight ahead. Without turning, he said, "Hard to tell. Everything's too uncertain right now. Since I'll be shipping out to the Far East, I can't see how it can be less than a year, maybe longer."

When he looked over at her, she had a sad, little-girl expression that caused his heart to crumble. Having lost much of his shyness since that Mary Esther weekend, he ran his arm around her shoulders and pulled her against him. He stroked her face and hair with his left hand, looking into her large, sympathetic blue eyes, and said, "However long it is, I hope you'll write and won't forget me."

"I couldn't forget you."

They kissed and kept on kissing, as rain began pelting down on the car roof, drowning out all other sound, leaving them alone in the world.

One of his last stops on Center Street was the barbershop, the place to learn the local news.

"Joe Hicks got orders yesterday," Cecil Dawkins said as he was cutting John's hair. "They say he's pretty sick about it. He was in over three years during the war. Now he's got to go again just when he's got his insurance business up and going."

"But at least he'll go in as a captain, and he's in the Transportation Corps, so maybe he won't have too tough a time." The speaker was one of three elderly men sitting in chairs along the wall opposite the barbers. Only one was waiting for a haircut. The other two were part of the daily traffic in and out of the shop, dropping in to rest and trade stories.

The ancient barber at the next chair spoke up. "I hear there's folks who're going to be drafted. That Adams boy from out at Shiloh was in here this morning. Said a fellow out that way had just gotten a notice." He paused in his snipping as he spoke, but kept the scissors suspended in cutting position. "It's funny. It don't seem like a war."

"Folks are dying, and folks are going off. It sorta looks like a war," one of the drop-ins said.

"The president says it's a police action," John said. "When I get back I'll try to tell you the difference."

Mr. Cecil had been cutting his hair ever since his mother led him into the shop by the hand and the barber lifted him up to a board laid across the chair arms. Now he shook hands with the men working all three chairs. Another parting, another sense of something indefinable passing.

"OK, buddy," Mr. Cecil said, "take care of yourself. We'll give you a cut on the house when you get back."

The black arrows on the newspaper maps had not moved for

nearly a month. They remained pointing ominously at a postage stamp of territory in the southeastern corner of Korea containing the port city of Pusan. General Walker's "stand and die" order was working. Meanwhile, men and supplies were pouring into Pusan. The intensity of the fighting continued, and the press was reporting heavy casualties. Still, no trumpet call to arms had sounded; there was no rationing of food, gasoline, or tires, no big parades to send the boys off. Yet the boys were going, in the tens of thousands, to redeem, if possible, the disgraceful retreat of American forces in the face of a peasant army and, John liked to think, to vindicate the principle of collective action to repel aggression.

It was John's last weekend at home. Becky and Frank arrived on Friday evening. On Saturday they sat around the house talking.

Becky was of medium height with straight blondish hair and a broad, cheerful face that reminded people of her mother. She had gone to Agnes Scott and then, in the usual custom, transferred to the University. There she met Frank Brandon. He came from Jasper and had a touch of a North Alabama hill-country accent. His dark, unruly hair and tortoise-rim eyeglasses gave him a bookwormish appearance. He let his wife do most of the talking, although he chimed in with surprisingly witty comments at unexpected moments.

They had dinner at noon, the full panoply of summer eating: fried chicken, butter beans, snap beans with cucumbers in vinegar, sliced blood red tomatoes, corn sticks, iced tea, and more.

"Mr. Herbert," Frank said, as Annie May cleared the table for ice cream, "how are you going to manage the paper without John?" Humor was evident in his eyes.

"It's not going to be easy," Herbert said. "I've gotten used to him over the last year. He's leaving just when I'd decided that he's got the makings of a first-rate newspaper man."

"It's a wonder the paper managed to get along without me for all those years," John said, with a sarcastic laugh.

"You won't really be away all that long," Anna said, in a tone suggesting she was trying to convince herself of the point.

"Frank," John said teasingly, "why don't you take a leave of absence from the Birmingham paper and come on down here and fill in?"

"That's not a bad idea," Becky said, before Frank could respond. "Every time we're here, I think how much nicer living in Remberton is compared to Birmingham."

The telephone rang, interrupting the conversation, just as Annie May put the last dish of ice cream on the table. "It's for Mr. John," she called from the hall.

It was Bartow Simmons checking on arrangements for the night's gathering at the country club. Everybody was all set for eight, he reported. "Be sure to tell Becky and Frank to come on out. Looks like everybody you ever heard of is in town."

Built in the twenties, the clubhouse was a rustic structure, set on a slight elevation in the middle of a nine-hole golf course, surrounded by oak and cedar trees and flanked by a pair of tennis courts. It had a veranda on two sides, plentifully supplied with rocking chairs. Inside, the club consisted mainly of one large, all-purpose room.

On this Saturday night, several low, round tables, surrounded by chairs, were clustered together at one end of the room, and here the party raged. By ten it was in high gear, with thirty or more people on hand. The crowd ranged from those two or three years older than John down to those two or three years younger. A few were married but most were not. Many were still in school somewhere, just now ending up the summer and readying themselves for the annual September launching of another academic year. Several were back in Remberton to stay; others worked elsewhere and were home for the weekend.

They talked, drank, and danced to music from an endlessly playing jukebox. Every man had brought a bottle for himself and his date, since the club had no liquor service. Each table sported a small forest of upright brown paper bags, concealing fifths of bourbon, scotch, and gin, amidst a sea of soft drinks, water pitchers, and bowls of ice. The heavier drinkers rarely left their chairs, staying within arm's reach of the supplies. Those given to dancing spent intervals out in the cleared floor space, especially during the faster, jitterbugging numbers, returning to the tables sporadically to retrieve or refill a drink. A dense layer of cigarette smoke floated over the entire scene.

The smoke grew thicker, the talk louder, the din greater as the night wore on. A sticky slush was building up on the tabletops. John danced during some of the slow numbers. In between he moved from one chair and table to another, carrying on trivial conversation.

Time and again he was asked, "Exactly when are you leaving?"

"On the No. 3 tomorrow," he would say.

From somewhere deep in his mind a small voice seemed to be saying over and over, "This is the last, the last night with this crowd, the last night in Remberton."

"Hey, buddy, your drink all right?" barked Skip Johnson above the noise.

"Yep," John said, exhibiting a full glass as he slumped down in a chair beside Skip.

"See that son of a bitch from Montgomery over there?" Skip said, nodding across the forest of bottles toward a dapper-looking figure engrossed in conversation with Berta. John did not know him, but he had the air and dress of a man from elsewhere, from some supposedly more sophisticated place, such as Montgomery or Birmingham, a type who considered himself to be doing Remberton society a favor by appearing occasionally to date one of the more attractive gals, usually driving a Chrysler or Buick or even a Cadillac. He held a cigarette at what was considered a smart angle, moving it casually as he talked.

"I had a date with Berta for tonight," Skip continued in a disgusted tone, "then she calls me up yesterday to say that she had forgotten she'd promised this Montgomery joker and couldn't go back on her word."

"Well, I wouldn't let it get you down. Judging from her expression, I'd say he's not much of a threat."

"All right, John, you've been sitting around long enough. Let's dance." Sally Young pulled him up by the arm as she spoke.

They joined several other couples dancing slowly, a plaintive female voice welling out of the jukebox: "Faraway Places with Strange Sounding Names." The song had been around for some time, but at this moment the words struck John with special meaning: "Faraway places with strange sounding names . . . faraway cross the sea . . . faraway places, calling, calling, me . . ." Yes, strange sounding—Pusan, Taegu, Taejon, Naktong, Han, Seoul—but they were becoming gruesomely familiar.

Sally pressed against him, interrupting his momentary reverie. She radiated a sexiness that caused him involuntarily to tighten his arm around her back. Once again, they were in the water together, bathing suits off. She murmured, "Will you drop me a line when you get wherever you're going?"

He didn't hasten to answer, but kept moving slowly to the music, transfixed by the contradictory sensations of resentment and attraction. He mentally fumbled for what to say, not wanting to get entangled with her but not wanting to let go altogether either. Finally he said, "I'll try to. No telling where I'll be or how much I can write."

They danced alongside Bartow Simmons and Jeanie Harris. Bartow said, "Hey, that looks mighty cozy. What about a little swap?" He handed Jeanie off to John and moved in on Sally.

John enveloped Jeanie's cuddly form in his arms, and they swayed slowly to "Faraway places . . ." Her face was nuzzled in his neck. "Looked like you and Sally were having a mighty good time."

"Well, you know Sally, and you know my thoughts about her."

"It makes me uncomfortable to see y'all together like that."

He pulled her closer and pressed his mouth near her ear. "Don't worry about that. She can't hold a candle to you."

The music ended, and they went back to the tables. John got to talking with one of his favorite people, Craig Anderson. He was working on a Ph.D. in English at Chapel Hill. From some talk about the Fugitives and Vanderbilt they moved on to Thomas Wolfe and Chapel Hill. Craig had become infatuated with Wolfe and had decided to do his dissertation on him.

"Incidentally," Craig said, "did you know that Mr. Ben has a large collection of the Agrarians?"

"How do you know that?"

"I was over there a while back to take Jeanie to the picture show. I'm fascinated by that library."

"Yes. It is good," John said, surprised to hear that Craig and Jeanie had been on a date and surprised at how much he resented it.

Sunday was a cloudless early September day. The crepe myrtles were in full bloom, a profusion of watermelon reds and whites and pinks lining one side of their yard. The day promised to be hot.

The Presbyterian church was filling up, the summer doldrums being over, as the Winstons were ushered in to their usual seats. The Major had begun sitting here in this pew when the church was built in the 1880s, and the family had sat there ever since. Like nearly everybody in Remberton, they went to church on Sunday. It was part of life's routine, like going to school every weekday.

Although reared in the church, John considered religion to be remote and abstract, something about which he had not thought profoundly and which did not have much to do with his life. But the overseas orders focused his mind. He found it more interesting and meaningful now. This morning, however, he had difficulty keeping his mind on the scripture readings and the sermon. What kind of assignment would he draw in FECOM? Anything was possible. A base in Japan. Or some outfit around Pusan. But he knew deep down that he would almost certainly be sent to a rifle company in the line.

He heard Dr. Cowley's booming voice coming from the pulpit: "God is everywhere at all times. He is with us both in life and in death." He noticed that the scriptures had a lot to say about fear and life and death. The sermon seemed to focus on fear, or rather the injunction not to fear. As the words faded in and out between his mental wanderings, he heard that in more than two dozen places the Bible tells us to be not afraid or to fear not. "Yea though I walk through the valley of the shadow of death, I will fear no evil."

Tom Cowley had been the preacher here since John's high school days. He was everyone's idea of an appropriate spokesman for the Almighty: tall, gray-haired, with large, well-formed features and a strong, deep voice. Harrowing experiences as a navy chaplain in the Pacific added to his credibility.

The organ thundered forth and the congregation rose to sing:

> The Son of God goes forth to war,
> A kingly crown to gain.
> His blood red banner streams afar.
> Who follows in His train,
> Who best can drink His cup of woe,
> Triumphant over pain.

Fumbling his way into the hymnal, John joined in the singing of the next two stanzas.

He looked over the crowd to his side and front. Across the aisle sat Dr. Lucius Craighill, who had brought him into the world and was known to everybody as Dr. Loosh. In the row ahead was his high school principal, still on duty. On the side aisle was Edward Kirkman, law partner with his mother's cousin, Noble Shepperson.

The prayer was now under way. Again his mind drifted. Suddenly the sound of his name, borne by the preacher's voice, entered his consciousness, but he was not alert enough to catch the words that accompanied it. He felt self-conscious and ill at ease, suddenly realizing that this service must have been designed with him in mind.

As usual at the close of the service, Dr. Cowley was standing at the main church door to shake hands with the flock. "Well, John," he said with a special heartiness, "I guess this will be it for a while."

"Yes, sir. Quite a while."

Dr. Cowley looked John in the eyes with an unfamiliar intensity, lowered his voice so that despite the crowd milling around them it seemed that they were alone, and said, as though he were a direct conduit from on high: "Remember this—God is with you."

Their hands were still clasped together, and their eyes remained locked on each other for an instant. John felt a momentary chill sweep over his body. He could not speak. He simply nodded slowly, turned, and quickly moved away.

He now wanted to leave Remberton, to get on with this trip. He had been saying good-bye for days. The time had come to move on.

At four o'clock he was in his room, dressed in his uniform. They had called the station and found that the train was half an hour late. Forty-five minutes to go.

He felt unreal, on edge. He wanted to leave, but he didn't want to leave. How had all the others felt at this moment? What thoughts had been in his father's mind as he left from this very house in 1917, exactly thirty-three years ago? They had never discussed it. And what about his grandfather in 1861? For that matter, what about the millions who shipped out for God knows where in 1942 and '43? It was reassuring to realize that he was not unique. This moment of leave taking from home to go off to war must be one of the most common experiences of mankind across the centuries.

He closed his single canvas bag and gazed around the room at the pictures and artifacts of his life to date, on display as in a museum. The dark leaves of the magnolia tree spread before his windows in the drowsy September afternoon. From somewhere beyond, he heard the familiar squawking of a blue jay. What would he see and do before he stood here again? If, that is, he were ever to stand here again. He was overcome with a sense of last things, of time passing, of a long chapter in his life being closed.

With a final glance around, he picked up his bag and walked down the stairs and out the front door to the car.

The day had become oppressively hot and heavy, suggesting the possibility of a late-afternoon thunderstorm. He thought he caught the faint, far-off rumble of thunder. They were all gathering at the car as he put his bag in the trunk.

He looked at the house, taking a final mental photograph. It was designed to be what it was, a town house, a large two-story home, set close to the street, its red bricks darkened by a century of weathering. So farewell to 53 Taylor Street, he said to himself, the only home he had ever had, except for his student days at the University.

At the station, he was surprised by the turnout. He knew that at least a handful of his friends would come, but there was a crowd of a dozen or more. They clustered around him on the long concrete station platform next to the tracks, all talking and laughing at once.

"Say, John, I didn't recognize you in that monkey suit."

"They say any man looks good in a uniform."

"We'll save a good coast trip for you."

"Watch out for those slinky Oriental women."

"Looks like you may get wet before you can get away."

The sun had gone. Dark, gray, low-hanging clouds now covered the sky. Thunder rumbled with ominous closeness. A half-mile to the north the train appeared from around the curve, its whistle sounding. In another minute, the locomotive thundered past them with a braking roar and metallic screeching, the noise drowning out all else.

John shook hands all around with the men and embraced the women. Sally Young grabbed him around the neck, mumbling in his ear, "Write me, you hear!" She quickly kissed him full on the mouth and backed away.

Embarrassed, he turned to Jeanie Harris, who had been standing beside him the whole time. She gave him a quizzical look. Despite his aversion to public displays of affection, he put his arms around her, hugging her firmly and kissing her on the cheek. He whispered, "Don't forget to write. I'll send you my address."

His mother and father and Becky and Frank pushed up to him

through the group. They all hugged and shook hands. He saw the tears welling in his mother's eyes and thought that if he didn't get on this train quickly, he himself might break down.

The whistle sounded a series of deafening blasts. The conductor, putting away his biscuit-sized pocket watch, called out the long-practiced command, "Board!"

Herbert's eyes were fixed on his son's insignia: shiny brass crossed rifles and gold bars. John knew what he must be thinking—they had talked about it in the past—that on the western front in 1918, that combination carried with it a 70 percent casualty rate and a life expectancy measured in weeks. He gripped John's hand and said simply, "Son, take care of yourself."

The coaches snapped forward at their couplings as John sprang up the steps. The train was moving. He turned and waved back at the little group for a few seconds before they were cut off from sight.

The first wet splats of the thunderstorm were falling as the train picked up speed in the graying afternoon. John remained on the platform between the cars watching familiar sights of Remberton slide by—the back of the wholesale grocery, the ice plant, the lumber yard, a straggling collection of run-down houses, and the pasture where he had often come with his Boy Scout Troop on overnight outings.

Then the woods closed in, and Remberton was gone. For how long, he wondered. For months? For years? Forever?

He stood on the platform between the cars amidst the deafening clatter of the swaying train, gazing distantly into the now pelting, slanting rain. A long, mournful series of whistles came back from the engine far ahead as the train approached a crossing. He turned slowly, picked up his bag, pushed open the door to the coach, and made his way along the swaying aisle to find a seat.

PART TWO
Kunu-ri

Chapter 5

STANDING ON A PIER just off the Embarcadero, John watched endless lines of soldiers streaming up the gangways into the troopship. Down the way an army band played marches interspersed with popular tunes. The air was clear and cool, the sky a cloudless blue—a perfect San Francisco day, he was told.

He milled around with a group of officers on the pier where a dozen attractive, stylishly dressed young women were serving coffee and doughnuts. Much of their talk was about the upcoming weekend, when they would be going down to Stanford for a football game, giving him a twinge of homesickness for games at Tuscaloosa.

He had hardly gotten a sentence out of his mouth when one of them said, "What part of the South do you come from?"

Trying to be clever, he said, "Take a guess."

"Mississippi," one of them said, laughingly.

"That's close. It's right next door."

They were all good-natured, laughing and joking as they poured coffee. But they seemed to view Southerners as an exotic species.

"Take a good look at 'em," one of his fellow officers mumbled. "The next female flesh you see will be slant-eyed and brown-skinned."

On deck he stood with hundreds of other men, crowding the rails, as the ship began backing away from the pier, with long, deep, bellowing blasts from its whistle. Then the band struck up "Auld Lang Syne." Misty-eyed, he pondered the awesome fact that they were now truly leaving home, heading for an alien world, not knowing when or if they would return. For a long while they stood silently at the rails, watching the water slowly widen between the ship and the pier, as the heart-tugging music faded into the distance.

Days later, at mid-Pacific, they heard the electrifying news that on September 15 two American divisions—one army and one marine— making up X Corps, had landed at Inchon, just west of Seoul, deep in the enemy's rear. This changed everything. Instead of being thrown into a desperate defense of the perimeter, he would join in a breakout already under way.

Then came Pusan and his first sight of Korea and Asia. The harbor was crowded with cargo ships being unloaded by antlike droves of Korean civilian laborers. The docks and streets were filled with the military paraphernalia of the industrialized world—jeeps, tanks, artillery pieces, and trucks. Here were all the features of Korea he was to come to know so well: shabby buildings long in need of maintenance; worn-out pavement in the streets; throngs of white-clad men and women—Asian yet different from Japanese and Chinese; and a unique, almost indescribable odor—unpleasant, ever-present, and pervasive, a combination of cooking smells, human excrement, and other unidentifiable ingredients. The raunchier aspects of Western culture had begun to appear here and there, as women in short, tight dresses lurked in shadowy doorways under signs reading Bar.

At the replacement depot—Repl Depl, in army lingo—on the outskirts of Pusan, John found himself in a room full of newly arrived officers presided over by an overweight captain. All of them had just been issued their gear—fatigues, combat boots, steel helmets, canteens, mess kits, and carbines.

"Too bad," the captain boomed sarcastically, "you men are too late for the really good action. You missed life in the perimeter with a chance to fight off the North Korean gooks." A low muttering was audible around the room, with some whispered aspersions on the captain's legitimacy.

"But with a little luck," he continued, "you might get a taste of action before it's all over. Anyway, we're going to give you a chance to see the sights and smell the night soil between here and Seoul. Come forward when your name is called and get your orders."

At a long table beside him were two sergeants with stacks of papers. It had already become evident to John at Camp Stoneman that the army cannot function without reams of paper and limitless coffee. When his name was barked out, he went forward.

"Well, Winston," the fat captain said, glancing over the orders with a smirk, "looks like you'll get a specially good look at things. They're sending you to an infantry battalion, and you'll probably be given a rifle platoon. They always need replacements for platoon leaders."

He set out on the long ride up the Korean peninsula to reach his unit, first by train some fifty miles north to Taegu, then by two-and-a-half-ton truck—deuce-and-a-half in the lingo—west and north, the convoy churning up immense clouds of dust as it moved along unpaved roads. With no paved roads outside the cities, the motorized American army brought everything in Korea under a blanket of dust.

The scars of war and its aftermath were everywhere—entire villages leveled and hundreds of refugees trying to return to their homes, many now nonexistent. He sickened at the sight of a mass grave just uncovered, containing over two hundred bodies of American and ROK soldiers and Korean civilians, hands tied behind their backs and shot through the head by retreating North Koreans.

He reached his battalion south of Seoul and was given command of Second Platoon, Baker Company. He felt green and unprepared, but he was saved by the platoon sergeant, Sgt. Steve Sewenski from Allentown, Pennsylvania. He had been in the invasion of the Philippines and had spent most of the time since the war on occupation duty in Japan. He complained that Korea had disrupted the nice life he had established with a Japanese wife and undemanding duty near Osaka. John wondered what these men—he had encountered several complaining like Sewenski—thought the army was for.

Despite his disgruntled attitude, Sergeant Sewenski was a godsend. He immediately gave John a detailed rundown on the platoon, its equipment, and men.

"These are pretty good guys," he said, in his tough-guy way of talking. "Some greenhorns, a few goof-offs, but basically an OK bunch."

With his battalion convoy, John crossed the Han River on a pontoon bridge—all previously existing bridges having been blown—and passed through Seoul, a depressing sight of urban ruin. Twice fought over, its buildings were badly damaged, the railroad station was gutted, and the dead bodies of its inhabitants were still in the streets.

They had thought they would stop near there, with South Korea having been cleared of Communists. But then came word that the United Nations General Assembly had adopted a resolution calling for the unification of all of Korea. So they were ordered north, crossing the Imjin River and the 38th parallel. Some waggish GI had erected a crudely lettered sign announcing the now-famous line and welcoming them to North Korea.

In Pyongyang, capital of the Democratic Peoples Republic of Korea, the battalion convoy passed near the government buildings. Giant pictures of Kim Il-sung and Joseph Stalin became targets for rocks thrown by the passing GIs. They met no enemy soldiers as they rolled ever northward.

He saw elements of the Middlesex Battalion and the Royal Northumberland Fusiliers, and they passed a detachment of Aussies, all part of the British Commonwealth Brigade. He heard rumors that Turks and Filipinos and units from Thailand, the Netherlands, and other nations were on the way. He saw the U.N. flag flying alongside the U.S. and ROK flags. He was tempted to shout, "Woodrow Wilson, we are here!"

So far he had seen no combat, had heard no shots fired in anger. It was only the luck of the draw, he reflected—always an important factor in one's fate in the army—that had given him a free ride, with little responsibility or danger. It was a magnificent sightseeing trip that stretched over more than five hundred miles, from Pusan to the remote northern corner, almost within sight of Manchuria. Along the way, summer had turned into fall, and fall was rapidly descending into winter.

Gusts of chilling wind snapped the top and sides of the dark green squad tent. Inside, at one end, stood the battalion commander. In front of him, filling the tent, sitting low on their steel helmets or on folding stools, were the officers of the battalion's three companies. A small, portable oil stove in the middle of the tent kept the outside chill at bay.

"Gentlemen, this will be the final briefing before we jump off tomorrow," Maj. Russell McKittrick, West Point '43, announced crisply. Unlike most of the officers in fatigues and field jackets, he wore wool ODs, neatly pressed, as though he had just dressed to go to an office at post headquarters. He had a boyish face and crew-cut hair and stood with military-academy erectness.

"Here is Kunu-ri," he continued, pointing with a stick to a spot near the lower edge of the map, which rested on a flimsy easel to his side. "And we are here," he said, moving the stick to the north of the village. "Here is the Chongchon River." He drew the pointer along the line of the river coming out of the northeast and running south and then westward. John sat with Baker Company commander, Capt. Howell Grimes, and the company's other lieutenants: Malcolm Mason from Terre Haute, Indiana, the executive officer, Alex Puccini from Milwaukee, commanding First Platoon, and Chris Ridley from San Jose, California, commanding Third Platoon. Ridley had just arrived the day before, making John feel like an old-timer. Mason alone was a West Pointer.

Captain Grimes was a Texas A&M graduate from Amarillo. He was stocky, rumpled, and seemingly unconcerned about what his superior officers thought about him. John had liked him from their first meeting.

The major continued. "The battalion's objective tomorrow is this string of three hills to our northeast. Here we have, running from west to east, Hill 314, which is assigned to Able Company; Hill 274, assigned to Baker; and Hill 417, assigned to Charlie. The three companies are in line abreast. There is no battalion reserve. We're relying on regimental reserve. The battalion CP and aid station will be approximately here," he jabbed at a point on the map south of the three hills, "1,800 yards to the rear of Baker. I want one squad out of Charlie detailed to the battalion CP to beef up security there."

Grimes mumbled quietly to his lieutenants, in his flat Texas drawl: "For once we won't be following in somebody else's dust."

The major went on. "Breakfast is at 0600. Our deuce-and-a-halfs will truck you up one company at a time. Able will move out at 0630, Baker at 0700, and Charlie at 0730. You'll be trucked up this road to this point." He moved his stick along a road leading north. "But that's as close as we can get you to your positions. From that point on you're doing what the infantry is supposed to do—proceed on foot. It's about four miles on the map, as the crow flies. But remember, this is up and down country, and there are no straight lines. We're probably looking at a six or seven mile hike. The companies will move up different valleys. Old Japanese maps are all we've got. Better make notes on them in English to identify these places. I want all companies to be in position not later than 1500 hours to allow time to dig in and put out patrols before dark. Any questions so far?"

Grimes spoke up. "Yes, sir. From the looks of things on this map, each of these hills is separated from the others by some sort of ravine or cut, maybe a stream. Won't it be hard to set up a continuous front or maintain contact?"

"Good question," shot back the major. "You're right. This damn country is so cut up that a continuous line might be impossible. The tactical situation is not good. I hope at least your radios are working and you can keep contact that way, if no other. We'll try to run wire to each company from my CP."

The tent flaps rattled under a sudden gust of wind, and a draft of cold air passed through the tent. Grimes and his lieutenants examined the maps. He whispered, "Be figuring out how to get to your position from the trucks."

"Sir?" came a voice from the other side of the tent. "What about ammo? We're pretty low."

"Another good question. I'm going to ask the Four to step up and talk about that and other supply matters."

Capt. Eugene Tompkins, the battalion S-4, moved up beside the major. He was from Phoenix, Arizona, one of those officers who had gone into the army near the end of the war and had retained a reserve commission. His family ran a building construction business from which he had been suddenly plucked by the reserve call-up in August. He spoke like a well-organized businessman.

"We know we're short of a lot of things," he began, "but we're not alone. Division G-4 tells us that the whole Eighth Army supply system is clogged. There's only one road up here from Pyongyang. They promise that more is on the way. We have a couple of dozen Korean litter-bearers that will be up on the morning of day two, we hope, with more ammo and rations. Winter clothing is, of course, a big problem. We are told that wools and parkas are on the way. We'll move them up to you just as soon as they arrive. On the ammo point, we've tried to spread it out evenly among the three companies. Every man should have at least one grenade and a minimum of thirty rounds for the M-1s and sixty rounds for the carbines. See me if you're shorter than that."

"OK, thanks, Gene. You know that we've been understrength and undersupplied all the way. In fact, ever since I've been with this outfit, since right after the breakout, we've never been up to strength or fully equipped. A big difference now, though, is that we've always been tagging along in somebody's wake. Now we're moving on the front line. When you get to those hills tomorrow, there will be no Americans in front of you. We really don't know what's out there. There may be nobody. But small North Korean groups have been harassing some of the other outfits on this move north, and they could well appear. Division G-2 doubts there are any Chinese forces of significance in front of us. Aerial reconnaissance hasn't spotted any or any sign of troop movements south of the Yalu. But I don't want you to let your guard down. Carelessness and overconfidence can spell disaster. Assume that there are enemy troops on your front and act accordingly."

"Sir?" came a voice from another part of the tent. "What happens on day two, after we've occupied the objective?"

"Orders from regiment are that all units are to hold on the day-one objective until further orders. The brass wants to keep a coordinated line of advance. Presumably, if all goes well on day one, as we expect, we'll move on to another phase line to the north. But we'll be taking this one day at a time."

The S-3 reported on the Eighth Army order of battle, pointing out that between them and the high mountains to the east were three ROK divisions, forming the right flank of the army. The Turkish brigade was also moving up to the eastern flank. Another ROK division, two American divisions, and a British Commonwealth brigade were to their west, between them and the Yellow Sea. He went on to explain that on the east coast, across the mountains, X Corps would also be advancing north toward the Yalu.

Major McKittrick took charge again. "Some of you have asked about artillery support. Where's our forward observer? We've got only one."

"Here, sir!" snapped a young red-haired lieutenant in the back of the tent.

"Good," the major said, "come up and brief us."

Lt. Mike Forney made his way to the front and stood beside the major. The redness of his hair seemed to have drained down over his face, covering it with red freckles and giving it a slightly pink cast. He was another fresh ROTC product, hailing from Bowling Green, Kentucky, and had recently finished a forward-observer crash course at Fort Sill. "The Forty-Sixth FA Battalion is supporting the regiment. One battery of 105 howitzers is assigned to this battalion. But there's a problem. There aren't many flat spaces in this country where howitzers can set up. They're working on this, but I won't know until tomorrow exactly where they can be put into position and how many we'll actually have available for support. Anyway, we'll do the best we can."

"We know the artillery won't let us down. Keep my CP posted just as soon as you have more information."

"Yes, sir. Also, sir, I can't tell from the maps we have where the best place is for the FO post. I'll have to find that after we reach the objective."

"All right. We need to remember that we have the possibility of air support. There's an air liaison officer at regiment. You have to request that through battalion, but don't be reluctant to do so if you think you really need it. That could be the case if the howitzers can't get in position—and if you hit some heavy going. Another point: We have four medium tanks and two quad-fifties assigned. But they face the road problem. To say the least, this is not good tank country. We'll try to position them to give you some support, but don't count on it."

After a few more questions, Major McKittrick was ready to conclude. He was, John thought, the truly professional military man.

"Although nobody would guess it," he continued, "this is Thanksgiving Day. Pass the word to your men that Protestant services will be here in the battalion CP area at 1000 and Catholic services at 1100. Thanksgiving dinner—and I'm told it'll be the army's finest—will be at 1200."

He was interrupted by a gust of wind that snapped the tent flaps with unusual force. He continued. "Now let me say this to wrap us up. I know we're understrength and short of supplies. Also, we have a lot of new men. We're not as well trained as we should be. The terrain is not what we would like. But the test of leadership lies in achieving the objective with what we have, not in moaning over what we don't have. Morale is not built by brooding over our disadvantages. Military situations are rarely ideal. But the army expects us—and I expect you—to carry out this mission in the best traditions of the American military. Remember this: Whatever our shortcomings, we are still a superior fighting force to anything that can oppose us. We are the first army in all history to fight in the interest of collective security under the United Nations flag. With good leadership—and some luck—we should wrap this mess up in a few weeks. I'm looking forward to standing with you on the banks of the Yalu. So, good luck and God bless you and your men!"

After the army's Thanksgiving feast, eaten out of aluminum mess kits, John spent the remaining hours of daylight inspecting his platoon, assembling his own gear, and talking with Captain Grimes about the next day's movement. By 2200 he was in his sleeping bag on the dirt floor of the tent he shared with the other Baker Company officers. In the darkness the cold was penetrating. He had removed none of his clothes except his boots.

Sleep came fitfully. The day had filled his mind with thoughts of home, and they lingered. This was the first Thanksgiving he had not been in Remberton with his family.

Until now, the novelty of army life, the exotic land, the scenes of death and destruction had absorbed all his attention, crowding out thoughts of home. He had felt exhilarated that he was here at a great historic moment, something he could not have remotely imagined six months earlier.

He had been in Korea nearly a month before receiving any mail. Now letters arrived once or twice a week. His mother was the most frequent writer, always urging him to take care of himself, as though he would not otherwise think of such. He had written Jeanie Harris as soon as he got his APO number and address pinned down. Her reply had come just a few days ago. She was enjoying the usual fall activities at the University. Football season was in full swing, with the attendant parties and so far one Saturday in Birmingham. "All this would be a lot more fun if you were here. I do miss you badly."

Her letter—which he had read several times—brought back fond memories, making him, at least momentarily, wish he could be back in that pleasant land of mild fall days, old friends, parties, football weekends, early-morning dove shoots, and, most of all, Jeanie. His mind drifted over her charms and attractions. Why hadn't he seen more of her during the summer? What a fool he had been. Now, though, she gave him something special to look forward to.

Someone in a nearby sleeping bag snorted and shifted position, bringing his mind abruptly back to the present. Tomorrow would be different. Whatever danger might be involved, he would be out there, for the first time with no buffer ahead. He was grateful that he had had these weeks to get used to the military service, to observe and learn from other officers and Sergeant Sewenski, and to develop a feel for his role as a platoon leader. He had gained a confidence that had been lacking a month ago. He was actually beginning to feel comfortable as an infantry lieutenant.

Yet, lying sleepless in his tightly zipped bag, contemplating the operations ahead, he sensed the presence of that unwanted intruder. He shrank from it, yet he knew it was there. It did not help his anxiety to remind himself that it was natural, that all men have fear in combat. He shifted restlessly, calming himself with the thought that the likelihood of encountering serious enemy opposition was slight and that this "home-by-Christmas offensive" would soon wrap it all up without difficulty. In the cold darkness, amidst the breathing of those around him, he finally fell asleep.

The Baker Company men stood around in the early-morning chill, stamping their feet and swinging their arms, looking for the trucks. Some were smoking cigarettes. They had breakfasted on hot corned beef hash, a welcome relief from the C-rations of recent days. They numbered 110, about half the authorized strength of an infantry company. They had six BARs, three light .30-caliber machine guns and one 60-millimeter mortar. Every man, except those with the heavier weapons, carried either an M-1 rifle or a carbine. Many sported bandoliers over their shoulders filled with magazine clips. They had one or two hand grenades apiece. Somewhere along the way, driven by the cold, most had discarded steel helmets in favor of pile caps.

"Hey, Puccini, you were bitching about the heat at Benning. You happy now?"

"Yeah. Ain't nothing to this. You oughta see a winter in Syracuse."

"Sarge?" asked another voice.

Sewenski turned in his direction. "Yeah, what is it?" He was helping one of the men readjust the sling on his M-1.

"When are the taxis coming?"

"You boys are getting soft. We're going to do a little walking today. Good for you. Remind you that you're in the infantry."

Muffled growls and curses followed.

Sewenski raised his voice. "Every man here got an extra pair of socks?" Heads nodded. "Hey, Edwards, you and Broderick," he called out to two men in the back with the LMG, talking to each other. "You got extra socks?"

"Right, Sarge, don't worry. We're big boys," one of them said. "What about our bedrolls and rations?"

"Battalion's sending up some Koreans with all that," Sewenski said.

"Well, now," muttered one of them, "giving us room service."

"What's this 'home-by-Christmas' stuff we hear?"

"Believe it when you see it."

"Ain't you looking forward to Christmas on the Yalu?"

"Man, them kimonos and hot baths in Japan look mighty good right now."

"They always did."

"Sounds like you mighta left something back there."

"He did. Ain't that right, Bud? Cutest little pair of almond eyes you'll ever see."

"Knock it off!" shouted Sergeant Sewenski. "I want to remind you to keep the grease off your weapons. This weather freezes everything. Grease is a sure ticket to jamming. Tonight, put your canteens inside your sleeping bag or you'll wake up with a chunk of ice inside a busted canteen."

Off to the side, talking with the newly arrived lieutenant, stood John. On the web belt strapped around his waist over the field jacket hung a holstered .45 automatic, two pouches with extra clips of ammo, and a canteen. A departing officer had given him the .45, not normally issued to lieutenants. Slung on his left shoulder was a carbine for which he carried two extra magazines. Like most of the men, he wore a pile cap.

John had taken an instant liking to Chris Ridley. He had a California beachboy look: a scrubbed face, a lithe, athletic build, a happy-go-lucky air.

"Well, Winston, too bad. Looks like Charlie Company will have a better view than you do. Our hill is higher," Ridley said, with a twinkle in his eyes.

"Fine with me. You've got to climb farther."

They were startled to see Major McKittrick walking briskly toward them, accompanied by the battalion supply officer, Captain Tompkins. He carried a wooden clipboard holding several sheets of paper.

"Well, gentlemen," McKittrick said in his crisp military voice and with a slight smile, "is Baker ready to move out?" With his crew-cut hair covered by a pile cap, he looked more mature than he had at the briefing. A major's gold leaf was in the middle of the cap's upturned bill.

"Yes, sir," John snapped back. He felt a touch of pride in being in an outfit commanded by his idea of a model officer.

"Good. Gene," he turned to Tompkins, "is there anything they need to know about supplies?"

"We've given them everything we can put our hands on. We have no reserve. Regiment says more is on the way—by the end of the day, we hope."

"Actually, we're in pretty good shape compared to First Battalion. They're really short. Now let me tell you this." He looked intently at the two lieutenants. "You may think of yourselves as lowly shavetails. I felt that way myself. But that's wrong. The infantry platoon is the basic unit in the army. That's where the job gets done or doesn't get done. No army is stronger than its platoons, and no platoon is any better than its leader." Suddenly shifting to a lighter tone, he said, "Where're you from, Ridley?"

"San Jose, California, sir."

"Great place. I was stationed at the Presidio a couple of years ago. How about you, Winston?"

"Alabama, sir."

"My roommate at the Point was from Mobile. Grand fellow. Killed at Bastogne. I always thought he would be a general. Great loss."

The sound of trucks grinding along in low gear came from behind them. They turned to see a line of deuce-and-a-halfs coming around a bend and moving slowly toward them along the narrow dirt road at the base of the ridge. Captain Grimes came up. "Good morning, sir," he said to the major. "Look's like we'll be getting under way." His paunchy face and loping gait were in sharp contrast to the major's bearing.

"Great. Right on time too," the major said, looking at his watch. "Able ought to be well on its way."

Turning to John and Ridley, he said, "You're lucky to have a fine company commander. He can be relied on to get the job done."

"Thank you, sir," said Grimes. "With your permission, sir, I'll see to this loading operation."

"Right," shot back the major. "Good luck!" He shook hands all around, saying "This is the most important operation in Korea since the Inchon landing, and I know you'll do yourselves and the battalion proud."

John walked over to the squad of eight Korean soldiers standing off to the side, a KATUSA detachment assigned to his platoon. Corp. Han Soo-Ho, the only one who spoke any English, commanded it. They were all in American-supplied uniforms indistinguishable from the rest of the platoon except for the ROK insignia. They all had M-1s slung over their shoulders. The small stature of the men gave the rifles a disproportionately long appearance.

"Corporal Han," John said, "are your men ready?"

Han snapped instantly to attention. "Yes, sir, we ready."

"Good. Just pile on the trucks with the rest of the platoon and stick with the Second Squad when we get off."

Shouted orders erupted all up and down the line as the trucks, six in all, pulled in and stopped. Tailgates clanged down, and the men of Baker's three platoons scrambled into the tarp-covered trucks, rifle butts banging on the metal flooring. The officers climbed into the cabs with the drivers, and within five minutes they were rolling slowly north back up the narrow road. The village of Kunu-ri, a distant collection of squat, thatch-roofed huts with smoke drifting from their low chimneys, dropped out of sight as they turned a curve into another valley.

The piercing cold of the night had moderated as the sun rose above the steep ridges. The day was clear except for scattered clouds. A light snow had fallen some days earlier, and thin patches remained here and there. John was invigorated by the cool, bright weather and the excitement of moving on foot into the unknown North Korean wilderness. As his platoon scrambled out of the trucks, lined up, and headed into the hills, he was seized with a sense of command that he had not previously experienced. He felt a heightened confidence as he barked out the words drilled into them at Benning: "Follow me!"

They had been on the move now for three hours, with only one fifteen-minute break. The company was strung out in single file for several hundred yards. Captain Grimes was in the lead—a point man well out ahead—with the First Platoon and the company's first sergeant, Wylie Hutchens, a longtime regular army man from Knoxville, Tennessee. Then came Second Platoon, with John at its head, followed by Third Platoon, led by Lieutenant Ridley.

The terrain was beginning to tell on the men. It was mostly up and down—up hillsides covered with scrub pine and boulders and down the other side, along rough trails through sharply defined valleys, then up another ridge, and then another. The hills and ridges were not of great altitude, but they were steep and rocky and never-ending. Despite the cold, men were now sweating. They were breathing hard and tiring, especially those carrying the heavy weapons.

"Captain says halt for a fifteen-minute break," announced First Sergeant Hutchens as he moved along the line toward the rear. "He wants to see all officers at Second Platoon right away."

The long, snaking line had entered a trail beside a rock-filled dry creek bed. The 110 men of Baker Company flopped down instantly, as if controlled by a single switch, emitting curses, complaints, and fatigued sighs. Most of the men lit up cigarettes, and all drew deeply on their canteens. Some took off their boots and massaged their feet.

Across the dry creek bed in the distance was a handful of Korean huts, clustered together, thin smoke rising from somewhere among them. A high ridge rose behind them and ran north and south parallel to the creek bed. White patches of snow splotched its sides in the shadowy defiles. The sky was blue and the air was clear and cold. Rice paddies were fewer here than in the south, and they were frozen over. The stench of human excrement had gone. The peaceful scene had probably not changed for several hundred years, except for the presence of these alien figures from ten thousand miles away, all dressed in green and olive drab and armed to the teeth. They must surely have been the first men from the Western world to set foot in this hidden valley.

Captain Grimes gathered with the lieutenants amidst a grouping of rocks just off the trail. They sat in a circle with a map spread out in the middle.

"As I figure," Grimes said, "we're here." He pointed a pencil at a spot on the map. "Hill 274 is here." He moved the pencil a bit to the north. "I reckon with all this up and down we've walked over three miles to cover about two miles."

"Look's like we're not much more than half way there," said Lieutenant Mason. "If I may say so, sir, I think we need to maintain more march discipline. The company's strung out." He seemed to want to show off his West Point background.

"Another three hours of this will probably do in these troops," said Lieutenant Puccini, the most anxious looking of the group.

"Well, we don't have any choice," Grimes said. "We've got to keep moving and occupy that hill before dark."

"Sir," John said, "the men with the heavier stuff are especially tired. What about rotating the BARs and machine guns? The mortar too."

"We could do that. Not a bad idea. Each one of you work out some system in your platoons for passing them around. Maybe we ought to give them five more minutes here."

"Good idea," Lieutenant Mason said.

"I agree we're too strung out," Grimes said. "When we get under way I want you to close it up some. Second Platoon move up on First, and Third move up on Second."

"Yes, sir," John and Ridley responded simultaneously.

They all lay back to relax for the few remaining minutes of the break. High above, out of the south, appeared a formation of three F-80 Sabre jets, streaking noiselessly northward.

"I can't get used to airplanes that don't make any sound when they're coming at you," Captain Grimes said.

"It's just as hard to get used to planes without propellers," Ridley said.

"I guess jets just keep up with their own sound," Mason said.

As he spoke, the planes came directly overhead. A crack of thunder broke over them, echoing and re-echoing across the hills and gradually dying out, as the trio of fighters disappeared to the north.

"What are they up to?" asked Ridley.

Grimes said, "Patrolling up along the Yalu to be sure they spot any Chinks coming across. I'm glad to know they're on the lookout. We don't want any surprises." From the far distance to their rear came the faint sound of engines of some sort. "Do you suppose that's our tank support?" asked Puccini.

"I wouldn't bank on it," Grimes said. "You may have noticed it would be pretty tough to get a tank up here."

"It would be," interjected Mason, "but we've seen signs of a couple of rough roads where I think they can make it."

"Sir," Puccini asked, "do you think the artillery boys can get some 105s in position to support us?"

"Well," Grimes drawled, "that's doubtful too. Look at this stuff we've come through. There aren't many spots level enough to set up even a couple of howitzers."

"By the way, sir," spoke up John, "where's our FO?"

"What about that, Mason?" asked Grimes.

"He's with Charlie. Says he thinks their position might give him the best vantage point on the battalion front."

Grimes rose to his feet. "OK," he announced, "let's get moving. We'll never get there sitting here."

Noon came and went. After a short break for C-rations, Baker Company plodded on, men scrambling over rocks, pushing through scrub growth on trackless hillsides. Fatigue was now strongly etched on their faces.

In his own sweating weariness, John thought of all of the army's twentieth-century motorized transport that was of no use here. These infantrymen were plodding onward, tired and dispirited, no different from soldiers of millennia past, as though the internal-combustion engine had never been invented. And what a grain of sand they were on the great beach of an army. This handful of men was a mere fraction of this force of nearly two hundred thousand, all moving northward, hundreds of handfuls like Baker Company. Major McKittrick was surely right, he thought. The infantry platoons were the critical elements. Despite his fatigue, he felt an undercurrent of exhilaration at being part of this advancing, victorious army, men from many parts of the globe here to make good on the U.N. commitment.

His reverie was broken by the halting of First Platoon in front of him. Top Sergeant Hutchens came hurriedly back along the line. "Captain wants to see all the officers up front."

On command, the entire line flopped down on the rocky trail. John, Ridley, Puccini, and Mason all gathered around Captain Grimes at the head.

Grimes was looking alternately at a map and through a pair of field glasses slung around his neck. "All right, look's like we're finally here. Unless I'm badly reading this Jap map, there's 274." He pointed to a distant ridge lying across the head of the narrow valley in which they had halted. Like the countless other ridges they had seen and climbed, it was covered with scrubby trees with dark, dull evergreen foliage, bare in spots where there were rocky outcroppings.

Grimes spread his Japanese map out on a flat boulder. "Here's how we'll move in."

The lieutenants clustered around the map. Grimes explained that Puccini's First Platoon would occupy the western end of the ridge, Ridley's Third Platoon the eastern end, and John's Second Platoon the middle. They would split up here and proceed to their positions by separate routes.

"Puccini, see this stream here," Grimes said, running a pencil along a line on the map. "It's probably a dry creek bed. Take that and it should bring you up on the left flank. Ridley, here's what looks like a saddle between 274 and Charlie's position. Go up that way and you should get on to our right flank. Winston, you can keep straight on this trail to the middle of the position. Any questions?"

Mason spoke up. "I assume we want to set up a continuous line once we're up there."

"Absolutely. It's now 1430. I want everybody in position by 1530. Sergeant Hutchens and I will check you out then. Get dug in and organize your guards. I want each platoon to post two guards at all times. You can rotate the men on two-hour shifts."

The First and Third platoons moved off. The captain, Sergeant Hutchens, and a radio operator sat down on some rocks to talk about establishing the company CP. John, left alone with his platoon, was now on his own. "Get Corporal Han up here," he directed Sergeant Sewenski, who was standing beside him. "He probably doesn't know anything about this place, but he'll know more than we do."

In less than three minutes Sewenski returned with the diminutive Korean corporal in tow. "Do you know anything about this country?" John asked, knowing full well what the answer would be.

"No, sir."

"Did they teach you anything about this area in the army?"

"No, sir. I South Korea. This North Korea."

"Yes, I know. Anyway, I want you to stay with me just in case."

"Just in what case, sir?"

John was mildly taken aback. Was this Korean trying to be fresh or was there a communication problem here? "Any case. Whatever may come up. Just stick with me."

In another twenty minutes Second Platoon was approaching the base of Hill 274. The men were strung out single file. In the lead was John with Sergeant Sewenski and Corporal Han. They were followed by the First Squad, in the charge of Corp. Robert Donovan, a lanky country boy from Arkansas. John had developed a special liking for him. He was quick, had a good sense of humor, and was firmly in command of his men.

They came out of a defile and moved along an open stretch parallel to the hill. When they were hundred yards from the point where John planned to begin the ascent, rifle shots erupted suddenly from the slope ahead.

"Hit the dirt!" Sewenski shouted. The command was unnecessary. Every man had instantly dived off toward the cover of underbrush and rocks.

Within seconds another volley crackled from the hill. This time John heard the close-by sound of ricocheting bullets.

He lay flat on his stomach, pressed up against a slight rise in the ground, his heart pumping fiercely and his breath coming hard. It had finally happened. Someone up there was intent on killing him. His mouth had gone dry. He gritted his teeth, resolving to stay under control.

"Was anyone hit?" he whispered to Sewinski.

"Can't tell. Don't hear anything." Next to Sewinski was Han and beyond him was Donovan, both hunched behind rocks. "Say, Donovan, pass the word along to see if anybody was hit."

John spoke again to Sewenski. "See that clump of rocks halfway up? Sounded like the shots came from there."

"Sounded that way to me too. What about putting a few rounds up there and see what happens?"

"OK."

"Hey, Donovan, get your men to put a couple of dozen rounds up on that knoll," Sewenski said, pointing up the hill.

The rifles in First Squad crackled for several seconds, stirring up dirt and chipping off rocks along the lip of the knoll. "OK," Donovan called out, "that's enough."

A full minute passed. Eight men abruptly leaped up from behind the rocks and fled to their rear. Rifle fire instantly broke out all along the platoon line. Two of the running men pitched forward. The others disappeared into the trees. They reminded John of a flushed covey of quail, two birds shot down on the rise.

The platoon moved up the hill, line abreast. "Keep on your toes!" Sewenski shouted. "More gooks might be up there!"

They reached the rocky outcropping. Beyond, they saw the two soldiers sprawled out, face down. A bullet had caught one in the back of the head and taken off the top of his skull. A bloody mess of brains spilled out on the ground. The other showed no wounds. Han rolled him over. At least two bullets had struck him in the back, passed through his body, and ripped open his front.

John had never seen death so close and so recent and so gory. He thought he would vomit, but he kept it down. He couldn't get sick in front of his men.

The dead soldiers wore brown quilted jackets, the color of dark mustard, and cloth caps and rubberlike shoes. Each had a bandolier of rifle ammunition. Han searched the pack each was carrying and found entrenching tools and a quantity of cooked rice.

"Look here, Lieutenant," Sewenski said. "This one has an M-1. That's a helluva note. Being fired on by our own weapons."

"What's that other rifle?" John asked.

"Japanese," replied Han.

John looked at Han. "Are these men from some North Korean unit? Do you know which?"

"No, sir," Han said, "They not Korean. They Chinese."

Chapter 6

THE LATE NOVEMBER DUSK SETTLED over Hill 274, and the thermometer dropped. Baker's three platoons were stretched out along two hundred yards of the hilltop. Instructions to dig in had not been followed. The rocky ground did not yield readily to entrenching tools, and the men were too exhausted to continue the effort for long. Instead they had piled up rocks and tree branches to create makeshift defensive positions.

Along its crest the hill was treeless and relatively level. In front of them it sloped down into rocks and scattered, scrubby trees. The floor of the small valley they faced was obscured by the growth. Other hills loomed ahead and to their right and left. Charlie and Able were somewhere out there on their flanks, but there was no contact.

Captain Grimes had established his command post about fifty yards behind Second Platoon, where the hill began to slope downward to their rear. There he gathered his lieutenants for a briefing. He would not bother with patrols now, he said, because of the coming darkness, but in the morning he wanted patrolling out to their front and flanks. It was important that they make contact with Able and Charlie. Telephone wire had not yet been run up from battalion, so he had no idea where the battalion CP was. The Korean bearers had not shown up, so there would be no bedrolls and additional rations until the next day. Then they talked about the Chinese flushed on the hill that afternoon.

"I thought MacArthur said the Chinese wouldn't come in," Puccini said, looking worried as usual.

"He did," Grimes said. "Told the president last month at Wake Island."

"Now the intelligence folks are talking about forty-eight thousand out there somewhere," John said.

Mason chimed in. "They think they're a screening force, mainly to delay our advance, maybe to try to scare us away from the Yalu. There's nothing left of the North Korean army."

"Forty-eight thousand doesn't amount to much in face of the whole Eighth Army," Ridley said.

"Unless they're all right in front of us," Grimes said with a slight laugh.

Night came on, and the cold deepened. It got down to fifteen degrees above zero. No fires could be built. Without sleeping bags or bedrolls and with insufficient winter clothing, the men were miserably cold. But, except those who rotated on guard duty, they slept, exhausted after the taxing daylong march.

Asleep, John dreamt he was on a quail hunt back home. It was a golden autumn afternoon, with the cool feel and smell of fall in the air. He was at the climactic moment; the English setter had pointed. He walked slowly forward, past the rigid dog, its tail stretched out, one front foot lifted, nose extended fixedly ahead. He held his shotgun high, almost in firing position, ready to be leveled on one of the rising quail. The covey suddenly thundered upward.

He awoke, his body shaking in the frigid air. Sergeant Sewenski was standing up and swinging his arms.

"Lieutenant, one thing you can say about this Godforsaken country, besides being damn cold, is that it's quiet," Sewinski said in a hushed voice. "I mean quiet like you ain't never heard before."

The only sound was the occasional shuffling of some soldier trying to get comfortable. It was as though all sound had been sucked from the earth. Primeval man, ten thousand years ago, could not have had it quieter.

"You're right," he whispered, "but I wouldn't complain about it. It would be fine if it were like this all the way to Manchuria."

A nearly full moon had risen, illuminating the entire landscape. It was almost light as day. The rugged, forlorn land took on an eerie beauty in the cold moonlight. The valley stretching out before him, and surrounding hills, could be seen in vivid detail.

Godforsaken, Sewenski had said. He recalled from somewhere in Psalms: "If I make my bed in hell . . . if I take the wings of the morning and dwell in the uttermost parts of the sea . . . Thou art there. . . . The darkness and the light are both alike to thee." Under that view, no place on earth could literally be godforsaken. But if any place could be, this desolate corner of Asia would surely be a candidate.

After an endless night of cold and fitful sleep along Hill 274, the men finally saw dawn creeping in from the east. Having dreamt of quail hunting, he now thought of dove shoots in the country near Remberton. This was their time of day, and it was his favorite kind of hunting. He could see himself and a half-dozen friends ringing a cornfield with their shotguns just after daybreak, the doves coming in high and fast, making unusually challenging targets. A good dove shoot sounded like a small war.

The cold abated as the day wore on, but it was never warm. The Korean bearers arrived with bedrolls and C-rations, but no ammunition.

"Hey, fellows, all the comforts of home for tonight."

"Yeah, they'll be spoiling us if they ain't careful. Next thing you know, they'll let us get a shower." Nobody in the company had taken a shower in nearly two weeks. "Maybe even a hot meal."

"Now you're really being ridiculous. Next thing you know, you'll be expecting geisha girls."

"Don't these C-rations beat that rice those Chinks had?"

"That's a close question."

A wiring team made it up from the battalion CP and hooked up Captain Grimes by field telephone. He talked with Major McKittrick, reporting that his patrols had made contact with Able and Charlie, each more than half a mile away over sharp ridges.

"What about radio contact?" the major asked.

"Can't reach either one on my SCR 300. The hills are apparently blocking transmission. The radio's not in the best shape either."

"This is the damnedest country," the major said. "Anyway, I expect we'll be moving on tomorrow."

Night came on again and with it the freezing cold. A full moon emerged, again illuminating a desolate and eerily beautiful landscape. In the distance, frost glistened on dead stalks in a corn-field at the far end of the little valley.

Not long after moonrise, the silence was broken by the sound of firing far to the east. It grew in intensity. The heavy throbbing of artillery blended with mortars and small-arms fire.

Captain Grimes stood listening with Mason and John. He said, "It's over where the ROK divisions are."

"Sounds like something big's going on," Mason said.

Half an hour passed. The noise from the east was continuous and undiminished. Then suddenly they heard firing on their left, much closer at hand. The crackle of rifles and submachine guns was clear.

"That's over at Able," Grimes said, looking to the left.

The firing kept up for ten or fifteen minutes and then stopped. All was quiet in that direction. Then through the moonlit night came a weird and startling sound: the forlorn notes of a bugle: "Ta-TA ta-TA ta-TA." Firing resumed to their left with greater intensity. A whistle sounded. Exploding mortar shells could now be heard.

John turned and went back to his platoon. Surveying the valley to his front, he was startled to see a long column of men coming out of the north and moving quietly across the moonlit cornfield at the far end of the valley. They were out of Baker's firing range. The column quickly passed from sight into a defile. He immediately reported to Grimes, who got the battalion CP on the phone. "Two hundred enemy soldiers in a column of twos heading south between Able and Baker."

As he put down the phone, the tinny blare of a bugle came from their right. Again that weird sound: "Ta-TA ta-TA ta-TA." Within seconds, rifle and submachine gun fire broke out and rose in intensity.

"That's Charlie," Grimes said. "Get all your men on double alert."

Another half-hour passed. It was now near 10 P.M. Heavy firing in the vicinity of both Able and Charlie companies continued. But now fire broke out to their rear. "Could that be back at the battalion CP?" John blurted out.

Grimes was already cranking the field telephone. After listening for a long minute, he put the phone down. He turned to his lieutenants, grim-faced. "The CP's under attack. The Chinks are all around us. I don't know how long our little island of tranquility will last. Winston, pull out one of your squads and set up an outpost along our rear."

Suddenly a half-dozen grenades exploded down toward Third Platoon. "My God," Grimes exclaimed, "now we're gonna get it!" Ridley took off at a run. "Hutchens! Where's Hutchens?"

"Here, sir." The first sergeant stepped forward, his breath luminous in the bright moonlight.

"Get over there and find out what's happening."

John, back with his platoon, looked down the long slope to their front and thought he saw shadowy figures moving amid the rocks and scrub trees two hundred yards away. "Sewenski," he called in an urgent voice, "look! Are my eyes playing tricks or are those men down there?"

"No tricks. This is it." Without hesitating a second, Sewenski ran along the line, issuing muffled commands: "Everybody up! We got trouble!"

He came back to John. The ghostly figures milled around in the shadows. John whispered, "I think we ought to hold fire. It's too far. What do you think?"

"Right," Sewenski said. "Let's watch it."

A cloud passed across the moon, darkening the scene. The figures became obscure in the gloom of the distant trees.

This is it. Sewenski's words played back through his mind. This is it . . . this is it. This was the moment he had imagined a hundred times, the moment for which he, an infantry lieutenant, had come ten thousand miles. His mouth was dry. His stomach felt queasy. Blood was pounding in his ears. His breath was short and rapid.

He lay flat behind a low pile of rocks, his numbed finger on the frigid trigger of his carbine. Stay in control. Stay calm. Maybe talking would help. "Sewenski, are all the men ready?"

"Yes, sir. I moved the KATUSAs between the Second and Third squads. They were on the end."

At that instant a bugle sounded from somewhere out in the valley below. It was that same chilling sound: "Ta-Ta ta-Ta ta-Ta."

"Here they come," said Corporal Donovan in a hushed voice. He was crouched behind a pile of rocks a few feet from John.

The figures grew larger and more numerous. The cloud passed, and the landscape was again lit with a near-daylight brilliance. Coming up the rugged slope at a run were at least a hundred Chinese.

Grimes came running along the line. "Open fire! Let 'em have it!"

Rifle and carbine fire poured from the Baker Company front, throwing up a wall of bullets in the face of the oncoming Chinese. Tracers from First Platoon's machine gun cut a diagonal path through their double rank. Some of the Chinese pitched forward; others spun around and fell back down the slope. But many kept running upward, hunched over and firing their Soviet-made burp guns.

"Get that machine gun going!" Sewenski yelled.

"It's jammed!" came back the answer.

"Pull the bolt back," called Sewenski.

Broderick, the gunner, yanked the bolt a couple of times and got off a half-dozen rounds. "It's jammed again."

"Keep working the bolt!"

Another voice called out: "The BAR's frozen up!"

John, flat on his stomach behind the rocks, heard the buzz of bullets overhead and the zing of bullets glancing off nearby rocks. He was seized with a single thought: This is kill or be killed. He shoved his carbine through a break in the rocks, set it on semiautomatic, and began firing at the oncoming Chinese, who were now within a hundred yards. Smoke was accumulating, and he could not be sure that he hit anyone.

"Pick your targets," yelled Sewenski. "Save your ammo."

From down the line came an anguished cry, "I'm hit!" From the other end, "They got Broderick!"

More Chinese were falling. Perhaps half their number had gone down. Suddenly whistles blew somewhere down the hill, and they blew again. The onrushing Chinese abruptly turned and ran back, stumbling over their dead, several more pitching forward, as the firing from Baker continued.

"Hold it! Hold it!" shouted John as the figures merged into the trees. In the quiet that followed, the only sounds were the moans of wounded men. The fight had lasted less than a quarter-hour.

John and Sewenski took stock. Broderick, the machine gunner, was dead, hit squarely in the forehead. Nausea again welled up in his stomach as he looked at the bloody face of a man he had been talking to only an hour earlier. Two other men were dead, both of whom had arrived only a week before and were hardly known to anybody. Six others were wounded in the shoulders and arms; two had superficial scalp wounds. Their buddies had broken out first-aid kits and were patching them up.

Sewenski came upon a man urinating on the BAR. "What in the hell are you doing?"

"Thawing out this son of a bitch. See, there it goes." He forced the bolt back.

"Hey, Lieutenant, what's that?" asked Donovan, fingering a hole in the left arm of John's field jacket. "Look's like a near miss."

John looked down at the hole. "Too near," he mumbled.

Sewenski came up with Corp. Han Soo-Ho in tow and announced, "Lieutenant, three KATUSAs bugged out."

Han blurted out, "I try to stop. No could do. They too fast."

"Tell the rest of them that's a court-martial offense. They could be shot."

Captain Grimes assembled his lieutenants. "Good job. We turned them back, and hit 'em pretty hard. But we took some casualties. Hutchens, what's your count?"

The first sergeant reported: "Three dead in First Platoon, three dead in Second Platoon, five dead in Third Platoon. We've got twenty-one wounded, about half of them out of action. So we're down about twenty men, counting dead and wounded."

"We got an expensive answer to one question we've been wondering about. We now know there are Chinese out there."

"But we don't know how many or what they're up to," Mason said. "Could be just a hit-and-run screening force."

"I'm inclined to think something bigger's going on. They're all around us," Grimes said. "Listen to that firing still going on in the east."

John spoke up. "Captain, you've got to subtract from the strength three KATUSAs who bugged out."

"I'm sorry to have to tell you, sir," Ridley said, "but two of my men bugged out. I tried to tackle one, but he got away."

"Too many new men here with too little training," Mason added.

"Bugging out is one thing this army can't stand for," Grimes said with unusual seriousness. "I've heard about it in other outfits, but not here. I expect you to stop it." He looked squarely at each lieutenant as he spoke. They all nodded their understanding, wondering how they could guarantee that no man would bolt and run in the midst of a fight.

They discussed the wounded. There were two problems. They had no assurance that the aid station was still there. The firing from that direction had stopped, but the telephone to the battalion CP was now dead. Even if the aid station were still in business, the company had no litter-bearers and no stretchers. The wounded could be taken back on makeshift stretchers, using blankets, but the company could not undertake that in the middle of the night, not knowing whether there were Chinese in their rear, and with the possibility of a renewed attack still alive.

"We don't have any idea what shape Able and Charlie are in," Grimes said. "It sounded like they were getting hit harder and longer than we were. At first light I want to send out patrols to make contact with them and the CP. Mason, what do you think we ought to do about our position here?"

"I recommend that we get all the wounded over toward the rear of the hill and then tighten up the line." He spoke with his usual assurance. "We should probably move the First and Third platoons in toward the middle."

"Puccini and Ridley, what do you think of that?"

"I was going to suggest it myself," Ridley said. "The grenades got my machine gun and the BAR."

"If we move in, I think we ought to keep our flanks covered," Puccini said.

"That's right," Grimes said.

They went on for a while discussing the deployment. Grimes suggested the men get some sleep, with guards posted and rotated through the night.

All around was quiet, except for distant rumbling in the east. Zipped up in his sleeping bag and warming up at last, John couldn't sleep. Chinese soldiers lay crumpled and dead in the moonlight only a short distance down the slope. They would be frozen stiff by morning, preserved until spring or until buried. Who would bury them? They were all dead at the hands of Baker Company, himself included. Had he actually killed a man, maybe more than one? Probably so, but he was not sure. He steeled himself with the thought that they were "the enemy." He could not permit himself to think of them as fellow human beings. If they had not been killed, they would have killed him and his men. It was his life or theirs, kill or be killed.

He was interrupted by shouts from the direction of the Third Platoon. He squirmed out of his sleeping bag and ran toward the sounds. In the moonlight he saw Lieutenant Ridley and several of his men surrounding a half-dozen American GIs with ripped clothing, blackened faces, and no head gear; they carried no weapons. Lt. Mike Forney, the forward observer, was one of them.

"These men are from Charlie Company," Ridley said. "They just broke into our line—a miracle we didn't shoot them."

The bedraggled group had a harrowing story. Charlie had been hit by the Chinese. They held them off for a long while, but their ammunition ran out. Hand-to-hand fighting ensued. The captain was killed. Many were wounded. They did not know what happened to the other officers. When the situation became hopeless, they and a few others managed to break out and run for it. In short, Charlie Company had been overrun and wiped out. A somber Grimes summoned his lieutenants. "With Charlie gone, our right flank is wide open. God only knows what's happened to Able. So . . . boys," he dragged out his words slowly and emphatically, "we might be sitting here all by ourselves. For all we know, we don't even have a battalion CP anymore."

They stood silently in a small circle for a few moments. Then Grimes asked, "What's the ammo situation?"

The lieutenants gave similar reports. The M-1s were down to about twenty rounds apiece. The carbines had maybe thirty or forty rounds. Most of the men had one hand grenade. The BARs and machine guns—the two left—were running low.

"I want half the men awake at all times," Grimes said. "Check your positions and build them up with rocks or whatever you can find. Too bad we can't dig foxholes in this stuff."

Distant firing in the east was still audible. The news of the Charlie Company disaster and the realization that they were now isolated and exposed made sleep impossible.

John looked at his luminous watch dial: a few minutes after 4 A.M. The moon had gone, and the night was now black. The silence was total. The temperature was just a little above zero.

The silence was shattered suddenly by earsplitting explosions of hand grenades all up and down the Baker Company line. Shrieks of pain and shouts of "I'm hit" mingled with the noise. John, coming out of his sleeping bag, felt the blast of a grenade on his back. He knew the Chinese could be no farther than fifteen or twenty yards away—right in their faces, concealed by the darkness.

They opened fire straight ahead, not seeing anything and not knowing whether they were hitting anything. They began heaving back the Soviet-style potato-masher grenades before they could explode. Shadowy forms of men began to appear to their front, no more than ten yards away. Many were firing bursts from Soviet-made burp guns into the Baker line. John put his carbine on full automatic and began spraying the oncoming forms. The advance halted as Baker's fire became intense.

First one and then another voice and still another could be heard above the cacophony of rifle and carbine fire and grenade explosions: "I'm out of ammo!"

Someone shouted suddenly, "They're coming in behind us."

John wheeled to the rear. The thickening smoke combined with the darkness made it hard to tell friend from foe. But there was no time to deliberate. He saw two men running toward him. He raised his carbine and pulled the trigger, but he got only a click. He had no more clips. He threw down the carbine and snatched his .45 from its holster. He leveled the heavy automatic at the chest of one of the oncoming figures and fired. It bucked upward in his hand as the figure stumbled to the ground. He swung to the other onrushing form and again fired, bringing the man down at his feet.

Chinese were climbing over the rocks from the front. Sewenski slammed the butt of an M-1 against the head of one, making a ghastly, crunching sound.

The Baker men were using rifles and carbines as clubs and pikes, slashing and stabbing. A few men still had ammunition and were firing into the heads and chests of the Chinese, often within touching distance, and the Chinese were firing back. The air was acrid with the smell of cordite. Smoke obscured muzzle flashes and produced a ghostly half-light. Shouts, curses, screams, and sounds of firing intermingled in a hilltop bedlam.

Above the wild melee, John suddenly heard Captain Grimes shouting at the top of his voice: "We've got to get out of here! . . . Get out of here! . . . Follow me! . . . Take off!"

John shouted to Sewenski, "OK, let's go! Pass the word! To the rear!" Then he broke into a run, yelling to the men to follow him and shoving a fresh clip into his .45. He ran headlong into a Chinese, knocking him off his feet, but kept on going.

Sewenski ran alongside him. Suddenly out of the murkiness a burp gun crackled, the burst catching Sewenski in the middle. He pitched forward, landing on his side. John instinctively dropped to his knees and turned him over on his back. His chest and stomach were ripped open; blood and guts were everywhere. He was dead beyond any doubt. John was transfixed by the gory remains of his sergeant.

Shouts in Chinese and English were all around him, mingled with rifle and burp-gun fire. The sickening thought struck him: I'm deserting my men. But there was no time to think. The captain had ordered them out. It was get out or die.

He lunged to his feet but was stopped instantly by a violent jab in the chest. Another painful jab caught him in the back. In the dim flickering light cast by the nearby burst of a burp gun, he saw that he was ringed by a half-dozen Chinese soldiers, each pointing a rifle straight at him.

Chapter 7

Two of the Chinese soldiers nudged him with their rifles toward the rear of the hill and motioned him to sit down. Their rifle muzzles remained pointed at his chest.

The shouting and firing died gradually out, but moaning and cries of pain from the wounded of both sides continued. Along the crest, Chinese soldiers talked and yelped at each other as they rummaged with glee through the Americans' abandoned packs and bedrolls. They had no apparent interest in pursuing those—however few there might have been—who got away.

John sat on the frozen ground, stunned by the awful incomprehensibility of what had happened. Suddenly, an American voice was beside him in the darkness: "Lieutenant, I thought you were dead or gone! This is Donovan." Two Chinese with rifles prodded him down beside John.

"My God, Donovan, it's you! What about the rest of the men?"

"Mostly dead or wounded. I saw the Chinks rounding up three or four still walking. I don't know how many got away."

John felt tears rolling unexpectedly down his cheeks, turning into icy rivulets. "What went wrong? We failed. I failed these men. How could this happen?"

"We were outnumbered and overrun. It's not your fault. We put up a pretty damn good fight. Nobody told us we would run into a buzz saw like this."

The Chinese poked at them with their rifles, motioning them to

be quiet. John asked, "Anybody here speak English?" There was no
response and no sign of understanding.

"We've got to get out of this," he whispered quickly.

Time passed. The Chinese on Hill 274 quieted down, and only muffled voices could be heard, along with the pained sounds from the
wounded. John and Donovan shifted positions to relieve the numb-
ness from the cold. Each time they moved, the Chinese guards jabbed
at them with their rifle muzzles, as if commanding them to be still.

As he slumped there in the numbing cold, a strange realization
came upon him. He remembered the fear that gripped him as the
first Chinese attack began; he now saw that in the last melee all fear
had gone. He had been oblivious to everything except the fight to
stay alive, to kill Chinese before they killed him. Not only fear but
all thought had been suspended. He had been functioning on pure
instinct and adrenaline. There must be a lesson in all this about fear.

The first hints of a cheerless dawn appeared in the east. Sounds of
stirring picked up along the hilltop. Chinese voices became audible. As
the light grew, he could discern the features of his guards for the first
time. They sat impassively in brown quilted clothing and cloth caps.
With the light, the carnage around them came into view. Dead Chinese and American bodies lay helter skelter in all sorts of contorted
positions, some crumpled, some bloody and torn. He was both hungry
and sick at the stomach, and he had never been as cold in his life.

Three Chinese approached. The guards prodded John and Donovan to their feet. One of the Chinese, who appeared to be in charge,
spoke to the guards. He was dressed like the others, but with red
piping on his collar and a small red star on his cap. Discussion and
gesturing went on for several minutes. The man with the red star
kept pointing along the hill toward the east.

John looked at him and asked, "Do you speak English?" Again
there was no response.

The guards punched John and Donovan in the back with their
rifle muzzles, motioning in the direction their leader had been pointing. They moved off. Donovan was in the lead with a guard behind
him, followed by John, with a guard at his back. They passed through
the milling Chinese and dead bodies, American and Chinese
intermingled, now frozen in their distorted positions. Around them
rose the harrowing groans of the wounded.

They left Hill 274 and moved in single file along a lower ridge.

Donovan and his guard were five yards ahead of John. He was firmly resolved that he would not let himself be marched off and shot or become a Chinese POW. He formulated his escape plan. He began to sing in a made-up, lilting melody: "We're leaving . . . to our right . . . when I say go, turn around and grab your man . . . I'll first count up one, two, three . . . then we'll run to the right, to the right." The guard jabbed John hard in the back with the rifle muzzle. He stopped singing, and they kept on walking.

They were now a couple of hundred yards away from Hill 274, and all was quiet around them except for the crunching sound of their boots on the rocky soil. To the right, the ridge sloped down steeply into scrubby trees, rocks, and underbrush. That was south, the way he wanted to go, the way toward Americans, he hoped.

Suddenly he sang out, "All right, Donovan, one, two, three . . . go!"

He wheeled and savagely charged headlong into the guard behind him. They crashed to the ground, the Chinese dropping his rifle and falling flat on his back. John slammed his fist into the man's face. His knees were in the man's stomach. He grabbed the rifle and with all his might rammed the butt into the man's head.

He leaped up and saw that Donovan was on top of his guard. He yelled, "Let's get out of here!" He plunged down the slope and into the thick growth.

Down and down he ran, stumbling over rocks and underbrush, barely staying on his feet. Branches of trees tore at his field jacket and face. As he hurtled downward, he hoped that Donovan was with him, but he wanted only to put as much distance as possible between himself and the Chinese.

The ground leveled out, and the trees thinned. He emerged into a small valley. Ridges rose on both sides. He stopped, his breath coming in great gasps, tearing at his lungs. He heard the crashing sounds of someone running through the underbrush behind him. He squatted in a clump of brush and waited. In a moment Donovan came into view. John hailed him, and they sat down together, not saying anything until they recovered something like a normal breathing rate.

In the far distance, in the direction from which they had come, they heard shots, random, single shots.

"Sounds like that's coming from 274," John said.

"You know what those bastards are doing, don't you?" Donovan said.

They sat in silence. After a few minutes the shooting stopped.

"Donovan," John began slowly, "I left the dead and wounded." Tears welled in his eyes.

"Damn, Lieutenant, you didn't have any choice. The captain ordered us out. Anyway, you didn't leave. You were captured."

"But I was trying to get out."

"Are you bound to commit suicide? We were finished."

"I could have stayed and fought on."

They sat without talking. All around them was now quiet, but sounds of distant firing came drifting in from the west and the southeast.

"I don't understand what that can be," John said, gesturing eastward. "It sounds like it's to the rear of those ROK divisions."

The temperature had not risen above freezing. They had had no sleep for over twenty-four hours and nothing to eat since some C-rations the evening before. They had no food or water, and they had lost their headgear somewhere along the way. But they each had an M-1 rifle taken from the Chinese guards. Between them they had eight rounds in their magazine clips.

All morning and into the afternoon they walked in what they hoped was the direction of Kunu-ri. By keeping the sun on their left before noon and on the right after noon they could maintain a generally southward course. But it was impossible to travel in a straight line because of the crisscrossing hills and ridges. Most of the time they were either climbing up steep hillsides or working their way down them. They proceeded cautiously, ever alert for enemy troops. They figured that with the entire Eighth Army stretched out from the mountains to the sea, they were bound to eventually intersect one of its units. Yet the absence of any sign of American forces thus far and the continued sounds of firing to the east and the west stirred within them an eerie feeling that something strange and ominous was afoot.

They did occasionally see American Sabre jets flying northward. "I'm mighty glad they're looking out for Chinks," Donovan said. "We'd like to know if any of 'em are around here."

"Yeah," John said, "those jets were a big help last night. Just as good as the artillery."

At midafternoon they crested a ridge and saw in a small valley below them several rice paddies alongside a lone farmhouse—the usual low, thatch-roofed hut. They were beginning to feel weak from their exertions and having had nothing to eat for nearly twenty-four hours. There was no sign of human life except a thin wisp of smoke curling up from one end of the house. So with their hunger and thirst mounting and with no other prospects, they decided to take the risk of seeking food and water.

They went down a trail that led between the paddies and the house. When they reached the door, Donovan stood to one side, his rifle at the ready, while John knocked, his rifle also poised for action. A small elderly Korean man opened the door just wide enough to see out.

John was uncertain how to get across his message. He stammered, "We Americans. Need food." He motioned into his mouth as though he were eating and also patted his stomach.

The Korean looked puzzled for a moment and then turned and said something back into the house. The door opened wider, and an equally elderly Korean woman appeared at his side. The two stood together looking at John and Donovan as though they were seeing creatures from outer space. John repeated his statement and gestures of hunger with added vigor. The couple murmured "Ah!" and nodded their heads affirmatively. They opened the door wider and motioned the Americans to come inside.

The door closed behind them, and they found themselves in a warm, cozy, but exceedingly plain space. They saw no one else. The room had the unmistakable odor of kimchee, that distinctive concoction of fermented cabbage and garlic, whose pungent, unpleasant aroma they had whiffed in numerous villages. They had not imagined that they would ever eat the foul-smelling stuff, but now they would take anything they could get.

The man gestured for them to sit on the floor against the wall. To their surprise they found the floor itself to be heated. They leaned back against the wall, warmer than they had been for more than a week. Yet they did not feel altogether relaxed; there was no way to know who else might be around or who might show up. There appeared to be another room to the rear, but they sensed no sign of life in that direction. They kept their rifles in their laps, safeties off, but as a matter of courtesy not trained on their hosts.

The woman went to a pot sitting on a low stove at the other end of the room. She began ladling into two bowls. Much to their relief they saw that it was hot rice and not kimchee. The man handed one to John and one to Donovan. They were so hungry that they immediately dug their fingers into the rice and began eating it in large gulps. It tasted flat and unseasoned, but the taste was irrelevant; it was food. The couple served them a second bowl, and they wolfed it down as well. They shook their heads when offered more, but they made motions of drinking. The woman then brought them bowls of water, which they drank in rapid swallows.

They sat there, warm and relaxed. Drowsiness descended, and their eyelids grew heavy. To stay on this warm floor and sleep was tempting; indeed, it was getting harder by the minute to resist. Yet they knew they dare not. They must keep moving. The Chinese might be everywhere, and chances for escape diminishing by the hour.

John wanted to compensate these lifesaving people, but he could think of no way to do so. He had no money, and even if he had, it would mean nothing here. He reluctantly concluded that he could only try to express their gratitude by gestures.

Through the walls of the hut he suddenly became aware of a faint yet rising sound. It was the sound of voices mingled with the clinking of some kind of equipment. He and Donovan snapped awake and were on their feet immediately. He cracked the door a tiny bit and instantly closed it.

"Chinese!" he said in a hushed voice. "At least a company-sized group."

The two headed toward the rear door. John put his finger to his lips, signaling the Korean couple to remain quiet. The door led into a dim room where there appeared to be sacks of rice and farm implements. They stood out of sight, their rifles at the ready. John's pulse was pounding.

The sounds of tramping feet and Chinese chatter grew louder, coming from the north down the trail heading south. Would they stop at this lonely farmhouse? What could two Americans do against a Chinese company? He mentally prayed that they would keep going . . . keep going . . . God, keep them moving on.

Then the column was even with the house. He held his breath.

The footsteps did not slacken. They passed on by, and the sounds gradually receded and then were gone. He let out a huge sigh of relief.

He and Donovan came out of the back room, and he stepped over to the Korean couple. He put his hand on the man's shoulder, saying, "We thank you. We thank you," bowing his head at the same time.

After quickly surveying the scene through the cracked door and finding it deserted, they stepped out into the frigid air. Instead of continuing south along the trail, they struck out west over the ridge behind the house.

An hour later they found themselves in another valley with dusk coming on. As they came from behind an outcropping of rock, they saw not more than seventy yards away a group of Chinese soldiers sitting in an open area. They ducked back behind the rocks and then crept carefully to a gap in the ledge where they could get a good look. Fifty or sixty men were gathered around a large black pot, all in the now-familiar brown quilted jackets and cloth caps. Some were walking back and forth to the pot and dipping into it. They were having an evening meal of rice.

"We could pick off some of those sons of bitches," Donovan whispered.

"We could, but I don't think we want to commit suicide yet. We better keep moving."

They backtracked and went north until they found a saddle running westward between higher ridges. It was rapidly growing dark, and they decided to hole up until daylight. They found a thick growth of trees in a narrow ravine. They broke off tree limbs and covered themselves with a dense layer of evergreen foliage and curled up as tightly as possible to try to pass through the freezing night.

Never had he felt so alone and abandoned. There must be thousands of their fellow countrymen close by, certainly within a few miles, but where were they? Surely the entire Eighth Army could not have evaporated. Though he felt profoundly alone, he knew they were not; the countryside was crawling with Chinese.

Curled up and shaking in the bitter cold, the moonlight eerily filtering down through the trees, John was hit with the full force of the disaster. Where were other Baker officers? Dead, wounded, cap-

tured? Was it possible that only he and Corporal Donovan were still
alive? Death had been all around them, in their midst, brushing
against him—he himself had killed men—and now he knew death
was out there in these desolate hills and valleys, standing by to claim
them. He thought of a First World War poem he memorized in high
school:

> I have a rendezvous with death
> On some scarred slope of battered hill
> And I to my pledged word am true
> I shall not fail that rendezvous.

In his desolation, he realized he was ready for the rendezvous. The
desperate fight on Hill 274 had given him a peculiar sense of immu-
nity against fear. If death wanted him, it could take him. But he
would not yield easily. He would do whatever it took to survive, and,
God willing, he would get himself and Donovan out of this alive.

Daylight finally began to seep through the trees. They had slept
only for short intervals, probably no more than three hours altogether. But it was just as well. It would not be difficult for a sleeping
man to freeze to death out here, where it was ten degrees above zero.

"Listen, Lieutenant," Donovan said suddenly as they were sitting
up and getting ready to move. "Do you hear that?" He pointed off
to the west.

"Yes. What do you make of it?"

They sat still for a few seconds, listening intently to the sound of
intermittent firing. It was something other than rifles or machine
guns, but it did not have the booming tones of the 105s or the bam
of mortars. Rather, the explosive sounds had a loud, cracking quality,
reverberating through the valleys.

Donovan said, "I'm thinking it's 90-millimeter guns on our tanks."

"Could be," John said, his ears cocked toward the west. "I'm not
familiar enough with them to say."

He pulled the crumpled map from his field jacket pocket and
spread it out on the ground in front of them. "Here's Hill 274," he
said, pointing with his finger. "It's hard to figure exactly where we
are. We've been going south and west. Here's the Chongchon. If we
keep going west and south we're bound to hit it, and then we can
go south along it to Kunu-ri. Does that make sense?"

"Makes as much sense as anything else. I ain't got no better idea."

"Here's a road along the river, so our tanks could be over there. How far do you guess it is to where that firing is?"

"Hmm." Donovan listened for a moment. "Maybe a mile or so. Hard to tell in these hills."

"OK, let's go."

The ravine intersected a dry creek bed. They followed it downstream.

"Looks like it might be a tributary that could take us to the river," John said.

"Looks like a place where Chinks might be," Donovan muttered.

They spread out and kept walking, slowly, saying nothing, their eyes searching both sides of the defile through which the stream ran. They were getting closer to the firing. It had intensified, now including heavy machine guns and mortars.

"We're heading away from the sound," John said after a while. "We better strike out to our left."

They climbed a small hill into a narrow valley and then struggled up a long, high ridge. After twenty minutes of climbing over rocks and through straggly brush, they reached the top, breathing hard. Below them, several hundred yards away, was the river, flowing from their right in an angry white froth, splashing around boulders. Any ordinary stream would have been frozen solid, but the current was so swift that it defied the near-zero temperature. They were transfixed by the drama being played out on its banks. On the far side of the river—which was perhaps seventy yards wide—two tanks were firing their turret guns into a hill upstream. "At last! Thank God!" exclaimed John when he saw the white star on the tank's side. A group of American soldiers huddled on the ground behind one of the tanks. Just then a couple of mortar rounds exploded nearby but apparently did no damage. On the near side of the river another tank was also firing its gun into the hill across the river. A quad-fifty unleashed streams of tracers in the same direction. Amidst the smoke on the hillside from the explosions of the 90-millimeter shells, enemy machine guns put intermittent fire down on this cluster of men and vehicles. A half-dozen American soldiers suddenly came running from the trees on the far side and dived for cover behind the tanks.

"Let's get on down there," John said.

They started down the hill but had gone only a few yards when Donovan said, excitedly, "Look, Lieutenant!" He pointed off to their left down the ridge. They both instantly dropped to the ground.

About a hundred yards away and a little below them they saw two Chinese soldiers. One was setting up a machine gun on a tripod. The other was bringing up ammunition boxes. They had an excellent angle of fire down on the quad-fifty and the Americans crouching behind the tanks.

"We've got to get them," John whispered. "You take the one at the gun, and I'll take the other one."

As they were settling themselves into a good firing position, they heard voices behind them. Looking back they saw two Chinese coming along a dip in the ridge only fifty yards away. It was obvious the Chinese had not yet seen them.

"Take the one on the left," breathed John.

The two Americans turned 180 degrees and flattened out. Donovan's M-1 cracked, and the soldier in the lead pitched forward. The other turned and bolted to his rear. John fired but missed.

"Now the fat's in the fire," John said as they turned back toward the pair of Chinese mounting the machine gun. They were now looking up this way. John and Donovan were flat on the ground, peering through scrubby bushes and so could not be seen.

"OK, fire right after me," John muttered.

He was prone, in the best, stablest firing position. Having turned to look their way, his man now presented an optimum target. He carefully lined up the front post of the sight on the brown quilted jacket covering the man's chest. He had always been good with a rifle, but only against a black bull's-eye on the target range. He squeezed the trigger ever so gradually. That was the trick with a rifle, just squeeze gently, no jerking, then hold the breath at the last instant. The M-1 bucked hard against his shoulder, followed in a split second by the crack of Donovan's rifle. One of the Chinese sagged to his knees and went over on his side, clutching his chest. The other fell backward over the machine gun.

"Good shooting!" snapped John. "Let's go!"

Chapter 8

LIEUTENANT WINSTON AND CORPORAL DONOVAN ran half-stumbling down the steep slope, waving their arms and shouting to identify themselves as Americans. They fell to the ground breathlessly behind the sheltered side of the half-track where a small group of GIs were clustered for protection.

"You guys are a sight for sore eyes," Donovan gasped.

"We don't look so damn good to me," one of them muttered.

"We thought the U.S. Army had disappeared," John added.

"It damn near has, and what's left's on the run," said another, who, like the rest, was dirty, disheveled, and unshaven.

"What's going on?" John shouted, raising his voice above the renewed hammering of the .50-caliber machine guns and the ear-stabbing crack of the tank's 90-millimeter gun.

"All hell's broke loose," said another. "The Chinks routed the battalion on the other side of the river. We're trying to get out what's left."

Another chimed in. "Nobody can wade across. Current's too strong. Freezing too. They got to ferry 'em over."

One of the tanks on the other side started into the river and sank up above its treads but kept coming. Men covered its back and sides, desperately grabbing for handholds and clutching each other. Although the current's force kept the river from freezing, the protruding rocks were ice-covered from the spray, which now lashed against the men.

Just then the remaining tank on the far side was hit in its engine.

Flames shot up instantly, and the men crouching behind it scattered, two of them falling from the machine-gun fire pouring down from the hill.

A man wearing captain's bars emerged from the turret of the tank near John. He ran up to the tank grinding noisily out of the roiling river water, like a sea monster emerging from the depths, icy water dripping copiously from its treads. A head popped out of its turret.

"Turn around and go back for the rest!" the captain shouted above the engine roar. "And shake it up. We've got to get out of here fast!" The men clutching onto the tank slid off, some of them helping the wounded.

At that moment, the burning tank across the river exploded with a blast that showered debris in all directions. The men who had run from its cover were cowering behind rocks and trees farther down stream. They ran forward to climb on the tank returning across the river, some pulling others on barely in time to make it as the tank turned and ground back into the frothing water.

The fire-hoselike stream of bullets from the quad-fifty churned up the sides of the Chinese-infested hill to protect the crossing. The crack of the 90-millimeter gun accelerated in tempo, pumping high-explosive rounds into the Chinese positions, tearing trees apart, and throwing up clouds of dust and debris. Wispy clouds of gun smoke hung over the scene, and the air was heavy with the acrid smell of cordite.

The human cargo hanging on to the swaying tank made it safely across the river just as a three-quarter-ton truck came racing up the narrow dirt road from the rear. A steel-helmeted lieutenant jumped out, yelling, "Orders are to pull back to the regimental CP pronto!"

The men filled the three-quarter-ton truck and the half-track. Those with shoulder, arm, and leg wounds were helped on. Several others, more badly hurt and maybe even dead, were laid on the metal floor. The remaining men clambered up on the back of the lead tank. The other tank held back to provide covering fire for the withdrawal.

As the last few men scrambled into the back of the half-track where John crouched beside the quad-fifty gunner, he looked up to the ridge where he and Donovan had come from and saw a line of at least twenty Chinese coming from the crest down toward them. He jabbed the gunner in the side and pointed upward. The Chinese dropped behind rocks and into kneeling positions. Before the gunner could swing the four .50-caliber barrels in that direction, he saw muzzle flashes from the Chinese rifles, and bullets ricocheted off the sides of the half-track. A man climbing in at the rear screamed horribly and fell over on to other men. Corporal Donovan, squatting beside him, lurched backward, moaning and clutching at his head.

The quad-fifty erupted into action, raking the hillside. Poured out at the rate of two thousand rounds per minute, the torrent of steel chewed up everything in its path. The enemy soldiers were blown violently backwards and dismembered.

The half-track jerked forward and quickly rounded a curve, leaving the hills, the river, a burning tank, and an unknown number of dead American soldiers to the Chinese People's Volunteers.

John leaned over Donovan, lying flat on his back. He called to him, but saw it was no use. A bullet had caught him in the left side of his head, ripping away half his face. His eyes were wide open, but staring blankly into space. There was no pulse.

He nearly vomited. Tears gushed out of his eyes. He was enraged at his powerlessness to do anything, either to save his corporal or to get back at those who had killed him. Sitting beside Donovan's body as the treads bumped and clanked along the dirt road, he was overcome with anger and humiliation.

At Kujang-dong they found clumps of American soldiers hastily setting up machine guns and maneuvering half-tracks and tanks into northward-facing defensive positions. A major shouted, "Keep moving south! We're setting up a blocking position here!"

Their column of vehicles, now joined by others, inched its way through narrow dirt streets. Low, thatch-roofed houses pressed in close on both sides, leaving barely enough room for them to make their way through passages never intended for such twentieth-century mechanical monsters. The odors of Korea filled the air—mainly kimchee and human excrement. But the place seemed deserted. Not a native inhabitant was to be seen. Yet smoke rose from some of the houses. Koreans must be hiding inside, John thought, overawed and frightened by these strange-looking armed men and the unearthly roar of massed engines, something they had never seen or heard before.

Yet the village was not devoid of life. In a small deserted court-
yard stood a lone ox—huge, motionless, uncomprehending. Several chickens gawked at these bedraggled and dispirited remnants of
American units.

At the southern outskirts of the village they were joined by still
more remnants of other units. The lengthening line of vehicles continued southward along the dirt road, moving slowly; they could go
no faster than the tanks. Darkness came, but they kept moving, inching along. Flashes of firing continued in the hills to their west, across
the Chongchon.

Near midnight the convoy reached the vicinity of Kunu-ri. Vehicles
of all sorts were there in profusion, getting in each other's way—
trucks, jeeps, half-tracks, and tanks. All was in confusion. The pounding of artillery, holding back the Chinese, could be heard
continuously to the east and north.

Rumors were rampant. It was difficult to sort out reality from wild,
baseless stories, but the reports were consistent on a few big points.
The three ROK divisions to their east had been overrun and deci-
mated, and the Chinese had broken through to their rear. The Turkish Brigade had also been destroyed, leaving the whole right flank
of Eighth Army exposed. The entire division front—all the battalions
that had gone forward three days earlier in the "home-by-Christmas
offensive"—had been badly mauled, if not totally routed. Their remnants were now gathering around Kunu-ri. Rumors about what was
happening toward the west were hopelessly confused.

When daylight came, cold and gray, John set out to find whatever
survivors of Baker Company or of the battalion there might be. He
encountered a field kitchen serving breakfast and wolfed down
corned beef hash and coffee, his first hot meal in three days. He
also stumbled into a quartermaster unit and was able to talk them out
of a parka, relieving some of the racking chill. He found a discarded
steel helmet and decided he would be well advised to wear it, even
though a pile cap would be warmer. He secured a carbine and three
extra clips of ammo from a stack that had been collected from the
casualties.

He wandered through tents, parked vehicles, and clumps of soldiers, looking for any sign of a familiar unit or face. Everywhere he

saw bedraggled men with sleepless eyes and weary faces, dirty, unshaven, covered with smoke and grime. He had never seen such a disorganized scene in the army.

"Winston, Winston!" His name was being shouted from somewhere behind him. He turned and saw Capt. Eugene Tompkins, the battalion supply officer, running toward him.

"My God, Winston, it's good to see you." He grabbed John's hand. "Are you all right?"

"Yes, sir, but my outfit is not. Have you heard what happened to Baker Company?"

"Afraid I have. But it's worse than that. It's the whole battalion."

"Have you seen anybody from Baker?"

"Grimes is here and about fifteen men. No other officers as far as we can find."

"Is Captain Grimes all right?" John said with concern.

"Yes. He's the only company commander left in the battalion. So far we've found only about eighty men left out of the three companies. I've put all of them under Grimes' command. I'm acting battalion commander."

"Where's Major McKittrick?"

"Dead."

The word shook John, and for a moment he had difficulty speaking. "Dead? The major dead? What happened?"

"The Chinks overran the CP. We had a terrific firefight—grenades, machine guns, burp guns, the works. We held our own for a while. But they kept pouring in, so the major ordered us out. I was standing near him, and when I turned to run, a grenade went off, knocked me off my feet. When I got up I saw that it had hit the major full in the side, cut him open."

They stood without speaking for a few moments to let a deuce-and-a-half make its way past them, groaning in low gear. It was pulling a trailer filled with a ragged assortment of duffel bags and cartons of C-rations.

"Winston, what we've got here is an unmitigated disaster. The top brass has bungled this operation. Why didn't they know about the Chinese? It makes me fighting mad, all this loss of men."

They walked on. "Let me get you over here with Grimes and what's left of the battalion," Tompkins said.

"What about our KATUSAs?" John asked.

"Never been heard from. Either killed or captured, I guess. But they could have bugged out."

Artillery rumbled steadily to the east and north. "Thank God for those 105s," Tompkins said. "They're about all now between us and the Chinks. Our flank is wide open."

They threaded their way through a couple of dozen men, some lying on the ground asleep, others sitting disconsolately and silently, smoking cigarettes. Several bullet-marked trucks were parked helter skelter alongside them. Captain Grimes stood there talking with Sergeant Hutchens. John could hardly have been happier if he had seen his own father.

Grimes stepped forward and gave him a hug. "Winston! I thought you were gone!"

"I almost was."

"Come on over here and sit down. Hutchens, see about some noontime chow for the men."

"Yes, sir," replied the sergeant. He left Grimes, Tompkins, and John sitting on the ground by a three-quarter-ton truck. They exchanged accounts of what had happened to them since the attack. Grimes described how he managed to get off Hill 274 with Sergeant Hutchens and a half-dozen other men. They worked their way back to Kunu-ri over the next day and night. They encountered two sizeable columns of Chinese, whom they managed to avoid by hiding. Since getting back they had collected a dozen more men from Baker and the remnants of Able and Charlie. From what some of the men had told him, he was fairly sure that Lieutenant Puccini had been killed on the hill. He had no clear information as to the fates of Lieutenant Mason and Lieutenant Ridley. Nobody knew what had happened to the forward observer, Lieutenant Forney. He figured there were four possibilities: dead, captured, hooked up with some other unit, or still wandering in the hills.

Sleeping again in a tent, as John did that night, was a minor luxury. The tent blunted the icy wind but did little to ward off the near-zero cold. A sleeping bag and the newly acquired parka helped.

He thought he might sleep better, being back in relative safety among Americans. But Hill 274 and the Chongchon came flooding back, bringing nightmarish memories of mass death—dismembered bodies, mangled limbs, and blood. Donovan's caked blood on his fatigues was an ever-present reminder. All those men of Baker Company who sat around laughing and wolfing down Thanksgiving dinner, less than a week ago, were no more. Why had he, among a tiny handful, been spared?

He heard, from somewhere off in the distance, soldiers' voices singing raggedly:

> Lordy, Lordy, listen to me,
> While I tell of the battle of Kunu-ri!
> We're buggin' out—
> We're movin' on!
> When mortars started falling round the CP tent,
> Everybody wondered where the high brass went.

What had gone wrong in this army of the mightiest nation on earth? Did they not have the moral high ground, here by warrant of the civilized world? He was overcome with a sense of shame and humiliation for himself and his country. Having been disgracefully defeated last summer by a backward peasant country, they now faced a similar disaster from another peasant army. As he brooded about it all, he was beset not so much with fear as with anger—anger with the high command for blundering into this catastrophe, anger at his country for being so unprepared to meet its responsibilities, anger at being a participant in a looming defeat. What morning would bring, no man, of course, could know. He might yet have that rendezvous with death. He was getting to know that old fellow, and if and when that supreme moment came, he resolved to stand him down, at least not to flinch or fail. Beyond that, it was out of his hands.

Two roads led out of the remote village of Kunu-ri. One ran west toward the sea, the other south through steep hills. As daylight came on this grim, cold morning, this crossroads was the scene of a vast aggregation of disorganized American army units, many battered and radically diminished in strength. To them all, down through the chain of command, came the urgent order to withdraw. The entire division was to move south immediately along the single dirt road to Sunchon, some thirty miles away.

Confusion reigned as units attempted to line up and move out in accordance with the specified order of march. But the order did not hold. Soldiers became separated from their units and grabbed rides on trucks and tanks as best they could. It was every man for himself. Captain Tompkins had given John command over half the battalion's remaining men—amounting to little more than a normal platoon. But they too became separated and strung out along the snaking column of vehicles. Most of the trucks, half-tracks, and jeeps also carried wounded, from those with minor injuries to the nearly dying. Some wounded were crowded onto the backs of tanks, along with other soldiers.

Finally under way, the column stalled. Word drifted back that a roadblock had been encountered and was being cleared. The column began to move again. A rear guard had been left near Kunu-ri, supported by several howitzer batteries. Their continuous booming gave a comforting assurance to the hundreds of men riding helter skelter on the assorted vehicles that the Chinese would be held at bay.

The column abruptly stopped again, as John, riding in a jeep, came around a bend. To his amazement, he saw flames and black smoke rising from stalled two-and-a-half-ton trucks, blocking the road. Far ahead he saw streams of tracers coming off the hills flanking the road. He jumped out of the jeep and ran forward. Two hundred yards ahead he found Captain Grimes standing beside a three-quarter-ton truck filled with some of their men. He was scanning the hills to their front with a pair of field glasses.

"What's up?" John asked, alarmed and breathing hard from his run.

"Looks like Chinks are on both sides of the road."

"I thought the roadblock had been cleared."

"That was another one back up the way. This is something new. It's beginning to look like they've cut our route in strength."

A major ran past them toward the rear. "Stand fast," he shouted. "We're going to get some artillery on those hills."

Minutes later two trucks came inching forward along the road towing 105-millimeter howitzers. They stopped near Grimes and John. Soldiers jumped out and unhitched the howitzers and maneuvered them off the road by pushing and pulling them into the shallow ice of a frozen rice paddy. It took the men an agonizing quarter hour of straining ankle deep in the frozen muck to get the two black snouts positioned toward the hills ahead. The first shots were wide of the mark, but they adjusted and began putting high-explosive rounds on the hills where the tracers originated. The men worked furiously, ramming the heavy 105-millimeter projectiles into the breeches of the two pieces. Their intermingled booming rolled across the hills, echoing and re-echoing, mixed with the crashing of the explosive rounds on the slopes ahead. The tracers gradually subsided.

"Good work!" Grimes called out. "Now let's get going."

At that moment shouts broke out up and down the line near John: "Chinks! Chinks coming in!" All eyes turned to the west across a long stretch of rice paddies, beyond the howitzers. There, several hundred yards away, emerging from a scattering of scrub trees at the base of a hill and coming toward them was a line of Chinese infantry, maybe two hundred or more.

"All out!" yelled Grimes to the men in the truck. "Winston, form a skirmish line along that bank and hold them off."

The men clambered out of the truck. Grimes rousted more men out of two other trucks. They all ran with John to an embankment parallel to the road along the edge of a large paddy. The Chinese were advancing at a run.

"Let 'em have it!" John called out. "Aim carefully! Conserve your ammo!"

The three dozen men sprawled on their stomachs behind the bank began firing their rifles and carbines. Some of the Chinese went, but most kept coming.

"Get those howitzers on them!" yelled Grimes, running toward the men manning the two pieces.

Straining and slipping in the slush, the artillerymen managed to slew the barrels around toward the oncoming enemy without having to reposition the carriages; in the muck the wheels had sunk almost to the axles. They began firing at point-blank range. Ammunition was fed to them from the backs of the trucks by a line of men functioning like a bucket brigade. White phosphorous rounds exploded in the midst of the oncoming Chinese with murderous effect, and within minutes the line was cut down. The few remaining Chinese turned and ran.

Ahead, tanks cleared the road, shoving the burning trucks off into the ditch. Exploding gasoline tanks added to the din. The artillery officer yelled, "Leave the guns. We'll never get them out of this mess." The men removed the breechblocks and set off thermite grenades in each barrel.

"Listen to that," Grimes said to John, motioning to their rear.

From the north and east, back toward Kunu-ri, came the sound of automatic weapons. "Isn't the rear guard supposed to keep us covered back there?" John asked.

"We might as well face it. We've got Chinks on our flanks and rear and front. All we can do is get the hell through them south as fast as we can. The British Commonwealth Brigade is supposed to link up with us down there somewhere."

The column started to move again. Men scrambled back onto any vehicle they could. Movement was in fits and starts, no faster than fifteen miles an hour—the tanks could go no faster—skirting by wrecked and burning trucks.

Riding in the back of a half-track, John began to see men lying in the ditches on both sides of the road. Vehicles halted sporadically to pick up wounded. He jumped out and ran over to the side of the road, looking ahead to an appalling sight. As far as he could see ahead the ditch was filled with prone figures. Some were calling for help; others were groaning in pain. Many were dead. Most were Americans, but there were also ROKs and Turks—all, he concluded, victims of an earlier ambush. He got some men off the half-track and loaded on five of the wounded before the column lurched forward again. It stopped again, and they jumped off and put three more wounded aboard. All had the same story: They had been told that this road to the south was clear. They had been hit unexpectedly by Chinese mortars and machine guns.

The line of vehicles abruptly halted again. Above the sound of engines came the rattle of a machine gun. Rising from the bed of the half-track and looking forward, John saw that a burning truck blocked their way. In the distance, the convoy had moved on, creating a gap in the column. Machine-gun bullets kicked up dirt in the road.

"Take cover!" he shouted. Men jumped from the vehicles into the ditch on the left side, shielding themselves from the raking machine-gun fire coming from their right.

A lieutenant colonel made his way along the protected side of the vehicles. He paused and called out in a loud voice, addressing no one in particular. "A machine gun has us pinned down. We don't have any mortars or anything else to take it out with. I'm asking for volunteers to go up there and get it."

A voice mumbled from somewhere in the ditch, "Go get it yourself." No one else spoke.

The officer added, "We're not going anywhere unless we take out that gun. If darkness catches us here, we've had it."

John peered over the hood of the half-track toward the hill some hundred yards ahead, on the far side. It rose sharply from the road at about a sixty-degree angle. At forty or fifty feet up it leveled out into some rocks and scrub trees. The machine gun was firing from what appeared to be a well-protected, rocky nest. Immediately across the road from where he crouched was a slope downward, leading to a cut that seemed to circle around toward the rear of the hill.

Seconds passed. The machine gun kept up its chatter. The colonel said, "We're going to lose a hell of a lot of men if we try to move forward without knocking out that gun."

More seconds passed. John took a deep breath and exhaled. "All right," he said in a quiet voice. "I'll go."

"Good," the colonel said, grabbing him by the shoulder. "Get some men to go with you."

John looked up and down the ditch. "OK, men, we take out that gun or we stay here and die. I'm asking for volunteers to go with me."

At first no one stirred. There were a few mumbled curses. Then a corporal lurched up from the ditch; a couple of PFCs followed. John did not know them; they were not from his company.

"Three ought to be enough," he said. "Anybody got some grenades?"

Several men lying in the ditch readily handed up grenades, obviously pleased to send them instead of themselves.

The four darted across the road and into the cut. After five minutes of half-running and stumbling along, they came to the rear of the hill. They faced an old cornfield, an expanse of open ground with rows of dead stalks, bent and withered in the wintry air.

"There may be Chinese up there looking down on us," John whispered, "but we've got to take a chance."

They broke into a full run, one behind the other, John leading. They reached the base of the hill and plunged into the trees. They began to climb toward the sound of the machine gun. The scrubby evergreen trees ran all the way up and gave them good cover.

"We've got to get within grenade distance." He motioned the men to spread out alongside him and move forward together.

They heard heavy firing in the distance to the south. "Sounds like this won't be our last problem," the corporal said.

The trees thinned out, and they saw ahead an open stretch of rocky ground. It sloped gradually upward toward a cluster of boulders. Behind those they saw several bobbing heads. The loud staccato firing clearly identified this as the machine gun's position.

"Too far for grenades," John said. "See that dead log," he said, pointing up the slope. "When I give the word, we'll all run to that point, throw grenades, and then run like the devil back the way we've come."

Two Chinese soldiers came into view, fifty yards off to the right. They were walking toward the machine-gun emplacement. Both men carried ammunition boxes. They had rifles slung over their shoulders. They seemed to be in no hurry. They sat down to the rear of the emplacement and lit up cigarettes.

"My God, what're we going to do now?" the corporal whispered.

"Let me think a minute," John said. He studied the two Chinese. They were smoking and talking to each other. The dilemma was stark. Once John and his men rose to rush toward the log, they would be in the open and there was no way they would not be seen. But if they shot the two before rushing the machine-gun nest, they would alert the gunners and the game would be up.

"OK, Corporal, you and I will get to the log and throw grenades. You others stay here and cover us. Don't shoot until they see us and go for their rifles. Then let them have it. OK with everybody?"

They nodded. John and the corporal slung their carbines over their shoulders. Each took a grenade and pulled the pin, holding down the firing mechanism. He took a deep breath and hissed, "Let's go!"

They leaped up and ran. The log was twenty yards across open ground in plain sight of the smoking Chinese.

John fixed on the machine-gun emplacement ahead. That was the objective; all else was blocked out of his world. He heaved the grenade, arching it upward, and watched it land just behind the rocks where the machine gun was rattling away. As he turned to run back, he heard it explode, followed immediately by the explosion of the corporal's grenade.

At that same instant, his left arm was slammed with a burning, painful jolt above the elbow. Shots rang out. He ran stumbling toward the two PFCs. All four of them plunged downward, back the way they had come, tree branches tearing at their faces. They reached the open cornfield and stopped, panting.

"Damn, Lieutenant," one of the men said, "sorry about that Chink. We didn't hit him soon enough, but we got 'em both."

"Think we better put a tourniquet on that arm?" the corporal said. John looked at his left arm. His parka was torn open just below the shoulder, and blood was oozing out. He saw blood dripping over the back of his left hand.

"Don't know. Bleeding's not too heavy. Don't think it got the bone. Let's get on back, then I'll see about it."

They made their way around to the road. The column had begun to move. They crawled into the back of a slow-moving deuce-and-a-half.

John felt faint. Despite the cold, he pulled off his parka. The torn sleeve of his fatigue jacket was soaked in blood. He got his arm out and saw the hole punched through the outer skin. "Superficial, I think. No artery hit. Can't tell about the bone." From somewhere in the truck somebody produced a first-aid kit, and he put a tight bandage over the wound.

The truck jolted along, stopping to pick up wounded until there was no more room. They were already piled on each other on the metal bed of the truck. The dead were being left behind.

Time passed, perhaps an hour. It was now late afternoon; darkness was not far off. The column halted. Engines stopped, and in place of their sound came a cacophony of mortars and automatic-weapon fire. John eased out of the tailgate and stepped into the road to look ahead. In the distance, nearly a mile away, the road entered a narrow defile. Cliffs rose immediately on either side, up to fifty or sixty feet. At the entry of the defile, and for some distance this side of it, the road was filled with burning vehicles. Mortar shells were exploding in the road and on the trucks and tanks for as far as he could see. Streaks of tracers came down from the cliffs on both sides. He was looking at a deadly gauntlet barring their escape route.

A formation of American jets came in low from the south. They divided, a line of three approaching on each side of the road. They unleashed napalm along the line of cliffs. Great balls of yellow flame boiled up for hundreds of yards. He heard the pounding of the planes' guns, spraying the hilltops as they raced along. They circled and came over again, three in a line on each side, gunfire saturating the hills.

The air strikes quieted the mortar and machine-gun fire from the cliffs. The column began to move again. Tanks shoved aside disabled and burning trucks and jeeps. But as John's truck neared the entry to the defile, enemy fire picked up, and the vehicles halted once more.

"Hit the side!" someone yelled. They piled out frantically and dived toward the ditches that ran up to the edge of the high embankments.

A mortar hit the truck next to them, showering them with metal and leaving them momentarily deaf but otherwise unhurt. He threw himself prone in the ditch, crowded to overflowing with men— wounded, dead, and dying. Alongside him was another lieutenant with bandaged head and arm in a sling. "Say, buddy," the lieutenant said in a remarkably calm voice, "want a drink?" With his one good hand, he pulled a pint of Old Granddad from his parka.

"Thanks," John said, not hesitating an instant, and took a long swallow. It burned down his throat and set up a pool of comforting warmth in his stomach.

The jets came in low again. They skimmed the cliff tops, leaving a string of napalm canisters that sent great balls of billowing fire soaring skyward. At the same time their .50-caliber machine guns sprayed the line of Chinese positions. Brass shell casings clattered in the road, on the vehicles, and on the men in the ditches, one bouncing off John's helmet. The unearthly thunder of the low-flying jets smothered all else as they pulled out of their run and circled back toward the south. Once again the fire from the hilltops subsided.

"All right, let's move!" yelled someone. "We've got to get through here before dark!"

It was now dusk. They knew they had seen the last air strike of the day. From now on, they were on their own, alone with their remnants of men and vehicles, the coming darkness, and the Chinese-infested hills.

John climbed on the back of a tank. The heat of its engine felt good but did nothing to ease the growing ache in his arm. It had now begun to throb, but despite the pain he had to use his left hand to help hold onto the lurching monster. He had lost his helmet in the mad scramble to get aboard.

Cliffs rose ominously on both sides. Dusk deepened into darkness. Mortar and machine-gun fire began to come down again on the struggling line of vehicles and their human cargo.

"Damn it!" yelled one of the men hanging onto the tank beside John. "The air strikes should've knocked all that out!"

The tank engines filled the canyon with an unearthly roar. Through it could be heard the whine of bullets ricocheting off the rocky walls and tank treads and turrets. A quad-fifty unleashed intermittent bursts upward at the source of the Chinese fire. Every man who could hold a rifle or carbine was firing upward from the backs of trucks, tanks, and jeeps. The ear-splitting crash of exploding mortar rounds sporadically punctuated this horrendous symphony of fire and engine noise. Smoke filled the darkened roadway, illuminated eerily by muzzle flashes and mortar explosions. In this nightmarish scene, the screams of men being hit were barely audible.

John, with an unknown number of other men, held precariously onto the back of the jolting, swaying tank. Bullets buzzed and zinged in the air all around him like a swarm of bees. Keep moving, keep moving, he muttered to himself, as the tank clanked on. To stop would be certain death. The only hope for life is to get out of this hellish canyon.

The man next to him shrieked, an agonized shriek so penetrating that it rose above the roar of the tank engine beneath them. He slid off the side as John clutched frantically with his left hand to save him. But he was gone, gone into the blackness of the road, as the column ground on.

At that instant, he felt a mighty blow in his side, like a powerful fist being driven into him at maximum force, but sharper and more painful than anything he had ever known. He gave an involuntary cry of pain. He grabbed at his side and felt a warm wetness.

A second later a red-hot poker seared the side of his head just above the right ear, shooting a bolt of pain through his skull. He saw a sudden flash of light and then all went black . . . black and quiet.

Chapter 9

SOMEWHERE NORTH OF PYONGYANG, astride the unpaved road, sat one of the lonely, innumerable, and indistinguishable Korean villages. Low brownish yellow huts with straw-covered roofs lined the road for a mile, and behind them the ever-present rice paddies, now frozen and deserted. But the village was by no means deserted, for at this hour an endless line of trucks, jeeps, and other military vehicles streamed down the single road through its middle, some pulling artillery pieces, most filled with men—American, South Korean, British, Turkish—what was left of Eighth Army, all withdrawing south. Everything—sky, houses, vehicles, men, road—merged into a grim gray-brown wintry landscape. MPs stood at intervals to keep the motorized procession moving night and day.

Just off the main road a large, weathered schoolhouse, constructed years earlier by the Japanese, was the center of hurried, life-and-death activity. Olive drab ambulances with large red crosses on their sides arrived and departed, along with numerous trucks, all discharging their cargo of wounded men. In the schoolyard to the rear lay row upon row of stretchers, each bearing a bundled figure, some covered with blankets, others in parkas and field jackets. Many were swathed in dirty, blood-caked bandages. Gusts of icy wind swept across this array of human misery.

Inside, oil stoves warded off the cold. The classrooms, now empty of school furniture, were filled with portable waist-high tables. On each was stretched out a wounded man, some stripped down, others still in dirty and blood-caked fatigues. Bottles of blood plasma hung over some, tubes feeding downward into arms. Men and women in white surgical masks bent over the inert bodies and moved urgently from one to another.   John opened his eyes. He was looking straight up at a wooden ceiling. Disoriented, he became aware of voices all around him. "Over here . . . Ready to operate . . . What's the blood pressure . . . OK, take him out . . . All right, over here, next . . ."

On all sides were groans and gasps of pain and an occasional scream. Still more voices amidst the noisy hubbub: "Nothing we can do for this one . . . Come on, move it! . . . Get him on this table here . . ." The air reeked of alcohol, ether, blood, and sweat.

A face appeared in front of his eyes. It was directly above him, with eyes looking down at him. He realized it was the face of a woman, the face of an American woman. A white surgical mask drooped around her neck just below her chin. Her curly brown hair was cut short. The sensation was strange, as he had not seen an American woman since the pier at San Francisco months ago.

"How do you feel?" she asked in a husky and tired but businesslike voice.

"Not sure," he half-whispered. Morphine had left him in a dreamy, detached state. "Where am I?"

"The evac hospital. We're going to operate on you in just a minute."

"Operate?" He shifted his position slightly and winced as pain shot through his middle. "For what?"

"Got to clean out your insides and sew you up . . . and you need patching up in a couple of other places."

"Where is this place?"

"In the boondocks, above Pyongyang."

"Pyongyang! We were way north of there. Are we near Kunu-ri? Or maybe Sunchon?"

"Don't think so, but I don't know those places."

She looked at one of the metal dog tags hanging around his neck and resting on his chest and then looked at the bottle of blood plasma suspended beside him, its tube running down into his arm. "Just double-checking the blood type," she said.

A weary male voice from his side interrupted. "What do we have here?"

The nurse said, "Stomach wound, scalp wound, and arm wound." He suddenly realized he was undressed down to his hips. The doctor put his hands on his side, then in turn on his head and arm, feeling around the bloody areas. He flinched at the pressure on his stomach.

"OK. Start the anesthesia."

Two other figures bustled around him. One of them said, "Smitty, how long since you slept?"

"Maybe twenty hours. Have you done any better?"

"Nope. Hobson got four hours this morning. Think we better knock off a while when you finish this one."

"Where's the chance? They keep coming." He waved toward the window and the yard filled with stretchers.

John felt a needle going into his arm. All began to grow cloudy. Within moments he was again in darkness and quiet.

He came to in a room overcrowded with men on stretchers. Two figures moved among them, taking pulses and fastening tags on some. He became aware that they were women. It was hard to tell because they were dressed in the same fatigues and combat boots that the men wore, and their hair was very short.

One of the women bent over him. "We've got to ship everybody out as fast as possible. Orders are to evacuate this position pronto. With luck, you'll get to a hospital unit in Seoul and then to a ship." She scribbled on a paper tag and pinned it to the blanket covering him.

Minutes later two men hoisted his stretcher and bore him out into the cold. "We're putting you on a deuce-and-a-half. No more ambulances. Lucky to have anything that rolls."

They shoved his stretcher onto the bed of the truck. Others were shoved in. They ended up with six stretchers jammed into the truck. More than a dozen other men, bandaged in varying degrees, sat along the sides. The tailgate was hitched up and the tarp drawn down.

The sounds of running feet and shouting voices came from alongside the truck. "Get this convoy moving! Do you want to hang around and meet the Chinks?"

With his right hand he gingerly explored himself. A thick bandage was on the right side of his head above the ear, held in place by adhesive tape running from the middle of his forehead to the back of his head. From his navel around to his right side, just below the ribs, was a huge swatch of bandage. The upper part of his left arm was firmly wrapped.

Among the wounded on the truck there was only desultory talk. One of those seated on the side said, "Anybody know what's going on?"

"Word is that the whole army is falling back on Seoul."

"I thought they were going to form a defensive line at Pyongyang."

"That was the first plan, but they didn't reckon the Chinks would keep on coming."

"That ain't all they didn't reckon on."

The convoy began to move. Their truck proceeded unevenly and jerkily, sometimes stopping, at other times speeding up. As the morphine wore off, the jolting over the unpaved road became increasingly painful. A recurrent chorus of curses welled up as the truck swerved around sharp curves and hit deep ruts.

At one of the halts they heard shouting and mingled American voices outside the truck. "Get those refugees out of the way. They're holding up the whole convoy . . . Must be hundreds . . . More like thousands . . . How come they don't stick around to welcome back Kim Il-sung? . . . Look's like they don't want to see their great friends, the Chinese . . ."

The truck jolted on. To the wounded men enclosed by the tarp, night and day were the same. Time meant nothing. Hours passed. Finally the truck stopped and its engine cut off. Voices were all around outside. The tarp went up, and the tailgate was lowered. "All right, men, here's the end of the line for the time being. Let's get unloaded."

Those sitting on the sides began to climb down with the help of somebody on the ground. Then the stretchers were taken off and carried into a building of some sort.

Thank God for morphine, John thought. He was now living from shot to shot.

The next few days he passed in a haze. He was loaded onto another truck, then came more bumpy roads and streets. "Inchon," he heard. Then he was carried onto a launch in the harbor and out to a hospital ship, part of the stream of human wreckage from the Eighth Army, ferried out day and night until the ship was full.

There for the first time in nearly three months were beds with mattresses and white, clean sheets. And there was real food served, and medical people walking around in clean, white clothing. They were all bathed and shaven and wore normal shoes, not combat boots. He was now in a fresh, white hospital gown. Even before the ship left the harbor, Korea seemed far, far away.

Two months later, in early February, the *Remberton Progress* carried the following front-page story.

LT. WINSTON AWARDED SILVER STAR

The Department of the Army has announced that Second Lt. John H. Winston has been awarded the Silver Star for "conspicuous gallantry" in Korea. Lt. Winston, son of Mr. and Mrs. Herbert Winston of this city, was seriously wounded in action in North Korea at the end of November and was transported to an army hospital in Japan where he is presently recuperating. He had earlier been reported as missing in action.

The citation accompanying the medal stated that Lt. Winston voluntarily undertook to eliminate an enemy machine gun that was holding up the withdrawal of an entire American division, then surrounded by enemy forces in North Korea, and that his successful action saved innumerable lives and equipment. According to the citation, Lt. Winston acted "in the finest tradition of the military service." The full text of the citation appears on page 3.

The Silver Star was pinned on Lt. Winston by Gen. Douglas MacArthur during an awards ceremony at the Tokyo Army Hospital.

In a letter just received by the *Progress,* Lt. Winston writes that he will be discharged shortly from the hospital and will be assigned for duty at Camp Drake, near Tokyo.

Camp Drake was a transit post, the first stop for the thousands of men arriving as replacements from the states by troopships docking at Yokohama. Nine months into the "police action," most of them were draftees and reservists. It was not a happy stream of humanity.

He was given a desk job, shuffling reams of paper, receiving and dispatching officers and enlisted men. Once a week he reported to the medical unit to be checked over. He was on the mend, but his strength had not fully returned.

He was in no mood to socialize and kept to himself as much as possible. His waking hours were punctuated by sudden memories of the horror that had followed Thanksgiving Day. His mind still struggled to come to grips with the magnitude of the catastrophe, with the death and suffering he had witnessed, with the loss of Major McKittrick, of his entire outfit—Mason, Puccini, Ridley, Forney, and the men of his platoon. Would he ever be the same again? Would those ghastly memories ever fade?

Occasionally, he was unavoidably drawn into a conversation.

"Winston," a man at his mess table said one day, "do you know why in the hell we're in Korea?"

"I thought I did."

"Well, I never did. Left a new business I just started, big mortgage on a new house, wife and baby. I can give up a lot for my country, but not for that sinkhole Korea."

He was in no mood to respond, so he said nothing.

At another meal he overheard a conversation between two majors. One said, "Word around the Dia Ichi is that about one hundred-eighty thousand Chinese hit Eighth Army along the Chongchon, and another one hundred-twenty thousand were what got X Corps at Chosin."

"Do you mean that there were three hundred thousand Chinese south of the Yalu?"

"That's what they think now."

"My God. What were they thinking last November?"

"They were estimating as many as sixty thousand."

John thought about his Silver Star. It was hard to be proud of an award for taking part in one of the most humiliating defeats the American army had ever suffered. At the awards ceremony in the hospital he had watched the Great Man come down the line pinning on medals and shaking hands with the recipients—some in wheelchairs, some on crutches, one blind, a leg missing here, an arm there—all in hospital-issued robes. He wanted to blurt out, "Why didn't you let us know about the Chinese? Why did you send your entire command into that death trap?" Instead, of course, he said nothing but "Thank you, sir." It was a moment that in his wildest dreams he never could have imagined. Here he was hearing that sonorous voice call his name, literally touching the hand of history. He was awestruck, despite a smoldering resentment that the supreme commander, a hero of his youth, had let them down.

Spring came. The cherry trees bloomed, and all around nature came back into life. But it left him cold. He did go into Tokyo one Saturday with a couple of other lieutenants, though with little enthusiasm. They walked the Ginza, surveyed the grounds of the Imperial Palace, and passed the Dia Ichi Building—where it was decided whether men would live or die in Korea.

They wound up in the bar of the Imperial Hotel, designed by Frank Lloyd Wright in the thirties. As they finished their second gin and tonic, one of the lieutenants said, "We ought to try the geisha scene."

"Great idea," the other said. "Are you game, Winston?"

"I'm feeling pretty tired. Think I ought to head back to the post."

Seoul was liberated again, and the U.N. forces at last regained the 38th parallel, where it had all begun ten months earlier. Casualties were staggering on both sides.

In April came news that hit Camp Drake like a giant thunderclap: President Truman had relieved General MacArthur. Disbelief and shock abounded.

In the officers' club, John stood at the edge of a huge crowd gathered around the radio to listen to the high drama of the general's farewell address before a joint session of Congress ten thousand miles away.

In his mesmerizing voice, MacArthur sketched the global dimensions of the conflict and the strategic situation in the Far East, putting it in historical perspective. The decision to intervene in Korea to repel aggression was sound, he asserted, and our victory was complete. The intervention of Red China created a new war, one not contemplated when our forces were committed. "I called for reinforcements," he intoned, "but was informed that reinforcements were not available."

Again and again, he was interrupted by thundering applause in the House chamber.

To those who said he was a warmonger, he responded that nothing could be further from the truth. He knew war as few other men knew it and had long advocated its abolition. But if war cannot be avoided, the deep resonant voice went on, it must be pursued and won. "War's very object is victory, not prolonged indecision."

As the Great Man approached the end of his oration—noting that his military service of fifty-two years was now concluding—the chamber of the House of Representatives was hushed, as was the crowd clustered around the radio in the officers' club:

> When I joined the army, even before the turn of the century, it was the fulfillment of all my boyish hopes and dreams. The world has turned over many times since I took the oath on the Plain at West Point, and the hopes and dreams have long since vanished. But I still remember the refrain of one of the most popular barrack ballads of that day, which proclaimed most proudly that "Old soldiers never die, they just fade away." And like the old soldier of that ballad, I now close my military career and just fade away, an old soldier who tried to do his duty as God gave him the light to see that duty.

Then, after a dramatic pause, came the final words: "Good-bye."

The House erupted into prolonged and tumultuous shouting and applause. In the officers' club there were eyes that were not dry, including John's.

It took a moment for the spell to pass. Then the officers stirred and began shuffling away from the radio.

"Old Doug really let 'em have it."

"I hope they got the message."

"You know, in the end the president didn't really have any choice."

"Yeah, he's the commander-in-chief, but I don't know about the advice he's getting."

"I think we ought to get out. We've done our part."

"You mean tuck tail and run?"

"Win it or leave it, I say."

"I say we should've never been there in the first place."

One day at mess he sat down beside a captain wearing the wreathed sword and quill insignia of the Judge Advocate General's

Corps. He had a broad, friendly face, tortoise-shell glasses, and an unruly shock of black hair, an unmilitary appearance not uncommon for JAG officers, especially reservists called to active duty. Extending his hand, he said, "I'm Carter Gordon."

"I'm John Winston. Glad to meet you."

"Where're you from?"

"Alabama. How about you?"

"Virginia . . . Richmond, Virginia."

"Are you just passing through like everybody else?"

"No. Not so far. They've got me assigned to the Post JA office. Said they're shorthanded for the moment. The intimations are that I'll probably be going on to Korea at some point. Seems to be a notion around here that you have to pay your dues by a hitch over there." He had a whimsical look about him that interested John. "What's your situation?"

"Well, I've had a turn over there. Maybe paid my dues, as you say. They've got me here pushing paper, marking time, I would say, until I rotate home."

They talked on, lingering over the meal. For John, it was the longest conversation in months.

Although Gordon was seven or eight years older, John found in him a mind and personality more compatible with his own than any he had encountered in the army. Thereafter they often sat together at meals and rambled over a wide range of common interests.

Carter Gordon had been born and reared in Richmond, attended St. Christopher's School and the University of Virginia. He had gone through OCS and had gotten to Europe in the Transportation Corps at the tag end of the war, just before V-E Day, where he helped in trucking supplies through France. After the war he had finished law school at Virginia and was now with his father's firm in Richmond. Or at least he was there until the army reclaimed him the previous winter, sent him through a JAG training course and then on to the Far East. It had only been a month since he left the states.

"This war hasn't touched most people. None of my friends in Richmond has gone. I think folks are getting tired of it and beginning to wonder why we're here."

"My guess is that most folks don't have the remotest idea what Korea is like. The war might as well be on another planet."

Their conversations gradually moved into lighter subjects. Knowing
that Gordon was from Richmond—he had never known anybody
from Richmond—he could not resist questions about his favorite historical subject. Did he, for example, know Douglas Southall Freeman?

"Oh yes. He and my father are friends. I see him around town a
good bit."

Gordon turned out to be as well read in the Civil War as John.
They quizzed each other in a jocular fashion and exchanged trivia
and anecdotes.

"Jackson's last words?"

"'Let us cross over the river and rest in the shade of the trees.'"

"And what about Lee's?"

"'Strike the tent.'"

Their banter about the Civil War made him think of his grandfather. On sleepless nights he imagined the Fifth Alabama in the late
June of '63, marching northward through the lush green hills of western Maryland into Pennsylvania, spurred on by the prospect of victory
deep in enemy territory, with flags and band music to lift their spirits
and stir their souls—"Dixie" and "The Bonnie Blue Flag," and the
white-starred St. Andrew's crosses flapping in the summer breeze—
moving unknowingly to their doom at the Peach Orchard and Cemetery Ridge, to defeat but not defeated in their native land, becoming
instead the stuff of legend and valor and honor, memorialized in ora-
tory and countless statues from Virginia to Texas, inspiring old men
even in his time to leap up yelling at the sound of "Dixie."

He and the men of Baker Company had likewise advanced northward with high hopes of victory, had likewise stumbled into disaster,
but, unlike those men of the Lost Cause, had no flags or bands, lacking what he had always considered to be the romantic aura of that
gray-clad army of long ago. But he now knew, as he could never have
known before, that there was nothing romantic about war. With or
without bands and flags, men suffered and died. And of one thing he
felt certain: there would be no speeches or statues to memorialize
the army of the Chongchon, an army of the most advanced nation on
earth, routed by a horde of peasants, traveling on foot, living off rice,
without trucks, tanks, artillery, radios, or airplanes. Every time he
thought of it, he was overcome with shame and anger about this war
that had not even been declared as such.

As the days passed, he found himself increasingly drawn to Gordon, who was not only a good conversationalist but also downright funny. He liked to imitate public figures—Truman with a flat Midwestern voice, MacArthur saying, "Armageddon will be at our door," all done with a twinkle in his eyes and mock seriousness.

They took the train to Kyoto one weekend. It was picture book Japan—snowcapped Fuji and scenes he had looked at in books innumerable times as a child. They toured the ancient sites in Kyoto's gardenlike setting, plodding from one Shinto shrine and temple to another in rickshaws, one-passenger contraptions, each pulled by a wizened Japanese man moving along at a trot. It was a glorious spring day, with a clear blue sky overhead and the smell of flowers and the song of birds in the air. In the quiet of this venerable Japanese seat, away from the sounds of the twentieth century, he forgot for the day that guns were pounding and men were dying not far away in Korea.

That weekend and his growing friendship with Carter Gordon wrought a change. Physically he was feeling better, and his spirits brightened. He could smile and even laugh again.

One evening in the mess hall, a captain who worked in the adjutant's office and who lived near him in the BOQ came over and said, "Say, Winston, we got some preliminary rosters on stateside shipments today, and I see your name there." He was a cynical type, overweight, with a stomach straining at the buttons on his khaki shirt, a common specimen among the occupation troops.

"Stateside?" He was surprised, not expecting such orders for weeks to come. "When?"

"Don't know. Maybe two or three weeks or so. You got some PI?"

"PI?"

"Yeah. Political influence. We see a good bit of it."

He bristled. "No. What makes you say that?"

"Well, for a good infantry lieutenant like you to be going stateside right now looks like somebody important back there has said something in the right places." He spoke sarcastically, as though he himself was suffering under a hardship assignment.

"I can tell you that's not true, and I'd appreciate it if you wouldn't put out any rumor like that."

The next day Carter Gordon sat down beside him in the mess hall at lunch. "Well, I'm on my way on the big venture. Got orders for Korea."

"Where?"

"Eighth Army HQ, but that's probably just for processing. I imagine I'll be shot out to some other place."

How unevenly, John mused, the burdens and dangers of war are distributed. Thousands of men would serve in Korea and never hear a shot fired in anger. He had seen them streaming through this transit center—quartermaster, ordnance, transportation, and others. Those wearing the crossed rifles, the crossed cannon, and the armored track would bear the burden, would put their lives on the line. But even in the combat branches there were those who would draw staff assignments or some rear-area duty and never get near the action. He took a certain grim satisfaction in knowing that he, and those like him, were where it really counted, that all those others, that legion in the rear, were there for one purpose only—to keep the men in the line, the men with the rifles, machine guns, and grenades, supplied and functioning. For men like Carter Gordon, going to Korea would mean an unusual, even an exciting or bizarre, experience, but one involving little danger, unless, of course, rear areas were overrun, as they had been last November. But that seemed highly unlikely now. No, Carter Gordon would be quite safe, even though he might well suffer the hardship of sleeping in a tent on a hard canvas cot.

The night before Gordon left, they went to the officers' club, picked up a crème de menthe for an after-dinner drink, and sat down to await the showing of the movie. It was *A Place in the Sun*, starring Elizabeth Taylor, Montgomery Clift, and Shelley Winters.

Sipping their drinks, they came back to a recurring subject—the United Nations. Gordon thought it was probably an empty shell that eventually would go the way of the League of Nations.

"The only reason the U.N. is in Korea is that the Soviet delegate was absent."

"I view that," John retorted, "as one of the truly providential events of our time. If he had been there and vetoed this step, the U.N. would have been dead."

Gordon said, "Have you thought any more about MacArthur's proposition?"

"I'm inclined to think he's right. Isn't victory the only point of war?"

"It may depend on how you define victory."

They sat in silence for a few moments, sipping crème de menthe. Then John said, "I've often wondered whether I could go back into it again. Lots of men who have been wounded have been sent back. I don't know how I'd react. Guess I'm lucky not having to face it again. Look's like I'll be shipping out soon."

The movie started. Elizabeth Taylor, the irresistible young woman, and the fancy parties she and her crowd attended set off nostalgic yearnings in John for what had been and stirred his imagination for what might be after the army.

In his musings in the days following the movie, Jeanie Harris played a prominent part. She, along with almost all else, had been crowded out of his mind in North Korea and in December during his painful weeks of recovery and preoccupation with the death and destruction he had witnessed. But then in mid-January, mail began to arrive from home, the first since before Thanksgiving, and it included a letter from her. Its warm and sympathetic tone revived his memories. He got another letter from her in February expressing continuing hope for his recovery. He had not heard from her since, and that puzzled him a little. Now, though, stimulated by the movie's portrayal of the glitzy romantic life, he savored the thought of her and what they might do together when he got back, savored the image of her short blond hair, her sunny face, her cuddly body. She was something to look forward to across that uncertain divide that had opened between him and Remberton.

How deep and lasting that divide would be, he could not tell. Leaving home on the train back in September, he could see, was the closing of one chapter and the opening of another. But the point of critical rupture with the past was Thanksgiving Day, 1950, in those forlorn North Korean hills. That day separated all that had gone before from all that came after. What happened to him, what he saw and experienced, in the ensuing days had changed his outlook on life, his view of human nature, and had left him wondering whether he could ever return to Remberton and resume what might be considered a normal life. But the near avalanche of mail that poured in during January and February, as people there learned he was hospitalized and not missing in action, all wishing him well, had softened his thoughts and reduced his sense of alienation from the past.

At the same time, his association with Carter Gordon, his improved physical condition, and the coming of spring had combined to lift his mood. And in that brighter picture, Jeanie Harris stood out.

After Carter Gordon left, he was again beset with a sense of loneliness. There was no one to talk to. Spring faded into summer. Fighting continued in Korea, and he continued in his desk job.

"Good news, Lieutenant!" The sergeant who headed the noncoms in the office advanced toward John, seated behind his desk struggling to reduce the pile in his in-box. The ever-present, heavy white coffee mug was at his right hand. It held at least two normal cups. The sergeant handed him a clump of papers.

"Are they finally rotating me home?"

"Not quite that good. But it's a good consolation prize. You'd better get yourself over to the PX and get some silver bars."

He hurriedly glanced down the usual array of mimeographed gibberish. There it was: John H. Winston 02205008 promoted to 1st Lt., Inf. He smiled at the unexpected news. He had anticipated being a lowly shavetail for quite a bit longer.

The sergeant said, "I guess they wanted to give you a nice going-away present. Congratulations!"

The mild euphoria from the promotion ended a few days later. A letter arrived from Jeanie Harris, the first in weeks. He opened it eagerly and began to read her account of various activities at the University and in Remberton. Then, with rising concern, he read her description of "the fine boy" from Decatur she had met this past fall. He was president of the Phi Delta Theta chapter and so on and so on. Then the bombshell: They had become engaged. The wedding would be in late summer. She went on to say how fine she thought he, John, was, how much she valued their friendship, and how she wished him all the best.

He sat for a while, letter in hand, looking emptily into space. He had heard of "Dear John" letters men overseas received from supposedly loyal girlfriends, but it had never occurred to him that he would be the recipient of one. The letter punctured the pleasurable dream that had been growing in his mind since the movie. Another link with the past cut, more evidence of a fissure between him and his previous life.

He slowly read the letter again. He imagined the painstaking effort she must have made in choosing appropriately diplomatic language to explain this turn of events. Her words of last September rang mockingly in his ears: "I couldn't forget you." Jeanie Harris, of all people, how could she do something like this? She, so genuine, understanding, trustworthy, lovable, professing to be so concerned about him. This was the kind of thing Sally Young might do, but not Jeanie. It defied explanation. But there it was—those stinging words: engaged . . . married . . . stated with such a ring of finality.

He ran his eyes once again over the critical passages. After an indeterminate time, lost in thought, he rose, sighed deeply, and dropped the letter in the wastebasket.

He was still getting accustomed to wearing silver bars and enjoying no longer being at the bottom of the heap—though unable to get Jeanie's letter out of his mind—when, a couple of weeks later, the sergeant approached his desk with a sheaf of papers.

"Got some more orders for you, Lieutenant. You may not like these as much as the last set."

His eyes ran quickly down the page. His breath caught in his throat. Could this be right? He slowly read and re-read the text. There was no uncertainty about it: He was being ordered back to Korea.

PART THREE
Hill 1080

Chapter 10

THE C-47 DESCENDED through the near cloudless sky on its approach to the airstrip at Taegu. John Winston twisted around in his bucket seat and pressed his face against the window to watch the Korean landscape pass beneath. It was full summer. The rainy season was over, and the rice paddies, stretching out as far as he could see, were green and vigorous. Here the landscape was gentler, the hills lower, and the valleys wider than in the north—a beautiful sight, he thought.

Despite his catastrophic experiences, he found something entrancing about this Asian peninsula. The people, their clothes so different from Western garb, the thatch-roofed villages, the haunting music, and the never-ending hills, valleys, and rice paddies gave this Land of the Morning Calm a bewitching quality.

He was on this flight by sheer happenstance. From time to time officers at Camp Drake, bound for Korea, were randomly tapped to act as couriers, and he happened to be one of those. He was to take in hand a large pouch of documents, board a C-47 at Haneda Air Base, and deliver it to a staff officer at Eighth Army headquarters in Taegu. He was pleased at the assignment because it gave him his first opportunity to see Korea from the air.

Minutes after the C-47 taxied to a stop on the airstrip, he was in a jeep heading into the middle of Taegu. The day was hot, very hot, the opposite extreme from the Korean temperature he had last experienced. Once again the stench of the countryside smote his nostrils,

143

the dominant odor being from the "night soil." On the riverbank, Korean women in their long white dresses were washing clothes. Old men in white with wispy gray goatees and tall black birdcage hats walked along the dusty road. Others trudged along, bent under heavily loaded A-frames.

The city had escaped serious war damage, but it had that run-down, gray-brown, dusty look of all Korean towns. The American military presence, army and air force, was everywhere evident. After threading his way through streets clogged with olive drab trucks and jeeps, he found the appropriate staff officer in the EUSAK headquarters and relieved himself of the document-filled pouch.

Three days later he was on the hard wooden seats of an antiquated train chugging north toward Chunchon, its cars filled with military personnel. Once again he was fully equipped—steel helmet, fatigues, combat boots, canteen, and carbine—heading into he knew not what, except that he had been assigned to an infantry regiment in the eastern sector. Remembering that a .45 pistol had saved his life, he had spent hours in Taegu looking for one and had finally wangled one from an officer who was headed stateside. It now tugged heavily at his web belt.

The pair of metal dog tags again hung on their chain around his neck. Dog tags were a curious military invention. They were the link between a man and his existence as a person. Without them, he was nothing, either living or dead. Apparently the army considered four pieces of information, and only four, to be of the essence: name, serial number, blood type, and religion. What a vast import was captured in just two letters on his tags—B for blood type and P for Protestant. One identified the fluid that was the key to life on this earth—that little B had saved his life when he lay unconscious in the evac hospital—and the other connected him to things not of this world.

The heat in the railroad car, crowded with replacements heading north, was oppressive. Perspiration ran copiously down his arms and legs, draining into the tops of his boots. The green fatigues that provided little protection from the cold last November now had the effect of sealing him in a sauna.

The landscape passing the train windows gave him a powerful and uneasy sense of déjà vu, bringing back what he had gone through last fall—the movement north through the countryside, hills getting steeper and valleys narrower, moving toward unimaginable disaster. The hellish cacophony flooded his mind—the clanking of the train and the babble of voices around him blotted out—and all he heard were booming artillery, staccato machine-gun fire, and earsplitting mortar explosions. Emotions he thought he had quelled forever now resurfaced. His hands trembled, and his mouth went dry. Despite the sweltering heat, a chill swept over him, and he shivered.

The reality on the ground was now very different. The U.N. forces had recovered and driven back north to the 38th parallel and even comfortably beyond it in the east, inflicting huge losses on the Chinese. For the first time in the war, the U.N. had a continuous line across Korea.

He had wondered whether this newfound momentum could carry them back toward the Yalu. But then in July had come the announcement that armistice talks with the enemy would begin. It sounded like the U.N. Command was ready to call it quits.

Yet at a briefing in Taegu for newly arriving officers, he was told that the fighting was by no means over. The pressure had to be kept up on the Chinese and North Koreans, the line straightened in spots, and positions improved.

He gazed at the valleys and hills that came and went as the train progressed northward. A village appeared occasionally in the distance, a cluster of thatch-covered houses and huts. In the rice paddies stretching away to the hills, men and women were working. Here and there was an ox. It was all so peaceful. What a huge price has been paid, he thought, to permit these simple folk to pursue their ancient ways free of Marxism-Leninism.

When the train pulled into Chunchon, he and a group of lieutenants and captains climbed on the back of a two-and-a-half-ton truck for the remaining journey to the north and east. With the tarp off, they got the full benefit of dust and hot sun and wind. The truck threaded its way through the congested streets of the town, which had changed hands four times in less than a year. Now Korean civilians had crowded back in, along with an overwhelming military presence. Enterprising entrepreneurs had wasted no time trying to capture American dollars from the troops, including establishments featuring the tawdry side of Western culture.

As the truck snaked its way along the dirt streets, it passed a stretch of bars. In front of one stood two young women wearing short skirts, slit up the side, with tight, low-cut blouses. The red lipstick and heavy rouge on their cheeks didn't go well with their Korean complexion. They waved, smiled, and called out, "Hey, GI, No. 1 girls! Have beer. Short time, long time!"

"Hey, Joe, looks like she's waving at you," one of the lieutenants said.

"Maybe we need a rest stop after that train ride. A little R and R," another said.

"Do you boys think the quality's improved over Pusan?"

"Looks all the same to me."

"The prices might be better here."

They picked up speed in the countryside, and their dust enveloped the low, straw-roofed houses, set close by roads never meant for such a never-ending stream of motor vehicles with their grinding noise and dust. There had been heavy fighting here the previous spring, and the mark of war was everywhere. Some villages were now only rubble, with nothing standing. In one, the gutted walls of an old Japanese bank were the only upright remains. They unceremoniously crossed the 38th parallel and continued north.

At corps headquarters it was apparent to him that the army was settling in. A tent city had arisen on the valley floor, with streets and drainage ditches laid out on a grid and long rows of tents in perfect alignment. He stayed there overnight in a transit tent and then went by truck the next morning still farther north to division rear and from there to the regimental CP and then still farther north to the battalion CP. Living conditions for the troops became increasingly crude as he moved down in the command structure. All civilian inhabitants had been removed to the south.

Signs grew that he was approaching the combat area. His truck passed a line of eight Sherman tanks pulled off the road, their helmeted crews standing around talking and smoking. Soon they skirted a battery of four 155-millimeter howitzers setting up a booming crescendo as they belched smoke from their black snouts pointed at a 45-degree angle, lobbing their high-explosive rounds over a steep ridge in the distance and onto enemy positions on the hills beyond.

An artillery officer riding on the truck said, "They like to put a little fire on 'em from time to time to keep 'em on their toes. We don't want 'em to forget we're here."

Lt. Col. Leonard Burkman, Second Battalion commander, sat in a folding wooden chair behind an army-issue folding wooden table. Across from him sat John with his helmet in his lap and his carbine leaning against his leg. The tent flaps on all sides were rolled up, permitting a faint breeze to pass through at intervals. Outside, the midafternoon sun baked the earth. Sporadic sounds of jeeps and trucks arriving and departing came from somewhere out of sight, mixed with soldiers' voices.

"Well, Winston, I see you've got quite a record." The colonel was looking at the 201 file. "Silver Star, Purple Heart, some pretty heavy action last fall."

"Yes, sir. It wasn't a picnic." The dirt floor of the tent was uneven, causing his chair to wobble.

"I'm glad to see you. We need some experienced officers. What I've been getting in recent weeks are green men from the States. This rotation policy we've got now sends 'em home just about the time they get enough experience to be worth something. In fact, the whole army here has turned over since last winter. You'll be the only officer in the battalion who saw action up around the Chongchon."

"That's easy to understand. Almost all the officers I knew are either dead or missing."

Lt. Colonel Burkman put down the 201 file and leaned back in his chair. "We're the center battalion in the regiment. Here, let me show you." He got up and took two steps over to a wooden tripod supporting a large map of the regimental position. A celluloid overlay bearing numerous black grease-pencil markings covered the map. "First Battalion is on our left, to the west. Here we are, and here is Third Battalion on our right, to the east. We occupy this string of ridges you see here, running roughly east and west right along the MLR."

New terminology had crept into army jargon. He had learned in recent days that MLR was Main Line of Resistance. Then there was the MSR—the Main Supply Route—a road constructed by army engineers, wider and better surfaced than Korean roads.

Lt. Colonel Burkman was tall and heavyset, with a broad face capped by dark, crew-cut hair. As a freshman at the University of Nebraska, he had been drafted during the war, obtained an OCS commission, and stayed in the regular army after the war. It occurred to John that the war had deprived the Nebraska football team of a good tackle.

The colonel sat down. He pulled a pack of Lucky Strikes from his fatigue pocket and offered one to John. "No, thanks," he said. "Sir, if I may ask, how is this battalion organized?"

Burkman lit up with a Zippo lighter, snapped it shut, and exhaled a line of smoke. "We've got three companies—Dog, Easy, Fox. Right now Dog and Fox are in the line. Easy's in reserve just to the rear of the ridge line. I'm putting you in Fox. One of its lieutenants just rotated home, and they need a good platoon leader."

"Yes, sir."

A jeep took John from the battalion CP up to the base of a steep, rocky ridge. There he was met by a sergeant who took his duffel bag and led him on foot up a winding path to the Fox Company CP on the south slope of the ridge, just below the crest. The CP was a bunker, mostly underground, roofed over with logs and sandbags.

Inside in the dim light he found Capt. Bruce Waller, West Point class of '47. He had been with the battalion since the beginning of the drive back north in the late winter and had seen some intense action. He was a blond six-footer with an eaglelike face. A holstered .45 was strapped around the waist of his dusty, sweat-streaked fatigues.

"Well, Winston," he said with enthusiasm, shaking hands, "I'm damn glad to see you. We're short a platoon leader and especially short on experienced officers. The old man told me about your record. It's impressive."

Captain Waller sat down on a stool and waved John onto a low stack of metal ammo boxes. "Let me explain our mission here. Mainly it's to hold our position and repel any attacks. We're facing North Koreans. We thought their army was destroyed last fall, but they've come back and are very formidable. The Chinese are off to the west, so we don't have to worry about them, at least not for now. Another mission is to run patrols to maintain contact and snag some prisoners all along to satisfy the intelligence boys. The gooks send out patrols, and we send out patrols. The trick is to stay out of each other's way, but sometimes we have little firefights. You'll be leading some of the patrols, but I want you to go along on one or two first to get a feel for how they work. They're all at night."

"What about offensive operations?"

"Not going to be any big offensive as far as I can tell. The brass is hoping for an armistice soon, even though the negotiations seem to have hit the skids at the moment. But I expect we might be ordered to take some of this terrain out in front of us. That kind of operation is limited, but it could be right nasty. The gooks are really dug in."

An explosion in the distance interrupted the conversation. "You hear that?" Captain Waller said. "North Korean mortar round. They lob them over here at irregular intervals. Can't tell when one will drop in on us, and can't hear them coming."

It was the first hostile fire John had heard since running the gauntlet below Kunu-ri. He flinched, noticeably he feared, and his stomach tightened.

"You can't expose yourself around here," the captain continued. "A couple of weeks ago one of our men was sitting out there not far from this bunker. It had been a quiet day. Without warning he was wiped out when a mortar hit right beside him. Their artillery can be bad, but you can at least hear the incoming."

Captain Waller went on talking, explaining how the defensive position was set up with barbed wire, trip flares, and outposts. He described the system of bunkers and connecting trenches, constructed to afford protection from enemy artillery and mortar fire.

"Sounds like the western front in the First World War," John said.

"Good analogy. The men on the Somme in 1916 would be right at home here."

"How did we let ourselves get in this situation?"

"It's this whole damn peculiar war, or police action, as we're supposed to call it. Just between you and me, I think MacArthur had a point. But that's not for us to say. We're here to obey orders. So let me get down to business. You'll take over First Platoon, on our left flank. You're lucky to have a first-rate platoon sergeant—Sergeant Alton. He's a regular army man, came in around the end of the war. I don't think he saw any action then, but he's seen plenty here since spring. Pay attention to him. He can give a lot of good advice. You've also got our ROK liaison officer in your bunker—Lt. Kim Yung Suk. Seems like a bright fellow who knows what he's doing. Speaks good English."

They stood up and shook hands. Waller said, "Good luck, Winston, I'm looking forward to working with you. Keep your head down and your wits about you. By the way, where're you from?"

"A small town in Alabama. You probably never heard of it."

"I'm from Augusta, Georgia." He smiled. "Glad to have another Southerner aboard."

John returned the smile. "I thought I detected a touch of that."

"Are you married?"

"No, sir. Never had the chance, but under the circumstances I think it's just as well."

"You've got a point there. I just got married a year ago. Might have been better if I hadn't until this is over. Wife is expecting a baby in another two or three weeks."

"All right, gentlemen," Captain Waller announced to his three platoon leaders and the forward observer gathered in his bunker, "I've just come back from a briefing at battalion. We're going to get up out of these bunkers and trenches and see some action. Eighth Army has decided that the MLR needs to be straightened and our defensive positions improved in this sector. I'm sure you've heard all the fireworks off to the west in the last couple of days. First Battalion tried to occupy Hill 820." He pointed to a map spread out on some ammo boxes. "They got to the top but couldn't hold it. That attack has been called off. The big reason is that the North Koreans are on Hill 969 out here on our left front, and they can put fire down on 820 and deny it to us. Therefore," he paused and took a deep breath, "Second Battalion has been assigned the objective of attacking and occupying Hill 969. Dog and Easy will carry out the attack. We'll be in reserve."

They all bent over the map to examine the terrain features. John had been in Fox Company only a week and had scarcely met the other lieutenants. Each platoon was dug into its own complex of bunkers and trenches, and there was little opportunity for contact among the officers.

The captain continued. "The attack will commence at 0700 tomorrow. It will be preceded by a one-hour artillery preparation combined with air strikes. Dog will move up this spur from the west, and Easy will hit the hill head-on from the valley. We'll move down at 0800 and take up a position at approximately this point"—he indicated on the map—"about two hundred yards from the base of 969. I want every man to have as many hand grenades and as much ammo as he can carry."

The briefing lasted half an hour. When it was over, John scrambled back up the slope and into the network of trenches to his bunker to get his men ready. The week since he had taken command of the First Platoon had been relatively quiet, with only some light enemy shelling. He had been on one uneventful patrol out across the valley floor, which was about two thousand yards wide. He had spent time getting to know his men and getting used to the molelike life under constant and unpredictable threat of artillery and mortar fire.

Captain Waller had been right about Sgt. Richard Alton. He quickly oriented John to the peculiarities of staying alive on the MLR.

"Lieutenant, don't show your head above ground in the daylight."

He had a sense of humor. "We try to send every man back for a shower every two weeks, whether he needs it or not."

Lt. Kim Yung Suk turned out to be unexpectedly interesting. This was the first chance he had to talk at length with a Korean. At night, lying on their bunks—dirt shelves cut out of the wall of the bunker—they talked.

Kim's father had been a Presbyterian minister in a small town near Pyongyang. Presbyterian missionaries from America, Kim explained, arrived in Korea in the 1880s and built churches and hospitals. After 1945 his father found life under the regime of Kim Il-sung increasingly difficult. So he and his family and most of the congregation made their way to Seoul in 1948 and founded a new church there. Kim enrolled in Seoul National University, hoping to study medicine.

After the North Korean attack, Kim and some of his fellow students escaped to the south, and he joined the army. He never heard of his father and mother and younger brother again. He assumed that they had died in the fighting or had been murdered by the invaders, like hundreds of other Seoul inhabitants.

On this eve of his first action with Fox Company, John said good night to Kim, and they extinguished the lantern. Sergeant Alton, who shared the bunker, was out checking the guards. John found it difficult to sleep.

At Kunu-ri, before they moved northward on that ill-fated offensive, it was fear of the unknown that threatened. Now it was the known.

"Kim," he whispered, hearing the Korean turning on his dirt bunk, "are you awake?"

"Yes."

"Have you thought much about fear?"

"Very much."

"What do you think?"

"I have never known a man without it, but my father would say that fear of death is pointless because in both life and death, God is with us."

They lay silent. After a few moments John said, "We better try to get some sleep. We've got a busy day tomorrow."

As the sky paled with the coming dawn and the men of First Platoon finished their C-ration breakfast, John moved through the trenches and bunkers with Sergeant Alton, inspecting every man. At precisely 0600 hours, the air overhead was rent with the shrieking of artillery shells, followed by an awesome thunderclap as the shells exploded simultaneously on the slopes and crest of Hill 969.

"Time on target," Sergeant Alton said. "The artillery likes to do that. Supposed to shock the enemy. Makes a good show."

From that moment on for the next hour, the firing was steady, 105- and 155-millimeter high-explosive and white-phosphorous shells bursting all over the face of Hill 969. The booming roar echoed and re-echoed across the hills and valleys. Near the end of the hour-long artillery saturation, silence suddenly fell across the hills, but only for a few minutes. It was broken by the deafening thunder of jet fighters skimming in from the south low over the heads of Fox Company. Wave after wave of F-80s strafed Hill 969 from bottom to top with .50-caliber machine-gun fire and unleashed canisters of napalm. Huge orange and yellow balls of flame billowed up and enveloped the hill. The firing, the flames, and the screaming roar of jet engines transfixed the Fox Company observers.

"God Almighty," John said to Sergeant Alton, raising his voice above the din. "Can't be anything left alive on that hill."

"Don't be too sure. In those bunkers they can survive a whole hell of a lot of pounding."

At 0700 all suddenly went quiet. Through his field glasses, John saw elements of Easy Company emerging from the brush and rocky crevices at the hill's base to begin the ascent. Dog Company was out of sight somewhere to their left, presumably starting up the spur. Fox's three platoons—two hundred steel-helmeted men weighted down with weapons and ammunition, with Captain Bruce Waller in the lead—began moving down into the valley to take up their reserve position. The sky was blue, dotted with high white clouds. The sun, now above the eastern ridges, promised another hot day. John knew that many a man seeing that sun rise would not live to see it set.

For a while all was quiet. Then the sound of machine-gun fire and exploding grenades broke out on the hill. It intensified and continued through the morning and into the afternoon. John sat with his platoon in a brushy defile listening to the heavy firing up ahead but not knowing what was going on.

Shortly after midday, the radio crackled into life. The radioman responded and then handed the set to John. It was Captain Waller. The battalion CO, he said, had reported that Easy was bogged down and had already suffered 50 percent casualties. The artillery and air strikes had not knocked out the enemy bunkers. He was ordering that Easy be reinforced by Fox.

"I want you and Second Platoon to move up and join Easy. Third Platoon will stay in reserve. Move out simultaneously abreast at 1430, you on the left, Second Platoon on the right. Link up with Easy. They're about seven hundred yards straight up ahead of you. I'll be going up with Second Platoon. The objective is to occupy the top of 969 by dark. Battalion says they'll try to send up some flamethrowers, but we can't count on it. Got it?"

"Yes, sir. Suppose the flamethrowers don't come up?"

"We'll have to take out the bunkers with what we've got. Anything else?"

"No, sir."

"Good. See you at the top before sundown. Good luck!"

Again there was the dryness of mouth, the tightening of stomach, the quickening of pulse. The day was hot and he was sweating, but he shivered. Fear hovered around him, pressing in on him, like air stirred ominously by unseen wings. He must keep it at bay. Fear not . . . fear not . . . yea though I climb this hill of death, I will fear no evil.

Lost in thought, he stood silently near Sergeant Alton, the radio operator, and Lt. Kim Yung Suk, and stared vacantly ahead, waiting, only vaguely hearing the distant firing.

"Lieutenant! . . . Lieutenant!" Sergeant Alton shouted at him. "I think it's time to move."

"Huh? What?" He looked at his watch. 1430. He snapped out of his reverie. "OK. Pass the word. Let's go! Follow me!"

Chapter 11

SPREAD OUT IN SKIRMISH LINES, the men of Fox's First and Second platoons scrambled up the rough incline. Artillery preparation and air strikes had left shattered tree trunks and shell craters everywhere. Rocks and earth had been churned and reconfigured.

They met litter bearers half stumbling down the slope with their wounded burdens. One man lay on a stretcher with a blood-soaked, mangled leg, a tourniquet strapped around his thigh. Another had a bloody bandage covering his entire forehead and eyes.

"It's pretty hot up there, boys," yelled one of the bearers. "Try not to give us any more work."

The platoon's recently arrived replacements stopped and stared grimly at the inert figures on the stretchers. A young private looked ashen and sick, as though he might vomit.

"Keep moving!" John called out.

Climbing on, they began to encounter Easy's dead. Bloody fatigue-clad bodies hit by hand grenades, mortars, and machine-gun fire were sprawled in all manner of contorted positions, legs and arms torn off, stomachs ripped open, intestines spilling out. A decapitated body had dog tags hanging around the bloody stump of neck. Bodies lay upturned with open mouths and vacantly staring eyes.

John sickened, gritted his teeth, and fixed his eyes straight ahead. Off to his side he heard two of his men retching. "Keep moving!" he yelled.

The firing ahead had died down. They moved in among Easy's

survivors crouched in shell holes and behind a line of rocks that formed a protective ledge across the slope. John found a lieutenant who told him what was going on. They were pinned down and hadn't moved for the last hour. They'd found bunkers still in business and plenty of enemy on hand. Easy's captain was dead. The other lieutenants had been wounded and taken to the rear. He was the only officer left.

The radio operator spoke up. "Captain Waller, sir." John took the radio.

"Hold tight where you are," barked Waller. "Air reconnaissance reports enemy reinforcements moving up to the top of the ridge from the north. We're calling in a fire mission. I'm taking command of what's left of Easy."

Minutes later they could hear artillery rounds shrieking overhead and crashing on the far side of the ridge and along the top. After a quarter-hour the barrage ceased.

Captain Waller was on the radio again. "All right, Winston, we're going to move up. I'm ordering Third Platoon up to join us. Keep going. If you hit any serious trouble, let me know."

Just then a mortar round exploded right behind John's men. A few seconds later another exploded to their front. It threw up dirt and small rocks that clattered off his helmet.

Sergeant Alton said, "They've bracketed us. We'd better get out of here fast."

"OK! Up and at 'em!" he shouted. "Fast! Let's move!"

Several dozen men sprang forward, running in a crouch. They had gone only a few yards when they heard the rattle of machine guns from up the hill and the sound of buzzing and ricocheting bullets all around them. They hit the dirt, flattening out, some behind rocks and fallen tree trunks, others in open ground. Then came a succession of earsplitting explosions in their midst. Bam! . . . Bam! Bam! . . . Bam!

Sergeant Alton shouted at a man who stood up and began to run down hill to the rear. "Come back here!" The man kept going.

John turned and saw the soldier—one of the new replacements— breaking in panic. Without thinking he bolted up and sprinted after him, half stumbling and plunging over the rough terrain. "Stop! Get back here!" He tackled the man and threw him to the ground, football style.

Keyed up himself, he grabbed the front of the man's fatigue jacket and shook him. "Get back up there and pick up your rifle!"

"I can't," the man sobbed, tears bubbling out of his eyes. "I can't do it."

John slapped him hard across the face. "Pull yourself together. Everybody's scared. But we've got to do our duty."

The man shook his head sideways. "No, no. I can't." He was sobbing, terror written across his teenage face.

John impulsively jerked his .45 from its holster and thrust the muzzle into the man's chest. "You're going to die right here if you don't get back with us." He yelled to be heard over the crash of mortar rounds. "You may or may not live up there, but you're sure to die here if you don't get back."

John pulled him to his feet by the front of his jacket and shoved him uphill. "Now get going!"

Running bent over back to Sergeant Alton and the radio operator, he was knocked sideways off his feet by a mind-numbing explosion. His ears buzzed. The world darkened for a few moments. He lay face down, flat on the ground, stunned, unable to think or move.

"Lieutenant, Lieutenant!" Sergeant Alton was beside him. "Are you all right?"

"Think so," he said, weakly, "Just shook up." He lay there for a few seconds, testing his arms and legs.

Cries of "Medic!" were coming from all sides, mixed with screams and moans that could be heard between explosions and over the staccato hammering of machine guns.

"These mortars are killing us. We've got to move on," Sergeant Alton said.

"Right." He rose unsteadily to his hands and knees, still feeling woozy. "Tell 'em to move on."

The men scrambled ahead to the next line of rocks. John regained his footing and caught up. A shower of Soviet-style potato-masher hand grenades descended on them. They frantically threw them back.

Through dust and clouds of hovering smoke, heavy with the acrid smell of cordite, they saw flamethrower teams going into action. They watched as the long, hideous tongues of orange and yellow flame shot forward into the slits of the bunkers. Screams such as John had never heard before told them that the fire was doing its work.

They moved ahead, running, stopping, firing, and moving on again. Slowly the enemy fell back. They passed brown-clothed North Korean corpses left from the artillery barrages and their own fire. They were bloody, mangled, and contorted like the American corpses they had seen earlier. Except for the uniforms, they were indistinguishable from South Koreans. The god of war takes its toll indiscriminately, without regard to race, creed, or allegiance.

After a last long, steep climb they reached the razorback ridge line at the top of Hill 969. The sun was touching the western horizon. The survivors stood there, breathing hard, filthy with sweat, dirt, and gun smoke. To the north, east, and west there was an endless succession of high ridges with valleys in between. On and on into the distance they ran, like incoming waves at the seashore.

At daybreak, as they had watched the awesome display of artillery and air power, none could count on seeing this sun set.

Those who stood at the crest of this high ridge could only marvel at being alive. Easy Company had lost three-fourths of its men, and Fox had suffered nearly 50 percent casualties. Breathing with relief and gratitude, they watched the glowing western sky, with its changing medley of gold and peach and pink reflected on the high clouds over the ridges and valleys of North Korea.

The left leg of John's fatigues had been torn badly by the mortar blast. His canteen was punctured, and two bullet holes were in the right side of his jacket. Once again he had come within millimeters and split seconds of death. Once again he had looked death in the face and stared him down.

"Great going, men! Good job!" Captain Waller walked among his grimy and bone-weary survivors, slapping some on the shoulder. "Fine job, Winston. That was touch and go for a while."

"Thank you, sir."

The captain's helmet was dented and scarred, its chin strap broken and dangling loose. Beneath the helmet, his face, streaked with gun smoke and dirt, showed the strains of the day. "Now look, here's what's next. Dog has linked up with us to the west." He pointed off toward the sunset. "The CO has ordered us to jointly form a perimeter and be prepared for a counterattack tonight. You know the gooks nearly always counterattack, and they love to hit us at night on hilltops."

So, as dusk came on, the men of Fox Company, weary and dispirited, spread out into a defensive perimeter, piling up rocks and remnants of trees and digging in. Machine guns and BARs were set up at intervals, with riflemen in between.

Korean laborers, bent under heavily loaded A-frames, came up from the rear with rations and a fresh supply of ammunition. They ingratiated themselves with the GIs, hoping for cigarettes. When given a Lucky Strike, they would proclaim, "Lucky, No. 1." They had had an uncommonly busy day clearing the dead and wounded from the hillside, overloading the battalion aid station and the graves registration unit.

Guards were posted, to be rotated on one-hour shifts. The rest of the men fell into deep sleep. The night was starlit. All was quiet, an unearthly quiet.

John was jolted out of sleep by the eerie sound he had never forgotten, a sound that had lived in his mind since that night north of Kunu-ri—the far-off blowing of bugles: Ta . . . ta, Ta . . . ta. He was instantly on his feet. "Alton, are you there?"

"Yes, sir. I hear it."

"Get everybody up and ready."

A cry came from one of the machine gunners. "Here they come!"

In the dim starlight, they saw figures coming up the steep slope, a long line stretching from left to right. Behind those were others. The rim of the ridge erupted with fire as Fox went into action. Flares burst overhead, turning the scene into daylight. The North Koreans fell as in a shooting gallery, although many were returning fire, and a few got within grenade distance. But the attack was repulsed, and the action was over in less than an hour. As such things went, it was a relatively light counterattack. Three men in First Platoon suffered minor wounds.

Over the next few days and nights, the men of Fox worked to recreate trenches and bunkers similar to those they had left on the last hill, making themselves ever more impervious to enemy artillery, mortars, and ground attacks. Soon they were dug in again, World War I style.

"I'm told we're getting a new lieutenant in the next couple of weeks," Captain Waller said. He and John were sitting on ration crates opposite one another in the newly established company CP, dug into the south slope of Hill 969. The blanket covering the bunker's opening was pulled aside to let in daylight and fresh air. The day was hot, but it carried a hint of approaching fall. It was the kind of day that made John think of upcoming football games and hunting season.

Waller continued. "Since you got here, the company has been functioning, as you well know, without an exec. We've been short of officers. When this new man arrives I'm thinking of making you company exec."

"That's quite an assignment for a ROTC product who's been in the army only a year." John spoke matter-of-factly, at pains to hide his surprise and pleasure at the prospect.

"Well, you've proved yourself. I've been keeping my eye on you. Have you ever thought of a career in the regular army?"

"Not seriously in recent times. I did think of West Point during high school, but I gave up on it. Without that, I assume I wouldn't get very far."

"Not true. Look at Gen. George Marshall. You can't do better than that. Our own battalion CO has done all right. By the way, we're about to get in a bunch of replacements. God knows we need them. But they'll be green, and we've got to work fast at fitting them in."

Waller stood up, indicating the conversation was over, but then quickly said, "Oh, one more thing." He motioned John to sit back down.

"I think it's generally not appropriate for me to bring up personal matters here," Waller said with a faint smile, "but I have a special piece of news I want to share with somebody. You're a good candidate."

"I'm honored. What is it?"

"A letter came from my wife in the morning mail. We have a baby daughter, born ten days ago."

"Congratulations!" John was on his feet, shaking hands. "That's great news. Are mother and daughter all right?"

"Fine. She went back to her parents' in Charleston when I left, and the baby was born there. Seven pounds, four ounces. It's tough not being there, but she's in good hands."

"That's a nice-sized little gal. What's her name?"

"Henrietta Montrose Waller. Named after my wife's grandmother. We're going to call her Henny. It's a rare occasion when I feel like celebrating anything up here, but this is one. Would you join me in a drink?"

"Gladly," John said, with mild surprise. Drinking, he had thought, was a real no-no here in the line.

"Pass me your canteen cup," Waller said as he rummaged in his duffel bag. He pulled out a half-full fifth of I. W. Harper and splashed a generous portion of bourbon into their cups.

"Here's to Henrietta Montrose Waller," he said. The two clinked their tin cups together and took a big swallow. The burning warmth ran down John's throat and into his stomach. He had taken too large an initial swallow, and his eyes watered.

The conversation mellowed as the two men talked. Waller wanted to know more about John's family and his work before being called up. In turn, he talked about his own background.

"I grew up during the war," he said, "had a bee in my bonnet to go to West Point. When I graduated from high school, I was on the young side and missed out on an appointment in favor of an older fellow. So I went to The Citadel. It was a good alternative. But then one of the senators came through the next year with an appointment, and I felt I had to take it. So it turned out that I had two plebe years—one at The Citadel and then the whole lowly way of life all over again at the Point. I can say one thing: I was well prepared for that second year of hell. In some ways, The Citadel was better at drilling and the manual of arms. And that's where I met my wife. We were married in the chapel there."

Their conversation drifted back to the war. "What do you think about the operation the other day?" Waller asked.

"I suppose the appropriate military response is to say that we accomplished our mission. But I'm very uneasy about it. We left a lot of good men back down this hill. Are we better off—or is the cause better off—because we're here instead of on the last hill?"

"For all we know," Waller said, "the taking of this hill may have had significant influence in getting the Communists to talk seriously. Those Chinese and North Koreans might be a little more impressed with our determination and capability than they were before. In any case, the decision as to what's worth doing and not doing is for those in position to know what we can't know—those who have the responsibility."

"I can't dispute that," John said. "But I have to say that I'm getting more and more uncomfortable at seeing all these lives lost for such limited objectives."

"Brooding over your misgivings will get in the way of your performance. Incidentally, have you seen the book by Marguerite Higgins?" Waller asked.

"I read some extracts just before I left Japan. Her diagnosis at the end is about right, I think."

"You mean the part about American unpreparedness?"

"That and the part about American softness compared to the Communist world," said John. "She quoted a Communist as saying that they would ultimately prevail because what American soldiers want more than anything else is a hot shower."

"I'm afraid there's something to that. Showers are good for morale—I would sure as hell love to have one right now—but we've got to learn to live as tough as our enemies. You've seen the truckloads of cigarettes, candy, beer, and other goodies for the troops," Waller said with disgust. "You can be sure there's nothing like that up north of us. The gooks don't know about hot showers and PXs. I've been amazed at how they can keep throwing men into the face of certain death. Lives are expendable for them, like ammunition. But I think they learned a lesson after Wonju and Chipyong-ni. We got them out in the open there, and it was a real slaughter pen."

Waller splashed more bourbon into their canteen cups and stuffed the bottle back in his duffel bag. He crossed his legs and took a sip. "One thing this war shows to me," John said, "is that a willingness to throw away unlimited manpower, even if they have only small arms, can make a formidable enemy. We better be careful how we discount these so-called primitive armies."

"You're right. This war is fortunate in one way. It's an alarm clock to wake us up. Everybody in the army knew we were being reduced to a dangerous level. The folks in Washington assumed we'd never have to fight. We had the atomic bomb, and that was supposed to be the answer. But here we are, on the ground on foot, where men in war have been since the beginning of time. This is the way it has to be, whether you have spears or M-1 rifles. Anyway, we have the message now, I hope, before it's too late."

The shadows were growing long outside the bunker as they drained the last drops from their cups. John was left with a pleasant glow. For a fleeting interlude, grim reality had been pushed back a bit.

"Thank you, sir, for the drink," he said as they stood up, shaking hands. "Congratulations again on the big news."

As he turned toward the opening, slinging his carbine over his shoulder, Waller said, "I hate to bring us back down to earth, but you might want to know that Division G-2 has sent down word that Hill 1080 is being reinforced by enemy forces. Not clear whether they're Chinese or North Korean. The intelligence folks think this is part of a general buildup all along the front."

"Isn't 1080 that massive, high ridge to our right front?"

"Right. The highest peak around here. It looms up out there, something like the rock of Gibraltar. Sooner or later they might want us to do something about it."

Lieutenant Kim was reputed to have a fine singing voice and had sung recently at a church service somewhere in the rear. So it was no surprise when the chaplain requested him to sing at the upcoming Sunday service at regimental headquarters. With Captain Waller's permission, John went with Kim in the jeep along the winding dirt road, bulldozed by the army engineers, back through two small valleys to the sprawling regimental base.

On rows of crude, wooden benches sat some two hundred young, fatigue-clad American men. John saw every kind of visage—the tough street kid, the craggy farm boy, the effete scholar. A few were black, but most were white, reflecting every strain of European stock—Nordic, Celtic, Mediterranean, Slavic, Anglo-Saxon, peasant and aristocrat alike. They sat with steel helmets in their laps and rifle butts resting on the ground between their feet.

Kim stood on a low wooden platform at the front. His high, melodious voice floated the familiar words over the assemblage, hauntingly touched with a Korean accent: "I have seen Him in the watch fires of a hundred circling camps, They have builded Him an altar in the evening dews and damps; I can read his righteous sentence by the dim and flaring lamps: His day is marching on."

The men on the wooden benches sat motionless, their attention riveted on the diminutive Korean figure with the ROK insignia on his fatigue collar. He concluded with heightened volume—"Glory, glory hallelujah, His truth is marching on!"—leaving these dozens of combat soldiers transfixed by the moving words, raised to a universal significance by the Asian voice. Many eyes were moist, including John's.

Back with his platoon, he studied Hill 1080 with his field glasses. It was a formidable landmass, looming well over a hundred feet higher than his position. It rose steeply from the valley, about three thousand yards to the northeast. For most of the way up, he figured, the climb would be at about a 45-degree angle. The rocky slope was cut by ravines, and the usual scrubby growth of evergreens appeared at places.

Running down the middle of the valley between Fox Company and Hill 1080, from east to west, was a small creek, the water now low; in the winter it probably dried up completely. Parallel to the creek was a narrow dirt road, little more than a trail. Beyond, near the base of 1080, was a small straw-roofed farmhouse, abandoned amid surrounding overgrown rice paddies. There were other neglected rice paddies scattered across the valley, untended for many months. Outwardly, the valley and its surrounding hills and ridges presented an appearance of tranquility, a scene of natural beauty, a scene at odds with the presence of two hostile armies with their instruments of mass death.

Fresh rolls of barbed wire had been brought up to John's First Platoon, and his men were busy stringing the wire out below their trenches, foxholes, and bunkers, which had been improved by continued digging. Sandbags had been filled and piled up along the line and on top of the bunkers. The Korean laborers had finally finished burying the enemy dead from the night counterattack. Because the job had taken several days and the days were hot, Fox Company had been subjected to the sight of rotting and bloated corpses strewn on the slope below and to the stench of decomposing human flesh.

After dark in his bunker, he finally found time to write home, for the first time in two weeks.

> Sorry I haven't written sooner. We have been busy changing hills. It's a seesaw contest, back and forth, trading hills. We can't use our strengths—mechanization, mobility, firepower. We're on

their level, slugging it out on foot. The enemy have the advantage because they have more foot soldiers and they don't care how many die.

You cannot imagine the conditions we live in on the MLR. It's been nearly three weeks since anybody in this outfit had a shower or a change of clothes, and that includes me! And you have to remember it's hot and we've been working hard. If things stay quiet, we'll start trucking men back to a shower unit near the regimental CP. If any man here appeared as he is on the streets of Remberton, he would be arrested for gross lack of sanitation.

Of course, we've got water. The Korean litter-bearers pack it up here in five-gallon metal cans carried on their backs on A-frames. This time of year nature provides a fine hot-water heater. All we do is put a can outside the bunker where the morning sun will hit it, and we have hot water. A steel helmet makes a good wash basin. I shave out of it and try to do some washing up. So much for the news.

You asked for a report for the *Progress,* but the scene is so grim here I am not in the mood. I'll keep it in mind. At least I've got a great company commander. His wife just had a baby girl. This is no place for a married man. He should be home right now.

Our Korean liaison officer is very interesting. We have long talks. I now know far more about Korea than I would ever have known without him. We share the same bunker, along with my sergeant, Dick Alton. He's out now checking on the guards. I'm sitting here on the ground beside a candle, using a C-ration carton as a writing desk. Incidentally, despite all the grousing about it, this is not bad food, although beans and franks can get old. At this moment, Kim is sitting by his own candle reading a small book, probably something on philosophy or religion. A fine fellow and a great singer.

I think it's grand that Becky and Frank are moving back. Frank'll be an enormous help.

Thanks, mother, for the details about Jeanie's wedding. I can imagine that Mr. Ben was in his finest hour. From what you say, I gather this war is finally being felt a bit, because several of the crowd couldn't be at the wedding because they've been drafted. I haven't heard from many lately, although I did get a letter from Sally telling me she's on the way to New York. I always thought that school teaching in Montgomery would be too quiet for her.

He finished the letter and sat back against the rough dirt wall, thinking of Remberton. Thoughts of home had been pushed out. But now he found himself reflecting on what seemed from this far distance to be an extraordinarily pleasant, even idyllic, place, one where everybody knew everybody else, not only knew each other but knew each other's parents and grandparents, knew the good and the bad, the sad and happy, all the sunshine and shadows of their intertwined lives. It looked good now from this battle-swept hilltop in Korea, even without Jeanie.

His reverie was broken when Kim blew out his candle. "You've got the right idea," John said. "We better try to get some sleep." He blew out his candle and slid into his sleeping bag.

After a few minutes, John said softly, "Kim, are you asleep?"

"No."

"May I ask you a theological question?"

"Yes, but I am not a theologian."

"You're more of one than I am. Anyway, here's my question. The other day, in our attack up the hill, do you think God was present right there?"

"My father would say that God is present everywhere, that it is impossible to be anywhere that God is not also there."

"Then do you think God had anything to do with what happened there?"

"If I knew the answer to that, I would be God."

"Who lives and who dies seems like pure chance."

"Since I cannot know, I find comfort in believing that I am in God's hand. Whether I survive this war, I have decided, is beyond my control. At least I am a little less worried."

"Maybe you're right, but I can't make sense of all the killing."

"I believe we are fighting pure evil, the forces of darkness. I cannot believe that God will permit those forces to prevail. But many lives may be lost to defeat the evil. Why that is so, only God knows."

Sergeant Alton pulled aside the poncho covering the bunker entrance and came in, carefully placing the poncho back in place. "All OK?" John asked. The men could not see each other in the bunker's total darkness. But he heard Alton's carbine being laid down and the unbuckling sound of combat boots being removed.

"Yes, sir. All's quiet right around here. Some artillery fire way off in the west. I ran into the Second Platoon sergeant, and he says he hears we're going to start doing some patrolling tomorrow night."

"I heard the captain mention it. It's not a bad idea. We've got reports about a buildup on Hill 1080."

Sergeant Alton slipped into his sleeping bag, and the bunker fell into silence.

Lt. Colonel Burkman came up the next day from the battalion CP to inspect Fox Company's position. After poking into the foxholes, trenches, and bunkers of the Second and Third platoons, he wound up in John's First Platoon. Getting through the narrow trenches was not easy for him. He was a big man—tall, large-boned, and heavy. He was cleaner looking and wearing noticeably fresher fatigues than anyone in Fox, obviously a man with more ready access to the rear-area showers.

"Looks like you boys plan to stay here for a while—found yourselves a home with a view." He was addressing John. They were clustered—Colonel Burkman, Captain Waller, John, and two sergeants—in the trench outside the entrance to the bunker.

"Well, sir," John said, "No telling when the gooks might swarm up here. We'd rather be dug in too much instead of too little."

"That's good thinking," Burkman replied. He turned to Waller. "Now, Captain, regiment wants us to start more active patrolling. I went to a briefing back there yesterday. They see enemy buildup all along the line. We've got to find out more about what's going on out there."

"Things seem pretty quiet right here," Waller said. "We've been peppered with a little shelling, but nothing really serious."

"Don't be fooled by this rustic tranquility. Those hills out there are probably crawling with invisible North Koreans. The French battalion had a nasty encounter a couple of days ago. It turns out that the enemy is tunneling in on these hills—deep tunnels where dozens of men can hide and withstand artillery barrages and air strikes. Their bunkers were tough, but these tunnels can really give us fits."

The colonel turned to go, but then paused. "By the way, Winston, I'm glad to have such good reports about you in the action the other day. Keep it up."

"Thank you, sir."

"We're going to need all the leadership we can muster if we have to take on Hill 1080. I see you've got a good view of that monster from here. But if the North Koreans are on top of it, they've got an even better view of you. Ten eighty could be a real bitch."

The colonel extended his hand. John shook it and then watched the group trundle its way back along the trench.

Captain Waller was back in an hour. "OK, Winston, we're going to begin putting a patrol out every night. We'll rotate among the platoons, starting with you." He spread a map out on the ground at the bottom of the trench, and they bent over it on their knees. After talking over the various terrain features, they agreed that John would lead a patrol out to the base of 1080, or as close as he could get to it, using the abandoned farmhouse as his target. The objective would be to find out whether there were any enemy outposts or movements in the valley. If there were, a secondary objective would be to bring back a prisoner for interrogation.

"Move out at 2100," Waller said. "It should be good dark by then. The password for tonight is 'Blue Sky.'"

With dusk, the sky became overcast. Rain appeared to be a prospect. Darkness came earlier than usual. There was no moon, and the stars were obscured by clouds.

"It's as black as the bottom of a coal mine," cracked one of the men.

At 2100 hours John led the patrol down the slope, through the barbed wire, past the machine-gun outposts, and into the valley. The patrol included seven men and Lieutenant Kim in case they snagged a prisoner. Leaving their canteens and stripping themselves of anything that might rattle or clink, they proceeded single file, several feet apart—"Indian style," as the men called it. Each carried an M-1 rifle. John and Kim carried carbines.

He had studied the valley carefully with his field glasses and the map, memorizing its undulations, overgrown areas, rice paddies, and the location of the creek and the trail. But in the darkness he could not be sure that he was where he thought he was. They moved slowly, not talking, stopping every few minutes to listen. In the stillness the crunch of their boots was alarmingly loud. He was relieved, after an hour's tedious progress, to come upon the trail. He was about half-way across the valley and going in the right direction. Before pushing on, they explored the trail for a little distance to the west and the east. They found nothing. They moved on. The creek turned out to be a slowly flowing stream, ankle deep and about fifteen feet wide. They waded across and kept moving. In a quarter-hour they came to the edge of overgrown rice paddies.

He halted the column and edged over to the corporal next to him. "Newton," he said in a low whisper, "pass the word to sit down and rest a few minutes. I think the farmhouse is just up ahead."

They sat in silence, straining their senses to the maximum. A slight breeze moved some of the undergrowth bringing a faint hint of long-ago night soil.

A handful of stars became visible. The clouds were thinning. The threat of rain was receding. A few more stars appeared. Their faint illumination eased the total blackness. He thought he could make out the shape of the farmhouse, about a hundred yards away. Beyond loomed Hill 1080, ominous and foreboding, its high ridge line just visible against the sky.

He cupped his ears. Could it have been a metallic click? Yes, he heard it again. Was it the click of a bolt? The silence had been so deep he could not be sure. "Hear anything?" His whisper was barely audible.

Newton said nothing. They both listened, focused intently on the farmhouse. Then there was no mistake about it. There came the faint sound of human voices, low and far off, possibly two or three men talking to each other.

"Somebody's at that house," whispered Newton.

The sound ceased. But in a minute it resumed. John was thinking hard.

"Here's what. You take one of the men and go off to our right about fifty yards and then turn and approach the house from that side. The rest of us will sit tight."

"What do you want me to do when I get near the house?"

"See if you can figure out how many are there. It might be just a two- or three-man outpost. Or maybe a squad or, for that matter, could be a whole company getting ready to hit us."

"If it's just a handful, do you want us to knock 'em out?"

"OK, but try to nab at least one prisoner. We're not here to fight. If it's more than three or four, come on back."

"Should I take Lieutenant Kim?"

John paused. "Good idea. Tell him I asked him to go along."

The three moved off and were lost immediately in the darkness. Long minutes passed. Low voices could be heard sporadically from the direction of the house. The silence was split suddenly by two rifle shots from the right. A few seconds of jabbering voices followed. Then came a fusillade of fire from the house—rifles interspersed with a burp-gun burst. Silence for a few seconds. Then another burst from the house.

All was then quiet. Minutes passed. Was his threesome dead? He was in a quandary. Should they stay where they were, go forward to help the men, or withdraw? He decided to wait a little while longer to see what developed.

Sounds of heavy breathing and crunching boots came from his right. "Lieutenant, it's us," Newton said breathlessly. "We better get out of here. We thought there were only three, but a whole flock came out of nowhere."

"Is everybody all right?"

"I took a hit in the arm, but I'm OK," Newton whispered. "How about you, Schmidt?"

"A crease in the thigh, but I can make it."

"Kim, are you all right?" John asked, still whispering.

"Yes," came the faint Korean voice.

"Let's move out then," John said. "I'll get the details later. We'll go back the way we came."

They came to the creek, waded across, and then crossed the trail. They moved more rapidly than before but still trying to make as little noise as possible.

They reached the base of their hill. More stars had appeared, and they could now easily see the outlines of the terrain and the ridge looming against the sky. John halted the group.

"Is everybody here? Count 'em off, Newton."

Newton moved back along the line, checking off the men. "All here, sir, except Lieutenant Kim."

"Where's Kim?" asked John anxiously. "Anybody seen Kim?"

One of the privates spoke up. "Last I seen of him was when we was crossing the creek. He was bringing up the rear."

"Anybody seen him since the creek?"

Nobody spoke. Seconds passed in silence. John said quietly, "I'm going back."

Corporal Newton said, "Sir, those gooks might have moved out this way on our tail."

"Never mind," John said, "take the patrol on in. Don't forget the password, 'Blue Sky.' Get Captain Waller on the phone and tell him that I request a fire mission on that house—a dozen rounds of HE ought to be about right."

With added light from the stars, John felt confident he could retrace their steps. He saw the trees, dips in the land, and unused rice paddies that they had just passed. He half-ran, spurred by a sense of urgency to find Kim.

He came to the trail and paused, listening. Hearing nothing, he crossed and in another hundred feet was at the bank of the creek. He looked up and down and saw nothing. The water was not swift enough or deep enough to have carried Kim away. He had to be on this side, unless the North Koreans had seized him.

He stood beside the creek, puzzling. He heard nothing except the low gurgle of the water flowing along its rocky bed. Then suddenly he caught the sound of a faint groan to his rear. He wheeled and moved up the bank toward the sound. There off to his side he made out a crumpled human form, lying face down. Despite the darkness, he was certain the uniform was American.

He knelt down and rolled the body over. The helmet had fallen off. "Kim . . . Kim," John whispered urgently. There was no answer. The eyes were closed. He ran his hand down the chest and stomach. The fatigue jacket was warm, wet, and sticky. He put his fingers on Kim's pulse and found, to his relief, that it was throbbing.

Why hadn't Kim told them he had been hit? He should have spoken up. Maybe it was an Oriental variety of stoicism, or perhaps some extreme view of Presbyterian predestination. In any case, he had to get him out of here fast. To lift him might inflict more serious internal injuries, but there was no choice. If left here, he would die, either by bleeding to death or at the hands of the North Koreans.

John hurriedly slung his carbine over his shoulder and ran his left arm under Kim's back and his right arm under his knees. He rose and headed back toward the trail, glad that Kim, like many Korean men, was small and light.

Near the edge of the trail he stopped to listen. His heart took a quick leap as he heard, faintly but unmistakably, the sound of moving feet. He quickly ducked into some trees, dropped to his knees, placed Kim on the ground, and unslung his carbine. He pushed the safety off and held it at the ready.

The sound grew, coming from his left. Kim groaned softly. He clamped his left hand over Kim's mouth, holding the carbine in his right.

Shadowy figures came into view on the trail. They were moving past him in a column. He counted twelve. They were less than twenty feet away. They passed on, and soon all was in silence again.

He gathered up Kim and struck out across the trail and into the underbrush on the other side, moving faster now, with a single-minded determination to get back to Fox Company as quickly as possible. He had to pause every few minutes to catch his breath and readjust his hold on Kim. He checked the pulse, and it was still beating, but the fatigue jacket was getting wetter.

From far to his rear, toward Hill 1080, came the crashing boom of an artillery round. It rolled down the valley like a bowling ball and bounced off the opposite hills. In a minute came another echoing boom. The firing battery has bracketed the farmhouse, he surmised. The howitzers should be firing for effect at any moment. And then there it was—a cluster of night-shattering explosions, at least a dozen rounds, he guessed, maybe more, singly and overlapping in a chorus of high-explosive power. He visualized the flimsy straw-roofed structure and the ground around it being pulverized, along with any enemy soldiers who might have been lurking there.

In less than half an hour he was at the base of Fox Company's hill. He began to ascend, panting heavily. From out of the dark came an American voice: "Who goes there?"

"Blue Sky. Lieutenant Winston."

"Come on in."

John moved uphill through the barbed wire and past the outpost and foxholes. His arms felt as though they might drop off.

"Got a wounded man!" he yelled. "Get a medic quick! Litter bearers!"

Chapter 12

"WINSTON," CAPTAIN WALLER ASKED WITH CONCERN, "what's the blood? Were you hit?"

"No, sir. Kim took a bullet in the stomach on the patrol last night, and I had to pick him up."

"How is he?"

"The medics took him back to the aid station, and they sent him on to the MASH. I haven't had any further report."

"Too bad. I liked him. Seemed like a good officer."

"Yes, he was. Good company too. A fine fellow. I'll miss him."

John had just come into the company CP in answer to a summons from Waller. Within a few minutes all the company officers were gathered there. Waller seemed unusually tense. It was obvious that something important was brewing.

"I've just come back from a meeting of the company commanders and the battalion staff. Here's the word: The battalion has been ordered to attack and occupy Hill 1080. This is part of a regimental-wide assault. The other two battalions will be attacking the lower hills to the east and west of 1080." He spread a map out on a folding canvas cot. "Easy and Dog will hit the hill on the flanks. We are honored, if I may put it that way, with the center, a head-on frontal assault right up the main face."

They all looked at the map. John felt a queasiness in his stomach.

"Based on what we know about 1080, I think this will be the toughest assignment this outfit has had since last spring," Waller said.

The attack was to be in two days. In the meantime, the artillery would work over the hill, and there would be air strikes. The intelligence estimates were that a North Korean regiment occupied the string of hills. There were bunkers and probably tunnels, so it was uncertain what effect the artillery and air strikes would have. They discussed timing and coordination.

"I'll be coming around to inspect each of your platoons tomorrow," Waller said. "The Korean bearers will be bringing up more ammo and rations. Be sure every man is fully equipped. This might be more than a one-day operation."

After several questions from the lieutenants, the captain dismissed the group, saying they would meet again the next day.

John lingered as the others left. "Captain, may I talk to you for a minute?"

"Sure. What is it?"

"This is an unusual thing to say, probably inappropriate, but I've got to say it." He paused, taking a deep breath.

"Go ahead. What's on your mind?"

"I don't know any way to say it except to put it bluntly: This mission is suicidal. I've studied 1080 for days. An assault up that monster will make our operation on this hill, bad as the casualties were, look like a preliminary warm-up. I hate to think what our losses will be. And for what? Another hill? Then after that, what? Still another hill? We'll never run out of hills, but we'll be going nowhere." He suddenly realized his voice was rising.

Waller listened impassively. He waited a moment after John stopped, and then spoke softly and calmly, as if to draw a contrast. "Look, Winston, we've talked about this before. It's not for you or me to decide whether this operation is a good idea or whether it will achieve anything of importance. Those questions have been decided higher up. We have our orders."

"This is not a spur-of-the-moment reaction. No one believes more strongly in this cause than I do. We have a U.N. mandate to unify all of Korea. Why aren't we doing it? If we were pursuing that mandate, I would not hesitate to do what we were ordered. But we're not." He stopped, realizing again that he was talking excitedly.

"I'm not going to argue with what you say. We must leave those matters to the constituted authorities. We follow their orders regardless of what we think."

The CP was quiet for several seconds. John could hear his heart beating. From far down the slope to the rear came the sound of a deuce-and-a-half grinding along. "I would like to request permission to speak to the battalion commander."

Surprise flashed over Waller's face. "What for? To give him the same argument you've just given me? The old man is tough. He would probably throw you out of his tent."

"I'm prepared to risk that. But I can't rest until I've at least had a chance to tell him that I think this attack is wrong. It's pointless."

For a moment John thought that Waller might do what he said the battalion commander would do. "It will be considered highly irregular for me to ask the CO to see one of my officers. He'll think it's up to me to handle their problems and not bother him. I might end up getting chewed out." He paused, as though debating with himself. After what seemed to John an interminable time, he said, "I won't be doing you any favor, but, all right, I will put the request through. I wouldn't do it if you weren't such a good officer."

"Thank you. I hope it doesn't get you in hot water."

"Now get on back to your platoon and start getting ready for this operation. I'll send word."

In the First Platoon bunker the field telephone jangled. It was Captain Waller. "OK, Winston, Colonel Burkman will see you this afternoon at 1600. I hope you'll get this stuff off your chest and come on back and get down to business. I warn you, the old man has been known to eat lieutenants for breakfast."

"Well, I'm glad it's not mealtime. I do appreciate your putting me in the lion's den. Hope I get out alive."

He slipped the receiver back into its case and sat down on an ammo box. What was he doing? Had he lost his mind? What could he hope to accomplish by seeing the battalion commander? His views would have no effect on anything. Once he said his piece—and probably got a first-class chewing out—he would have no choice but to come on back and go forward with the planned attack.

It was not true, he reflected, that there was no choice. He could refuse to lead his platoon up Hill 1080, thereby disobeying an order—the ultimate military sin. Yet if he really believed that to carry out this attack would be to throw away dozens of lives to no good end, shouldn't he stand up for his belief and take the consequences, whatever they might be? For a fleeting moment he actually thought the unthinkable.

Sergeant Alton came in as the sound of artillery in the east grew louder. "What's that artillery?" asked John.

"Enemy shelling on Third Battalion. The gooks like to keep reminding us they're still there. We've been pretty lucky so far, but I predict we're going to get a heavier dose soon."

"Are we ready?"

"About as ready as we can be." He leaned his carbine against the bunker wall, took off his helmet, and wiped his forehead with the sleeve of his fatigues. "Still hot out there but getting a little better." He dropped to the ground and said, with an air of concern, "Sir, I've been keeping a close eye every day on 1080. The gooks are good at digging in so you can't detect them from a distance. But in the last couple of days I notice some differences. Stuff up on that hill has been moved around. My guess is they've built at least several bunkers."

"We've got reports of tunnels, too. You put all that together with the height of the hill and the steepness of the slopes and you've got something that will make our trip up this hill look like a picnic."

"I've been up and down the line talking to the squad leaders and the men, to get them ginned up for the effort. A lot of them are nervous."

"Aren't soldiers always nervous before an attack?"

"Some more than others. I get it myself."

"So do I," John said with a slight smile. "What do you think about this attack?"

"That's not for me to say. But since you asked, I think it's going to be pure hell."

"How do you think our green men will work?"

"Always hard to say. We've seen some of these types break and run. That could happen again. On the other hand, a lot of them will be good."

"I've got to head back to the CP now. Be sure that every man has as much ammo and as many grenades as he can carry. One thing you can say about the army now is that it has plenty of ammo. The enemy has unlimited men, and we have unlimited supplies. Try to figure how that comes out."

He slung the carbine over his shoulder, pulled the steel helmet down on his head, and went out.

Battalion headquarters was a cluster of squad tents in a narrow valley about two thousand yards behind Fox Company. Several of the large rectangular tents—olive drab and dusty, designed to accommodate an infantry squad—were filled with the usual array of unsteady folding tables, typewriters, and a seemingly endless supply of paper. Here, with tent flaps rolled up all around, the various battalion staff officers and their underlings were at work. Off to the side were the tents housing the aid station. A makeshift motor pool contained at the moment a jeep, several trucks, and three half-tracks on which quad-fifties were mounted. Parked off to themselves were a half-dozen Sherman tanks. Down the valley about half a mile away was a howitzer battery. The black snouts of its 105s, comfortably separated from each other, were angled upward and pointed northward.

The day was sunny and clear, with only a few white clouds drifting overhead. Light gusts of wind stirred up swirls of dust along the road leading south. The leaves on a line of poplar trees showed yellow tints, signaling the approach of fall. The second summer of the war had gone and soon it would approach its second winter. It had been a year since the Inchon landing and all the high hopes of quick and total victory.

John sought out the battalion adjutant, Capt. Arthur Zander. An unsoldierly figure and unlikely prospect for an infantry outfit, his paper-pushing position was the only imaginable slot for him. He delivered John to Colonel Burkman's tent and left.

John came to attention and saluted. Colonel Burkman said, "Have a seat. What is this you want to see me about?" He spoke impatiently, as though resenting the intrusion. He stamped out a cigarette in the sawed-off brass base of a 105-millimeter casing.

As John sat down on a stool across the table from the colonel and laid his helmet and carbine on the ground, he wondered why he had ever had this crazy idea. He wished he were back up with his platoon. It even occurred to him to say, "Sir, the problem I had has been taken care of, and I really don't need to talk to you." But no, he had come this far; he could not turn back now. He took a deep breath and began, determined to remain calm.

"Well, sir, it has to do with the proposed attack on Hill 1080."

The colonel interrupted brusquely. "It's not proposed. It's been ordered by regiment. Actually, I think the order came down from army."

"Yes, sir. I understand it's set for day after tomorrow."

"Correct. We plan to jump off at 0600. I hope you folks up at Fox are getting ready. It's going to be a big show."

"Yes, sir. I don't know whether Captain Waller told you what I wanted to talk with you about, but . . ."

"No, no, he didn't. He just said you wanted to see me about something important. So what is it?"

"Well, sir, to get right to the point, I believe strongly that this attack is ill-advised. I would say also unnecessary and foolish."

The colonel, who had seemed bored and impatient, suddenly stiffened. A look of incredulity spread over his broad, large-boned face. "Since when does a platoon lieutenant think it appropriate to review Eighth Army's tactical decisions?"

"I know this is unusual, probably highly irregular, but . . ."

"You're damn right it's irregular. But since you've brought it up, I'd like to hear your assessment of the situation." He added sarcastically, "Maybe we could detail you to army operations."

He drew in another breath and launched into his theory about the war—his enthusiasm over the United Nations' cause, his view that the U.N. Command should carry out the U.N. decision to unite Korea, that obviously somebody had decided not to do so, that they were not to go forward to defeat the Communists, and that in light of all that it was immoral to throw away lives simply to take another hill. He then stopped, surprised that he had not been interrupted.

Colonel Burkman sat in silence for a moment, looking at John with a mixture of perplexity and irritation. Sounds of trucks and voices of soldiers milling about came in through the open tent sides. "What you say is interesting, but completely irrelevant. If I were Van Fleet or Ridgeway, there would be some point in discussing your ideas. But not here."

"Sir, I'm not just theorizing over this as an abstract matter. I've thought about the situation for a long time—ever since the armistice talks started. It is wrong to spend lives of Americans, or anyone else for that matter, under these circumstances. If we take on 1080, there's many a man in Fox this afternoon who won't be alive forty-eight hours from now."

"So you might think that. I might think that. And we might be right. But so what? We have orders. The attack will go forward, and you will do whatever you're ordered to do by Captain Waller."

He stared into space beyond the battalion commander. Somewhere down the road a tank engine roared into life. After a pause, he said, "Sir, if I lead my platoon up that hill and they are slaughtered, as I think likely, I will forever carry the blood of those men on my mind and conscience, if I survive. We saw what happened on 969. This'll be worse."

"Winston, that kind of thinking is dangerous for a commander. Nobody is happy about casualties, but if you start worrying too much about that it will impair your ability to do what you have to do. You did a good job on 969, showed you had what it takes. I've been thinking about putting you in for a Bronze Star. But now I'm wondering whether"—he lowered his voice into a tone hinting of sarcasm—"you're getting a little weak-kneed."

"Sir," he said, feeling himself go rigid and speaking in a voice louder than he would have liked, "I believe my record speaks for itself. With all respect, I have to say that I resent any suggestion like that."

"I didn't think you'd like that. But the way you're talking here might lead some folks to think you had developed a yellow streak."

With an effort, he controlled his anger. "My views about this have nothing to do with my own safety. I've long ago learned to forget that."

"Then can you forget all this high-level strategy and tactics you've been talking about and get back to business?"

"No, sir. I am convinced this back-and-forthing over these hills is not worth the cost."

"You've got to get it in your mind that we're not sitting in the National Security Council in Washington. We're an infantry battalion in the line, in direct contact with the enemy." He spoke with heightened sternness, a military commander irritated with an obstreperous subordinate. He continued in a carefully measured voice. "Are you intimating that you won't be able to lead your platoon in this attack? Or maybe that you'll just give it a halfhearted effort?"

John sat impassively. He stared blankly through the rolled-up tent flap at the motor pool in the distance. He then heard himself saying quietly, the words coming out of his mouth as though they were being put there by a ventriloquist: "I'm not sure."

"I've never had a conversation like this before," Burkman spoke with barely suppressed anger. "A lot of commanders would chew you out and charge you with insubordination. I'm going to end it now and just say this. In case there's any doubt about it, I am now giving you a direct order to go back to your platoon and to carry on, subject to the orders given you by Captain Waller. Is that clear?"

"Yes, sir. I think I understand what you say."

Colonel Burkman's face reddened. "Damn it, I'm not telling you to think! I'm telling you to act, to do your duty. We've got to take 1080. That's all that counts now. You are dismissed."

The sky had clouded over, and a light rain began falling at dusk. All across the MLR the rain fell, a cool, early autumn drizzle, falling indifferently on the just and the unjust alike—on Chinese, North Koreans, South Koreans, Americans, English, Scots, Australians, New Zealanders, French, Filipinos, Turks, Ethiopians, Colombians, and others from the four corners of the globe. It ran in rivulets down the hillside at Fox's position and formed puddles at the bottoms of trenches and foxholes, where men stood guard in ponchos and helmets, shivering from the dampness, water seeping down their necks and into their boots.

The rain stopped and the shelling began. It was the heaviest dose of artillery fire that Fox had received since occupying its present position. It lasted for thirty minutes. But the enemy gunners never seemed to get their range adjusted. Nearly all shells fell short.

"They must be trying to take out our wire or else they can't shoot worth a damn," Sergeant Alton said as he and John sat in the bunker riding it out. They were safe from everything except possibly a direct hit.

After the shelling stopped, Captain Waller ordered a special alert. "Can't tell whether that's just some harassing fire or whether they're trying to take out our wire in preparation for an attack."

But the rest of the night was quiet. Between remaining on the alert for a possible attack and being disturbed by his meeting with Colonel Burkman, he passed a sleepless night. He had probably ruined himself in the eyes of the colonel. But that was not really important. He was not a career officer. What did disturb him was the confusion in his mind about what he should do. The colonel had put it to him: Carry out orders—go forward with the attack. He found himself again thinking the unthinkable: Was it conceivable that he could bring himself to refuse to obey the order?

Morning came gray and overcast. There was a flurry of activity to replace and repair the barbed wire. At mid-morning the artillery batteries opened up on 1080. For an hour they plastered the hill from bottom to top with high-explosive and white-phosphorous shells—105s and 155s. The men of Fox watched the show with fascination, trees blown away and rocks and debris churned upward.

The artillery ceased, and within minutes came the air strikes. The jets thundered in from the south in groups of three, flying straight at the face of 1080, firing all their 20-millimeter and .50-caliber guns simultaneously, pouring a torrent of steel into the hill. They then swooped upward, unleashing canisters of napalm, turning the whole face of the hill into a fiery inferno as they banked steeply, their engines shrieking, and headed back toward their base at Suwon.

"If this war depended on who's got the firepower, we'd have won it long ago," John said, standing in a trench beside Sergeant Alton. "And if it depended on air superiority, it would have been wrapped up."

Shortly before noon, the field telephone jangled. Sergeant Alton picked it up, listened for a moment, and then handed it to John. "It's Captain Waller."

His voice was crisp and all business. "Colonel Burkman just called. He's pretty mad. He's ordered you relieved of all duty in Fox. You are to get your gear together and report to battalion immediately. I don't know what you told him, but it must have been dynamite. So get on back here to the CP right now with your stuff. I want to see you."

He sat down on his sleeping bag, stunned.

"What's the matter, sir?" Alton asked with concern.

After a long pause, he said, "The colonel has just ordered me out."

"My God, what a time for that. We can't hit that hill with a green platoon leader."

"I know. It's not good. I don't understand it."

He sat still for a minute or two, lost in thought: This he had never expected. He got up and slowly began stuffing his belongings into his duffel bag.

He went up and down the line, saying good-bye to his men. He was overcome by the thought that he alone would be spared 1080.

Minutes later he was in the company CP confronted by Bruce Waller. "Winston, this is the darkest day I've had for months. To pull you out now is insane, if I may speak off the record about the old man. He's sending up a new lieutenant to take over your platoon, but this is a hell of a time for that. What happened yesterday?"

"All I said to Colonel Burkman was what I said to you. I knew he didn't like it, but I never thought he would do anything like this."

"He said he couldn't trust an officer in this operation who had your attitude. It would jeopardize the mission. He was really hot under the collar. Thinks you would go so far as to refuse to lead your platoon in the attack."

"I never said that."

"I tried to talk him out of this, but I didn't get anywhere. The fact is, Winston, that I need you on 1080. It could make a lot of difference."

"I'm sorry. I really am sorry to let you down. I should never have gone to see the colonel."

They looked at each other for a moment. "Well," Waller said, "you better get moving. He wants you back there pronto."

They shook hands, in a long, lingering grip. He picked up his duffel bag and started toward the opening. Then pausing, he said, "I hope all's well with your wife and baby Henny."

Waller nodded. "Yes, fine. I'm due to rotate out in a month, so it won't be too long before I see them."

Once again John stood before the battalion commander in his tent, this time accompanied by the adjutant, Captain Zander. From somewhere in the distance, over a radio tuned into the Armed Forces station, came the strains of "The Tennessee Waltz."

Looking grim, Colonel Burkman said, "Winston, I was upset by our conversation yesterday, and I've given it a lot of thought. I've concluded that an officer with the kind of attitude you exhibited cannot be relied on to lead men in combat, especially in a difficult mission like that coming up tomorrow. So, I have relieved you, although I know that places an added burden on Captain Waller."

Burkman had not asked John to sit down, so he stood stiffly, still wearing his helmet and with his carbine slung over his shoulder. His duffel bag rested on the ground at his feet.

Colonel Burkman paused for a moment and then went on, in his sharpest military voice: "But that's not all. I am charging you with insubordination and disobedience of orders. I've got a jeep waiting to take you on back to division. You'll be delivered to the provost marshal, and I assume the JAG will take it from there." He stopped again for a second and then added, "The army cannot tolerate any thought of disobeying orders. We would disintegrate if that were permitted in even the slightest degree. This is particularly true of officers. I regret this turn of events, but I have no choice, in the interest of this command."

He turned to the adjutant. "OK, take Lieutenant Winston to the jeep, and you go along with him to division."

Turning back to John, he said, "You're dismissed."

PART FOUR
Justice According to Law

Chapter 13

AT THE CENTER OF the sprawling corps headquarters, just north of the 38th parallel, three tall flagpoles stood side by side. They bordered a large, open area where helicopters carrying generals landed and took off. On the first, flapping in the autumn breeze, was the blue and white banner of the United Nations. On the middle pole was the Stars and Stripes. On the third was the flag of the Republic of Korea, white with the red and blue halves of its circular design representing the yin and yang, the eternal dualities: male and female, heaven and earth, light and dark, mountains and valleys, active and passive—the Asian view of the interdependence of the world of nature and of human beings, the complementary forces that make up all aspects of life.

Nearby were the tents of key staff officers. Between the chaplain and the provost marshal was the Judge Advocate section. In its front tent were the enlisted men busily typing the multitude of documents essential to keep the machinery of military justice functioning. A narrow connecting link led to the rear tent where the officers sat, also at folding wooden tables, each with the ever-present in-box and out-box.

Positioned at the far end was the head of it all, the staff judge advocate, Lt. Col. Albert Jameson. A handsome man, tall and lean, a West Point graduate, he had served in the field artillery in Italy during the war and was afterward sent by the army to the University of Michigan Law School. He had that mixture of affability and toughness much admired in the military service, a predictable prospect to wear a star. His neatly pressed fatigues and polished boots set him apart from the other JAG officers in the tent, most of whom—rumpled and unmilitary—were reservists called up for a couple of years.

Lt. Colonel Jameson was bent over his table, examining a file with unusual intensity. A corporal from the front tent appeared and laid a sheaf of papers in the colonel's in-box, his approach causing the table to shake from the uneven plank flooring.

"Tell Captain Sloboken to step back here," the colonel said.

Capt. Oscar Sloboken was a graduate of the Ohio State Law School and had been an assistant U.S. attorney in Akron. He was stocky and had a fleshy face with deep-set dark eyes and dark hair. As a thorough and careful lawyer, he had won the admiration of Lt. Colonel Jameson.

"Sir, you want to see me?" Sloboken said.

"Yes. Have a seat." The colonel motioned to a chair against the end of the tent. In these close quarters, a private conversation was possible only by talking in low voices while facing away from the other occupants.

Colonel Jameson looked worried. "Here's a curious and sensitive case. General Willard called me up and personally handed me the file. It involves a lieutenant charged with disobedience of orders. His division commander wants the case out of his command, thinks it's too hot a potato to handle at that level, and has asked us to take it over and try it here." He handed the file to Sloboken, who began to flip through the papers. "You can imagine General Willard's reaction to a case like this. He got red in the face talking to me about it. Wants it prosecuted to the hilt."

"I see they've completed the Article 32," said Sloboken, still turning papers.

"Right. They did that at division. So it looks like we're pretty well set to go. But before we do anything, I want you to study the file and come back to me with your views on the case. I don't have to tell you that prosecuting an officer for disobedience of orders, especially in a combat situation, is extremely serious business. As far as I know, there's been only one other case in Korea, and that one's caused a ruckus in Washington."

Captain Sloboken took the file and went to his table at the other end of the tent. A couple of hours later he was back with the colonel.

"This is a curious situation," he began. "There's an affidavit in the Article 32 investigation from the accused's battalion commander. He preferred the charges, and he's apparently the main—maybe the only—witness. He says that the lieutenant objected to an operation ordered by regiment and himself. He says the accused indicated that he would refuse to carry out the order, so he relieved him as platoon leader and sent him to the rear."

"Exactly what did the lieutenant say? Did he actually refuse to obey the order?"

"That's not clear from these papers." Sloboken spoke with an air of mild disgust over the inadequacy of the investigation. "I think I should interview the battalion commander myself to find out more precisely what his testimony will be."

"Sounds like a good thing to do. We don't want to go off half-cocked. So get on up there as soon as you can. In the meantime, it's my understanding that division is sending the accused here. We need to make arrangements for keeping him until the trial. I don't quite see him in the stockade."

"An arrest in quarters might be appropriate."

"Check it out with the provost marshal. We could cut an order assigning him to the transit quarters, with access to the mess tent and the showers. The officers' club doesn't sound quite right under the circumstances."

"Considering where he's been, that should be only a mild hardship."

"As soon as the man gets here, we ought to hook him up with defense counsel. Gordon may be the best choice. What do you think?"

"I agree. He's good, and he's had more experience than the others."

The colonel nodded his head slowly. "We don't want any questions raised later about the quality of the defense. This is one of those cases with potential for a lot of political flack." He paused for a moment. "OK, get going and let me know about your interview with the battalion CO. Send Gordon over here."

In a corner of the tent, by the narrow passageway to the front, a frame had been constructed out of two-by-fours and sheets of burlap nailed on it to create a small room for the defense counsel. The point was to create a measure of privacy for consultations with the accused. The privacy, however, was mainly visual, as voices traveled easily through and over the burlap walls. So talk here was carried on in whispered tones.

Capt. Carter Gordon emerged from this cubicle and approached Colonel Jameson. "Well, Gordon," the colonel said, with a twinkle in his eye, "here's a good one for you, the most sensitive case we've had since I've been here." He handed Gordon a duplicate set of the papers in the case and signaled for him to sit down.

"Has the chief of staff been caught in a Korean whorehouse?"

"Maybe not quite that bad," Jameson smiled slightly. He had learned that he had to put up with irreverent comments from these civilian lawyers who were short-timers. "But it's troubling and could give us some headaches." He lowered his voice. "I want our best defense counsel to take the case, and that's why I'm assigning it to you."

"I appreciate the compliment. I'm a little weary of desertions, assaults, and sleeping on post, so I hope we've got something different here."

"Something really different. An infantry officer, right in the line, charged with willful disobedience of an order."

"That's pretty heady stuff." He thumbed a couple of pages into the file, glancing quickly at the key entries. Suddenly his eyes widened, and he blurted out, "Lt. John H. Winston! My God! Is he the accused?"

"That's what it says. Is there something special about that?"

Carter Gordon sat mute for a moment, continuing to look at the papers. "This is extraordinary. It's unbelievable. I got to know a Lieutenant Winston last spring at Camp Drake. Saw a lot of him. He's about the last person in the world I would ever suspect of disobeying an order."

"Sounds like you're in the right frame of mind to handle the defense."

"I really can't get over it," Gordon said, as he continued to turn the pages. "If this Winston is the man I remember, he's good material for defense counsel. He saw some rough action and acquitted himself well."

"Well, you've got yourself a client. He's on the way from division. Sloboken will let you know when he gets here."

At midmorning the next day, Carter Gordon walked across the road and went into the deserted courtroom tent. It had occurred to him that it would be unnecessarily demeaning to bring an accused lieutenant into the JA tent to see him, as was the practice with run-of-the-mill accused charged with the more traditional offenses. So he had called the MPs and asked that Lt. Winston be brought to the courtroom, which was not in use this day.

He pulled a chair up to one of the tables and sat down and waited in the milky white half-light from the translucent plastic covering the entrance. Light breezes rippled the top and sides of the tent. In the distance was the chop-chop-chop of a helicopter taking off. Otherwise all was quiet.

Gordon had often mused over this so-called courtroom. All the way from Pusan up to the remote mountains and valleys of the north, an entire legal system had been laid down, wholly alien to this Asian land. It was the courts-martial system of the American armed forces, ordained by the Constitution. It functioned in dusty, windblown tents, its libraries in footlockers, its judges and attorneys in fatigues. Despite its military trappings, it was a manifestation of the rule of law and embodied the essence of Anglo-American criminal jurisprudence: Men could be convicted and imprisoned only if the government proved them guilty by legally admissible evidence beyond reasonable doubt of violating known and definite laws, previously enacted, through an established process that gave the accused a full opportunity to be heard in his own defense and to cross-examine witnesses against him, with the assistance of trained legal counsel. The system was marvelously portable; it could go wherever the army went.

On the table in front of him was the book he carried everywhere. Bound in a sturdy red cover, it bore the words, *Manual for Courts Martial, United States, 1951*. In this one volume were all the statutes and procedures governing the military justice system. It even laid out a script, step-by-step, for the conduct of trials. Like the circuit-riding lawyers of old, with Blackstone in their saddlebags, he could stick this book in his ditty bag, climb in a jeep, and do business in Yang-gu or Chunchon or anywhere in Korea.

He heard voices outside the tent. The plastic-covered door was pulled open, and two men entered. One was a soldier wearing an MP armband. The other was Lt. John Winston.

The MP addressed Captain Gordon. "Sir, do you want me to wait?"

Gordon and John stared at each other. Surprise was written all over John's face. Gordon, distracted and only half hearing the MP, mumbled, "Uh . . . no . . . no. I'll get him back."

The MP left, and the door swung shut behind him. John said, "I don't know what to say." He stood stiffly, his arms at his side.

Gordon wore his whimsically bemused look. "You can imagine the shock I got when I saw the name of the accused in this case."

He reached over and grabbed John's hand, shaking it warmly. "I guess I'm in a tough spot," John said, glad of Carter's friendliness.

"It's not good. But there are a lot of unanswered questions here. Before we go any further, I have to ask you whether you are satisfied to have me as your defense counsel."

"Satisfied? I should say so." Not yet recovered from his stunned surprise, he added, "I thought we'd never meet again. It's just plain dumb luck."

"That remains to be seen. But if you're satisfied, we'll proceed on the basis that from now on I'm representing you. At some point I'd like to hear all about what you've been doing since Japan. But right now we'd better get down to business. Have they given you a copy of the order about your stay here?"

"Yes. I have it right here." He patted the pocket of his fatigue jacket. "It restricts me to corps headquarters. What a joke. Where else could I go? Wandering in the boondocks? I notice I'm excluded from the officers' club. Didn't realize there was such a watering hole anywhere this side of Seoul or Taegu."

"It's nothing to write home about. You have the mess tent and the showers and the PX, so you're not in bad shape."

"This seems like a resort compared to where I've been. I can't tell you how good it feels to get washed up and get rid of all that gear. I feel downright nude without my helmet and carbine."

"I take it you've read the report of the Article 32 investigation."

"Yes, and let me say right off that I am not guilty."

"OK, I assumed not. Let's get down to specifics. He flipped through the papers to the charge sheet. "I know you've seen this, but I want to read the exact wording of the specification. There's only one. This is a standard form. 'In that 1st Lt. John H. Winston,' and here it gives your serial number and outfit, 'having received a lawful command from Lt. Col. Leonard E. Burkman, his superior officer, to participate in and perform his duty as platoon leader in a scheduled attack on Hill 1080, did, at APO 301, on or about 22 September 1951, willfully disobey the same.' Some people think the law is verbose, but that's pretty simple and straightforward. Now, I want you to tell me exactly what happened, as best you can remember it. Give me all the details."

John told his story, beginning with his conversation with Captain Waller and then describing his meeting with Lt. Colonel Burkman. "I can't recall the exact words he and I used, but I've told you the general thrust."

"So here's what we have. Colonel Burkman takes the stand and testifies that you said you refused to obey his order. Then you take the stand and deny that you said anything like that. It will be the word of a lieutenant colonel against the word of a first lieutenant, the word of a senior regular army officer against the word of a junior reservist on a two-year tour."

"Doesn't sound too good."

"That's a fair statement. But I still have a lot to look into. Most of the law involved in courts-martial is right here in this manual." He tapped the red book on the table. "But not quite all. We have some other books, and I want to study everything we have on this offense."

"What might be the sentence here?"

Gordon sighed and said offhandedly, "Theoretically, could be death."

"Death? Has anybody ever been sentenced to death in Korea?"

"In only one case I know of. But this case is not nearly as clear-cut as that one. I can't imagine a death sentence here. But a stretch of time at Leavenworth is quite imaginable."

They sat in silence for a few moments. A truck in low gear passed along the road beside the tent. Then John said, despondently, "The sad part is that all of this is self-inflicted. I was a fool to talk with the colonel."

"Maybe so, but that's water over the dam."

"Well, where do we go from here?"

"There are two things to be done. First, Captain Sloboken—he's the trial counsel—is going up today to interview Colonel Burkman in detail. When he comes back, I'll talk to him. We need to know more specifically what that testimony will be. Then I need to do some research into possible legal theories. I hope I'll be able to talk to you again by tomorrow afternoon, if I get back in time from the MASH. Got to run over there in the morning to interview a witness in another case."

Gordon reassembled the papers. He put them together in a file folder and stood up. "OK. Come on. I'll walk over with you to your quarters."

Chapter 14

JOHN LAY ON A FOLDING COT, stretched out on his back, staring
vacantly at the slanting tent top just overhead. He had never known
a darker hour, had never felt more alone. The full weight of his
plight had now fallen on him. He was facing a general court-martial
for a capital offense.

He longed to undo what he had done, to have stayed with his platoon, to have shared its fate, whatever that might have been. He was
clearly wrong to have wasted time analyzing overall strategic and
tactical decisions. No matter how ill-conceived he thought they were,
he should have soldiered on, come what may.

He was filled with remorse. He longed to know what had happened to Fox Company, especially its First Platoon. He would never
see any of those men again, dead or alive. He had let them down.
He was haunted by Captain Waller's last words: "I need you on 1080."

He tried to console himself by recalling that Colonel Burkman
had made it impossible for him to take part in the action by sending
him to the rear. He, John Winston, did not quit or run away. Was it
possible that he had actually said what the colonel reported? He had
to admit that the moment had been so stressful he found himself
unable to recall his exact words. Whatever they were, they must have
been misunderstood.

He thought of Remberton, of home, of family and friends, how it
was and how it might have been. How could he ever return? He shud-
dered as he imagined the news sweeping over town—John Winston

court-martialed in Korea, John Winston sentenced to prison for disobeying orders.

He thought of his grandfather, who went home in defeat but with
his honor intact. "As at Thermopylae," a Confederate monument
proclaimed, "the greater glory lay with the vanquished." He, though,
would be going home in dishonor as well as in defeat—he still considered the retreat of last fall and the abandonment of the effort to
unify Korea a defeat. Of course, at home at this moment no one
knew of this looming disaster. But it could not be kept secret forever. His only hope lay in the chance that Carter Gordon might yet
save him.

Captain Sloboken and Lt. Colonel Jameson sat close together in
chairs resting unevenly on the wooden planking next to the SJA's
table. Sloboken's fatigues were flecked with dust from the open jeep
ride.

"Colonel Burkman is exercised over this case," Sloboken said. "My
guess is that if everything had gone all right in their operation on
1080, he might not feel so strongly about it. But the way things
turned out makes Lieutenant Winston's action—in the colonel's
mind—doubly reprehensible."

Jameson interrupted. "What is the exact order that Colonel Burkman says he gave Winston?"

"He says the order was to go back to his platoon, to take part in the
operation on 1080, and to follow orders of Captain Waller, his company commander."

"And what does he say that Winston said or did?"

"I pressed him hard on this. He says that Winston said in effect
that he couldn't do it. I asked him whether Winston said expressly
that he refused to obey the order. He said he didn't remember Winston's precise words, but that was their upshot."

"Upshot may not be good enough. We need testimony as to what
Winston actually said or did."

"Yes, sir. I agree. It gets particularly fuzzy when Winston denies that
he said he refused to obey."

Jameson pulled a Lucky Strike from a pack lying on his table and
tapped one end on the back of his hand. "Am I right in remembering that nobody else was present during this conversation?"

"Correct. I talked with a couple of the battalion staff officers who knew about this incident. Colonel Burkman had told them about it. But all they know is his version of it. That would be hearsay, of course, and inadmissible."

Jameson lit the cigarette and exhaled a stream of smoke. "What about Captain Zander, the adjutant? He has a statement in the file."

"I talked to him too. He was there when the colonel relieved Winston but not at the earlier meeting. He doesn't help any."

"Well, how do you size it all up?"

"We've obviously got a credibility question the court will have to resolve. But I see another problem with the prosecution's case. Colonel Burkman relieved Lieutenant Winston of all duty on the morning of 22 September. The attack on Hill 1080 commenced at 0600 on 23 September, the next day. After Winston was relieved and sent to the rear, it was impossible for him to obey the order. In other words, the time for performance of the order had not yet arrived when Winston was removed from the scene."

"Isn't there some concept of anticipatory disobedience? In the case of an announced intention to disobey, is a commander helpless to do anything?"

"The commander needn't stand by helpless. He can take steps to meet the situation. That's what Colonel Burkman did here by relieving Winston. The question, though, is whether an orally announced intention to violate an order in the future can amount to a violation of Article 90."

"But isn't this where a theory of anticipatory disobedience comes in?" Jameson stood up and shuffled around nervously in his confined corner of the tent, drawing on his cigarette.

"Frankly, I think it's shaky. The law, as best I can tell from our limited library, is not clear. I can imagine an Article 90 conviction on this evidence being set aside by the military review court. Or by our new military appeals court looking to make its mark. On the other hand, I think we can probably make out a case under Article 133, some theory of conduct unbecoming."

"Are you saying that is what I should recommend to General Willard?"

"Yes, sir. That's what I would be inclined to do. He might not like it, but it's our job to give him the best legal advice we can, like it or not."

"To say he won't like it is a gross understatement. But I think I should at least discuss it with him and tell him about your thinking."

"Isn't a commander supposed to take his SJA's legal advice?"

"He can take it or leave it. He has the final say. Anyway, I'll think some more about it." Jameson sighed. "I don't look forward to that conversation."

At the top of the high wooded ridge that formed the backdrop for corps headquarters, a construction unit had recently finished building a small chapel. Steps had been cut in the hillside at intervals to make a long, winding walkway from the base of the hill. Protestant and Catholic services were now being held there every Sunday morning. At other times the ridge top was deserted. Carter Gordon and John had climbed up the winding path in the late afternoon and seated themselves on a clump of rocks near an old Korean burial ground. Dark, strangely shaped stones loomed in the underbrush.

From their rocky perch, the two men looked down on the entire corps headquarters, the grid of tents and roads stretching out along the MSR. Beyond was the river where the shower tents stood with their long and monstrous hoses extending into the water. Down the road was the short dirt airstrip, its windsock hanging limp in the afternoon stillness.

Looking at the three flags in the center area, Gordon said, "They say that red and blue circle on the Korean flag represents yin and yang. What do you make of that?"

"Kim talked a little about it. It has something to do with the dualities of life—things like male and female, night and day. But they don't include life and death. It seems to me they are the ultimate duality."

"Aren't they different, though? Life and death are not together on this earth. They don't coexist like the other dualities. A person is either dead or alive."

"A person is also either male or female. Believe me, I've seen life and death coexisting, been side by side with death. Anyway, if I understand the Scriptures, it's all life—first life on earth and then life hereafter. Death is merely a junction point between the two."

"The Victorians used to say that life on earth is simply a vestibule to eternity. But speaking of Kim, I found out something for you at the

MASH. Their records show that a Lt. Kim Yung Suk was operated on there for a stomach wound and then shipped off to a hospital in Seoul."

"Well that's good news. I hope he made it. He was in bad shape."

"And I have news about your outfit, but I'm afraid it's not so good."

John's face clouded. "Tell me about it."

"The battalion kicked off the attack on Hill 1080 as scheduled. They hit heavy opposition, especially Fox Company. On the first day they didn't get more than halfway up. But they held on there overnight and resumed the attack the next morning. Regiment sent up reinforcements, and by the end of the second day they had gotten to the top. There was a counterattack during the night, but they managed to hold on, and they're there now."

"What about casualties?"

"That's pretty bad news. Fox lost over half its men—counting both killed and wounded. Captain Waller was killed on the second day."

He sat mutely for a few moments, looking emptily into the distance, unable to speak. Tears welled up in his eyes. Then he lost control and broke into sobs. He cried in a way he had not cried since childhood, bending over, head in hands, elbows on knees, his body shaking.

Struggling to get hold of himself, he pulled a handkerchief from his pocket, wiped his eyes, and blew his nose. "I'm sorry," he gasped. "That just got to me. I've known a lot of men killed in the last year, but this one is different. His wife just had a baby. He was due to rotate out in a few weeks." He blew his nose again. "On top of that, he was a fine officer. I thought he would surely make general."

Gordon shook his head and sighed. "You needn't be embarrassed. You've had a lot on you lately. This just goes to show that this is no place for married men with children."

"Been married only a year." He had regained his composure. "Did you hear anything about a Sgt. Richard Alton?"

"No. I don't know about anyone else."

They sat in silence for a minute or so. In the distance, two deuce-and-a-halfs passed along the MSR, churning up dust that settled on the tents. Shadows were lengthening across the ridge and on the valley below.

John shook his head slowly. "So we've got another hill. So what? It's all crazy. But I should have been there. Now I'm alive and they're dead. I guess I deserve what I get. Maybe I should plead guilty and get this all over with."

"Not so fast. I know you're upset, but there's no point in pleading guilty if you're not legally guilty."

"But maybe I am—at least guilty in some sense."

"Listen, John, we're not dealing here with ultimate justice. We're concerned with justice according to law."

"Is there a difference? Aren't you just splitting hairs? I should have been with my men and with Waller."

"Let me ask you this: If Burkman hadn't relieved you, what would you have done?"

John thought hard for a few moments. "I think I would have gone back and done what I was supposed to do—but who knows? And besides, that's not what happened."

"There you have it, can't you see? No one can know the whole truth, only God. All that we imperfect humans can do is set up an institution we call a court and have it determine through established procedure whether you are guilty beyond a reasonable doubt under the law and the evidence—guilty of a specific charge under the statute. The result is justice according to law."

"So, a person found not guilty in court could still be morally guilty, couldn't he?"

"That's not for us to say. We have to leave that to a higher court. Right now we need to put our attention on what's facing us here."

"Do you have anything new?"

"A little bit. I decided to go to your old battalion headquarters and talk to Colonel Burkman myself."

"Oh? What does he say?"

"He's going to testify that you refused to comply with his order to go forward with your duty as platoon leader in the attack on Hill 1080."

"And I dispute that."

"Yes, I know. That's your main defense, but there may be another possibility. Colonel Burkman relieved you the day before the attack, so when the time came to take part in it you were not there to obey the order."

"Do you think they'll go for that?"

"I'm not sure. The books here don't give a clear answer. It's like many questions that come up in the law. There are a surprising number where the question has to be put to a court before we can know the answer."

"But how strong do you think this argument is?"

"I would give it 50-50 at this point. But you can be sure," Gordon said, patting John on the knee, "that I'll put forward the strongest defense possible under the court-martial law. We've still got three days before trial so," he said, as he stood up, "keep your spirits up and hang in there. Now let's go. It's chow time."

The hours dragged by, night and day, day and night. Alone, with nothing to do, he was in a state of limbo. Three times a day he went to the mess tent. He ate in silence, avoiding conversation. In the morning or the afternoon, depending on his mood, he walked to the shower tents, taking off his T-shirt, shorts, and socks, discarding them into a laundry bin, and picking out a clean set from a jumbled pile in another bin. A man did not need to own any clothing in this military version of socialism.

In between, he lay on his cot thinking. Again and again his mind went back to Bruce Waller and Fox Company and Hill 1080. Waller had said that he might make a difference. He was bedeviled by the illusion that maybe he would have, although he could not say how. At least he would have shared their fate.

He thought of that baby girl called Henny. The name had stuck with him, the name of a little girl who would never know her father. It was when he thought of her that the tears flowed again.

Hill 1080 reinforced his belief about the war. He was convinced he was right, and he took some solace in having had the courage to stand up and say so. But was that really courageous? Had he been subconsciously running away? Had he gone yellow, as Burkman suggested? He cringed at the thought. He was confused and began to think that he didn't know what to think.

All that he had to read was a paperback collection of hymns and readings issued by the United Nations Command, something he had picked up at the chapel. The foreword was by the Great Man himself, stirring in John all those ambiguities he had felt for the past year—

the Inchon triumph, the Chongchon disaster, the prolonged indecision inveighed against in the farewell address. But there was unquestionably the command of the English language. Here it was demonstrated again—John could imagine the deep and cadenced voice intoning: "No race or nation or creed can claim the authors and composers. Here is the language of unshackled spirits, the voice of God's free men in the sanctuary."

He thumbed through dozens of the old favorites, in Korean on the left-hand page and in English on the right. He perused lines he had sung innumerable times since youth—admonitions to trust in the Lord, injunctions against fear, and great words of praise and thanksgiving. He no longer needed to speculate about fear. He had experienced it, knew firsthand that valley of the shadow and, more to the point here, those ridges of death. And here was that curious line from the 91st Psalm: "A thousand may fall at your side, ten thousand at your right hand; but it will not come near you." Dozens of times he had asked himself the unanswerable question: Why should he be spared when others all around him were falling? He could not fathom the mystery of it all. The abyss looming ahead seemed as dark and threatening as had death on those North Korean hills. Had he been spared there only to meet his doom here?

At night as he lay sleepless on his cot, he could hear the far off rumbling of artillery. He saw in his mind the bunkers, foxholes, trenches, and barbed wire on the high rocky ridges where shells were crashing, flares drifting downward, giving a surreal whiteness to the night. Those ridges were forever imprinted in his memory, up and down and up and down, on and on without end. The rising and falling of the distant artillery reminded him vaguely of the distant pounding of surf coming to him on the night breeze from across Santa Rosa Island as he lay half-asleep in Bartow Simmons' cottage. For an instant, his and Sally's naked bodies again pressed together in the water at Mary Esther. How pointless now seemed his concern about being disloyal to Jeanie. How far away and long ago all of that seemed, part of a world lost forever.

And so he waited and brooded, waited for the three days to pass, waited to confront his judges and to learn what lay in or beyond this dark abyss.

Chapter 15

MORNING CAME GRAY AND OVERCAST, matching John's mood. Summer had gone, and autumn chill was in the air. The yellow leaves on the poplar trees by the river were starting to fall, and men were wearing field jackets over their fatigues.

Inside the courtroom tent, the brown and olive drab scene was bleakly illuminated by two electric light bulbs dangling on wires hanging between the tent's two supporting poles, standing like skinny tree trunks in the middle of the uneven plank flooring. Sporadic gusts of wind rattled the side flaps and rippled the top, causing the light bulbs to dance and sway crazily. Here, in this enclosure of poles and canvas, in an isolated valley of a remote Asian peninsula, ten thousand miles from their point of origin, the laws of the United States were to be enforced, and justice done according to law, by military officers attired in scruffy green fatigues and combat boots.

"The court will come to order." The voice was that of Col. Morris Hedley, sitting at the center of the nine officers lined up behind the burlap-fronted plywood structure serving as the court's bench. A silver eagle was on one collar of his fatigue jacket, and the wheeled insignia of the Transportation Corps on the other. He was one of those seasoned colonels, nearing retirement, who had long ago been reconciled to never getting a star. He had about him the aura of a wise sage, one possessed of judicial temperament.

The president was flanked by two lieutenant colonels, three majors, and three captains. Unlike Colonel Hedley, these men had the intense look of ambitious officers, exhibiting a hint of impatience at being drawn away from their units to while away time at this lawyers' business.

Sitting alone at a small table was the law officer, Maj. Grover Sampley. A large man with the gait and look of a farmer, he came from Valdosta, Georgia. He had served in the army at a desk job during the war and had come back home to practice law, staying in the reserve as a sociable outlet in an otherwise quiet town. "Don't let that country-boy appearance fool you," Gordon had told John. "He's plenty sharp." He sat here now as the judge, required to rule on all questions of law that might arise. Indeed, in this tent he was the law, responsible for seeing that the trial was conducted under law, conducted in accordance with the statutes and rules in the red-bound *Manual* open on the table in front of him.

Sloboken sat alone at trial counsel's table. Gordon and John sat a few feet away at the defense table. Off to the side was the court reporter, a corporal seated at a small table on which lay a stack of steno pads and a collection of sharpened pencils, one gripped in his hand, poised to record every word said. Behind him at the entrance to the witness tent stood an MP at parade rest.

Captain Sloboken rose and moved through the routine steps to get the court organized and the trial under way, adhering precisely to the script laid out in the *Manual for Courts Martial,* from which he was reading. He recited the order appointing the court and all its personnel, and administered oaths to the reporter, the law officer, and the members of the court, who were to act as the jury. In turn, the president swore in trial counsel and defense counsel.

Sloboken announced that he had no challenges to any member of the court. Then Gordon rose. "The defense strikes Maj. Anthony Marella."

From the law officer's table Major Sampley intoned, "Major Marella is excused."

A wiry, crew-cut infantry major rose and left the tent, not concealing his irritation over the idea that anyone could question his objectivity. The remaining members of the court rearranged their seating to accord with the new order of seniority.

Earlier Gordon had explained to John why he would exercise his one peremptory challenge to remove Major Marella. "He's a hard-nosed combat type who believes that no case would be prosecuted unless the accused is guilty." He said there was also a tactical advantage in getting him off. Under the two-thirds rule, with nine members the prosecution needs six to convict. With eight the prosecution still needs six because a fraction is counted as a whole. "With nine, we need four for an acquittal. With eight, we need only three."

Sloboken read the charge and specification in the case of *United States* v. *John H. Winston, First Lieutenant, Infantry,* alleging that he willfully disobeyed a lawful order of a superior officer in violation of Article 90 of the Uniform Code of Military Justice. The accused and his counsel rose together. Gordon announced: "The accused pleads innocent to the charge and specification."

John resumed his seat in a near trance. It all seemed like a dream—a nightmare, to be precise. Despite days of thinking about it, he still had difficulty comprehending that he was actually here before a general court-martial, charged with one of the most serious of all military offenses, with his entire life on the line. He did not find it reassuring to look at those grim-faced officers sitting behind the improvised bench.

The moment at last had come for the prosecution to present its case. Sloboken hesitated, seemingly flustered. "May it please the court," he began, uncertainly, "the first and only witness for the prosecution is Lt. Col. Leonard Burkman. It was my understanding that he would be here at this time, but he has not yet appeared. Therefore, I must request a brief recess."

"Very well," the president said, "the court will be in recess for ten minutes."

Sloboken started for the tent door but was met just inside by an anxious and hurried-looking lieutenant from the JA Section. He handed Sloboken a note and whispered to him. They immediately stepped outside.

When the court came back into session a few minutes later, Sloboken stood at his table, somber and shaken. "May it please the court, it is my sad duty to inform the court that Lt. Colonel Burkman was killed this morning by an enemy mortar round while inspecting his position. In view of this unexpected development, the prosecution requests a recess until 1400."

For long moments a stillness enveloped the tent, disturbed only by the wind rippling the top. The members of the court sat motionless and stony-faced. Finally the president cleared his throat and said, "Did you say that Colonel Burkman was your only witness?"

"Yes, sir. As I saw it, he was. But in view of this startling development, the prosecution now has to reassess the case and to consult with the SJA. At this moment I cannot say what our next move will be."

"All right," the president said, "the court will be in recess until 1400."

John and Gordon rose and stood at their table as the members of the court filed out. They remained in place, stunned, while the tent emptied. They were left alone, and for some seconds neither spoke.

Then Gordon said in a hushed and deliberate tone, "Burkman was the only way they could hope to prove the charge. I see no choice for the prosecution but to dismiss the case."

"But he signed a sworn statement. Why can't the prosecution use that?"

"Inadmissible under the hearsay rule."

Neither man moved or said anything. John stared vacantly at the empty chairs behind the bench, trying to comprehend the enormity of what had been wrought by a random mortar round.

When the court reconvened at 1400, Sloboken rose and recited the words required by the script in the *Manual.* "All persons present when the court recessed are again present."

John was in a state of confusion and turmoil. The shocking turn of events had pulled him back from the abyss, had released him from this dark ordeal. Yet he could find little solace in the dramatic reversal of his fate, because it had come at the price of a man's life. A dismissal of the case now would give him no vindication.

Hesitating and somber, Sloboken continued. "The prosecution calls as a witness, Capt. Arthur Zander."

Startled, John whispered to Gordon, "I thought you said no one but Burkman could testify to what happened."

Gordon whispered back: "That's so, based on everything I know. I don't see how Sloboken can salvage this case with Zander."

The MP admitted Captain Zander from the witness tent. Portly and looking overage in grade, Zander awkwardly came to attention in accordance with protocol and saluted the president. He raised his right hand, took the oath, and sat down in the witness chair.

Through a series of questions, Sloboken established that Zander was the battalion adjutant on 21 September and that he escorted Lieutenant Winston to Lt. Colonel Burkman's tent that day. Then he said that instead of leaving, he lingered outside the front of the tent and overheard the exchange between Burkman and Winston.

"We never heard this before," John whispered nervously.

Gordon shook his head and held up his hand, cautioning silence, his eyes riveted on Zander.

The examination then proceeded as follows:

> TC: What did you hear?
>
> Witness: Lieutenant Winston was describing his views about the conduct of the war. He said there was no point in wasting lives in taking these hills when a decision had been made not to win the war and unify Korea but to settle where we are.
>
> TC: Was it your impression that Lieutenant Winston was objecting to an operation scheduled on Hill 1080?
>
> DC: Objection. The witness's impression is irrelevant and inadmissible.
>
> LO: Sustained.
>
> TC: Did you hear Lieutenant Winston say anything about a proposed operation on Hill 1080?
>
> Witness: Yes. He said he thought it was foolish, that it would accomplish nothing, and would cost us a lot of casualties.
>
> TC: Did Colonel Burkman at any point give any orders to Lieutenant Winston?
>
> Witness: Yes, sir. Colonel Burkman ordered him to return to his platoon and to prepare for and carry out his duties in the attack on Hill 1080.
>
> TC: When he was given that order, what did Lieutenant Winston say?
>
> Witness: He said in effect that he could not take part in that operation.
>
> TC: Did you understand the accused to be refusing to carry out the order?
>
> DC: Objection. The witness can testify only to what was said, not what he understood.
>
> LO: Sustained.
>
> TC: Did the accused say anything else in response to Colonel Burkman's order?

Witness: As I recall, he just said that he could not lead men to
their slaughter when there was no point to it.
TC: To the best of your recollection—and this is an important
point—did the accused say that he would refuse to obey the
order to take part in the attack on Hill 1080?
Witness: I would say that he did, but I do not recall his exact words.
TC: After the accused had gone, did Colonel Burkman say anything to you about this conversation?
Witness: Yes, he said it looked like Winston was going to disobey
a direct order.
DC: Objection. That is strictly hearsay. I move that the witness's
answer be stricken from the record.

Major Sampley sat silently, brow furrowed, mentally wrestling with
the legal question presented. A deuce-and-a-half ground its way
along the road outside the tent. Then he spoke, in the overly
emphatic tones of a Southerner in an official role. "Sustained. The
answer will be stricken. The court is admonished to disregard the witness's last answer."

Sloboken completed his examination of Zander by having him
describe the events of the following day when Colonel Burkman
relieved Winston of his duties and sent him to the rear.

Gordon then rose and commenced his cross-examination. He first
attempted to get Zander to admit that he himself violated Burkman's
order, or at least intention, that Zander leave him and Winston alone
and that Zander's eavesdropping was reprehensible. He then got
Zander to acknowledge that he had never mentioned having overheard this conversation until this very moment, after Burkman's
death, implying that Zander was simply repeating what Burkman had
later told him.

Gordon then continued:

DC: Now did you hear Lieutenant Winston say expressly that he
refused to obey Colonel Burkman's order?
Witness: Not in those words.
DC: Well, what were his exact words?
Witness: I can't recall his exact words, but he was clearly object-
ing to the operation.
DC: In other words, he was saying that the operation was ill-
advised?

Witness: Yes.

DC: Isn't it possible for a person to think that a proposed operation is a bad idea and yet not disobey an order to take part in it?

TC: Objection. Counsel is arguing with the witness.

LO: Sustained.

DC: You said that Colonel Burkman's order to Lieutenant Winston was to return to his platoon. Is that correct?

Witness: That was part of it.

DC: And didn't Lieutenant Winston return to his platoon?

Witness: Yes, as far as I know.

DC: And he was there in his platoon preparing for the attack on 1080 when Colonel Burkman sent for him the next day?

Witness: He was there. I don't know what he was doing.

DC: What was the extent of the casualties in Fox Company in the operation on Hill 1080? TC: Objection. Irrelevant.

LO: Does defense counsel care to respond?

DC: Yes, sir. The heavy casualties in Fox Company will show that Lieutenant Winston was correct in his assessment of the operation and its likely consequences.

TC: Whether the accused was right or wrong in his predictions is irrelevant to the question whether he violated Article 90.

LO: The objection is sustained.

DC: No further questions.

In a brief re-direct examination, Sloboken had Zander explain that he had not revealed the overheard conversation earlier because he was embarrassed about it and that he had come forward now only because he thought the information was important to this case and Colonel Burkman was no longer available to present it.

Gordon said that the defense had no further questions. Zander was excused and ushered out by the MP. Sloboken then announced that the prosecution rested. The president whispered to the officers on his right and left and then called a fifteen-minute recess.

The eight officers rose from behind the bench and filed out the front of the tent, several reaching in their pockets for cigarettes.

"Let's get some fresh air," Gordon said. He and John went outside and around the corner out of sight of the court members who were standing in a group, talking and smoking. The day was still gray and blustery.

"I think Sloboken was as surprised as we were at the sudden

appearance of Zander," Gordon said. "Left to his own devices, he might have dismissed this case. But he's under heavy pressure to prosecute. All I could do with Zander was to show his vagueness about what was said and to bring out facts to make him look bad and weaken his credibility."

John was emotionally whipsawed. "How does it all look now?"

"My guess is that Burkman's death doomed the prosecution's case. He would have given it the rank and status and credibility that is not there with Zander. Hard, though, to tell what they'll make of Zander. They may feel they've got to honor the deceased by finding you guilty."

The court and its retinue reassembled. Sloboken made the ritual announcement. "All persons present when the court recessed are again present."

Colonel Hedley leaned forward, his tortoiseshell reading glasses held in his right hand. "Is the defense ready to proceed?"

Gordon rose. "Yes, sir. The defense wishes to make a motion."

"What is the motion?" Hedley asked, with a note of curiosity in his voice. Motions at this point were rare in courts-martial.

"The defense moves for a finding of not guilty."

The faces of the eight officers all showed surprise. No one on the court or in the JA Section could remember having heard such a motion made before.

The president looked at Major Sampley. "Would the law officer instruct the court as to the proper procedure."

During the recess Gordon had alerted Major Sampley that he intended to make this motion. So he was prepared, and he proceeded to speak in his pompous style, looking at—virtually reading from—the *Manual*.

"Defense counsel will make his argument in support of the motion, and trial counsel will respond. The law officer will then rule on the motion. If the motion is denied, the defense will proceed with whatever evidence it has. If the law officer grants the motion, any member of the court can object. If an objection is made, the court will be closed, and the court will decide the motion by majority vote."

"Very well," Colonel Hedley said. "Defense counsel, proceed with your argument."

Gordon said that the motion was based on two grounds. The first was that there was insufficient evidence to permit the court to find that Lieutenant Winston had disobeyed an order. The order was to return to his unit. He did so. As to any announced intention to disobey, the testimony of Captain Zander was vague and fell far short of showing a clear-cut statement that the order would be violated.

The second ground, he asserted, was that Lieutenant Winston could not be found guilty of violating an order to take part in an attack on the morning of 23 September because he had been sent to the rear on 22 September.

Sloboken argued to the contrary. The harsh Rs of his Midwestern accent contrasted strikingly with Gordon's soft Tidewater Virginia voice. The court could find, he said, that the accused had expressed a clear intent not to participate in the attack on Hill 1080. There was a doctrine of anticipatory disobedience. Where there was an announced intent to disobey, a commander is justified in concluding that the order will be disobeyed, and there is a basis for charging a violation of Article 90.

Major Sampley declared that the court would be in recess for approximately fifteen minutes. He jumped up, left the tent, and dashed across the road to the JA Section.

He returned shortly, and the court was called to order. "All persons present when the court recessed are again present," intoned Sloboken.

Clearing his throat, Major Sampley announced in an appropriately solemn voice, "The motion for a finding of not guilty is denied at this time, with leave to the defense to renew the motion at the close of all the evidence."

Gordon stood up. "The defense calls the accused, Lieutenant Winston, as a witness."

John raised his right hand, swore to tell the truth, and sat down in the witness chair, his heart thumping. He had been over his testimony several times with Gordon, but he was not sure now that he would respond in exactly the same way under the pressure of the moment. Also, he did not know, of course, how the cross-examination might go. Like many nonlawyers, he suspected that a skillful trial lawyer could trip up a witness and make him say something he did not really mean.

Gordon began by asking John to outline his service in Korea since his arrival a year ago. His questions brought out details of John's participation in the "home-by-Christmas offensive" along the Chong-chon, the withdrawal from Kunu-ri, and the action that resulted in the award of the Silver Star. There followed an account of his wounds and hospitalization.

Sloboken intervened. "If it please the court, all these details about the accused's previous service are not relevant to the present charge. They would be appropriate at the sentencing stage but not on the issue of guilt."

"They are relevant," Gordon responded, "if it please the court, as showing that the character of the accused is such that he is a person unlikely to commit the offense charged."

Major Sampley brooded for a few moments amidst the windy flapping of the tent. The light bulbs gyrated at the ends of the wires. "To the extent that prior service shows, or may tend to show, the good character of the accused, it is admissible. But we can't go too far afield in the details. Counsel should confine the evidence to essential features of accused's record."

"Yes, sir," Gordon said. He then proceeded to have John describe his part in the action on Hill 969.

Sloboken again interrupted. "If it please the court, the details of that operation are not pertinent. I request that defense counsel be instructed to limit his questions to the essential features of accused's record and omit this multitude of details."

"The point is well taken," Sampley said. "Let's move on and omit the details."

So by questioning that drew out the reluctant John Winston, and thanks to the relative lack of objection by Sloboken, Gordon succeeded in developing a portrait of a brave young infantry officer, dedicated to duty, who had suffered much but had never complained or shirked responsibility.

"Now, Lieutenant Winston," Gordon resumed, "I want to bring you to the 21st of September, to your meeting with Lt. Colonel Burkman. Would you explain the circumstances that brought that meeting about and what happened there."

John took a deep breath and began describing his discussion with Captain Waller about the proposed attack on Hill 1080 and how he met with Colonel Burkman at his own request to make the same points.

"What order, if any, did Colonel Burkman give you?"

"He told me to get back to my platoon and to get ready for the attack on Hill 1080."

"Did you do that?"

"Yes, sir."

"Did you at any time tell Colonel Burkman that you would not obey his order?"

"I don't recall doing so."

"What do you recall saying to him?"

"My memory about that conversation is hazy. I felt under considerable strain. I felt strongly about my views on the proposed attack, and I was nervous in saying all that to my battalion commander."

"At that time was it your intention to refuse to participate in the attack on Hill 1080?"

"I can't say that it was."

"Did you say anything to Colonel Burkman that could have led him to think that you would refuse to carry out his order?"

"I can't believe that I did."

After several more questions, Gordon concluded by asking, "Is there anything else you want to say about your conduct that is relevant to this charge?"

"All I can add is that I have never disobeyed any order I have received. All I did in this instance was to express some views about this war that are shared by others. I think my record in Korea shows that I am not the type of officer who would ever violate a direct command."

Sloboken rose for the cross-examination. "Lieutenant Winston, you say that you do not recall telling Colonel Burkman that you would refuse to carry out his order to take part in the operation on Hill 1080. If you have no recollection, it is possible, is it not, that in fact you did say that?"

"It does not seem possible to me."

"But you cannot deny that you said such a thing, can you?"

"I can't deny it or admit it because my memory is not clear on the point."

"You did in fact express opposition to an attack on Hill 1080, did you not?"

"Yes, sir."

"And you felt very strongly about that, didn't you?"

"Yes, sir."

"Given those strong views, it is not unreasonable to conclude, is it, that you might have had in mind refusing to participate?"

"Views about an operation and disobeying orders are two different things."

"But strong opposition to an operation would be consistent with a refusal to participate in it, wouldn't it?"

Gordon was on his feet. "Objection. Counsel is arguing with the witness."

"Sustained," intoned Major Sampley.

Sloboken resumed. "Now you have testified about the actions in which you have been involved. You were wounded pretty badly?"

"Yes, I would say so, but not nearly as badly as some others."

"And the action on Hill 969 had just taken place about a week before you learned of the plan to attack Hill 1080. Is that correct?"

"Yes, sir."

"There's some chance, is there not, that you were getting a little shaky about such actions, that the wounds you had suffered and the casualties you had seen around you had made you somewhat less willing to go through another attack of that sort?"

"Nobody looks forward to something like that. But I don't think I was anymore reluctant than most. I've seen men break and run under fire. I've never done that."

"No further questions," Sloboken said as he sat down.

Gordon stood up. "I have no further questions."

The president said, "The witness is excused. Does the defense have further evidence?"

"No, sir. The defense rests. However, the defense wishes to renew its motion for a finding of not guilty on the same grounds as argued before."

"Does either counsel wish to submit additional argument on the motion?" asked Major Sampley.

Each counsel responded in the negative. Then, to the surprise of both, the law officer did not call a recess. He hesitated only a few seconds and then began in his most official voice. "On careful consideration, and taking into account arguments of counsel and such authorities as are available to me, I hereby grant the motion on the second ground. That is, I hold that as a matter of law a member of the armed services cannot be guilty of a violation of Article 90, the willful disobedience of an order, when it is not possible for that person to obey the order because of having been relieved of duty and removed from the place at which the order was to be performed. In other words, I find no basis for a doctrine of anticipatory disobedience as far as Article 90 is concerned."

Surprise was evident along the bench. "Is there objection to the ruling from any member of the court?" Colonel Hedley asked.

"Yes, sir," barked one of the lieutenant colonels. "I object."

"Very well," said Hedley. "The court will be closed for consideration of the motion."

All but the eight officers on the bench filed out. "That was a gutsy ruling by Sampley," Gordon said, as he and John reached a quiet spot outside the tent. "Especially in light of the strong interest in this case by the general. I really didn't expect it."

"What do you think the court will do?"

"It will take five votes to grant the motion. That's asking a lot. If they deny it, all is not lost. We need only three votes to avoid conviction. So it's possible for the court to deny the motion and then turn around and acquit."

The court took longer than expected. Twenty minutes went by before everybody was called back in.

Sloboken announced, "All persons present when the court was closed are again present."

Colonel Hedley, taking his glasses off, announced, "With all due respect, the court disagrees with the law officer's ruling, and it has denied the motion."

Trial counsel and defense counsel then proceeded to make closing arguments, each repeating the points made earlier in arguing the motion. Gordon stressed the requirement that, in order to convict, the court had to find every element of the offense beyond reasonable doubt, words dear to the hearts of defense lawyers, and he mentioned them more than once. At the end, he played his highest card: "This young officer, called from civilian life and sent to Korea with no special training or orientation, has not hesitated to lay his life on the line time and again. He has stood literally face to face with the Chinese and North Koreans and has never flinched. When men were dying all around him, he stood firm and attempted to rally them. His voluntary elimination of an enemy machine-gun nest cleared the way for most of his division to escape a certain death trap. For that he was awarded the Silver Star. His clothes had been riddled with enemy fire, and he suffered three serious wounds, requiring months of hospitalization and recuperation. Yet he returned to the front line and again led a successful attack through murderous enemy fire. It is inconceivable, I submit, that an officer of this character would consider disobeying an order of a superior officer. To convict Lt. John Winston of this charge would do a profound injustice to an exemplary officer, and I urge the court to preserve his honor and do the right thing by acquitting him."

Gordon sat down, scraping his chair across the plank flooring. Two members of the court coughed. Colonel Hedley looked expectantly toward Sloboken, who had the prosecution's privilege of closing. He rose and said, "I have no further argument."

After a moment of surprised silence, all attention focused on the law officer. He instructed the members of the court on the elements of the offense and what they had to decide in order to find the accused guilty, two-thirds of the members in this case—here six— being required to concur in such a finding. The courtroom was again cleared, leaving the eight officers to deliberate.

Two hours passed, and there was still no summons to return. No one in the JA Section could remember a general court-martial taking as long to reach a decision. They all had to stay close by because there was no way to know when they would be called back in. Every half-hour or so Lt. Colonel Jameson wandered through the front JA tent and across the road, with a quizzical and anxious look, to make inquiry, but of course no one could tell him anything.

The sky had grown darker and the wind stronger. Though it was midafternoon, the world around them had the appearance of twilight.

John's face was drawn and strained. "I just want to get this roller-coaster ride over with now."

They sat in silence for a while. Then he said, "If I'm acquitted, it will be because Colonel Burkman was killed. Isn't that right?"

Gordon hesitated, gazing toward the chapel on the high ridge beyond the vigorously flapping flags. Then he said quietly, almost as though talking to himself, "We'll never know."

Nearly three hours had gone by when word came that the court had reached a decision. "The court will come to order," said the president, taking off his glasses.

"All persons present when the court was closed are again present," recited Sloboken.

Colonel Hedley looked straight at John with the utmost seriousness. "The accused will rise and face the court." The faces of the other officers were inscrutable. John stood up at the defense table, erect as if he were at attention on the parade ground. For an instant the planking creaked under his feet. The wind suddenly died down, and there was not a sound.

"Lt. John H. Winston, it is my duty as president of this court to inform you that, after the most careful deliberation, the court in closed session has found you not guilty of the specification and charge."

He paused, glancing at the law officer for some indication of approval or of the need for other steps. But Major Sampley sat inert and expressionless, his silence signifying that all was in order, that there was nothing further to be done.

Satisfied that the court had done its job, Colonel Hedley spoke again. "This concludes these proceedings. The court is adjourned."

PART FIVE
The Ever-Rolling Stream

Chapter 16

STRAINS OF DANCE MUSIC WAFTED across the spacious and elegant lobby of the Fairmont Hotel as John walked in from Powell Street and made his way toward the ballroom. A placard announced a USO Saturday night dance for officers of the armed services.

He was dazzled. Dozens of good-looking young women in colorful, form-fitting dresses were dancing, talking, and mingling with drinks in hand among the many uniformed officers. Half the men were army, the rest divided about evenly between air force and navy, with a sprinkling of marines. He could hardly remember when he had seen such a collection of American women, all looking more glamorous than he remembered. His first night off the troopship back in the States, it was almost too much of a nearly forgotten world.

Like all the other army officers, he was dressed in pinks and greens. He relished the still novel feeling of being showered and in a clean shirt and tie and a clean, well-fitted, belted blouse with normal trousers and low-cut shoes. A man needed months of dirty fatigues and combat boots to appreciate it all.

He found the bar and ordered a bourbon and water, then edged off to the side amidst a gaggle of lieutenants, none of whom seemed to know any of the others. For a while he stood there, sipping his drink and absorbing the fairy-tale scene. The band was playing "On Top of Old Smoky."

"What's the system?" he asked an army lieutenant.

"I'm new here tonight, but I think you just go up to one of the gals and ask her to dance."

He got another bourbon and water and moved to the other side of the ballroom to get a closer look at the women. There were some really good lookers, he thought. For well over a year the only American women he had seen had been a handful of army nurses. A few officers were breaking in on couples on the floor, with expressions on their faces, he mused, conveying their belief that they were God's gift to women. But breaking on strangers was not his style. Anyway, at the moment the orchestra was pounding away at a tempo too fast for his taste.

It had been less than a month since he had walked out of that courtroom tent on the other side of the world, miraculously pulled back from the abyss. The next day Carter Gordon told him that word had come down from General Willard, who was fuming over the acquittal, that he wanted that lieutenant out of his command pronto, and in fact out of the army. As Winston was scheduled to ship out anyway in a few weeks under normal rotation policy, the corps adjutant cut orders immediately sending him back to the States and to Fort Campbell, Kentucky, for discharge.

Carter Gordon had gone with him to the airstrip by the river. The weather had changed dramatically, and it was a clear, sunshiny fall day, cool and crisp. Both world and he seemed to have been born anew. He climbed into the cramped rear seat of the small two-seat liaison plane. A maintenance crewman pushed his duffel bag in behind his seat.

"Here's hoping we'll meet again under happier circumstances," Gordon said as the two shook hands.

"The circumstances could be a lot less happy," John said, buckling himself in. "You saved my life."

"That's putting it a little strong. Don't forget that enemy mortar round. Anyway, the case came out the right way."

The plane's engine coughed, sending the propeller into a half-turn. Then it roared fully into life. They had to shout to be heard.

"Was this justice according to law?" John yelled.

"Right. But justice in any sense."

A soldier slammed the plane door and pulled the chocks from in front of the wheels. The pilot, sitting only inches in front of John, revved the engine up to full throttle, and the Piper Cub lurched forward into its short takeoff run. John looked back and last saw Carter Gordon's diminishing figure standing by the strip, hand upraised in a parting wave.

They flew westward toward Seoul, along and just below the 38th parallel, that invisible line that had forever found a place in history. They flew low, affording a good view of the lonely, scarred ridges and valleys and some still-intact villages, smoke rising from the thatch-roofed huts. Flying down the valleys, they were often even with the tops of the hills on either side.

He was struck with how little there was in the rustic scene below to suggest that within the past year thousands of men had died there in the agony of battle. How quickly it all might be forgotten!

In the throbbing beat of the plane's engine, those he had known passed through his mind, as though he were turning the pages of a photo album. Of most, he did not know whether they were dead or in one of those prison camps in the North, about which they had heard dark rumors. Then there were the endless lines of dead and dying on the road south from Kunu-ri, and all those who went down around him on that deadly climb up Hill 969. And on 1080 there was Bruce Waller—yes, Capt. Bruce Waller, who remained in his memory most vividly of all.

He was processed through the Repl Depl and on to a troopship in Inchon harbor. After a week's layover in Sasebo, he boarded another troopship for the twelve-day Pacific crossing.

He had plenty of time to brood. The dark cloud of disgrace had been lifted. Yet this gave him no joy. He was oppressed by his growing belief that he had abandoned his outfit, by Waller's death, by his realization that only through Burkman's death was he given life anew. These burdens he would carry within himself forever. But no one else need ever know. He firmly resolved that these events would remain a secret chapter of his life.

Now he had been magically transplanted to another planet, atop Nob Hill in San Francisco. What he saw before him in the ballroom was what men dreamed and fantasized about in the bunkers along the MLR.

"Hi. My name's Tina. What's yours?"

Preoccupied with the action on the dance floor, he had not seen the perky blond come up to him. He was momentarily flustered. "Oh, uh, my name's John—John Winston."

"That's a nice name. Are you stationed here?" She had a warm smile.

"No, just passing through." After so long an absence, he was finding it awkward to talk with an attractive woman.

"I see you've been in Korea." She touched the little blue-and-white-striped ribbon in the row above his breast pocket.

"And I see you know your ribbons."

"Some. My goodness, here's the Purple Heart. What happened to you?"

"Just got nicked like lots of other folks."

"What's this?" She touched the blue, white, and red-striped ribbon at the beginning of the row.

"Silver Star."

"What's that for?"

"It's another one of the medals the army gives out."

"Well, you must have done something to get it."

"Just did what had to be done at the moment, did the same thing lots of others did."

"Now this is impressive. I've seen a few of these but never knew what they were." She ran her finger along the thin blue rectangle above the row of ribbons, bearing the impression of a musket and encircled by a wreath.

"Combat Infantry Badge. That's the one that really counts."

He sipped his drink. She tipped her glass up, and the ice rattled.

"Would you like another drink?" he asked.

"That sounds good."

They walked together to the bar, and she ordered a gin and tonic. He was feeling a bit more relaxed now, and he looked her over. She stood about five five, had wavy blonde hair that came just below her ears, bright green eyes, and a nicely shaped body hugged tightly by a rose-colored dress. They moved away from the bar and stood sipping their drinks, looking toward the dancers.

"I'll bet you're from the South. Right?"

"I can't imagine why you'd think that," he said, with a faint smile.

"Now let me guess. Georgia? Alabama?"

"Right the second time. How about you?"

"Dallas."

"I thought I caught a touch of Texas there."

"Probably more than a touch."

They sipped again for a few moments. Then she said suddenly, with a note of enthusiasm, "Would you like to dance? The orchestra has slowed down."

He hesitated, still feeling a little ill at ease. "OK, if you can put up with somebody who hasn't been to a dance for a long time."

She laughed, and they put down their glasses and threaded their way through onlookers and dancing couples to a relatively clear spot. She looked laughingly up into his face, as he put his arm around her waist, and she ran her arm across his shoulder. She was a woman with a lot of sunshine about her, as his father would say.

They moved into a slow fox-trot. The experience felt novel, like the sensation one feels in beginning to walk again after being long in bed with an illness. It struck him, too, that he had not been this close to a woman in more than a year, had not touched a female at all. And except for brief medical discussions with nurses, he had not even talked to one.

She moved in closer, her arm reaching farther around his neck. He tightened his arm at the back of her waist. They were covering little space on the dance floor, just more or less swaying in place. Her soft hair against his cheek had a pleasant fragrance. The easy beat of the orchestra, their slow swaying, the warmth of the bourbon, and, above all, the sensation of her body clasped tightly against him—all had the effect of lifting him into a narcoticlike state of euphoria. Korea was far, far away—so far removed from this moment that for the first time in a year and a half it dropped altogether out of his mind.

The music stopped. The magic spell was broken. They walked, holding hands, over to the table and recovered their drinks.

"This bourbon's getting a little watery," he said. "Think I'll have another. How about you?"

"Thanks. I'll just nurse this one along a little more."

With fresh drink in hand, he steered her off to the edge of the crowd, where they watched the dancers and talked.

"You say you're from Dallas. What are you doing in San Francisco?"

"Came to work, to find something different and maybe more exciting."

"Have you found it?"

"Pretty much, although I have a humdrum sort of job." She said
she worked at an insurance company downtown in an unglamorous
secretarial position. They chatted on about her job and what she
found interesting about the city. He glanced at his watch.

"Say, this dance is about to end. It's almost nine. But there's something I particularly want to see."

"What's that?"

"Top of the Mark. Would you be interested in heading up there
with me?"

She smiled. "It is spectacular. Sure, I'd enjoy going along. I haven't
been up there in a while."

A cable car clanked its way up Powell Street from Fisherman's
Wharf as they came out of the hotel. The night was filled with that
peculiar moist coolness of San Francisco. They crossed California
Street, passed through the lobby of the Mark Hopkins Hotel, and
took the express elevator to the Top.

"I want a table facing west toward the Golden Gate," he said.

"That's what everybody wants," she said, with her musical laugh
that he had begun to find attractive.

From the elevator, they came into the great room, with the circular bar in the center, lined with long, high windows, through which
the lights from the city below sparkled in every direction. They
strolled along the right side, searching for empty chairs.

"Ah!" she exclaimed, as they spotted a couple rising to leave,
"we're lucky."

The location was perfect. They sat down, looking straight out to
the Golden Gate.

"Have you ever seen the bridge before?" she asked.

"As a matter of fact, yes. But from quite a different angle. I saw it
from water level, and got a good view of its underside." For an instant
he thought of all the men who had passed under that bridge who
would not be coming back.

A waiter appeared. "Gin and tonic?" he asked, looking at Tina. She
nodded. "Bourbon and water for me."

Turning back to Tina, he said, "Tell me about yourself in Dallas."
He was feeling increasingly relaxed.

"Not a whole lot to tell. I grew up there and went to SMU. After I graduated I decided I needed a change of scenery. A sorority sister of mine had been talking about San Francisco, so she and I decided to take the big step and come out here together."

"Do you all room together?"

"We did. But she had a very sad experience. She met a man stationed at the Presidio, and they fell in love. Then he was sent to Korea. To make a long story short, he was killed last spring. It was a devastating blow for her, and she decided to go back home. I've stayed on, but I'm not sure what I'll do in the long run."

He was curiously unmoved by the man's death. He had seen death wholesale, and one more meant little to him now. Dawn would be breaking there now. What had the shelling been like last night? Had there been any night attacks? What hills were they fighting over now?

Their drinks arrived. "Have some peanuts," she said, handing him a filled bowl. Her voice and smile brought him back to the Top of the Mark.

"Well," he said, raising his glass in her direction, "here's to a fine San Francisco evening." She clicked his glass with hers, and they took deep swallows. She talked more about her roommate and the now-dead boyfriend.

"He was killed near a place called Chunchon. Have you ever heard of it?"

Korea again. He answered impatiently. "Yes, but just to pass through." He saw shabby streets, dusty and choked with army trucks, bars, Korean whores waving at everything American.

She asked him about himself, and he fell into talking about Remberton, the newspaper business, and what he might do.

The waiter reappeared. "Another round?"

"I'm fine," she said.

He said, "Another bourbon and water, please."

"I bet you're really looking forward to getting on some gray flannel slacks and loafers and sitting down by the fire."

"That sounds pretty good. You can't imagine how good it feels to have on ordinary shoes. They're so light, so airy around the ankles. I feel almost unshod. And clean, white sheets on a real mattress! That's luxury."

"All those cute little gals in Alabama are probably just dying for you to get back."

"I doubt it. I was not much of a ladies' man."

"You underrate yourself. You're quite a handsome and appealing man. Women will be falling all over you."

He blushed and nervously took a drink. Her remark stirred sensations inside him that he had not felt in a long time. Hardly surprising after fifteen months in the boondocks living with nothing but men and death.

After a pause, she became serious and said, "It must give you a lot of satisfaction to know you did you part over there."

He hesitated. "Satisfaction is not a word I would use. Frustration is more like it. Maybe humiliation. Do you realize that the retreat last fall was one of the worst defeats—maybe the worst—the American army ever suffered? It was a disgrace, and I was part of it."

"But isn't it true that the United States—maybe I should say the U.N.—saved the Republic of Korea?"

He sipped his drink. "Well," he said reflectively, "I guess you would have to say that."

"And prevented the spread of communism?"

"Yes. But I better not get started on the war. I have some strong views about it. Why don't you bring me up on the movies and the hit tunes and anything else I'm behind on?"

She rambled on about movies she liked and didn't like and what she considered the best popular music.

"Another gin and tonic?"

"Oh, well, why not?"

He signaled the waiter for another round. He moved his chair closer.

They got on to books. She had majored in English at SMU. Her father had wanted her to study something practical, but she resisted, being just a little rebellious. After wandering through her recollections of life at SMU, she wanted to know about the University of Alabama.

Growing more loquacious—and vaguely aware that his hand had gotten onto her knee under the table—he recounted his college days. For a fleeting interval he was back in Tuscaloosa, and Korea had never happened.

The waiter was clearing the next table. John caught his eye. "A bourbon and water, please."

His eyes opened uncertainly, blinking several times before settling on the white ceiling directly overhead. It was broad daylight. His body felt stiff and cramped. He was flat on his back, and he gradually became aware that he was lying on a sofa. He lifted his arms and felt over his chest. He was wearing his light tan uniform shirt and pink trousers, but he had on no shoes or tie. He heard bells ringing in the distance, multiple bells continuously chiming and ringing. He turned his head and saw Tina standing by the sofa, looming above him.

"How do you feel?" she asked in a quiet voice.

He didn't answer immediately, but shook his head, sending shafts of pain through his skull. Then he spoke slowly. "Where am I?"

"In my apartment."

"Your apartment! Where's that?"

"Corner of California and Leavenworth."

"Good Lord. How did I get here?"

"You don't remember?"

"I'm absolutely speechless. I can't tell you how embarrassed I am. I remember being at the Top of the Mark."

"I mentioned that we hadn't had any dinner and asked whether you'd like to come to my place where I could fix something. The restaurants were all closed. You said fine, so we got up and came here. You did pay the bill, and you left a generous tip. You and the waiter had gotten to be real friends."

"How did we get here?"

"We walked. It's only a few blocks. You were unsteady, but we made it. I wasn't the steadiest myself."

"You've got to know that I've never, never done anything like this before. I can't believe it." He swung his feet off the sofa and sat up. Intensified throbs surged through his head. "This is terrible. I must have really tied one on."

"You did pretty well."

"I apologize. That's about all I can say. The first night back in civilization must have been too much to handle. Did we eat anything?"

"No. You sat down here on the sofa and took off your blouse and tie. I told you to get comfortable and went in the kitchen. When I came back in a few minutes you were lying down asleep. I took off your shoes and put a pillow under your head, and here you are."

He looked sheepishly over at his dark green blouse, with its colorful row of ribbons, draped over the back of a straight chair. His tie lay on top of the blouse, and his brown buckle shoes were on the floor under the chair. "Good God. This is unimaginable."

"Would you feel better with a shower?"

Focusing now on her, he saw that she was wearing a green flannel bathrobe. It matched her eyes. He rubbed his face and said, "It couldn't hurt, I suppose."

"Just a minute. I'll move a few things out of the way in the bathroom." She disappeared into a small hall but returned shortly with a bath towel and washcloth. "OK, the coast is clear."

He closed the bathroom door and undressed. He fiddled for some moments with the unfamiliar shower controls to get the water temperature suitably hot. For a long while he stood under the pummeling spray, soaping and savoring the hot water. When he thought he had exhausted its restorative effects, he shut it off, stepped out, and began toweling himself briskly.

She called from the hall. "Do you need anything?"

"Do you happen to have some kind of razor I could use?"

"Yep. This is a well-stocked place. May I come in?"

He wrapped the towel around his hips and opened the door. She rummaged in a drawer under the washbasin and pulled out a small case containing a safety razor.

"Thanks," he said. "I'm slowly coming back to the land of the living."

"I'm fixing some coffee. Would you like something to eat?"

"No, thanks, not yet. I'll try the coffee first." Then he added, "If you're serving aspirin, I wouldn't mind some now."

She reached in the medicine cabinet and pulled out a small bottle of Bayer. Looking at him with a sly smile, she put the bottle in his hand and closed the door.

He shaved, using the bar of soap. Also using the soap and his finger, he did a makeshift job of brushing his teeth. He then redressed, finding it distasteful to put back on the clothes he had slept in.

As he padded into the living room, she came out of the kitchen with a cup of coffee on a saucer. "Do you want cream or sugar?"

"Just black, thank you." He sat down in an armchair.

She leaned over and handed him the cup and saucer. He had the fleeting impression that she was wearing nothing beneath her loosely tied robe.

Getting herself a cup, she returned to an armchair opposite him, sat down, and modestly crossed her bare legs, tugging down on the short robe that would not quite cover her knees. He noticed her toenails were painted the same deep red as her fingernails.

"What are the bells?" he asked.

"Grace Cathedral," she said. "It's just up the street. As you may or may not recall, this is Sunday morning. They have an eleven o'clock service. Would you like to go?"

She had a twinkle in her eyes, and he couldn't tell whether she was serious or just kidding him. "I don't think I'm quite up to that. Do you go there?"

"Sometimes. It's impressive. But I was raised a Methodist, and it's a little stiff for me."

"I can understand that. I'm Presbyterian."

She stood up, tightening the sash around the bathrobe. "Here, let me get you another cup of coffee."

"I believe it's beginning to bring me around."

She returned shortly with a fresh cup. "Are you about ready for something solid? I can give you scrambled eggs and toast. That's about all I have on hand."

"Sounds fine. Come to think of it, it's been quite a while since I had anything except peanuts."

"Just give me a few minutes. Make yourself at home. The Sunday paper's over there." She went into the kitchen.

He moved to the sofa and picked up the front page of the *San Francisco Chronicle*. In the lower left-hand corner was a small headline: "Korean Truce Talks Continue." The article said that the U.N. representatives and the Chinese and North Korean Communist negotiators were meeting again at Panmunjom. Little progress, however, had been made, and no one was predicting early agreement, but fighting had subsided in recent days.

He called out to her. "Does anybody here pay any attention to this war? From what I've seen here, it might as well not exist."

She called back. "I regret to say that it doesn't seem to get much coverage. It's surely not like the last war."

He perused the paper for a few more minutes. Then she called him to the kitchen, and they sat at a small table. He wolfed down the scrambled eggs and a total of five pieces of toast heavily coated with strawberry jam. "That really hits the spot!" he exclaimed, as he cleaned his plate and leaned back with his third cup of coffee.

"By the way," she said casually, "who is Waller?"

He stopped his cup in midair. "Waller? What do you know about Waller?" His voice had an unpleasant edge.

"Nothing. I heard you call it out in your sleep."

He was relieved. "Oh, he was one of my company commanders."

"You mentioned a couple of other people last night."

"When? Who?"

"Before we left the Top of the Mark. You said Colonel Burkman was your battalion commander."

He tensed. "Did I say anything else about him?"

"You said he was killed but saved your life. I didn't understand what you were saying."

He sighed. "It's too complicated to explain. Anyway, I'm here, and lucky to be here."

After an awkward moment of silence, she said, "Let's go back where it's more comfortable."

They sat down together on the sofa. He leaned back and stretched his legs out full length. He was getting to a to a nearly normal state, although he still had a mild headache. She was close beside him, and he felt the warmth of her body and saw the curve of her breasts in the loose V of the bathrobe. This was heady business for a man fresh from the MLR.

The Grace Cathedral bells were chiming again. Sunday morning. Stores were closed, people were going to church. He would have to get used to it again. Along the MLR, Sunday was no different from any other day, except that when things were quiet, groups of soldiers were trucked in relays back to the battalion CP to attend services with the chaplain.

She asked, "Where are you staying?"

"The St. Francis." He half-laughed. "They should give me a refund for last night."

"Tomorrow I could take off from work and show you the city. How about it?"

He hesitated, looking off into space. Before he could say anything, the telephone rang. She jumped up and stepped across the room and answered. Between long silences, she was saying "Yes . . . all right . . . fine . . . OK . . ."

He thought of his father's advice one day when they were driving to Montgomery for a press meeting not long after he received his active-duty orders. "Don't get involved with women you meet in the army," his father had said. "What looks great in the Fort Bliss Officers' Club won't look the same back in Remberton."

She hung up the phone. "That was a woman from the office. We're planning a shower for one of the secretaries who's having a baby."

She came over and plopped down beside him. "Well, don't you think you can stay over?"

"Nothing I'd like better, but I don't really have a choice."

"Why not?"

"I'm on orders for Fort Campbell to be discharged. Can't afford to mess up right here at the end. To make it I've got to catch a train from Oakland this afternoon."

She looked disappointed. "What time is the train?"

"4:15."

"It's just ten now. We've still got some time."

From gazing into space, debating with himself over what to do, he turned and looked at her upturned face, smiling at him wistfully, her pale, smooth skin in the loose front of her robe. He slid his arm across her shoulders and leaned forward and kissed her lightly on the lips.

"Well," she whispered, "that's nice."

"I can't believe this. Here I am, twenty-four hours back in the States, sitting with a beautiful woman in her apartment in San Francisco. If I wrote them about this in Korea, they'd think I made it up."

"I hope you don't find it too unpleasant."

He said nothing. Something within him had changed, something that made him feel different at this moment than he had ever before felt in the presence of a woman. He looked intently into her green eyes; they seemed to be soaking up his gaze. Time and place ceased to exist. Breath coming short and heart pounding, he was lifted into some other plane, somewhere he had never been before.

He kissed her again, his fingers running lightly through her hair and down her neck and on to the soft skin beneath the robe.

Chapter 17

JOHN WAS ON A TRAIN heading south through the rolling hills and pastureland of middle Tennessee. He sat at a window, watching the scenery slide by. The brightly colored leaves of fall had gone. The bare branches were a reminder that winter was not far ahead. He still wore his uniform—he had no other clothes—but he was now again, as of this day, a civilian, having been honorably discharged from the United States Army at Fort Campbell.

Rain splashed sporadically in slanting lines against the train windows. It was a dismal fall day. He would be home in time for Thanksgiving, and how different this Thanksgiving of 1951 would be from the last. Many a man who had eaten turkey out of his mess kit a year ago—flushed with the prospect of early victory and the end of the Korean police action—would never see home or Thanksgiving again. Yet the war went on, the talking went on, and the killing went on. For the second Thanksgiving and the second Christmas, the blue and white United Nations flag would be flying over men and women from many nations, spread across those freezing hills where, he liked to think, civilization had taken its stand. However disturbed and frustrated he was, he had to admit that the far frontier was being held, albeit at a huge cost.

Home had loomed large in his mind on countless days and nights over the last year. Although he had come to feel cut off from it, irrevocably separated from it by his searing experience, it remained an idyllic place where all was bright and happy. Now that he was drawing nearer, nearer by the hour, his mood about it darkened. Home, that magical word and concept, had taken on a slightly ominous quality. The prospect of actually arriving there gave him an uncomfortable foreboding.

The town itself might be the same, although a lot of his friends had drifted away. But he himself was surely not the same. At times he had wondered whether he could ever laugh again, but he had found that he could. Maybe it was just a matter of time before the horrors would fade. But he doubted that he would ever again be the same. He did not know how it would be to live with the dark secret locked away in his mind. He had almost divulged it in his drunken state in San Francisco. One thing was certain though: The twenty-two-year-old boy who left Remberton in September 1950 was now returning as a twenty-four-year-old man.

His brooding was interrupted by the butch working his way along the swaying aisle, a drawn, ageless figure with a hoarse, froglike voice, calling out, "Coca-Cola, candy bars." John bought a Coke, paying a quarter for what would have cost a nickel off the train. He leaned back, sipping and watching the hills of North Alabama come into view. The rhythmic clickety-clack, clickety-clack of the wheels over the rails lulled him again into a reverie.

For two days and nights after leaving San Francisco, he had watched a large part of the American landscape pass by the train windows—first the Western desert, then the Rockies, and finally the Great Plains. There had been much time to think, as there had been on the troopship. But the thinking was different now. Getting back in the States put everything in another perspective. The Orient had receded, drowned out by the sights and sounds of the mid-century United States. San Francisco had been a rapid and dramatic reintroduction. The contrast with Korea could hardly have been more stark—the bright lights, automobiles, hotels, restaurants, and the glamour of the dance, but most of all, Tina. It would be a long time before he would forget her. Still in the pocket of his blouse was the piece of paper on which he had hurriedly jotted down her address as he had rushed out to catch the train: "Christine Barnes. Apt. 3A. Corner of California and Leavenworth."

But now his thoughts were on the future. It would take a while to get readjusted. There should be no rush. The *Progress* seemed to be in good hands with Frank and Becky back. Now he needed to rest, just take it easy in the quiet of home, back in normal clothes, food, and his own bedroom. The old zest for hunting had gone. He had shot enough and heard enough shooting to last several lifetimes. He would do some reading. They were all assuming he would come back with the newspaper. He had led them to think that, but he doubted more and more that he could do it. In any case, he figured that after Christmas would be time enough to face the question. He had to let the strangeness of home wear off.

The train pushed ever southward. Birmingham had come and gone. Now the train had left the Montgomery station, perched on a bluff above the Alabama River. It would not be long. He felt a quickening of his heartbeat and a queasiness in his stomach. How strange it would be to see his family again, and all the others, seeing them now after the experiences he had had. He wondered how his father had felt when he came home from France in 1919 and how his grandfather had felt coming home from Virginia in 1865. They did not come home, he assumed, burdened with the necessity of forever keeping secret a disgraceful episode in their lives.

"Remberton!" the conductor called out as he walked down the aisle. "Next stop, Remberton! This way out!"

Familiar fields and houses flashed by. From up ahead came the long wailing of the train whistle, blowing for the Mill Road crossing. He reached up to the overhead rack and pulled down his duffel bag. He put on his cap and made his way along the aisle toward the rear, the bag dragging against the ends of the green, felt-covered seats.

He stood with the conductor in the clanking, rumbling noise of the swaying vestibule between cars. The train, its whistle blowing, rounded the last long curve leading to the station. Then came the hissing of the air brakes and a precipitous slowing down, causing him almost to lose his balance. With a protracted squealing of steel against steel, the train lurched to a stop.

In the sudden silence, the conductor yanked the door inward, banging it loudly into the catch to hold it open. He pulled up the metal flap covering the steps. John, duffel bag in hand, followed him down and on to the platform. He stood there, looking at the station, the Railway Express cart being wheeled out, a slice of

Center Street—absorbing the unbelievable fact that at long last he was home.

In the distance, half-running toward him and waving, came his mother and father and sister Becky. He dropped the bag as his mother threw her arms around his neck. "Thank God, you're finally home," she half-whispered. He felt her warm tears on his cheek.

Then his father was standing beside him grasping his right hand and putting his arm around his shoulder. "Well, son, this is a great day," he said, smiling broadly. "Great to have you back in one piece."

Becky gave him a strong hug. "My goodness, you're mighty handsome in that uniform. And look at all those ribbons! Frank got tied up at the last minute and couldn't get here, but he'll be at the house in a little bit."

"Look's like something's going on here," John said, poking at a protrusion below her waist.

"We wanted to surprise you."

"Congratulations! When's it due?"

"April. I feel great so far. Morning sickness gone."

His mother grabbed him by the shoulders. "You're too thin. We'll have to fatten you up."

In the car all the way to the house they peppered him with questions. How was your trip? How are you feeling? What do you want to do first?

When he walked into the back hall of the house, Annie May burst out of the kitchen. "Lord, Mr. John, you are a sight for sore eyes. And don't he look good, Miss Anna?"

"He certainly does. But don't you think he could use a little weight?"

"Aw, we'll take care of that." Fingering the sleeve of his blouse with her large brown hand, she said, "Is them army wools you got on?"

"That's what they are, and I'm going to take them off in a minute for the last time."

"I'm sorry our friends can't see you in your uniform," Becky said. "You look so nice."

"I hate to deprive them of that pleasure," John said, "but I've been waiting a long time to get into civvies."

He went up the stairs, along the hall, and into his room. He closed the door and leaned back against it. Glad to be alone, he took a deep breath and exhaled. He stood there, surveying this museum of his life, of his life before Korea. It was all as he had left it—all the photographs and mementos still there. But it all seemed part of a distant past.

A chapter in his life had been written and closed. There was no doubt in his mind now; he had crossed a great divide, sharply separating all that had gone before from all that would come after. At this moment, though, he was dangling in limbo, poised between past and future, knowing where he had been and what he had done but uneasy over the unknown that lay ahead.

He stripped down to his underwear. As he laid his uniform on the bed, he was hit with a fleeting twinge of nostalgia mixed with pride. Whatever dreams he had about military service had been fully satisfied. Like his father and grandfather, he had done his duty, had paid his dues, so to speak. Now he would take his uniforms to the cleaner and then store them away in some trunk in the attic, heavily interlarded with mothballs, along with all his other army artifacts and souvenirs, to join the high-necked tunic, Sam Browne belt, and puttees from 1918 and the faded gray jacket from 1865. Just as he had come across those items with fascination when he was growing up, maybe his descendants would come across these. "Daddy, tell us about Korea." "Granddaddy, were you in Korea?"

He lingered long under the hot shower, relishing the privacy of his own bathroom. He went to the closet and pulled out a pair of gray flannel slacks and put them on. From the dresser drawers he got a pair of socks, one of his old shirts, and a maroon pullover sweater. He finished dressing by sliding his feet into his well-worn loafers that were right on the closet floor where he had left them.

Tina came to mind, as she would many times in the days ahead. She had hit it on the head—gray flannels and loafers, hard to beat. He thought of her in her San Francisco apartment, but his father had been right. That was another world, far from his room here in Remberton. She would remain a fantasy he could always summon up, but this was, after all, his world. Yet there was now a curious strangeness about it.

For the next few days he didn't want to see people around town. He spent time driving through the streets and nearby countryside.

They were all as they had been. Occasionally in passing he waved at someone he recognized, but he deliberately avoided calling on anyone. He had to get reaccustomed to the scene gradually, like a diver coming up from the depths slowly to avoid the bends.

Then he developed a sore throat. It got worse, and he had a fever. He took to his bed, eating little other than the hot chicken soup that Annie May brought him.

"I wonder if the boy has brought home some strange Oriental disease," Herbert said, with growing concern.

They sent for Dr. Loosh. He came and examined John at his bedside, holding a stethoscope against his chest and back, sticking a thermometer in his mouth, holding down his tongue with a stick, getting him to say "Ah," taking his pulse, and punching in various parts of his abdomen.

"You've got a beauty of a scar here," the doctor said. "Don't see many like that. Some surgeon had a real job. These stitch marks are a little rough."

"The operation wasn't done under what you would call ideal conditions," John said.

"What was the hospital?"

"32nd Evac, in an old Japanese-built schoolhouse. If the health authorities in this country saw anything like it, they'd go bananas."

Dr. Loosh finished his examination. "Contrary to what a lot of people think, medicine is not an exact science. Diagnosis is often little more than a guess. My best guess is that you have mononucleosis." He wrote out a couple of prescriptions and told John to stay in bed and let him know how he was in two or three days, unless he should get worse in the meantime.

He paused at the bottom of the stairs to report to Herbert and Anna that their son probably had mono. "I gave him a couple of things to take. Just keep him in bed and feed him." He added, as he opened the front door to leave, "From the looks of that scar he brought home, we're mighty lucky to have that boy here at all."

So for the next two weeks John was in bed except to get up to go to the bathroom. He was in bed right through the Thanksgiving holidays, much to the disappointment of his family and his friends who had come home for the weekend. The telephone rang often with their inquiries about him. He did manage to get to the dining room table for an hour on Thanksgiving Day to eat turkey with the family, finding it hard to keep his mind off his last Thanksgiving dinner.

One afternoon when he was lying in his room half asleep, Annie May stuck her head in the door and said, "Dr. Cowley's downstairs. Says he'd like to see you."

Although he had given instructions that he wanted no visitors, he said, "All right, send him up."

The last time John had seen Dr. Tom Cowley was when he said good-bye to him at the church door on the Sunday he left Remberton, a lifetime ago it now seemed. In the dark hours in Korea, he had often remembered his parting words.

"Well, John, it's grand to have you back, even though temporarily prone." Dr. Cowley spoke in the rich-timbered voice of a seasoned preacher. "There was a time when a lot of people thought we might not see you again, but I never gave up."

John propped himself up against the pillow and shook hands. Dr. Cowley pulled up a chair and sat down beside the bed.

"There were times when I wouldn't have bet a nickel on getting back," John said. "Plenty of others didn't. But I guess you saw a lot of stuff like that." He had often heard Dr. Cowley refer to his service as a navy chaplain.

"I surely did. Especially at Iwo Jima, where I went ashore with the marines. That was the worst. A chaplain is in a peculiar position. He's not a combatant but he can be—and I think should be—where the combat is."

Here John felt for the first time he could talk about Korea. "I wonder if you saw what I saw—men's intestines torn out, arms and legs and even heads blown off."

"I did, plenty of it. Nobody who hasn't actually been there and seen it can imagine the scene. The battlefield may be about as close as we can get to hell on earth."

"They don't show those mutilated bodies in the war photos and old paintings of battle scenes."

"No, they don't. I guess they figure the public can't take it."

"How can God permit such slaughter and suffering? Either God is all-powerful and could stop it or God cannot stop it, in which case he is not God."

"I suppose men have always asked how can God permit evil. How can God allow bad things to happen? The existence of evil is one of the most perplexing of all mysteries. You have to remember that man is free to do evil, to act foolishly, to do great harm."

John was silent for a moment, thinking. Then he asked quietly, "Do you have a good answer?"

"Not one that's really satisfying. It's not for us to know ultimate answers to all questions. I do know that good and evil both exist, and I'm convinced that sometime we have to stand up against evil at the risk of suffering and death. A woman with a lot of troubles told me years ago that God never promised us a bed of roses. The promise is to be with us, whatever happens. And there is the assurance that good will ultimately triumph. The devil cannot win in the long run."

"But in the short run he can surely wreak havoc."

"Christian thinkers have been troubled by war for a long time. You have pacifists who think all war is wrong. But the theory of just war gets a lot of support. They all agree that my war was a just war."

"What about Korea?"

"I think it qualifies. You have armed aggression, with conduct contrary to international law and ordinary human decency. And it was clear that it could not be stopped by any means short of force. "

"One question I'll always have is why I lived when many around me didn't."

Dr. Cowley spoke in a lowered voice. "Again, we don't know. But think about this. You may have been spared for some mission later in life, for some special purpose that we cannot now know, and may never know."

John said nothing, looking blankly at the preacher for a few moments, and then turned the conversation to other matters. As was often said by members of the flock, just being in Tom Cowley's presence made a man feel better. His imposing stature, wartime experiences, and deep voice seemed to authenticate him as a genuine representative of the Almighty, a man of sorrows, acquainted with grief.

By early December John was up, sore throat and fever gone, and feeling much better. But he was weak and thinner than ever.

Frank had come by to see him several times. He was brimming

over with enthusiasm about the newspaper. "It's a great thing to have a paper you can get your arms around. The whole operation is right there—news articles, editorials, sports, society, ads, the business side—all there in sight and within reach. None of this departmentalization where you're a small cog in a huge machine." He went on to say that, of course, they would need to agree on some division of responsibility, but that should be no problem. Each would still know what was going on in the other's domain, and they would continuously talk about the whole operation. John listened but said little; he found it hard to get excited about at all.

His strength gradually returned. He ate heartily, whatever Annie May put in front of him—plenty of fried chicken, ham, grits, and quail that his father had shot. He filled his days with reading. He sought out books on the shelves in the den that he had long seen there and intended to read some day but had not gotten around to: Tolstoy's *War and Peace*, Dostoyevsky's *Crime and Punishment*, and Arnold Toynbee's writings on civilization. He was glad he had not read them earlier, as he suspected he would not have appreciated them nearly as much as he did now.

Late one afternoon he and Herbert were sitting in the den perusing the newspapers. "Well, son," Herbert said, putting down the *Birmingham News*, "do you think you might be ready to get back with the paper after New Year's?" He had not mentioned the subject earlier. "We want you to get fully recuperated and plenty rested, so I don't mean to rush you."

John had just picked up the latest issue of the *National Geographic* as his father spoke. He let it lie in his lap. "I suppose so. Before I dive back into things I want to be sure I'm ready, physically and mentally."

"I understand the physical. What's the mental concern?"

"I just need some time to get adjusted to being back here. It doesn't seem to happen overnight."

"I think I know what you mean. I had a touch of that when I got back from France. The best thing to do, though, I think, is to get going with some active work. Sitting around the house for too long is not good. A man can have too much time to think."

"I can see that. Do you think we can work everything out with Frank and me?"

"Oh, I doubt there'll be any problem. If that's what's worrying you, I would forget it. I'll plan to phase out and leave it with you two. Of course, I'd be around and always available for help or advice."

Anna came in, much to John's relief. "John," she said, "you remember when you first got home we talked about having an open house here to give folks around town a chance to see you and welcome you back. That didn't work out then, but I'd like to plan on doing it during the Christmas holidays, when a lot of your friends are home."

"Do you really want to go to all that trouble? I'll eventually see everybody."

"I know, but a lot of people are anxious to see you. You probably have no idea of the reaction here to the word that you were missing. It was like a death in the family. All that night and for the next several days they came by here. They brought food just like they do at a funeral, and they sat and talked with us. It was a great comfort, and it showed how much people—all sorts of people—really love you. When word came that you were alive and not missing, there was rejoicing, like you had been raised from the dead."

"Well," John said reluctantly, "if that's the way you feel about it, OK."

"Fine. I suggest the day after Christmas Day. Most of those who've come back will still be here."

Christmas that year was as festive as ever, if not more so. The Winstons, as usual, had a giant cedar in the parlor, covered by a multitude of colored lights. Its pleasant aroma filled the room. A large green wreath with a red bow hung on the front door, and an array of smilax, mistletoe, and holly decorated the stair rail and chandelier in the hall. The weather had turned cold, so a log fire was kept going in the parlor.

During Christmas dinner they talked about Becky's baby—whether it would be a boy or girl and whether they had decided on names.

"John," Herbert said, "now that you're settling down, it'll be your turn next."

"Don't you think it would be a good idea if I got married first?"

"That's the usual order of events," Frank said.

"Well, are there some prospects of that?" Becky asked.

"Not that I know of," John said, looking put upon. "There don't seem to be any eligible females in sight."

"I'm not sure about that," his father said, with his familiar bemused expression. "Sally Young called up here several times during Thanksgiving to ask about you."

"Sally Young and I have never hit it off. Last time I knew anything about it, she was dating Bartow Simmons."

"That's all off," said Becky. "Word is that Bartow's dating some gal in Nashville."

"Anyway, Sally's up in New York."

"But she'll be here tomorrow," Anna said, raising her eyebrows.

The open house, at dusk the next day, attracted more than a hundred guests. All the women, young and old, had to hug John and tell him how thankful they were that he was safely back. "I knew the Lord would take care of you," one of the matrons said. One of the men said, "You really had us worried there for a while."

Then there were questions. Did you actually see some of those commies? Is it as cold over there as they say it is? Do those Koreans speak English? What was it like when you were wounded? When you were missing in action, where were you? He answered all of them as politely as he could and in generalities and platitudes.

Mr. Ben Harris came in the front door, shivering from the chill. "John, my boy, I can't tell you how good it is to see you!" He half-hugged him as he shook hands.

John had long thought that Mr. Ben liked the idea of having him as a son-in-law, and the warmth and effusiveness of the greeting suggested in his mind that this might still be the case. Putting Jeanie behind him, as he had determined to do, had not been easy. He had to acknowledge something he had not squarely admitted to himself before, that he had been in love with her. Time, though, was gradually easing the deep hurt he had felt at her defection, and he didn't care to reopen the painful episode. Yet politeness prevented him from ignoring her altogether. So he said simply and matter-of-factly, "How's Jeanie?"

"Fine, but she's not here. They're with her husband's folks in Decatur."

Craig Anderson appeared, home for the holidays from Chapel Hill. John said, "How's Thomas Wolfe coming?"

"Slowly. I've got the ABD degree."

"ABD?" said Baby Sister Carpenter, who had just walked up.

"All but dissertation," Craig said. "But I'm plowing along. Hope to have it done by next year."

The dining room table held many sorts of goodies to eat and a huge bowl filled with colorful fruit punch. Those were the only visible refreshments. To preserve the pretense—in accordance with Remberton protocol—that alcohol was not being served, Herbert had placed a table in an alcove off the rear hall, where it could not be seen from the front, and on it had put several fifths of bourbon and scotch and a stack of small paper cups. Word was passed discretely among the men that the stuff was there. Most of them managed to drift casually away from the women and duck to the rear. They would knock back a shot or two and then wander back to the front, circulate and talk for a bit, and then nip back to the rear for another shot. Most of the younger set—the men in John's crowd—however, seldom got back to the front.

Sally Young accosted John in the front hall. "I don't mean any disrespect to your father, but don't you think it's a little inhospitable for you and all your friends to be back there drinking without offering any to us girls?"

He gave her a worldly smile and then said in a whisper, "You have a point. Give me your cup." He took it and disappeared. In three minutes he was back with the cup half-filled with bourbon. "You better cover it up with some punch."

"Good idea," she said with a wink. "Thanks."

John thought she had taken on certain New York airs in the way she held her cigarette and moved her hands. Instead of being put off by her, as he used to be, he now found her surprisingly interesting, different from the other Remberton girls.

Guests came and went all through the two-hour open house. Numerous comments were addressed to Herbert and Anna, proud parents of the returned war hero. They beamed and nodded in agreement.

"Looks like the next generation is about ready to take over the *Progress*."

"John and Frank will make a fine team at the paper."

"Herbert's going to be doing a lot more hunting and fishing."

"It's grand to see another Winston carrying on at the *Progress.*"

The crowd gradually thinned. Most of the older guests—friends of Herbert and Anna—had left by the end of two hours. But the group in the back was getting louder. With the older folks gone, John decided the time had come to open the whole thing up and invite all the girls to the rear. By this time he had replenished Sally's punch cup twice with bourbon, and she was in a high holiday mood.

Anna and Herbert said good night and went upstairs, abandoning the party to the young folks. They were, after all, good sports, John thought. He had been pleased to find them in such good shape on his return. Anna had changed her hairstyle, getting rid of the bun and adopting a fluffed-out, wavy do. She was still pleasantly chubby. Tonight she had worn a fashionable rose-colored shantung dress. Herbert had changed little except for slightly thinner hair. If anything, he looked more ruddy and healthy.

In another hour, with Herbert's stock of bourbon and scotch exhausted, they all decided to go on to the country club. They drifted out of the front door, loudly talking and laughing. "John," Sally called out, "how about riding with you?"

Hours later, when he pulled up and switched off the ignition in front of Sally Young's house, she said, with an unusual lilt in her voice, "Would you be interested in a little good-night kiss?"

He was in a mellow mood—it was the most fun he had had since coming home from the army. He said without hesitation, "Why not?"

It was quite a kiss. Actually, it was not one kiss, but a series that went on for some unreckonable time.

She ran her fingers through his hair, then said suddenly with concern, "Goodness, what's this?"

"A souvenir from Korea."

"It's a long ridge. I didn't know it was there. It's all covered with hair."

"Finally. For a while it was a pretty raw-looking line."

"I thought Mr. Herbert said you were wounded in the stomach."

"That's another one."

"Do you have a scar from that?"

"You wouldn't believe it. It's a real prize."

"Can I see it?"

"Well, I don't think this is a good time. It's a little cold to take off clothes."

"Too bad we're not down at Mary Esther."

He chuckled but said nothing.

"You know I have to leave for New York tomorrow. Maybe some other time," she whispered, as she pressed her mouth hard against his, her arms tightly around his neck.

"We've rearranged the office, as you can see, to have three desks here." Miss Effie McCune was explaining the new setup to John. "We moved the file cabinets and shoved your father's desk down there. Now you are here." She pointed to John's old desk, midway along the wall. "And here's Frank's place."

It was the first week in January. John had decided that he could not put off his return to the *Progress* office any longer, out of respect for his father, if for no other reason. The three had talked at length about the whole operation and had mutually agreed on how they would work. Frank would handle the business side and have responsibility for various features such as society and the mill village news. John would be in charge of sports, although Rufus Scruggs would do most of the writing, as in the past. He would also take on book reviews and the Washington column—his favorites—and would share responsibility with Herbert for the front page and general news items. For the time being, Herbert would have the editorials, but he was planning on phasing out altogether over the coming year. "I'll stay around long enough to see that you boys have got the show up and running at full speed."

Later that afternoon Herbert corralled the entire *Progress* staff in the front office—himself, John, Frank, Miss Effie, Rufus Scruggs, and Booker Jackson. Thelma Parker, the society editor, came running in just as they were gathering.

"This is a great moment," he announced, "the beginning of a new era in the long history of the *Remberton Progress*. The old Major," he pointed to the formidable countenance looking down on them from the wall, "would be proud indeed. We've got a new team here, combined with the old team. The paper's future is bright, and I look forward to many years together, even though I myself will be moving over to the sidelines before long."

Through all this, John struggled to appear interested. But his heart was not in it. He had come to think that he could not remain in Remberton and live comfortably with the Korean secret he had resolved to lock away forever, that he would have to get away from his Remberton past to put Korea behind him or at least to live with it.

They soon settled into a routine. John's first assignment was to do a story on the senior class play at the high school and the upcoming session of the circuit court. For the story on the court, he went to the clerk's office in the courthouse and looked over the docket. It was about half criminal and half civil. A secretary there showed him the case files, and he became engrossed in reading the pleadings in the civil cases and the indictments in the criminal. He decided he would sit in on some of these trials and write stories about them. In the past, the paper had done only cryptic reports on court proceedings, giving little of human interest. He would introduce more complete coverage.

One day while he was wondering whether he would understand enough about these cases to write accurate accounts, the phone rang. "John!" boomed the voice at the other end. "This is Noble Shepperson."

"Yes, sir! How are you?" The call shot a current of excitement through John. He had been wanting to see this man, a lawyer and combat veteran.

"Fine. Welcome back! Sorry I couldn't get to your open house; we were in Mobile. But I've been wanting to talk to you ever since you got home. Can you come over to my office sometime?"

What a stroke of luck, John thought. Noble Shepperson was one of the few men around with whom he might talk realistically about Korea—he, Shepperson, having been a colonel in an armored division in Europe—and he was also someone from whom he might get help in doing articles on the upcoming trials.

The next afternoon John climbed the slanting wooden steps running up the side of the drugstore to the second floor offices of Kirkman and Shepperson.

"John, great to see you!" boomed the colonel, as the secretary ushered him into his office. He was a tall, athletic figure, with a military-style haircut and a voice that carried. "Have a seat." He pointed to a chair facing the front of his desk and seated himself on the other side in a swivel chair flanked by tables overflowing with disorderly piles of notes and books. "I followed you through Herbert. It was great news when it turned out that the MIA report was incorrect. I gather you got roughed up some, but you're fine now. You look in good shape."

They talked a while about John's experiences. Shepperson was especially interested in the use of tanks in the hills and narrow valleys.

"This is the damnedest war I ever heard of," he said. "Do you think MacArthur was right?"

John was slow in responding. "Hmm. Yes and no. He was right in his instinct that we should have finished the job and unified Korea. He was wrong in his failure to understand or anticipate the Chinese intervention. I got very frustrated and disenchanted."

"It's hard to argue against the supremacy of civil authority."

"Do you remember you once advised me against going to West Point? You said that with the war over and the army shrinking there probably wouldn't be much future in the military."

Shepperson smiled. "Guess I got that one wrong. The future does look different now. Are you sorry you took the advice?"

"No. I think I've satisfied my curiosity about the army and have had enough."

John finally turned the conversation to the upcoming court session. He asked a lot of questions about the procedure to be followed.

"How do you know as much about this as you do?" Shepperson asked.

"I got to know a lawyer in the JAG while I was in Japan, and we talked some about the law. He used to say that justice according to law was different from justice in general. That always puzzled me. Do you have any thoughts on that?"

"A good many. I live with it all the time. Who can say what justice is in some abstract sense? God only knows. All we can do in this flawed world of imperfect human beings is to set up an organizational structure, an institution—call it a court—and a procedure through which disputes can be settled without a fight in the streets. The trial is a substitute for self-help and violence."

"What about the rules of evidence?"

"They control what information the jury can consider. You'll hear it said that a trial is a search for truth. Not so. If the truth emerges, that's fine. But it sometimes does not, because of the rules of evidence. For example, those rules keep out communications between a husband and his wife. That can be very important information that any reasonable person would want to know about if we were seeking the truth. The reason has to do with protecting some other, presumably more important interest."

"So if a jury decides a case without some piece of relevant information of that sort, you would still say that justice has been done according to law?"

"Right. Justice has been done in accordance with duly ordained legal process. Who knows whether justice in some moral sense has been done?"

"What happens if a witness dies but he's already given a written statement, signed under oath? Can that statement be used at a trial?"

"No, the statement is hearsay because it was not subject to cross-examination. That's a peculiar situation. I had that happen to me once, and I lost the case because the witness had died. If he had lived and testified, I'm pretty sure I would have won."

"And that's justice?"

"It was a legally binding result arrived at under the existing rules. You can argue about whether it was justice."

"You're saying pretty much what Carter Gordon said."

"Who's Carter Gordon?"

"He's the JAG lawyer I met in Japan. All of this seems strange to a layman."

"I know it does. The law has its peculiarities, but we like to think that most of them make sense, once you understand the reasons. I'm surprised to see you interested in all this. You sound like somebody who might like to study law. Have you ever considered it?"

John hesitated, uncertain whether he should reveal the growing fascination he felt for the subject. "Maybe a little bit. It does seem to be intellectually challenging, more than I suspected."

Shepperson took the list of cases from John and went down it, case by case, explaining each.

As John rose to leave, Shepperson said, "When the trials are over and you have some more questions, come back."

At suppertime the next evening, Herbert, Anna, and John were sitting at the breakfast room table having vegetable soup. The big meal was still in the middle of the day, when Annie May was there to cook and clean up.

"I hear you had a long conversation with Noble Shepperson," Anna said.

"How did you know that?" John asked.

"I ran into Nan in the grocery store and she told me."

"There's an old saying that there are three ways to send a quick message: telegram, telephone, tell a woman," Herbert said.

"Now, Herbert," Anna chided, "that's a typical man's comment. You shouldn't repeat it."

"Well, anyway," John said, "did Miss Nan say anything more about it?"

"She just said that you all went over the cases coming up for trial. Noble was impressed with how interested you are in legal proceedings."

"Are we heading toward a legal affairs column in the *Progress?*" Herbert said with a smile.

"I doubt it, but I think we could give more coverage to what goes on in the court here."

"That's fine, if you can do it without insulting the local citizenry or stepping on anybody's toes," Herbert said. "It's hard to write about these court fights without doing that. That's why we haven't done more of it."

"Well, I'll give it a try this time around. Mr. Noble says he'll be glad to go over my report to be sure I've got the procedure right." He smiled and added, "You can go over it to eliminate the offensive passages."

He sat through several trials, wrote a story, and took it to Noble Shepperson.

"Say, this is good stuff," Shepperson said as he finished reading the draft, while John sat on the other side of his desk, waiting apprehensively for a reaction. "I think you've got the makings of a lawyer. Herbert wouldn't like to hear me say this, but I think you ought to give it some thought."

John had been doing just that, and this conversation strengthened his growing conviction that law and not journalism was where his future lay. He felt that a new career in a new place would let him put Korea behind him better than if he stayed at home. His time in the army had put a distance between him and Remberton. The divide between past and future was not as great as he had imagined while in the Far East, but the old closeness had diminished; the bonds had been loosened. Although he loved his parents no less, he no longer felt comfortable living there with them.

But he was in a terrible quandary. His departure from the *Progress*, as well as from Remberton, would no doubt be viewed as a renunciation of his heritage, an abandonment of his preordained role to carry on the family tradition. He knew that, to put it mildly, such a move would be upsetting and disappointing to his parents. The pulling and hauling on his heart and mind left him almost sick. He could hardly bring himself to contemplate the prospect of telling them.

A month passed, and there came a day when he realized a line had been crossed and there could be no turning back. It came upon him with unequivocal clarity: he must leave, go to law school, and pursue a life in the law. He could put off no longer the dreadful moment of telling his parents.

"Are you feeling all right, John?" Effie McCune said, as he sat preoccupied at his desk.

"Yes. Why do you ask?"

"You look a little peaked and distracted. Is something wrong?"

"No. Guess I'm a little tired. Stayed up too late last night."

His stomach was in knots. He could not concentrate. Yet he waited one more day, working up the nerve to break the momentous news to his parents.

The three of them sat at the breakfast room table eating ham sandwiches for supper. John had no hunger, and he only nibbled at his food. Herbert and Anna talked about the proposed rerouting of a highway on the edge of town, but he scarcely listened and said nothing. Compared to the confrontation just ahead, his meeting with Colonel Burkman now seemed like a breeze. When they had finished their sandwiches, he spoke up, first swallowing hard and taking a deep breath.

"I've got something I need to talk to you about."

"Don't tell me you've got an idea for a new column," Herbert said.

"No, I'm afraid it's more important than that." Then he plunged ahead, speaking rapidly and nervously, wanting no interruption until he got it all out. "For a long time I've been thinking about my future at the *Progress*. I thought about it a lot in the army, and I've been thinking more about it since I got home. I've wondered more and more whether I was cut out for newspaper work and whether I wanted to spend the rest of my life doing that in Remberton. Well, to make a long story short, I've finally decided that what I really should do is to study law and be a lawyer."

He stopped. His heart was beating rapidly. Only the ticking of the hall clock broke the silence. Herbert and Anna sat impassively—stunned, he thought. Then Herbert cleared his throat and spoke, slowly and softly.

"This is a pretty big step, a whole change in your life's direction. What makes you think it's the right thing to do?"

John explained his conversations with Carter Gordon in Japan and with Noble Shepperson and the reading and thinking he had been doing recently about the legal process. Not wanting to hurt their feelings unnecessarily, he said nothing about his attitude toward living at home or the detachment he now felt about the town.

"Well, John," Anna said, "you know we've always assumed you'd come back home to the *Progress* and eventually be editor. But"—he thought he detected a slight crack in her voice—"it's your life, and I want you to decide what's best for you and where you can make the best contribution."

He was in the midst of the moment he had dreaded. Disappointment was written all over his parents' faces as they sat looking at him. Again, he heard the hall clock ticking. "Well, son," Herbert finally said, "I wouldn't be honest with you if I didn't say that this bolt out of the blue is not what we ideally would have wanted. We just took for granted, without thinking about it, that the line of succession would continue. But I have to admit, deep down, that your mother is right. It is your life, and you have to make your own decisions."

"Actually, as I see it, the line of succession will continue with Frank and Becky here."

"Do they know anything about this?" Anna asked.

"Not yet. I wanted to talk with you first. I'm assuming that Frank will carry on, and the paper will still be in the family."

Herbert leaned back in his chair, took out a cigarette, and lit it. Anna sat unmoving, her eyes glistening with tears.

Impulsively, John got up and went around the table and gave her a hug.

"I hope you can understand, Mother. This is not an easy decision. I know you've always counted on me here, and I'm afraid I'm letting you down. But I'm convinced that in the long run it's the right thing to do. With Frank here, everything will go on in good shape." She pulled a Kleenex out of her dress pocket and dabbed her eyes, and he sat back down.

"This changes the whole ball game," Herbert said. "We need to talk to Frank right away. When are you thinking about leaving?" John detected a note of uncharacteristic irritation in his father's voice.

"They've invited me for supper tomorrow night. Let me discuss it with them then before you bring it up. I wouldn't be leaving until the end of the summer, so we've got a long time yet."

Anna, having recovered her composure, said, "I'll bet Noble talked you into this, didn't he?"

"Oh, no. Don't blame him. We did have some good conversations, but he never tried to persuade me about anything."

"What are your thoughts about law school?" Herbert asked, trying to make conversation.

"I haven't worked that out yet. I don't want to go back to Tuscaloosa. It's too familiar. Something new, a different setting, is what I want."

"What about the University of Virginia?" Herbert said.

"It's a possibility."

"You sit every day under a couple of its illustrious products," Herbert added. As John knew, he was referring to Woodrow Wilson and Hilary Herbert, both of whom had studied law at Virginia.

"Right. I'll begin looking into it."

Again, awkward moments of silence followed, and the ticking of the hall clock was the only sound.

John shoved his chair back and said, "I'm pretty tired. Think I'll go on up to bed. We can talk about this some more tomorrow." He kissed his mother and gave his father a hug across the shoulders.

Herbert said, "Good night, son."

The tone of voice and the look of ineffable sadness on his father's

face told John more than words could express: You are throwing
away what has been built over the last eighty years, what has been
handed to you to carry on, to serve this community and this state, a
solemn obligation you are now renouncing.

Upstairs in his bathroom he looked long at himself in the mirror.
"My God, I cannot believe what I've done. But it's done." Tears rolled
down his cheeks.

Chapter 18

THE FEBRUARY NIGHT WAS RAINY and blustery. Remberton seldom had freezing weather, but in winter it could be uncomfortably damp and chilly. John was at home alone. Herbert and Anna had driven to Montgomery in the afternoon to visit some old friends, have dinner out, and would be home late. John was slumped down in an easy chair in the den reading a book that Noble Shepperson had lent him to help him understand civil and criminal procedure. The more he read, the more he found his mind engaged in the niceties of legal process. Despite his nearly disastrous court-martial experience, he was coming to see a certain intellectual beauty about this rational construct designed to deal with irrational human behavior.

He had dropped his bombshell on Becky and Frank the night after he told his parents. Becky was as upset as his mother.

"John, are you serious? What does Daddy think?" Like their mother, she cried. "We've always counted on your being here. I can't believe it."

He tried to explain his thinking, going into it more fully than he had with his parents. She calmed down, and the three talked well into the night about the future, his and that of the paper.

"I'll miss you, but I'll carry on," Frank had said at the end.

Things had been a little tense around the house and the office for a few days after he broke the news, but he was relieved to see that his parents were gradually coming to accept the fact that he would be leaving. They did drop a hint from time to time that they

hoped he would eventually come back to practice law in Remberton. "I'm sure Noble would love to take you in," his mother said. To
this, John was noncommittal.

Once, his father had mildly tried to talk him out of his decision.
"I should have given you more responsibility," he said in a remorseful
tone. "Would it change your mind if I stepped aside right now and
turned all the editorial responsibilities over to you?"

John assured him that this had nothing to do with his decision,
that he had no complaints with the way they had worked. It pained
him to see the continuing disappointment in his father's face.

The hall clock struck 11:30. He read on for several more minutes
and then decided he was sleepy. No point in waiting up for his father
and mother. He left the hall light on and went upstairs to his room.

He was about to undress when he was startled by a loud, urgent
knocking on the front door. It reverberated through the hall and
up the stairs. No one ever knocked at the door this way; callers always
used the bell. And who could it possibly be at this hour of the night?
The knocking resumed, and he headed down the stairs.

Perhaps Korea had made him more cautious than he would have
been in small-town Remberton in past years, but in any case he called
out, "Who is it?"

Back came the answer in a male voice. "Officer Petty."

John had known him for years. Howard Petty was a state highway
patrolman who lived in town. Pulling open the solid wooden door,
John said, "Yes, sir, come in. What a raw night." The rain blew across
the porch as Petty quickly stepped into the hall and took off his cap.
John closed the door, and they shook hands.

"What can I do for you?" John asked.

Officer Petty, wet in his highway-patrol jacket and boots, looked
solemn and ill at ease. "John, there's been an accident up the highway involving your parents."

"Yes?" John said, apprehensively, "What happened?"

"They had a collision with a truck. Looks like the truck skidded
across the center line over on to their side."

"How are they?" John asked with rising alarm.

Officer Petty hesitated, biting his lower lip. "Well," he said slowly,
as though searching for words, "John, I don't know any way to tell
you this except to tell you." He paused, breathing in nervously and

swallowing hard. "I regret to say that Mr. Herbert and Miss Anna both died in the collision."

John was motionless for a long moment, looking into Petty's face. He half-whispered, incredulously, "Dead? Both dead? Are you absolutely sure?"

Petty nodded slowly before speaking. "I'm afraid so. It was a head-on. We got two ambulances out there with a nurse from the hospital as fast as we could, but it was no use."

The two men stood like statues, immobile, expressionless, neither knowing what to say or do. The wind-driven rain splashed against the windowpanes. Then the hall clock began to strike midnight.

In the days following that shattering news, John detached, moving as in a dream, unable to assimilate that his father and mother were suddenly gone forever, taken from him in the blink of an eye, abruptly and without warning. He had been in the midst of so much death, had brushed against it so intimately, that he thought he was inured to it. But this was different. Death had never before torn him apart as it had now done.

All during the day and into the night following the news and in the day and night after that, they came, a steady stream of the good folks of Remberton, flowing in and out of the Winston house on Taylor Street, bringing cakes, casseroles, fruit, and cookies. The typical outpouring of sympathy and friendship—mixed with a measure of curiosity—that erupted on the death of any well-regarded citizen was magnified by the shock of the double catastrophe. Becky moved back into the house to help deal with the callers, and numerous ladies—longtime family friends—took turns at the front door and at receiving the food. Annie May was on duty far longer than her normal hours. John spent much time in his room, coming downstairs at intervals to speak to the visitors.

All stores on Center Street closed the afternoon of the funeral. Newspaper editors from Montgomery, Birmingham, Mobile, and small towns in between assembled in a body as honorary pallbearers. In the church there was standing room only, and the crowd spilled out on to the sidewalk. At the front of the sanctuary just below the pulpit, the two caskets stood side by side, each covered by a huge spray of gladiolus and ferns.

Dr. Cowley's strong voice faded in and out of John's mind. "I am the resurrection and the life, he that believeth in me, though he were dead, yet shall he live . . . ." The assemblage sang with fervor, "For all the saints from whom their labors rest . . ." Music and words and readings came and went. More singing, "Faith of our fathers, living still . . ." Still more words and readings. Then the closing hymn: "Our God, our help in ages past, our hope for years to come . . . a thousand ages in thy sight are like an evening gone . . . Time, like an ever-rolling stream, bears all its sons away . . ."

The two caskets were rolled up the center aisle, followed by the pallbearers. The family was ushered out a side door and into waiting cars lined up behind the two hearses. The procession, over a mile long, moved down Center Street, quiet and deserted with all stores closed, and out to the cemetery.

The family sat in a double row of chairs beside the two open graves. John found himself sitting next to the weathered granite gravestone with the inscription:

> John Winston
> March 22, 1840
> July 6, 1930
> Major
> Fifth Alabama Infantry
> CSA

The crowd pressed in on all sides. A slight breeze deepened the chill of the February afternoon. The camellias were in full bloom, adding their colors of red and white and pink to the dismal winter day. Dr. Cowley's words drifted in and out of John's consciousness. ". . . with the sure and certain hope of the resurrection . . ."

At times over the next weeks John felt physically sick from the incomprehensible loss of his parents, especially at night when he was alone in the big house. He had illusions at times that his mother or father might walk in, that they were just downtown and would be home at any moment. He was overcome with remorse at having inflicted such pain and disappointment on them in their last days. If only he had waited, put off divulging his decision for a little while, they would never have known.

He felt a heightened sense of obligation to see to it that work at the paper went on without interruption. The time would soon come when Frank would have it all to himself, and he wanted to do everything he could to insure a smooth transition. In their wills, Herbert and Anna had left everything to John and Becky in equal shares. Sooner or later that would have to be sorted out. For the time being they agreed that Becky and Frank would move into the house when John left for school, but he would always have his room there.

Amidst all the grief and remorse and reordering of their lives, John had to give attention to law school applications. He pondered his father's suggestion of the University of Virginia. Carter Gordon had spoken fondly of it. But the very proximity of Carter Gordon and his connection with the school argued against it. He feared it would be an unpleasant reminder of his court-martial and the Korean experience that he hoped to put behind him. Also, he knew a couple of students there now. He wanted to get away from all connections with his former life. In the end, he applied to the Harvard Law School and was accepted for enrollment in the coming fall.

In the spring, Becky's baby was born—a boy weighing eight pounds, three ounces. They named him Herbert Winston Brandon and announced that he would be called Win.

John heard himself saying, unthinkingly, "Look's like we've got a future editor of the *Remberton Progress*."

The first year of law school was for John the most exhilarating intellectual experience of his life, an experience never quite equaled again. Classes and reading assignments were totally absorbing. He did little else but study, staying late into the night in the library. He learned the real meaning of that venerable adage, "The law is a jealous mistress. He who would win her must woo her . . . must live like a hermit and work like a horse." The all-consuming nature of law schoolwork alleviated the lingering grief over his parents and helped wall off the Korean episode.

It was in the class in civil procedure, a month after school started, that he was first called on. "Mr. Winston," the professor's voice boomed out. The sound of one's own name coming from a professor's lips was a sound that by this time every student had come to dread.

"Yes, sir," he said as he rose, trying to keep his voice under control.

It was a large, banked classroom, with about two hundred students.

"What has the due process clause got to do with in personam jurisdiction?" The professor stood behind a desk on a raised platform at the front of the room, his gaze fixed penetratingly on John, who felt very alone and vulnerable standing above the banked heads of his classmates, most of whom were thinking, "There but for the grace of God go I."

He gave an answer, not remembering later exactly what he said. The professor then pressed on. "Take this case," and he gave a hypothetical set of facts. "Is there jurisdiction over the defendant?"

John answered. "Then suppose that . . ." and some new facts were added. John was on his feet a good fifteen minutes. The ordeal was not quite like going up Hill 969, he thought afterward, but it was harrowing.

He had no doubt, though, that in the law he had found his calling. He was aware of the supreme irony that had he not been court-martialed, had he never known Carter Gordon, he would probably not be here, for that, he could now see in retrospect, was where the seed was planted. He must be the only member of his class, he thought, with the bizarre distinction of having been prosecuted for a felony, worse, a capital offense—a distinction they would never know about.

While he wanted to lock away the sense of guilt and remorse he felt over what had happened at Hill 1080, for a while he made an effort not to forget those lost men of Baker and Fox companies and especially Bruce Waller. Sometimes in the middle of the night he would wake up and think of Waller's wife and baby. He even had the idea of going home by Charleston on some future vacation and looking them up, but he never did. Then as time passed, his deliberate suppression of the court-martial caused all those other Korean experiences to fade.

One night in the winter he came back to his room earlier than usual. It was upstairs in a Victorian house on Highland Street, a twenty-minute walk from the law school. As he was settling down to study, he was called to the telephone downstairs by the ancient woman who owned the place. He wondered who it might be. He rarely got a phone call. He picked up the receiver. "Hello."

"John, it's Sally."

The surprise was total. He knew she was still in New York, but they had lost touch. He had not seen her since the night of that open house at Christmas over a year ago. "Sally Young! How in the world did you find me?"

"I called Becky and got your number."

"Where are you and what's up?"

"Still in New York. I hear you're just one of those serious and busy law students."

"I guess you'd have to say it's pretty serious stuff, and it keeps me right busy."

"Then you need a break. Listen, I'm in a group that's rented a house at Bromley so we can go up there and ski on weekends. I'm going up weekend after next. How about coming over?"

"I've never been on a pair of skis—except water skis."

"That doesn't make any difference. I hadn't either until last winter. They have a beginners' slope, and you can take instruction. Anyway, skiing isn't the whole thing." She laughed.

He finally agreed to come. It took more than two hours to drive from Cambridge. He arrived at dusk on Friday evening. Fresh snow was all around, and the temperature was well below freezing.

On the way over he had thought a lot about Sally Young. He realized now that his view of her had shifted, beginning, he thought, with her letters to him in Korea. When he got home she seemed more relaxed, not as snippy, ready to laugh more. Then there was the night of the open house when she asked to ride with him to the country club. He well remembered that little session they had in his car when he took her home, and he wondered as he drove through the western Massachusetts hills how much that had to do with his willingness to brave snow and freezing weather for a sport he cared nothing about, with a loss of valuable study time.

The turn-of-the-century farmhouse was a two-story frame structure set back from the road in a clump of trees, now starkly bare. His tires crunched over the snow-covered drive as he edged in beside three parked cars. The cold struck him almost tangibly as he stepped out of his car, provoking momentary, unpleasant memories of Korea. He picked his way as fast as he could over the icy snow, up the steps and into the house without pausing to knock.

He was in a large, plain, but comfortably furnished living room.

Logs blazed away in the fireplace. Several men and women stood around, talking. He saw Sally at the same moment that she looked over and saw him. She came rushing his way and gave him a warm hug. "Well, you made it! What does an Alabama boy think of all this snow?"

"Not much. But I guess it goes with skiing."

"Law school hasn't worn you down. You look great."

"Glad to hear it. You look right sharp yourself."

She laughed easily. "Come on over and meet these folks."

She led him by the arm toward the fireplace and introduced him. They were from the Midwest and upper New England. John guessed that although they were acquainted, they did not really know each other well.

They were having drinks. "What do you want?" Sally asked.

He would have liked bourbon but out of consideration for Sally's taste had brought a fifth of scotch. "I've got something here in my bag." He stepped toward the front door and rooted out the bottle. "Does Teachers pass muster?"

"It's fine, but you didn't have to do that. I've got some stuff."

"Well, I've learned that you can't know what to expect in these parts."

After one drink the group began industriously ladling out beef stew and then sat down at the one large table. The stew was wolfed down. Then some apple pie was brought out and consumed with like speed.

They sat on the chairs and two sofas for a little while, speculating over the skiing prospects for the next day and relating experiences on the slopes the last time they were there. Before nine o'clock they had all vanished, spreading out to the numerous bedrooms, leaving John and Sally alone.

"This beats all," John said. "I assumed this was going to be a big party weekend. My first break in months. Here it is Friday night and everybody's sacked out before the show's even started."

"I should have alerted you. These are serious skiers. Everybody who comes up here from New York on the weekends is the same way. They've gone to bed because they'll be up before daylight. I hate to tell you, but you'll be up then too. You're rooming with Joe, and he'll be rearing to get to the slopes by the time the sun's up."

"I guess that means we have to call it quits too."

"We probably should if we want to feel halfway decent in the morning. Now tomorrow night will be different. Sunday morning can be more relaxed, so we can make more of a party out of it Saturday night."

They chatted for another quarter-hour, and then she said, "I don't like to mention it, but I suppose we should get some shut-eye."

She moved around the room turning out the lights. "We leave one on here by the door."

"The last time I saw you," John said, "you asked me the question I'd like to ask you now."

"What's that?"

"How about a little good night kiss?"

"And what did you say?"

"I said, 'Why not?'"

"Then I'll say the same."

They hugged and kissed. "There'll be more time tomorrow night," she said in a whisper.

He found his room dark and heard Joe's heavy breathing. He located the next-door bathroom, then undressed and slid under the blankets.

Sally had been right. He felt as though he had barely fallen asleep when he heard Joe shuffling around in the pitch dark. Then the lamp was switched on.

"Time to rise," Joe announced in his Wisconsin accent. The voice had more life and cheerfulness in it than John thought natural or appropriate for the hour.

John joined the crowd downstairs for hurried coffee, doughnuts, and corn flakes, all gulped down. Then they were off to the slopes at Bromley, five miles away. Day was just breaking over the bleak landscape.

John rented skis, poles, and boots and signed up for instruction. All morning he went up and then down the short beginners' slope. Sally joined him a couple of times, but she stayed mainly on the intermediate slope. At lunch they ate hot clam chowder and then were back out. No long, leisurely lunch in front of the fire with a couple of beers, as he had envisioned. Only darkness forced them to the cars and back to the house.

The group milled around in front of the fireplace having drinks. This time John knew the system, so he saw to it that he and Sally had two scotches before the call came to sit down and eat. They had a mountainous heap of spaghetti smothered in tomato sauce. A couple of loaves of French bread made the meal, and there was apple pie again for dessert. Not long after they finished eating, John and Sally were once more alone in the living room.

"Do we have to go to the slopes tomorrow?" he asked.

She laughed. "You don't sound very eager."

"Today was a fine outing. Great break from the books. I'm glad you called. But when I was up around the Chongchon River in ten above, I swore I would stay warm the rest of my life. So I have a thing about snow."

"Well, it's certainly not necessary to go out there again. Everybody leaves right after noon anyway. Getting into New York on Sunday afternoon can be a slow go."

"I need to get on back to the books. Probably should leave before noon. Why don't we forget the slopes and enjoy the evening?"

She laughed. "Books over skiing? My, my! I know what the crowd upstairs would say."

"By the way, I didn't bring this scotch over here with the idea of taking any back. We need to give it some attention."

They went into the kitchen. John poured two drinks. She added ice and water. They leaned against the counter, sipping and talking about Remberton. She hadn't altogether lost her sharp tongue, and she was not reluctant to give a frank assessment of some of the town's citizens. Two years earlier John would probably have considered them sarcastic and unpleasant. Now he thought they were funny. They were less biting, and she was definitely mellower. He laughed more than he had in a long while, in fact, for the first time in several months. Harvard Law School did not afford many occasions for laughter.

They finished the drinks, fixed another for themselves, and went back to the sofa in front of the dying fire.

"What do you think you'll do after law school?"

"That's a good question. I'm not sure. A lot of students are all set to go to New York or Washington or Philadelphia or some other big city. Not many seem to want to go back home, wherever home is. They've got the Wall Street-type firms in mind."

"Does that appeal to you?"

"Not really."

"What about Remberton?"

"I doubt it. Too many ghosts there. I would always see my father coming out of the *Progress* office and see my mother there at the house. It's a great place to come from, but not to go back to, at least for me."

"That leaves you somewhere between Remberton and Wall Street. That's a big territory."

"Right. A big decision." He put his arm around her shoulders and said, laughing, "Somehow I doubt you're a Remberton type." She felt smooth and firm and warm under her sweater.

She laughed and put her glass aside. He had already put his down. He leaned over and kissed her lightly. "You know something?" she asked.

"What?"

"I've decided you're pretty nifty."

"Have you just decided that?"

"No. I've thought it for quite a while. I think it began to dawn on me on that last trip to Mary Esther. You've changed since then."

"For better or worse?"

"More mature. More serious. And," she paused, with a sly grin, "more appealing."

He looked into her dark eyes, ran his hand along her curly black hair, and kissed her again. "Let's move down where it's warmer."

They slid off the sofa on to the rug in front of the fireplace, where embers still glowed. She put her arms around his neck and pulled him to her. For a long moment they looked into each other's eyes. Then their lips met. All was quiet—the deep quiet of a frozen winter night—except for their whispering and breathing, the simmering of logs, and the rustling of clothes.

In later years, John looked back on that Bromley weekend as a watershed in his life. It had changed his perception of Sally Young. Maybe she had actually changed, but he doubted that she was much different. What had changed, he realized as he mulled it over, was himself. Korea, his parents' death, and law school in the East had all had an effect, although he could not quite say what it was. Whatever the explanation, he now saw her as a less abrasive, more appealing person than he had known before. What he had thought of as her sharp tongue he now saw as funny and interesting. And her undeniable physical charms seemed more pronounced than ever.

But the weekend had little effect in the short run. He again buried himself in his law studies, with virtually no social life. He and Sally kept up sporadic correspondence, and there were occasional long-distance calls. She and her roommate allowed him to sleep on the sofa in their apartment on East 86th Street when he passed through at vacation times, but he was too immersed in the law to run down to New York on weekends.

At the end of his first year in law school, John worked during the summer with an Atlanta law firm. At the end of his second year, he did his summer stint with a Birmingham firm. By the time he graduated and took and passed the bar exam, he had made the crucial decision: He would go with one of the large Birmingham law firms.

Along the way the Korean War dragged to its conclusion. On July 27, 1953—three years and one month after Kim Il-sung launched his surprise attack—an armistice agreement had finally been signed by the United Nations Command, the North Koreans, and the Chinese Communist forces. He had painfully followed the depressing news accounts of some of the bloodiest battles of the war, all for hills and ridges that might move the line a mile or so here and there, with thousands of casualties on both sides. He was heartsick but was so absorbed in his studies that he had little time to brood over something he could do nothing about.

It all ended with a whimper. No sirens sounded, no whistles blew, no parades welcomed the boys home—all in marked contrast to V-J Day in August '45 and November 11, 1918. The only discernible sound was a collective sigh of relief. No commiserating over traumatized and disabled veterans could be heard; nor was there a whisper of concern over the MIAs—more than 8,000—no demand that they be accounted for. South Korea had been saved from communism, and the Communists with Kim Il-sung still at their head were right where they had been. The line dividing the two was pretty much where it was on June 25, 1950. But it was over, gone, and soon to be forgotten.

Once John was settled in Birmingham and working hard to build a competence and reputation at the bar, he found that he was often lonesome, and his thoughts turned more and more to Sally, and their letters grew more frequent. A year later they dropped a bombshell: They announced that they would be getting married.

The news was the talk of Remberton. "I never would have imagined it," many said.

Jeanie Harris called John. He had seen her in Remberton only once since her marriage, and they exchanged genial pleasantries. He still carried a deeply buried hurt from her rejection—more than that, betrayal—and he was not eager to have anything to do with her. But she seemed to want to be genuinely friendly, as though to heal the breach.

"I want to have a party," came the soft voice over the phone, tinged with mock sarcasm, "and I'm going to serve gin and words."

"Words? What kind of words?" John asked.

"Your words. All those words you have to eat, after what you used to say about Sally."

He forced a half-laugh and said facetiously, "I can't imagine I ever said anything uncomplimentary about this fine gal."

"I could give you quite a list, but I don't think you want to hear it."

He considered for an instant telling her that she had some words to eat herself, but decided that this would sound like sour grapes. He didn't want to let her think that she meant anything to him. So he just chuckled and said, "Well, you ran off and got married, so what was I to do?"

On a visit to Remberton shortly after the news broke, John asked Becky, "What do you think Daddy and Mother would say about this?"

"I don't know what they would say, but I'm sure they would be quite surprised. They thought Sally had her eye on you for a long time, but they heard you throwing off on her all along." She paused reflectively, reminding him of their mother. "I'm wondering what you see in her now that you didn't see in her then."

"That's a good question. I've thought about it a lot. Maybe what's different is me."

"There's not much doubt about that."

The wedding was a large and splashy affair in Remberton. At her insistence, it was in the Episcopal Church. She had been reared a

Methodist, but in New York she had become fascinated with the Episcopal Church after attending services a few times with her roommate. John couldn't figure out whether she was attracted by the
theological doctrine or by the trappings of clerical garb and liturgy.

In Birmingham, they started out in an apartment near Mountain
Brook Village, the preferred beginning venue for many of the young
marrieds in the legal, medical, and business worlds. A couple of years
later, they bought a house in nearby Crestline Heights, typically the
next move among the same set. They anticipated, as did all their
friends, that children would be coming along. But time passed, and
there were no children. They were concerned and eventually sought
medical help. Tests suggested it was unlikely Sally would ever be able
to have children. They discussed adoption but with little enthusiasm.
John's disappointment was tempered by lurking but unconfessed
doubts over whether he would make a very good father, and he had
equal doubts about Sally as a mother. Gradually, they accepted the
fact that there would be no children. As the years went by, his practice grew dramatically, and they moved once again, this time to one
of the large houses on Cherokee Road, a pseudo-English manor
house set well back on a wooded hill. It was more house than a childless couple needed, but she wanted it, and he willingly went along.

The marriage was a bit odd from the beginning. He found Sally
interesting and attractive, had a genuine affection for her, and considered that he loved her. But in his heart of hearts he felt he was
never really "in love" with her. He doubted that he could fall in love
with anyone. After Jeanie Harris, he wanted never again to expose
himself to the possibility of being wounded in that way. The passion
that might otherwise have been focused on a woman was instead con-
centrated on the law.

Korea had erected an emotional barrier that the years had not
altogether removed and that he could not seem to cross. He had
long ago tried to put it out of his mind, but his effort was only partly
successful. There were occasional dreams or—more accurately—
nightmares in which bugles blew in the night, shells crashed around
him, and he saw men he had known, again and again Bruce Waller.
From time to time there would be a flash of recollection triggered
by something in the newspaper. Then, too, there was a tangible
reminder every time he combed his hair or took a shower. He found

it was not easy to live with a secret, telling no one and resolved to take it to the grave.

And so the years clicked by. He and Sally became involved in civic activities as his practice grew and professional standing rose. Their main recreational activity was tennis, often doubles with couples they knew. During his year as state bar president, Sally attended all the necessary functions in good style, laughing and talking with everybody. But in between those occasions she seemed depressed, and after the year was over she became increasingly morose and withdrawn.

He found it difficult, after years of detachment and preoccupation with work, to give her the emotional support he knew she needed and that he wanted to give her. He spoke confidentially about her with their Episcopal rector and a psychiatrist friend, but he got little help.

When she seemed low, he would ask, "Can you tell me how you feel?"

"No. Just don't feel good."

"Do you have any pain? Headache? Stomachache?"

"No. I don't know what's the matter."

Then came the day she drove to Montgomery for a church meeting. Hours after she was due to return, her car was found crashed into rocks down a deep embankment along the northbound lanes of the interstate. She was dead at the wheel. An exhaustive police investigation was unable to determine the cause. The weather was dry and clear. No other vehicle was apparently involved, and no mechanical failure in her car could be identified. An autopsy showed no trace of alcohol or drugs.

That had been more than a year ago now. He had been cast into despondency of a sort he had not known since Korea and his parents' deaths. He had led a secluded existence ever since, living alone in the stillness of the large, now lonely house on Cherokee Road, confining his activities to his practice and avoiding social occasions. Every now and then he went to Remberton and spent the night with Becky and Frank.

Each time, he visited the cemetery. There he would stand alone for a long while in the burial place of his forebears, close to the now-weathered granite markers on the side-by-side graves of his parents.

His attention, though, was focused on the fresh grave at the foot of his mother. The newly installed stone read:

Sally Young Winston
September 12, 1929
March 3, 1990

Lingering beside it, he would think of their life together, especially her last months. He should have given her more of his time and attention over the years, especially when it was obvious she was not well. Why hadn't he been able to get closer to her, to give her more love and emotional support? She had been a good wife, and he had tried to let her know of his gratitude. He missed her more than he could have imagined. His despondency was deepened by dark suspicions surrounding her death.

His law practice became all-consuming. Work was his refuge from grief and pain. And he avoided the darkness within by absorption in the woes of others who struggled against life's burdens and pitfalls.

But overnight everything had changed with that telephone call from Associate Attorney General Roger Evans at the Justice Department. The proposal that he be nominated to the federal bench had returned him to the land of the living. After virtually no hesitation, he enthusiastically embraced the prospect, deciding that becoming a federal judge was the right thing to do at the right time, the unexpected fulfillment of a longtime ambition. For the first time in more than a year, life took on a bright, positive aspect; there was again something to live for, a challenge to be approached with enthusiasm.

But the anonymous call from the drunken woman threatened his chance for the judgeship and indeed his career and his honor. The call had instantly peeled away the intervening years. Hill 1080 once more loomed before him—a forbidding landmass, high, steep, dark, ominous, the grave of Bruce Waller and most of his company, the grave of the men he had commanded, men he had abandoned. And looming up with it was the specter of that disgraceful court-martial made known to the whole world. Yet it was intolerable to think that a lifetime of honorable service in the law could be undone by ancient events on the other side of the world. In the short time since Evans's call, this judgeship had come to mean a great deal to him, and he would not lightly give it up. His dilemma was torturing, made all the more so because of his inability—or refusal—to discuss it with anyone.

As the days passed, though, he persuaded himself that the mysterious caller might never be heard from again. He began to see it as a phantom threat, a bogeyman that would never materialize. Without that caller, no one need ever know of that Korean episode. His anxiety subsided, and he determined to go forward with his life, to go forward with the judicial nominating process, with the exciting prospect of becoming a judge, and a federal appellate judge at that.

PART SIX
Reckoning

Chapter 19

AT HIS DESK A COUPLE OF WEEKS LATER, John perused the massive questionnaire he had just received from the Justice Department. Evans told him it was a routine questionnaire required of all prospective nominees. Burdensome, yes, but, he explained with an apology, an inescapable part of the bureaucratic process. Burdensome was an understatement, John mused, as he ran over the dozens of questions, page after page of probing into the details of his life: his practice, organizational memberships, family, financial holdings, physical and mental health, every place lived at since the age of eighteen, every job held. The minutiae were daunting. He could get all the information together, but it would take days, maybe weeks. However, if it had to be done as a ticket to the judgeship, then he would just have to do it.

But then, near the end of the document, his eye fell on this question: "Is there anything in your background that, if known publicly, would likely cause embarrassment to the administration or raise a question as to your fitness for the federal judiciary? If so, explain."

"Damn," he muttered, mild profanity having crept into his speech. Anything in his background? Only that which he had sworn to himself to keep secret forever. What do they mean by embarrassment to the administration, that amorphous entity sprawling across Washington? What about his own embarrassment? It was all the same, though, and he saw now with dismay that he could not escape what he feared. Forget the mystery caller. Here was the Justice

Department itself fishing for skeletons in the closet, and he had a beaut.

He pondered his options, trying to think clearly and rationally. He couldn't answer the question "No," as much as he would like to. To lie would hardly be the way to launch a judicial career. But to answer "Yes" could well be the end of his prospects for the bench.

He stood up and looked out the window, drawing a deep breath to calm himself. "Explain!" He muttered the word aloud with disgust. How could he explain to anyone today that complicated situation of four decades ago? He dropped back into his chair, clenching his teeth in frustration.

All the other questions he could answer without the least shadow of a worry. His life had been impeccable—impeccable, that is, with one glaring exception. But hadn't he been acquitted? Hadn't he received an honorable discharge? Hadn't history's judgment vindicated him? He knew, though, that the acquittal resulted from a quirk of fate.

He vacillated from one hour to the next and from day to day, putting off dealing with the questionnaire. When he imagined the outcome of exposure, he was convinced that nothing could be worth it and felt prepared to withdraw himself from consideration, explaining quite plausibly—though not truthfully—to Evans and the public that he had decided he really preferred to remain in law practice. He could then safely plod along in his well-worn routines and have nothing to explain to anyone.

But then he thought of those years stretching out ahead, years of doing over and over what he was now doing. He was increasingly certain that the judgeship was the natural next step in his career. Wearing the black robe would permit him to at last make good use of his life's experiences, experiences that had intimately acquainted him with the intersection of justice and morality, of chance and truth. In the days since Roger Evans's call, he had convinced himself that he would be a good judge. What's more, he wanted the position.

After days of tormented thought, he concluded that he had to go forward with the process, hoping to weather the exposure. But it was too painful and awkward to try to explain in writing what it was in his background that would embarrass the administration. He decided reluctantly that he should go to Washington and discuss the matter in person with Roger Evans, something he had determined decades ago that he would never do.

The office of the associate attorney general was on the fifth floor of the Justice Department building, a few doors from the attorney general's inner sanctum, along the wide corridor adorned with WPA murals. Its windows afforded a view across Constitution Avenue and beyond the row of museums to the Mall.

John sat in the reception room preoccupied by his upcoming conversation with Evans. He tried to read the morning's *Washington Post* but found it hard to concentrate. One of the two secretaries graciously supplied him with a cup of coffee. He sipped it, thinking it might reduce his anxiety. It's silly, he thought, for him, an experienced trial lawyer past sixty, to be nervous about this meeting, but nevertheless he was.

"Mr. Evans will see you now," the secretary said as she pushed the door open and stood aside for him to pass.

He entered a huge wood-paneled room with a high ceiling and tall windows. The furniture—upholstered in a colorful floral pattern matching the draperies at the windows—looked more like an upscale residence than an office. A gray plush pile carpet covered the floor. The decor was out of sync with his mood. Something funereal would have been appropriate.

A short, stocky man came from behind a massive desk. He had a shock of dark wavy hair and a pleasant open face. "Come in," he said, with a broad smile.

"I'm John Winston." They shook hands.

"Roger Evans. Great to have you drop by. We've heard some fine things about you. It's always good to see a prospective nominee in the flesh. Gives us a better feel for what we're getting." He steered John toward a conversational grouping of two wing chairs, a sofa, and a coffee table. Evans sat in one of the wing chairs, and John, following a signal, lowered himself into the deep cushioned sofa.

The secretary followed them over. "Mr. Winston, would you like another cup of coffee?"

"No, thank you. I'm fine."

"I think I'll have one, Brenda, if you don't mind," Evans said.

"I appreciate your seeing me," John said as she closed the door. "This is a new experience."

"You're not alone. It's new to everybody who comes through it. It can be trying, but most get through it unscathed."

John had checked out Evans in the lawyers' directories and found that he had been a partner in a medium-sized St. Louis firm concentrating on commercial litigation. He had the affability and appearance of a small-town politician.

Trying to hide his nervousness, John said with a smile, "I'll say one thing. You folks really know how to design a questionnaire."

"Isn't that a mess? This process has gotten more complicated over time. Forty years ago the people here in the department and the senators would have had a conversation, arrived at a nominee, sent it over to the White House, and the president would have made the nomination. Of course, there was an FBI investigation, but it rarely turned up anything worth talking about. Now it's gotten ridiculous— more checking out than necessary, a lot of duplication, too many cooks stirring the broth. But we're trapped in the system, so I'm afraid we have to ask you to do all that bureaucratic form filling. Here, let me show you one." Evans got up, went to his desk, and picked up a six-inch-thick bundle. "I won't tell you who this is, but he's a nominee for a district judgeship."

"I doubt that I'll inflict quite that much on you."

"From what we've learned, you should be an easy case. It's a pleasure to have one like that."

"That brings me to what I came to talk with you about. It concerns that question that asks whether there's anything in my background that might embarrass the administration."

Evans's countenance lost its sunny aura, and his bouncy voice switched into a serious mode. "Is there something there we ought to know about?"

Brenda returned and placed a cup of coffee on the table in front of Evans. He reached for it but said nothing. She turned and left the room.

John followed her with his eyes and waited for the door to close. Though he was older than Evans and a seasoned litigator, he felt like an embarrassed schoolboy about to confess to his teacher. He could hardly believe that he was about to divulge what he had thought he would never divulge, but he knew also that the moment of truth at last was at hand. He took a deep breath, exhaled, and began.

"I don't know how you'll assess it, but there is something I think I should tell you. If you want the whole story, it'll take a little time."

Evans, coffee cup in hand, leaned back in his chair with a resigned look, suggesting an apprehension that his dream nominee was about to go down the drain. "Go ahead. I've got all the time you need."

John cleared his throat and began. He laid out the whole story, from his conversations with Bruce Waller about his views of the war, through his meetings with Colonel Burkman, to his trial. He sickened and swallowed hard as he came unavoidably to the words "disobedience of orders" and "court-martial."

Evans listened attentively throughout. When John finished, he said with a sigh, "That is quite a story. We've seen a lot of unusual situations in these files, but nothing like that. Obviously, as you recognize, it could pose a problem. I should say there could be two problems—one here and in the White House, the other later in the Senate. In this job I always try to imagine the worst-case headline that might appear on the front page of the *Washington Post*. What comes to mind here is something like, 'Nominee for Federal Appeals Court Tried for Disobeying Orders in Korea.' You see what I'm saying?"

"I certainly do. That's why I'm telling you about it now. You should know that you are the first human being to whom I've mentioned this matter since the day I left Korea. Not even my late wife knew about it."

"I appreciate your candor. It's far better to know about it now than have it rise up and hit us over the head later. I'm not prepared at the moment to predict the reaction in the administration. It's clearly something we need to talk about."

Hesitating a moment, John found himself saying what he didn't really want to say. "I'm quite willing to withdraw my name if you all think that's the wise step to take."

"No, no. Don't do that yet. I want to talk to my assistant here, and we need to run it past the White House people. Do you object to that?"

"My concern is confidentiality. Can that be guaranteed? You can imagine what this disclosure might do back home."

"Confidentiality can never be guaranteed in this town. You've already seen that press leak. Unfortunately, we don't have any plumbers to fix those leaks. The last time that was tried, it didn't work out so well." They both smiled. "All I can say is this. I will keep this within as small a circle as possible. In the department that would be me and my assistant. In the White House it would be the counsel and maybe one other. They are all close-mouthed, but there's no absolute way to keep others from learning about it. Secretaries are involved in typing and filing. You've got to think whether you mind having it revealed, because, if it doesn't leak earlier, it could come out if we send your nomination to the Hill."

John nodded. "Yes, you can be sure I'm thinking about that."

"It would be helpful to have more details and some official documentation. Do you have anything like that?"

"We're talking forty years ago. So I don't know what I may have, but I think there's a transcript of the trial buried somewhere in a trunk. Would that help?"

"Right. That would be just what we need. Can you send me a copy as soon as you get back?"

"If it's there, I will. Now there's one more thing I should mention." He then described the phone call from the unidentified stranger.

Neither said anything for a few seconds. Evans drained his cup, put it on the table, his eyes squinting in hard thought, and said, "This telephone caller could turn out to be our major problem. Look at it this way. The White House crowd might want to go forward with your nomination without disclosing the court-martial. There would be no need to do so if we decided that it really doesn't adversely reflect on your qualifications to be a judge. I'm not at all sure that the FBI investigation would turn it up. They check military records but mainly to note the period of service and the character of discharge. Your record would show an honorable discharge. If that's the way the FBI report came in, the Senate Judiciary Committee wouldn't know of the matter, and you would zip right through . . . unless . . . unless this telephone caller breaks the news."

"Suppose the news comes out somehow in the Senate committee for the first time, and the senators or the press ask the White House why this information wasn't made known. Wouldn't that make the administration look bad?"

"We could handle that by saying that we examined the facts carefully and concluded that this long-ago incident had no significant bearing on your suitability for the federal bench, especially in light of your superb qualifications."

"Would that settle the matter?"

"Not necessarily. If some senator has a bee in his bonnet to get at the administration, he could make a big brouhaha out of it. It would have nothing to do with you. It would be a way of scoring some political points. And there are some senators like that."

"If I understand you correctly, you're saying that if this caller doesn't follow through on the threat, this court-martial episode might never be mentioned at all?"

"Right. Of course, I can't promise that's the way it would work, but there's a good chance it would."

"Well," John said, after a moment's silence, "I guess that's all we can do for the time being."

"I think so." Roger Evans rose, and John did likewise. They walked to the door, paused, and shook hands. "You look like my kind of judge," Evans said. "I hope it all works out."

"Thanks. I'll be back in touch soon."

Back in his office, John dived into the monstrous questionnaire-answering job, assigning a secretary the task of rooting through old files to assemble the necessary information. He wondered how many able and busy lawyers had declined nomination to the federal bench when confronted with this extraordinary volume of paperwork, just to reach the point of serious consideration, with nomination not guaranteed. Some of them might think that a judgeship was not worth the time and hassle.

He had mixed feelings about his conversation with Roger Evans. A cloud of fear hung over him, a vague apprehension that any day the episode might find its way into the news media. It would be a choice morsel for an aggressive and less-than-scrupulous TV or newspaper reporter. But at the same time, having told someone of his long-pent-up story gave him a sense of release, of having a burden lifted from his mind. There were moments when he actually felt good. After all, Roger Evans had not recoiled at his revelation, had not deemed it automatically disqualifying.

The evening after his return from Washington, the phone rang at his house. "Mr. Winston, this is Brenda in Mr. Evans office. Can you speak to him?"

He had not expected to be talking again to Evans so soon and had certainly not expected to be called at home at night. "Yes. Put him on." He glanced at his watch. It was after 8 P.M. in Washington. Those stories he had heard of long hours in the capital seemed to be verified.

Evans got right down to business. "John," the now-familiar voice said—first names came quickly and easily in Washington circles— "We've had a meeting on your situation. Before moving along we'd like to see what can be done to smoke out this person who called you and find out what he's really up to."

"Do you have some magic trick up your sleeve?"

"No, but we have various means of getting the newspapers to run stories. You've seen those lines that say according to sources that asked not to be identified."

"Yes, and they irritate me."

"I can understand, but they do have their uses. Our idea is to have a story about your rumored nomination run in some of the major dailies in your circuit and see whether that provokes another phone call."

"Suppose it does?"

"Our hope is that if another call does come, you can get more clues, enough to put us on his track or to help you to at least make an educated guess as to who he, or maybe she, is."

"It sounds like a long shot, but I can't think of anything better unless we forget that call and plow ahead."

"Well, I'll be frank with you. Some of those in the administration don't relish a committee fight over your conduct in the Korean War or your views about the war. If an open fight can be avoided, they are happy to send up your nomination, but if it can't, they are hesitant. They don't want to give those hostile senators any ammunition."

"When do you want to have the story run?"

"Within the next few days."

John hesitated, thinking about the reaction within his firm. "OK. Go ahead. My partners will be annoyed, and I sympathize with their view. But I myself don't see any great harm in another report of a rumor."

"Sorry about your partners. I know how they feel. You can always blame the irresponsible media and those anonymous sources."

Two days later, John was heading down the interstate highway to Remberton. He was going home to dig into a locked trunk in the attic, undisturbed for four decades.

It was late afternoon when he swung out of the line of tractor trailers and assorted RVs and cars into the Remberton exit. After stopping at two red lights and passing a shopping center, the Holiday Inn, Econo Lodge, McDonald's, Hardee's, Golden Corral, and Texaco and Exxon stations, he reached the tranquility of residential streets. Within minutes—he was always surprised now to see how small the town was—he pulled into the driveway of 53 Taylor Street The changes wrought on Center Street and out on the interstate had left this neighborhood untouched. Here all was as it had been for as long as he could remember.

He unlocked the front door with the key he always carried, stepped into the hall, and closed the door behind him. Becky and Frank were away on Ono Island. The quiet was tomblike; the thick walls shut out all external sound. Only the ticking of the grandfather clock could be heard, the clock that had been ticking all his life. He had the sensation of stepping into a time capsule. The voices of his mother and father came to him, and he could almost see them standing in the hall. He saw himself at the moment when he left for the army, and on the day he returned, Annie May—now long gone like the others—greeting him. "Is them army wools you got on, Mr. John?" He suddenly wished that Becky and Frank were here to dispel these ghosts crowding in on him from the long-gone past.

He found a bottle of Jack Daniels in Frank's well-stocked bar and poured a good shot into a glass. He went into the sitting room that Becky had redone with modern furniture. A television set had replaced the old cabinet radio. But his father's favorite chair was still there, the chair he always sat in to read the papers and listen to the radio, where he had sat on those long summer evenings of 1950 as they followed the news from Korea.

John sat down in that chair and sipped his drink. He leaned back and closed his eyes. Nostalgic thoughts flowed over him. The years of his growing up in this house passed mentally in review, along with

that time he had come back as a fresh and uncertain college graduate to work for the paper, supposedly its future editor, until a Sunday morning's events on the other side of the world changed
everything.

He got up out of the chair, walked back to the bar, and poured
another shot. It was high summer, still broad daylight at eight
o'clock. All the restaurants on Center Street had gone out of business, so he'd have to drive out to one of the fast food places on the
interstate. But he didn't feel like facing that garish commercial strip
that had grown up over the last two decades. Remberton, like countless towns all across the United States, had lost its center.

He found a pizza in the freezer and put it in the microwave. He
made supper out of it and a bowl of ice cream. He then went upstairs
to find the trunk and begin his search for the trial transcript.

When he unlocked the trunk in a far corner of the attic, he felt as
though he were exhuming a grave. He had packed and locked it
shortly before he left for law school, and it had never been opened
since. Through all the years he had kept the unused key with him in
a small jewelry box.

The hinged top creaked open, and the faint odor of ancient mothballs wafted up. There were his fatigues, khaki shirts and socks, the
dark green belted blouse, a pair of pinks. A box contained his
insignia: gold and silver lieutenant's bars, crossed rifles, the brass
U.S. for the lapels of the blouse, the row of ribbons, and the Combat Infantryman's badge. The medals themselves were there. Each
rested on satiny cloth inside a handsome box, much like those containing elegant pieces of jewelry at Tiffany's: the Silver Star, the Purple Heart, the United Nations Korean medal, and the army's Korean
campaign medal.

There were the two metal dog tags on their chain. Of all the items
in the trunk, these meant the most to him. They had been with him
every foot of the way, hanging around his neck, resting on his chest.
They had seen all the action he had seen.

He uncovered a large packet of letters tied with string. They were
the letters he had written his parents, all saved by his mother. He had
never gone back through them, and in fact he'd forgotten they were
here. He opened the first in the stack—they were lined up chrono-
logically—and began to read. Under the bare attic light bulb, sitting

on the floor beside the trunk, he became hopelessly engrossed in reading them. He had forgotten how he was careful not to say things upsetting to his parents, while still trying to say something of interest. He was struck by his optimism in the early letters, of his eagerness to participate in the U.N.'s reunification of Korea, and his vivid descriptions of rice paddies, villages, hills, and Koreans. The pungent smell of night soil came back. He found himself liking this young and idealistic letter writer, who seemed almost a stranger. But the last letter of that type was written on Thanksgiving Day, 1950, saying he would write again from the banks of the Yalu. After that there was a large gap before the letters resumed, and thereafter their tone was different. They were cautious, giving even less information about himself and the situation in Korea than the earlier ones. They gave no hint of the magnitude of the Chinese onslaught, of the disastrous withdrawal from Kunu-ri, or of the death-defying ascent of Hill 969. And there was, of course, nothing whatever about his court-martial.

He suddenly felt tired and emotionally drained. He'd been reading for two hours. He decided to go to bed, hoping to be fresh in the morning, when he would resume the exhumation.

He slept well in his old bed in his old room, long since redecorated by Becky and bereft of all the mementos of his life, pre-Korea. It was a neutral room now, devoid of personality, although the venerable magnolia tree still stood outside the window, and blue jays still squawked.

He rose, showered, made breakfast of instant coffee and toast with orange marmalade, and again ascended the attic steps.

Burrowing down deeper in the trunk, he came at last to the main object of this trip, the transcript of his trial before the court-martial. As he held the yellowing pages in his hand, chill bumps flashed over him. Here was the verbatim record of his darkest hour, a record on paper that had come from that very spot and had been prepared by human beings who had actually been there.

He took the transcript downstairs and settled into his father's chair to read. He put a yellow legal pad and pencil on the table beside him to make notes.

How quaint the transcript looked, typed on low-grade legal-size paper. Army typewriters, well-used and often battered, produced irregular lettering, looking primitive and antique. As he read, the scene and all the characters came vividly back to mind—the large windblown tent, the officers sitting behind the crude wooden bench, everyone dressed in identical fatigue jackets and trousers and combat boots. He had forgotten some of the details, and reading it now after years as a trial lawyer gave it fresh meaning. He had to agree that the prosecution's case against him was thin, but he was also startled at how he as a young lieutenant could have acted so brashly.

He wanted to put a hard, skeptical trial lawyer's eye on the proceeding and try to figure out whether anybody involved might have a memory of it and sufficient lingering hostility toward him to motivate an attempt to derail his appointment to the bench. So he went slowly through the transcript again. But he decided it was a hopeless task to pick out any likely suspects. Many of these people were probably dead now, and those still living would be difficult, if not impossible, to find. Anyway, he had no way of guessing motivations.

He went to the kitchen and got a Coca-Cola from the refrigerator. Becky and Frank had installed central air-conditioning, so the house was quite cool—almost too cool for his taste—even though the temperature outside was approaching ninety as the summer day wore on. He wanted isolation—he had parked his car out of sight in the back—and being shut up under air-conditioning served his purpose for the moment.

The pictures he found on returning to the trunk drew him ever deeper back into that time. One had been taken of the Baker Company officers when the unit was encamped at Pyongyang waiting to move north. There he stood with Capt. Howell Grimes and the company's other lieutenants. He had last seen Grimes on the desperate run south from Kunu-ri and never knew what had become of him. The other lieutenants were either dead or survivors of a Chinese POW camp. How young and carefree they all looked!

Another photograph, taken a few days after he joined Fox Company, brought back the grimness of the scene along the MLR. He and Capt. Bruce Waller and his platoon sergeant, Richard Alton, were in a trench just outside his bunker. Waller was, of course, dead, but he had no idea what had happened to Alton. He stared for some moments at Waller, seeing his face for the first time since they parted,

Waller saying, "I need you on 1080." He thought of that new baby girl, something that had not crossed his mind in years. What were they going to call her—wasn't it Henny? How old is she now? She had to be forty. God, how much time had gone by! A mature woman, having never known her father, she had nothing either to remember or to forget.

The last photograph—his father had said he ought to frame it— showed none other than General of the Army Douglas MacArthur pinning a Silver Star on the hospital robe of Lt. John Winston, the latter with an awed expression. With the picture was the citation asserting his "conspicuous gallantry." He could hear now the deep and resonant voice of the man wearing the small circle of five stars, "Congratulations, Lieutenant Winston." As he thought about this historic figure with whom he had at that moment stood face to face— the man who had proclaimed that "In war there is no substitute for victory"—all the ambiguities about him resurfaced—the military genius, the author of Inchon, who nevertheless had sent them unsuspectingly into the mouth of death.

He knew that most, and maybe all, of the men in these pictures were dead. It was startling to realize that he might be the only one of them still alive. For the first time in a very long while, he was remembering the men he had known and that host of other Americans who had died around him. Their country had forgotten them, and he realized with sadness that he too had largely forgotten them. The painful events of his last days in Korea and the shame of his court-martial had made him avoid all thoughts of that time. In locking away his personal secret, he had closed off remembrance of his fallen comrades, along with the idealistic young lieutenant he had re-encountered in these letters and pictures.

He could not have been closer to death—separated only by milliseconds and millimeters—yet he had escaped it and they had not. The old unanswerable question resurfaced: Why? He saw Dr. Tom Cowley sitting beside his sickbed soon after his return, saying in a quiet voice: Maybe you have been spared for some purpose we cannot now know and may never know. Here he was, though, sixty-three years old and unable to discern any divinely ordained purpose to his life. Sure, he had worked hard to improve the state's legal system, had contributed time and money to worthy charities, but there was nothing special about that; many others had done the same. If he had been saved from death all those years ago for some special reason, it ought to have become apparent by now, but he could not see it. Maybe Tom Cowley was wrong. Maybe his survival was nothing more than a fluke, sheer blind luck, with no meaning to it at all.

Replacing the photographs in their envelope, he came to the clump of his army orders, beginning with the order calling him to active duty and ending with the one sending him back to the states for discharge.

Clipped behind the last order was a slip of paper with his scribbled handwriting: "Christine Barnes. Apt. 3A. Corner of California and Leavenworth." A slight smile creased his somber face. Tina! All these years she had been tucked away in the remote recesses of his mind, to be remembered and fantasized about at odd times. Once when he was in San Francisco at a bar meeting, he wondered if she were still around, and he even walked by the corner of California and Leavenworth and scanned the names on the mailboxes, knowing he would not find her there and not knowing what he would do if he did.

He leaned back against another trunk and sat with eyes closed, reliving that lost time. The sluice gates of memory had been thrown open, and it all came flooding back: Baker Company on Hill 274, the gauntlet south of Kunu-ri, Fox Company on Hill 969. Howell Grimes and Bruce Waller were again alive in his mind. They should not be forgotten, he thought.

He got to his feet slowly, repacked the trunk, and closed the lid, again locking up the tangible remains of that searing experience, the greatest adventure of his life, but not now sealing off the memories. They were back in full force.

Chapter 20

JOHN SCOOPED UP THE RECEIVER. "An old friend of yours is on the line," the receptionist said.

"Put him on." It was a law school classmate, an Atlanta lawyer.

"Hey, John, you're in the *Atlanta Constitution* this morning."

"I didn't realize my fame had spread that far. What does it say?"

"It's a little thing on page two. Headline says, 'Alabama Lawyer, Korean War Veteran, Said to Be Next Federal Appeals Judge.' It goes on, 'A Birmingham lawyer, John H. Winston, is in line to be appointed to the vacancy on the U.S. Court of Appeals for this circuit, according to informed sources who asked not to be identified. Winston has been actively engaged in trial practice for many years and is a past president of the state bar. He is a graduate of the University of Alabama and the Harvard Law School. According to the sources, he had an outstanding military record in the Korean War, where he served as an infantry platoon leader. Once the FBI investigation is completed, the president is expected to send the nomination to the Senate. The court to which he is being appointed hears appeals from federal district courts in Alabama, Georgia, and Florida.'"

"Well, if the press doesn't treat me any worse than that, I can't complain." They chatted for a few minutes about the nomination and then hung up.

John had to chuckle to himself over the clever way Roger Evans had highlighted the Korean War angle in the headline, putting out the bait to entice the mysterious caller. But no call came.

Three days passed, and Roger Evans got him on the line. "Anything yet?"

"Not a peep. Where did the story run?"

"Atlanta, Birmingham, Montgomery, Mobile, Savannah, Jacksonville, Tampa, and Miami."

"That's pretty good coverage of the circuit. Either she hasn't seen the story or she's given up."

"Or she's just holding her fire until a later point. I don't think we can make much one way or the other by the lack of a call. Rather than spin our wheels I'd like to move to the next step in the vetting process, which is to get you up here for the interview."

"Interview? What sort of interview?"

"It's part of this elaborate bureaucratic process we talked about. All prospective nominees now have to be interviewed face to face by attorneys in the Department. This has to be done at an early stage, so I've got to ask you to come back for that purpose. The sooner the better."

A week later John was seated at a small conference table in a room on the fourth floor of the Justice Department, a plainer, more stripped down office than the ornate quarters of the associate attorney general. He was facing two young men and one young woman. The men wore starched white shirts, dark suits, and dark ties. The woman was in a female version of the dark suit with white blouse buttoned up around the neck. Her hair was pulled straight back. She looked very serious, as did the men. Not one, he guessed, was over thirty, and he doubted that any had ever tried a case or served in the armed forces.

"Mr. Winston," began the man in the center, who seemed to be in charge, "this is a routine interview, the kind we hold with all judicial nominees, or I should say, prospective nominees. DOJ and the White House will put the interview results together with your questionnaire responses, the FBI investigation, the ABA report, and other information in deciding whether to make the nomination."

"After working through that questionnaire, it's hard to imagine what other information could be needed," he said somewhat testily.

"The interview is designed to get at some intangibles, such as judicial temperament, judicial philosophy, understanding of the role of courts, and so on. Of course, we would not ask you to take a position on any matter that might come before the court. Do you understand?"

"I think so."

"All right, let me begin by asking you what you think the job of a court is in American society."

"The job of a court?" Are they joking? Is this a law school seminar?

"Yes. What is a court supposed to do?"

"Decide cases. People come there with controversies they can't otherwise resolve. The court's job is to resolve it for them."

The woman spoke up. "And how is the court supposed to decide the case?"

This was first semester, first year law school stuff. It was demeaning. "By deciding the disputed facts and applying the law to those facts."

"Where does the court get its law?"

And so the interview proceeded for nearly two hours. Finally the center man stood up, and all three shook hands with John. There had been no smiles, no jokes, no chitchat.

"Mr. Evans said he wants to see you. Would you like someone to take you up?"

"No, thanks. I think I know the way."

"Come in," said Roger Evans, rising from behind his huge desk. "How was school?"

They shook hands, and John said, "I don't know whether I passed or failed. They strike me as former law review types who got their questions out of the federal courts casebook."

"You've got it about right. When I first came here, someone said that we have a government of children. You can see what he meant."

"I hope you got my answers to the questionnaire."

"Yes, and the transcript too. Come over and sit down and let's talk about it." John sagged into the sofa, and Roger took a wing chair.

"The next step," Roger resumed, "is to get the FBI report. If that doesn't reveal anything about this court-martial, the White House would like to send your nomination to the Senate. The unknown factor is whether that person out there speaks up about this court-martial. If that should happen, the White House folks say they're prepared to meet it. In fact, they think there might even be some political mileage for the administration in having a nominee who thinks like you do about the Korean War, that we should have won the damn thing and gotten rid of the Communists while we were at it. Of course, we don't know what the committee would do about this if it comes out. It could get nasty. Now what do you think? "

John took a deep breath and exhaled. He was at the point of no return. "I've been thinking a lot about it. I've decided that I'm willing to take the risk and face up to it if I have to."

Evans nodded. "Good. We'll move ahead."

On a Tuesday morning six weeks later, in an ornate committee hearing room in the Dirksen Senate Office Building, the Senate Judiciary Committee concluded a hearing on pending judicial nominations. For the nominees—there were five—the proceeding had been nothing more than a formality. When the chairman gaveled the committee into adjournment, a mild euphoria came over John. All those weeks of apprehension were behind him; an enormous weight had been lifted. He had made it, free and clear, his Korean secret still safely buried, his honor and reputation unblemished.

Well-wishers gathered around him, laughing and shaking hands with congratulatory comments. He had to get used to the exhilarating idea that he was actually going to be a United States circuit judge.

Correspondents from newspapers in his circuit crowded in and sought statements.

"All I think it appropriate to say at this time is that I am pleased with the hearing. If the committee approves me and the Senate agrees, I look forward to serving on the federal bench."

Roger Evans came up from the front row where he had been sitting. "Congratulations. All is as we hoped. No surprises. It'll probably take the committee a couple of weeks to prepare a report, and then we could get a floor vote in another couple of weeks. So in a month you should be in position to put on the black robe."

The crowd had thinned, and they were gathering up papers and stuffing them into their briefcases, preparing to leave, when a woman walked up from the rear of the room.

"Mr. Winston," she said.

"Yes?" He saw before him a statuesque female in the mandatory dark jacket and skirt with white blouse.

"My name is Henrietta Waller."

For a long second he stared at her, his mind having difficulty coming to grips with the import of her words. Then he said slowly, in whispered wonderment, "Henrietta Waller?"

"Yes. Henrietta Waller from Charleston, South Carolina."

His eyes searched her face. In a soft voice, he asked, "Are you known as Henny?"

"Yes. Didn't you know my father in Korea?"

His eyes misted over. No words came to him. After a moment's hesitation, he reached out and took her right hand in both of his. "I cannot believe it. My God, Henny Waller!"

Roger Evans spoke up. "What's this all about?"

"It's a long story," John said, without taking his eyes off her. "Her father was my company commander in Korea. The finest officer I knew."

Henny and Roger Evans shook hands. "Well," Roger said, "I'll leave you to talk. I've got to get back to the office. We'll call you when we get the committee report."

He left, and Henny and John were alone in the now empty hearing room. "Sit down a minute and let's talk," he said, pulling a couple of chairs out from the table.

"So you're Bruce Waller's daughter?" he said, continuing to look at her as though she were a creature from outer space. She looked back at him with equal intensity. Her expression was serious and earnest, with no hint of levity. She nodded, and he said, "How did you know who I am and that I was here?"

"That's a little complicated. If you have a few minutes, could we talk in my office? I'm on the Antitrust Subcommittee staff, and my office is just around the corner."

"Sure. I'd love to. I've got plenty of time."

As they walked along the corridor, he said, "You say you're on the staff. Are you a lawyer?"

"Yes."

"Where did you go to law school?"

"University of South Carolina."

They went into a large room with several desks occupied by women punching away at word-processor keyboards. They passed through them and into a tiny room.

"This is my cubbyhole," she said as she closed the door. She went around the desk and sat down. He dropped into a chair facing her across the desk. On one side of her was a computer and on the other was a glass-fronted bookcase filled with Government Printing Office documents. On the wall was an abstract painting. The room had no window.

"Mr. Winston," she began, looking quite serious, "this is awkward for me to bring up, but I promised my mother I would."

Her cool and not so friendly air puzzled him. She paused, so he said, "How is your mother?"

"She lives in Charleston, alone except for a maid. She's not well."

"I'm sorry to hear that, but I'm glad to know she's still living."

For John, this scene had an air of unreality about it. His mind struggled to comprehend that this mature woman was Captain Bruce Waller's baby daughter. She looked younger than he knew her to be. But there could be no doubt about the connection. In her face he saw Bruce Waller's prominent cheekbones, wide, full mouth, and bright eyes, but in a feminine version, topped by a full head of auburn hair, swept back in a windblown fashion.

"To get to the point," she said, in a husky Charleston accent, "this is harsh, but I don't know any other way to say it. My mother believes you did a grievous wrong to my father in Korea, that you deserted him just when he needed you most."

The room went silent. John tensed. He searched for some appropriate words but could say only, "Why would she think that?"

"All I know is what's she's told me. Apparently she had letters from my father telling her what a fine officer you were, and then came a letter—the last she ever received—saying you had left him on the eve of this big attack, that he didn't understand it, that it was a serious loss at a critical moment. I'm afraid I have to say, to put it bluntly, that she blames you for his death."

John was stunned. He knew he had to stay calm. Keeping his voice level and low, he said, "Have you seen those letters?"

"No. Mama keeps them locked away."

"But how does this come up now? How does she know about me or this hearing?"

"Back in the summer she read about your nomination in the paper. She seems to have always had your name in her mind."

"What paper?"

"The Atlanta paper. She was visiting friends there."

"Had you heard her talk about me before now?"

"A few times vaguely in the past. But when she came home from Atlanta she was full of it, saying that you were not fit to be a federal judge. She knows both the South Carolina senators, and she was saying she was going to call them and tell them all about what you did to my father."

"Did she do that?"

"No, I talked her out of it, at least for the time being. I told her that she really needed to know more about the whole thing before she made such a damaging charge. I told her I would make a point of talking directly with you and hear what you had to say. She agreed to hold off until I could do that. So here we are, the first chance I've had. I'm terribly sorry to have to be the bearer of this unpleasant news. You probably don't need to be told that if she did call the senators, it could create problems for your confirmation."

"Yes, I don't have any trouble seeing that. So where does the matter stand?"

"I'm supposed to talk with you and then tell her what you say and what my reaction is."

They were startled by a knock at the door. "Come in," she called out.

A neatly dressed young man cracked the door and said, "The chairman wants to see the staff right now."

"About what?" she said, obviously not pleased.

"The markup tomorrow."

"All right. I'll be there in a few minutes."

The door closed, and she said to John, "This is a command summons, at least if I want to keep my job."

John was thinking fast. He couldn't leave the matter hanging like this. "Listen," he said with a hint of urgency, "we need to talk more about this. I'm staying over until tomorrow. Is there any possibility you could have dinner with me tonight?"

She looked quickly at her appointments calendar, then lapsed into thought for a few moments. He couldn't tell whether she was hesitating because she had a conflict or whether she was uncertain about wanting to have dinner with him. She turned back toward him and said, "I don't think dinner would work, but maybe we could meet again later this afternoon. I should be through here around four."

"That would be fine with me. I'm staying at the Hay-Adams. Why don't you give me a call there when you're available."

"All right. I'll call you."

She rose and gathered up a sheaf of papers and started around the desk. "Sorry I have to run." She didn't pause to shake hands, and there was still no trace of a smile.

From Capitol Hill he came back to the hotel, had a sandwich, and went to his room. He lay down, hoping to take a nap, but he was too disturbed. The nagging fear of disclosure that had dogged him for weeks and that had been lifted with the conclusion of the committee hearing that morning now gripped him again.

It was sad that this was the way he had encountered Bruce Waller's daughter. He would have liked it to be a joyous occasion. Instead, meeting her had brought him back under the dark cloud he thought he had just escaped. Worse than that, he was a man indicted by her mother for killing her father. No wonder she was so somber. What must she think of him?

Looking ahead, he was uncertain how to proceed. Somehow he had to convince Henny that he was not guilty. How much did she or her mother know? She hadn't mentioned the court-martial. Should he tell her about it? He regretted she was not available for dinner. If they could sit down in a more relaxed setting than her office, he might be able to break through her icy exterior and explain himself better.

He was half-dozing when the telephone rang beside the bed. He roused himself and picked up the receiver. "Hello."

"Mr. Winston?"

"Yes."

"I'm all finished now or will be in another few minutes."

"Could I get you to reconsider having dinner?"

There was a pause. "Just a minute." He heard a rustling of paper. Hesitatingly, she said, "Well, I guess now I can arrange that. We've taken care of the problem for tomorrow. What time did you have in mind?"

"Anytime. At your convenience."

"How about 6:30?"

"That's fine."

"Should I meet you in the lobby of the Hay-Adams?"

"Yes. I'll wait for you there."

He saw her come through the hotel's front entrance and walk briskly into the lobby—only five minutes late—her heels clicking sharply on the uncarpeted sections. From this distance he got a better perspective on her. She was of medium height and build. Beneath the dark professional suit, he detected the outline of a good figure.

They met in the center of the lobby and shook hands in a businesslike fashion. He said, "Shall we go right in to the dining room?"

She nodded, and they walked in that direction.

They were conducted to a table for two. The china, glassware, and cutlery all sparkled against an immaculately white tablecloth. The waiter laid menus and a wine list in front of them and asked, "Would you like something to drink?"

Looking at Henny, and thinking a drink might loosen up the situation, John asked, "What would you like?"

"What are you having?"

"A martini."

"Then I think I'll have a bourbon and water."

John was ill at ease. In view of the seriousness of the matter that had brought them together, he was in no mood for small talk. But after an awkward silence, he said, "That's quite a view," looking out the window near their table. Across Lafayette Square the lighted portico of the White House shone through the trees.

"Yes, it is," she said, seeming no more interested in small talk than he was.

"Maybe we ought to take a look at the menu," he said. Each opened the weighty listing of offerings.

When the drinks came, he said, "I was with your father the day he received word of your birth. He produced a bottle of bourbon—a rare item where we were—and we drank a toast to Henrietta Montrose Waller."

"I'm impressed that you remember that name."

"It was a memorable moment, something warm and personal in that grim setting. Anyway, to follow up on that toast, I want to propose a toast to him." He picked up the martini. "Here's to Bruce Waller, father of a fine daughter."

She looked slightly surprised and embarrassed. Saying nothing, she picked up her glass and touched his. They both sipped their drinks. She seemed to relax a bit, but there was still no smile.

"Those days are sharply etched in my mind," he said. "The experiences were so intense. Life was on the edge."

They again studied the menu. "What do you think you'd like to eat?" he asked.

"That salmon looks good."

"Fine. I think I'll have veal."

They sipped their drinks and continued to look at the menus. "You might want something to start with, an appetizer or soup or salad," he said. "They've got quite a list."

"I'll just have a green salad."

He was holding off plunging into the subject dominating his mind, the only subject they were here to discuss, until they were served, so he would not be interrupted by the waiter. In the meantime, he had to make up something to say. "Do you mind my asking how you happen to be in Washington?"

"No. When I graduated from law school, I married a man who was a year ahead of me. He had come here to work in Strom Thurmond's office. So I came up, first with a law firm, then on the Judiciary Committee staff, where I still am."

"What does you husband do now?"

"We divorced not long after that. The marriage was a mistake, and I think I realized it from the start. He was immature, didn't know what he wanted. He took up with a woman who worked on Capitol Hill, and that was that. Thank goodness there were no children."

The waiter reappeared. "Another drink?" Their glasses were nearly empty.

John would have liked another, but he thought it better to get on with the business at hand. "I think we'll just order dinner."

After they ordered, she said, "It's been quite a day. Meeting you was—I don't quite know how to put it—was an emotional experience, after I had heard all that my mother said."

"It must have been a pretty grim prospect."

"I tried to imagine what you'd look like."

"What did you expect?"

"I didn't expect what I see now. From Mama's talk, I envisioned a villain, perhaps a shifty, unreliable-looking character. I knew you had to be in your sixties, so I imagined an overweight slob, probably bald." For the first time, he thought he caught a flicker of a smile.

"Good Lord. You must have dreaded the meeting."

"I certainly didn't look forward to it. I'm not sure what to think until I hear what you have to say."

"Let me get right to that and tell you about your father and me and specifically about what bothers your mother."

"That's exactly what I want to hear."

"It will take a little while to give you the full picture, but I think that's necessary for you to understand what happened."

"Go ahead. I want to hear it all."

With the glow of the martini in his stomach, it occurred to him that wine might lighten up this odd confrontation still more, so he said, "First, let me pick out some wine." He looked at the list. "What do you know about Virginia wine?"

"Nothing. Never had any."

"Would you mind trying some? I've never had it either. Didn't know Virginia produced it."

"Sure. I'll try anything once."

The waiter arrived with their salads, and John ordered a bottle of Monticello chardonnay.

He finished off his martini and leaned forward, elbows on table, his eyes fixed on hers. "When I was with your father, it was my second tour of duty in Korea. To explain everything, I have to tell you about my first tour."

He began telling her the Kunu-ri story, recounting it in greater detail than he ever had before, telling her far more than he had ever told Sally or anyone else. He relived it, carried away by the rush of memory, sparing her none of the grisly details of killing and mangled bodies in the disastrous operation along the Chongchon.

He reached a stopping point. "I didn't really mean to get into all that. It just came out."

"It's fascinating, but grim and sickening."

He had barely finished his salad when the waiter put their dinner in front of them and filled their glasses with chardonnay. For a while they ate and said nothing. Then she asked, "Sounds like you were pretty badly done in. What happened to you after that?"

He told her about the Tokyo hospital and his recuperation, his stay at Camp Drake, and the surprising orders to return to Korea. The waiter appeared and pulled the bottle out of the ice bucket standing next to the table and refilled both their glasses.

"This gets me to your father. I was assigned as a platoon leader in his company, high up on the eastern side, right in the line—First Platoon, Fox Company, Second Battalion."

"Tell me about my father. What did he look like?"

"Tall, lean, rather handsome. You resemble him in the face. He was a crisp, businesslike commander, well organized. To me, he was the ideal officer. I thought he would surely be a general some day."

He described the attack on Hill 969, finding himself carried away by the memories of that deadly ascent, describing it in vivid detail. She was transfixed; her eyes never left his.

He finally paused, as though out of breath. The waiter emptied the wine bottle into their glasses and turned it upside down in the ice bucket.

He resumed in a calmer vein. "Your father and I hit it off quite well. The day he got word of your birth, we had a long talk in his bunker. He told me about meeting your mother when he was at The Citadel and how they were married in the chapel there. I got to see him more as a person."

"I knew him only through pictures and Mama's talk. I've never had a clear view of him. This helps a lot."

He was at last up to the point that really mattered. He would give her all the details, except the court-martial. As a lawyer, he was still intensely embarrassed over having been prosecuted for a felony. Anyway, it did not involve her father.

"After the operation on Hill 969, we got all dug in again. Then came word that we were being ordered to attack Hill 1080, a massive ridge in front of us. By this time I was convinced that it was pointless and immoral to waste lives on those hills, with no objective other than another hill. We were two days away from the attack, and I let all these thoughts out on your father. He understood me, but he really couldn't do anything but say that we had to obey orders. Then I did the most foolish thing I've ever done. I requested permission to see the battalion commander so that I could tell him what I thought. Imagine that—a lieutenant telling his battalion commander, a lieutenant colonel, how the war should be conducted! Your father thought that was crazy—and he was right—but he did arrange for me to see Colonel Burkman."

The waiter cleared the table of their plates and glasses. John ordered coffee for both of them.

Then he continued. "That meeting with the battalion commander was bizarre. I honestly can't remember exactly what I said. I did explain my views about the war, my frustration, and I told him bluntly that I thought the attack on Hill 1080 was wrong and would cost unbelievable casualties. God, it seems arrogant in retrospect, for me, a lowly lieutenant to be saying all that. He got angry, to put it mildly, a not surprising reaction, I might add. He ordered me to go on back to my outfit and get ready for the mission. I did. The next day your father sent for me and said that Colonel Burkman had relieved me of duty and ordered me to the rear. He had decided that I would refuse to do my duty, that I would disobey orders to take part in the attack." He sighed and stopped, looking vacantly out toward the White House.

She had not said a word for a long while, but she continued to stare at him. In a low voice she asked, "What happened then?"

"I went by your father's bunker to say good-bye. To my dying day I'll be haunted by something he said: 'I need you on 1080.' At that moment I would have given my right arm to stay."

His voice caught, and he paused for a moment. "I went on back to the CP, and Burkman told me he was relieving me because he could not be confident I would do my duty. He sent me on to the rear, and I never saw anyone from my company again. A week later I heard about the attack on Hill 1080. The casualties were high, more than half of Fox Company killed or wounded. When I found out Bruce Waller had been killed, I broke down. I had seen men killed all around me, but this was the first time I actually cried. I mean cried like a child. What got to me more than anything else was that his baby daughter would never know her father and that he would never see her."

He saw a tear roll down her cheek. She pulled a Kleenex from her purse and dabbed her face. They sat quietly, neither saying anything. The waiter set cups in front of them and poured coffee.

"Well," he finally said, "that's the story. I did not run out on your father. I was removed by Burkman. If I had not been, I would have been right there with him. Many times since then I wished I had been, and have condemned myself for talking to the battalion commander. I've sometimes wished I had died on the hill with Captain Waller. I've always felt guilty even though I know I didn't do anything wrong. Burkman was wrong in thinking I would have disobeyed orders."

She looked away from him and gazed out the window. He could see tears in her eyes.

He sat silently for a few moments and then said, "There's only one other person who knows of this episode beside you. That's Roger Evans at the Justice Department."

She turned back toward him. "I mentioned that Mama is not well. She has diabetes, and she had a mild heart attack a year ago. On top of all that, she has a drinking problem. She'll go along sober for days or even a couple of weeks and then go on a binge. It's hard to know how she'll react to anything. She's unpredictable and erratic. All of her family are gone, and she lives alone with a maid."

"I'm terribly sorry to hear that. During the first year or two I was back from Korea, I thought of going through Charleston sometime to see if I could meet the two of you, but I got busy and regret to say I never got around to it. Would it help now—at least help her understand what happened—if I were to go there and talk to her?"

"Hmm," she hesitated, "Maybe. But I better think about that some more."

"Didn't you say she was holding off calling the senators until you talked with me?"

"Yes. So I've got to let her know something or else when she's in her cups she might just haul off and call one of them. She knows Fritz Hollings best."

"I'm flying back to Birmingham in the morning. But if you think it useful, I could come to Charleston anytime. I've pretty much put aside everything else until this confirmation process is over."

"What about your family?"

"None of that around. Never had any children. My wife died over a year ago."

"Oh, I'm sorry."

"I'm getting used to it. Going on the bench—if I get there—will be a good tonic. Something fresh and challenging."

"Tomorrow is going to be a very busy day, so I must go. But I want you to know that I do appreciate your telling me all this. John Winston in the flesh is not the John Winston I was expecting to meet. It's something to talk to someone who knew my father in his last days. Mama is overwrought about this. Living alone she's let it build up in her mind." She pushed back her chair and stood up.

"May I see you home in a cab?"

"Thanks, but that's not necessary. I go around town at night by myself all the time."

"I'll at least get you in a taxi here."

They walked to the front entrance, and he had a doorman hail a cab.

As they stood on the curb waiting, she said, "It's going to take me a little time to absorb all I've heard tonight. I'll think about whether it would be a good idea for you to get together face-to-face with Mama."

He took one of his business cards out of his pocket. "Here's how you can get in touch with me. I appreciate your patience in hearing me out."

The cab pulled up to the curb, and he opened the back door. He stuck out his hand, and she clasped it briefly, saying, "Thanks for the dinner."

She got in, and he closed the door behind her. The cab lurched away, leaving him standing alone, puzzled over this enigmatic woman and wondering whether he had won his case with her.

Chapter 21

BACK IN HIS BIRMINGHAM OFFICE he plunged into the business of turning over all his pending matters to other lawyers in the firm. In the wake of newspaper reports of his trouble-free confirmation hearing, renewed congratulations poured in from all over the state and from law school classmates elsewhere. He felt a great sense of relief that he had made it unscathed through the Judiciary Committee. Yet his enjoyment of the moment was seriously dampened by the potential threat of Henny's mother.

A week had gone by since his dinner with Henny, and he had heard nothing. His anxiety was growing. He was tempted to call her, but he decided against it. Maybe no news was good news.

Then came a call from Roger Evans. He was not his usual jovial self. "John, something new has come up in the Judiciary Committee that we need to talk about as soon as possible."

"What is it?"

"I'd rather not go into it on the phone. I hate to ask you to do this, but can you come back up here right away?"

"If you think it's really important, I suppose so."

"It is, or I wouldn't ask you to do it."

John looked at his appointments calendar. "What about day after tomorrow?"

"That's fine. Would midmorning suit? Say ten o'clock?"

"Right. I'll be there."

He hung up with a queasy sensation. Had Mrs. Waller gone ahead and called a senator? Evans said it was something new. But what else could it be?

Late that afternoon while he was still worrying about what could have happened in Washington, Henny's much-awaited call came through.

"Mr. Winston, do you have a couple of minutes?"

"Yes," he said, trying to disguise his eagerness to hear what she had to say. She sounded less frosty than she had on their first meeting, but the "Mr. Winston" put him off a bit.

"I've been thinking about what we discussed and have finally decided that it would be a good idea for you to talk to Mama. I reported our conversation to her. She still has firmly in mind that you had some responsibility in my father's death, but she has agreed to see you."

"Good."

"I think I told you that she's unpredictable and has mood swings. So I can't guarantee how this will come out."

"I'll take my chances. When should I come?"

"I need to be there with you. Can you make it this Friday?"

"Yes. I'll have my secretary let you know my arrival time."

Waiting in the associate attorney general's reception room, he continued to puzzle over why he had been called back. It must be the court-martial. But if Mrs. Waller hadn't called, how could it have come to light? The FBI investigation hadn't revealed it; neither had the Judiciary Committee staff check. He could not imagine what else it could be.

"This is budget planning time, and things are pretty hectic," said Brenda. "All the divisions are trying to get more money." Two harried-looking functionaries emerged from Evans's room, one in shirt sleeves. Each carried an armload of files.

"All right, Mr. Winston," Brenda said, "you can go in now."

Roger Evans greeted him just inside his door and motioned him over to their usual positions on the sofa and chair. He immediately got down to business.

"I'm really sorry to burden you with this, but I thought it necessary to deal with it without delay." John nodded, and Evans continued. "To get right to the point, let me ask you this. Does the name Samuel Gilmore mean anything to you?"

John hesitated, furrowing his brow and thinking. "No," he said slowly. "Can't say that it does. Should it? How does it come up?"

"He's supposed to have been an enlisted man in your platoon in Korea, your platoon in Fox Company in September 1951."

"I tried to know the names of my men, but now I don't remember all of them. But why does this come up?"

"Here's the story. A staff lawyer on the Judiciary Committee called me and said that the staff had received a letter from one Samuel Gilmore claiming that you had threatened to kill him. He says that he was in your platoon and was attempting to get back to the medics to get a wound treated when you stopped him. He claims that you pulled your pistol on him and said you would kill him if he didn't get back up front. You shoved him back into enemy fire, and he was seriously wounded and paralyzed from the waist down. That's the essence of it. Under the circumstances, I'm obliged to ask you what you say in response."

John sat speechless for a long moment. "I hardly know what to say. I'm dumbfounded. My every effort was to protect my men, to keep casualties to a minimum. I never prevented any man from getting medical treatment."

"Do you see any possible basis for a report of this sort? Can you recall any incident that might lead a man to make such an allegation?"

For some seconds John looked through the tall windows at the sky. "The only thing I can think of is this. We had a problem with bugouts. When the going got heavy, with intense enemy fire coming in and men being hit all around, there were a few—fortunately not many—who would break and run. We were dealing with hastily trained draftees, some poorly motivated. My noncoms and I tried to stop it. It was not unusual for a sergeant to physically tackle a soldier who was bugging out. This was all in the midst of chaos, trying to hold together our line in the face of machine-gun and mortar fire. I can recall that on at least two occasions I grabbed a running man and forced him back forward. But I never stopped a seriously wounded man from getting medical attention. Scratches on the arm or leg didn't count. Everybody had those."

"Do you recall ever pulling a pistol on anyone?"

"That's possible. It's a life-and-death matter. There's no time to analyze and think rationally. I may have used my .45 a time or two to convince a man that I meant business. I heard of an officer who actually shot a running man when he couldn't stop him. I can understand that, but I never did it. The army doesn't like to talk about this sort of thing."

Evans had been gazing at the ceiling. He brought his eyes back to John. "You might recall that we talked about how hostile senators can take political potshots at the administration by digging up dirt on its nominees. This allegation gives them ammunition, if they're inclined to use it, and we don't know whether they are. I'm not even sure that any senator knows about it yet. This was a staff call. The reason for the call was to tell me about it and to ask whether I would be willing to get the FBI to investigate the matter. I thought I had no choice but to agree to that. The agents will interview Gilmore and you and get written statements. Can you think of any possible witnesses who could help you?"

"The only action I was in with Fox Company was on Hill 969. My platoon sergeant was named Richard Alton. From Kansas City, Missouri. I have no idea whether he survived the war. He was with me through this operation and would have likely seen anything of this sort."

Evans noted the name on a pad. "This one takes the cake! Here we've been worried all along about your court-martial. And we were barking up the wrong tree. My guess now is that this Gilmore was the unknown caller."

"No, that call was from a woman, and I think I now know who she is."

"Really! So who is she?"

"Well, I hope to be talking to her this week. If you don't mind, I'd rather wait until then to tell you about it."

"But does it have anything to do with Gilmore?"

"No, but I will let you know all about it after I talk with her."

After a momentary silence, John said, "This is really strange. I have no idea where this Gilmore thing came from. Do you think it's going to matter?"

"It certainly could. Imagine the headlines: 'Korean Veteran Says Winston Threatened to Kill Him,' or 'Nominee for Appeals Court Said to Have Threatened to Kill Soldier Under His Command.'"

"Not good," said John, shaking his head.

"The worst aspect of this is not so much the Gilmore problem but the fact that this new investigation will take them back to your Korean service, and sooner or later they're likely to stumble onto your court-martial. So I think there's a good chance we'll end up in the pickle we thought we had avoided."

"Do you think the White House will stick with me?"

"I can't speak for the White House, but I would guess that for now they'll stand behind you. We've come too far along the road to cut and run at the first few drops of rain. A lot will depend on the senators' reactions."

"I'm prepared to defend what I did. I had hoped the court-martial wouldn't come out, but I'm steeled to face it."

"All we can do is keep our fingers crossed and see if we can work this out quietly. If it gets into the press, all bets are off."

Henny was waiting for him at the gate as he emerged from the jet way. In a simple short-sleeve dress, she looked more feminine and less formidable than she had in the professional uniform.

"Hello, Mr. Winston. Was your flight all right?" She was more cheerful than she had been in Washington.

"Just fine. Is all well at your house here?" They shook hands.

"As well as can be expected."

They jostled through the crowd and headed along the corridor toward the baggage claim and ground-transportation signs. He had checked his bag through to Birmingham, so they made their way out of the terminal building and to her car in the parking lot.

John had to make a special effort to disguise the discouragement he felt after his meeting the day before with Roger Evans. He was now doubly burdened by this unexpected Gilmore complaint: the charge that he threatened to kill one of his own men, and the likelihood of the disclosure of the court-martial through the renewed FBI investigation. So even if Henny's mother could be mollified, the whole thing might still come to light and his appointment blow up in his face.

"It's fifteen years old," Henny said as she unlocked the doors to the Mercedes Benz. "But Mama's too attached to it to give it up."

She maneuvered the car out of the airport toward the highway.

"Mama tries to take a nap after lunch, so we should plan to see her later in the afternoon. In the meantime, is there anything you'd especially like to see?"

"As a matter of fact, there is. The chapel at The Citadel."

"That's easy."

After several miles she pulled off the interstate into the city streets. It was one of those delicious Charleston days of early fall, the summer heat gone, a cloudless blue canopy overhead, the air stirring gently. They drove along Moultrie Street, past the long wooded expanse of Hampton Park, and through the Lesesne Gate.

Immediately there opened up before them the sweeping vista of The Citadel's heart—the vast expanse of the grassy parade ground fringed with palmettos and oaks and bordered on the far side by the line of white, four-story barracks, their battlements suggesting Moorish castles.

Traffic was suddenly thick—pedestrians and cars. She said, "Looks like they're about to have a parade. It's quite a show. Would you like to see it? We can do the chapel after it's over."

"Sounds good. I like a little pomp and circumstance."

She turned into a rear area and parked the car. They walked along the road to the reviewing stands on the edge of the parade ground in front of Padgett-Thomas Barracks, whose tower dominated the scene. They climbed into the stands and took seats amidst the large crowd assembling.

"There's the chapel," she said, pointing straight across the parade ground to a tall building whose architecture carried a hint of the Spanish. Across the front, above the portico, were the words "Remember Now Thy Creator in the Days of Thy Youth."

He lapsed into silence and back into his foreboding. He knew the rest of the quotation from Ecclesiastes: "When the evil days come not . . ." Yes, in the days of his youth that's where it all happened, happened to that lieutenant who, from this vantage point of sixty-three years, seemed so very young, seemed now to be another person, not just an earlier embodiment of himself. Yet he was now being called upon to defend, to explain, the actions of that young lieutenant in a matter of life and death forty years ago. However unfair it might be, he would this day have to face a widow who had not forgotten.

The sound of bugles came from within the barracks, followed by an eruption of drums. The band emerged through a sally port and marched onto the field. Then out of the long line of barracks streamed the cadet battalions. In the autumn sunshine, the two thousand cadets, marching in formation with absolute precision, were a resplendent sight in their sharply creased white duck trousers, gray dress coats, white webbing, and shiny brass buckles, led by cadet officers wearing red sashes and carrying sabers. They gradually formed a long unbroken line facing the reviewing stands, stretching from one end of the parade ground to the other.

Shouted commands could be heard all up and down the line as the cadet corps took position. The band music stopped, and all was quiet.

Then a series of commands issued from the adjutant just in front of the stands, followed by a cacophony of relayed commands in the battalions. An artillery piece at the far end commenced firing a salute, a slow, measured series of thundering rounds, each booming and then echoing off the buildings at the far end, giving a double effect to each round. The sound took John far away, to the murderous artillery preparation on Hill 969, the explosions echoing up and down the valley.

Finally came the command, "Pass in review!" The band struck up its martial music with its throbbing drumbeat, and company after company passed in front of the reviewing stand, each responding to the command, "Eyes right!"

John looked at the fresh, intense, young faces . . . in the days of thy youth. Did they have the same innocent, idealistic views he had at their age and before Korea? Would any of them ever be called on to face what he had faced?

As the last company passed the stand, he roused himself and said, "You were right. That's an impressive show." He was glad to be here, glad they had happened upon the parade so that he could see and get a feel for the place where Bruce Waller had begun his military career.

They walked across the wide, grassy stretch of parade ground to the chapel doors and entered the long nave with its soaring ceiling. Stained-glass windows filtered the sunlight into a soft, ghostly hue. They walked slowly down the stone-floored center aisle. Overhead, along both outer walls hung the flags of the fifty states.

Near the front they sat down in one of the red cushioned pews. They were alone in the quietness of this vast space. For some time they sat in silence. John was absorbing the scene. High above the altar was a magnificent stained-glass window. He could barely make out the inscription underneath it:

> To the Glory of God
> and in memory of
> The Citadel's patriot dead
> this window is enshrined.

Here, it occurred to him, God and Caesar were in unusually close juxtaposition. Outside was Caesar—the rifle-carrying cadet corps, the flags, and the martial music symbolizing the armed might of the nation, ready on call to defend it against all enemies, foreign and domestic. But inside these walls was the realm of the spiritual. This entire edifice proclaimed that above Caesar's legions there is a higher authority.

In the silence and half-light of this place, where Bruce Waller and Nancy Montrose had been married four decades ago, John felt a strange closeness to that long-dead man. He saw again in his memory, as he nearly always did when Bruce Waller crossed his thoughts, that day of noise, death, and suffering on Hill 969, and he saw Captain Waller filling his canteen cup with bourbon to toast that new baby girl half a world away, the baby who was the mature woman now sitting beside him, whose body warmth he felt and perfume he smelled.

Her whispered voice broke the silence. "I think we should go along now."

In the car, they turned into Meeting Street, back into the eighteenth century, passing block after block of architectural gems, detached narrow-fronted houses with walled gardens in between. She parked along the street.

"Well, here we are," she said as she cut off the ignition. "Before we go in, I want to tell you that I read your entire file in the Judiciary Committee. I have a good friend on the staff who works on judicial nominations, and he let me see it. It has only a brief mention of your army service, no details. But it makes an impressive case out of your legal career. I can see why you're being nominated."

"I appreciate that. If the full story were in the file the picture might look a lot different. Right now, as I told you, only you and Roger Evans know the story. Unless you've told your mother."

"I have told her. I thought I had to."

"What was her reaction?"

"She's had so firmly in mind that you had something to do with my father's death that she has trouble seeing it any other way. She didn't say much, so I don't really know what she thinks. I suggest you get right to the crucial events she's bothered about."

"All right. Let's go in. I feel like a defendant on trial."

They went up three steps to the front door. It was a two-story frame house, flush with the sidewalk. It looked like all the other houses he could see as he looked up and down the street. Ahead, St. Michael's Church protruded over the sidewalk.

She unlocked the door, and they entered a long veranda running alongside the house and overlooking a small garden that extended to the windowless side of the house next door. The chirping of birds filled the air.

"Mama grew up in this house, and I did too. It's a typical sideways Charleston house."

Halfway along the veranda they went through a door into a large sitting room. "Mama," Henny called. But there was no answer. "Mama!" she repeated. Then, "Celie! . . . Celie!"

"Who's Celie?"

"Mama's maid and cook, been here forever." Turning to John, she said, "I don't know where they can be."

Abruptly, a door from another room opened. A woman middle-aged or older stood there looking at them. "Henny! It's you. Thought I heard somebody."

Henny looked disturbed. "Mama, where's Celie?"

"Let her go early. Didn't need her."

Henny shot an irritated and embarrassed glance at John and moved toward her mother.

"I told you to keep Celie until we got here," Henny said sharply.

"No point in it. Didn't need her."

Looking at John, Henny said, "Mr. Winston, would you come over and meet my mother?"

"Mama, this is Mr. Winston, John Winston. Remember I told you he'd be here this afternoon to see you."

As John came nearer, Henny said, "Mr. Winston, this is my mother, Nancy Waller."

"It's an honor to meet you," he said, extending his hand, which she took limply and without expression.

The woman standing before him had clearly seen better days. Her face had the leathery look that comes from too much sun tanning. Her hair, flecked with gray, could have used a comb. But he could imagine that thirty years ago this was an attractive woman, one that might have even had a regal air about her.

"I'm going to fix you some coffee," Henny said sternly.

"Too late in the day. What I need is a little wine. Matter of fact, I had a glass and don't know where I put it." She ran her eyes around the room. "Oh, there it is." She walked unsteadily to the mantelpiece and picked up a half-filled glass of white wine. She swayed slightly as she dropped into an armchair.

Henny threw a despairing look toward John and rolled her eyes. She motioned for him to follow her toward a side door. They came into a large pantry between the dining room and kitchen. She closed the door and said in a lowered voice, "I could wring old Celie's neck. I told her to stay here 'til I came back. But Mama probably ran her off. As you can see, she's half-drunk, probably been on wine all afternoon." Tears ran down her cheeks. "This is terribly embarrassing."

"Don't worry about it," he said.

She pulled a Kleenex from a box on the counter and wiped away the tears and blew her nose.

"Is there anything I can do?"

"Not much anybody can do," she said, still drying her eyes. "After she's started, she usually keeps on drinking until she falls asleep. I'm going to fix her a cup of instant coffee, but it won't do much good."

She put a kettle on the stove and ladled out a teaspoon of coffee into a cup. "Would you like some?"

"No, thank you." He leaned against the wall, wondering how this woman's inebriated state would affect the business he had come for.

Henny picked up the coffee, and they went back to the sitting room. Nancy Waller was still in her chair. He noticed for the first time that an opened wine bottle was on the table beside her. She refilled her glass.

"Here, Mama," Henny said, "put that glass down. I want you to drink this coffee." She put the cup on the table beside her mother.

John looked around. On a table behind a blue sofa stood two large framed photographs. One was of Bruce and Nancy at their wedding. The other was Bruce Waller in his West Point uniform. John stared at that face, the face of the man he had not seen since his parting in the bunker three days before his death. This face was slightly younger but very much the one he had known and the one imprinted on Henny.

"Have a seat, Mr. Winston," Henny said.

He let himself down in an armchair opposite the mother. Hoping to lighten the scene, he said, "I would feel more comfortable if you all just called me John. We don't need to stand on formality."

Nancy Waller ignored the coffee and took a swallow of wine. "Mr. Winston," she began, either not having heard his comment or choosing to disregard it. She spoke with a slow deliberateness, trying to articulate her words distinctly. She had a deep, whiskey voice. "You were with my husband in Korea, right?"

"Yes, I was. A long time ago."

"You don't have to tell me how long ago it was." Her voice was raised and irritated. "You were his lieutenant, his trusted lieutenant. He wrote me how much he relied on you. And then you ran out on him, left him when he needed you most."

He flinched, almost visibly, but his expression did not change. He wondered how it would be to talk with this woman when she was sober. Never mind, he had to deal with what was here. He had to stay calm, if possible. Henny sat impassively off to the side.

"Mrs. Waller," John said slowly and quietly, "I greatly admired Captain Waller, thought more of him than of any other officer I knew in the army."

"Then why did you do what you did?" Her voice rose still more. "Do you know Henny was only a month old, left me a widow with a month-old baby!"

"Yes, I know that, and back then I cried over it more than once. I want to explain. . . ."

"Now you want to be a federal judge?"

"I've been nominated to be one. I didn't seek the position."

"Do they know what you did? Do they want a judge who abandoned his commanding officer, left his men to die? Can a leopard change his spots?" Some of the wine sloshed out of the glass onto her lap.

"Mrs. Waller, Henny and I had a long conversation about this. Did she tell you how I explained what happened?"

"Sounds like you wormed your way out of the company just before the attack on Hill whatever it was."

"I didn't worm my way out. I was ordered out by the battalion commander."

"From what Henny says, sounds like you made up something to say that you knew would get yourself out."

Henny spoke up. "Mama, I didn't say that."

John said, "I felt strongly about wasting lives on pointless hill attacks, and I told him that."

"And you knew that would get you relieved!"

"That is not true." John noticed that his own voice was getting louder. "Maybe I should have known that's what would happen, but I didn't. I was young, idealistic . . ."

She took a swallow of wine and stared at him, her eyes boring into his. "Then you went on your way, merrily back to the rear, safe and sound."

That did it, triggered within him an irresistible impulse to complete the story, to get it all out. He stood up nervously, his back to the fireplace as though he were warming himself in winter.

"Listen to me," he said, looking down at her and speaking as he would to an obstreperous child, "I'm going to tell you a secret I've kept for forty years. I want you to know."

His loud voice, coming from his standing position, cowed her into silence. Henny's eyes were fixed on him.

"When the colonel sent me to the rear, it was not to a safe-and-sound sanctuary. It was to a general court-martial. I was formally charged with the willful disobedience of orders. The sentence could have been death."

Henny's lips parted in an inaudible gasp. Her mother sat somber and glowering.

"This is the most serious of all military offenses. If I had been convicted, I would have gone to prison, if not sentenced to death, and it would have ruined my life."

Nancy Waller, having just taken another swallow of wine, interrupted. "Guess you got out of that, too."

"I didn't get out of it. I was acquitted after a trial."

"Acquitted! My God, how could they acquit you?"

"Two reasons. It wasn't clear that I said I would refuse to carry out the order."

"Didn't the commanding officer say you refused?"

"More or less."

"Why didn't the court believe him?"

John hadn't intended to get into all the details, but he couldn't stop now. "The court didn't hear him. He was killed before the trial."

"My God," she exclaimed, "another officer killed, my husband killed, and you walk away. Never had to face up to what you did. And you think you're fit to be a judge! Somebody needs to know about this!"

Henny glared at him. "You didn't tell me about this."

"I just couldn't bring myself to talk about it. The trial didn't involve your father. But now I want to get it out so you'll know the whole story."

"But you don't want the committee to know, don't want it to block your appointment to the court, do you?" Henny said.

"No, I don't. I didn't seek this appointment, but once it was offered I came to want it."

"So when you say," Henny continued, "that you want to get the whole story out, you don't really mean it?"

Her words were like a jab in the stomach. They hurt. He was increasingly agitated. "I'm not sure what I mean. Am I guilty or not guilty? Morally or legally? Guilty of what? Of disobeying an order? No. Guilty of deliberately running out on my outfit? No. Guilty of saying something that I knew would get me removed before this horrendous attack? I don't think so, but who knows? Guilty of thinking the war was being run in the wrong way? Yes. Guilty of objecting to the slaughter of thousands of men for nothing more than another hill? Yes."

He was breathing hard, almost shouting. "I did my part! I gave it all I had!" He was losing control, just what he didn't want to happen.

Suddenly, impulsively, he dropped to his knees in front of Nancy Waller. "Look! Give me your hand!" He took her left hand and rubbed it along the right side of his head. "Feel that? Feel it?"

"What is it?" She spoke in a mumbled slur.

"The path of a Chinese bullet. One millimeter closer and I would have been dead instantly."

He jerked up his shirt and undershirt and pushed down the top of his trousers. "See, look!" The entire right side of his stomach, from his ribs down into his trousers, was covered with a purplish splotch of a scar, surrounded by irregular stitch marks. He grabbed her hand and rubbed it over the scar. She recoiled, quickly pulling it back. "Another piece of Chinese work. Two months in the hospital and weeks of recuperation. No, I paid my dues."

Henny and her mother looked at the scar in fascinated horror. Nancy Waller suddenly dropped the empty wine glass and flung her arms around John's, sobbing on his shoulder. "I'm so sorry," she gasped between sobs, "so sorry . . . I didn't know." Her voice was slurring badly now. He felt his own warm tears running down his cheeks. He ran his arms around her back and held her lightly. She mumbled, "But at least you're alive." She held on for another long minute, then slowly dropped her arms and slumped back in the chair.

In the silence John heard himself breathing. He remained motionless for some seconds and then slowly pushed his shirt back into his pants and got to his feet. He wiped his eyes with his handkerchief.

"Please excuse me," he said quietly with a sigh, looking at Henny. He backed up to the fireplace, regaining control of himself. "I could not have been any closer to death. But I survived, while a host of others right around me didn't. Why they died and Bruce died and I didn't, I'll never understand. The question has haunted me."

Henny, who had been riveted to her chair, now stirred and said, "I think you need a drink. I know I do. How about bourbon on the rocks?"

"Fine."

She left, and he slumped back down in the armchair opposite Nancy Waller. She had leaned her head back on the chair with her eyes closed, breathing deeply, her bosom rhythmically rising and falling. She was asleep.

John imagined the day this woman, then young and attractive, in this very house, maybe in this very room, with baby Henny in a crib, opened the telegram: "The Secretary of the Army regrets to inform you that your husband . . ."

Henny came back and handed him a short glass filled with bourbon over ice cubes. She sat down across from him with a similar glass. They both sipped in silence.

She was the first to speak. "Well, I hardly know what to say."

"There's not much more to say, I suppose."

They sat again in silence and sipped. Sounds of chirping birds drifted in through the open door. The afternoon had worn on toward twilight. Somewhere in the distance church bells were ringing.

After an interval he said, "What do you think your mother will want to do?"

"It's hard to say. It may depend on how much she remembers tomorrow." She paused reflectively. All was quiet except for the birds and the church bells. Then she went on. "After I read your committee file and thought about the whole thing, I decided that it would be a shame for this piece of ancient history to block your appointment."

"Do you still feel the same after hearing about this court-martial?"

"Yes. I don't think that really changes anything. I wish all our judges had the qualifications you do. So you can rely on me to stop Mama from doing anything to interfere with your confirmation. That is, I will do everything I can. She's not altogether controllable."

Her unexpected words touched him. "Thank you. I'm grateful for your help. I apologize for not telling you about the court-martial when we talked in Washington."

"I must say, it did come as a startling surprise. I thought you had told me everything. But I don't see that it matters. Is that the whole story?"

He thought of Sam Gilmore, now weighing on his mind, and was tempted to tell her. But it was unrelated, he reasoned, so he held it back. "Yes, as far as my relationship with your father goes, that's it."

He looked at his watch. Time to get going to the airport. But he didn't want to go. Here this afternoon, Henny had mellowed and smiled, had taken on a personality different and warmer from what he had seen in Washington. As she sat facing him, legs crossed, sipping her drink, he suddenly saw her not as Bruce Waller's daughter but as a mature, attractive, sophisticated woman. As he was thinking this, he became aware that this was the first time since Sally's death that he had looked at a woman in this way, his eyes contemplating her swept-back auburn hair, the swell of her bosom under the summer dress, and her crossed knees and legs. He was made slightly uncomfortable by a peculiar inner stirring he had not felt for a long time.

He rose, though, putting down his glass. "I have to run to catch my flight."

She stood up. "Normally I'd drive you to the airport, but I better stay here with Mama."

"I can get a cab at The Mills House." He extended his hand, and she took it. "This has been a memorable afternoon. Thanks for it all."

"Good luck from here on." She continued to hold his hand, making him aware of the warmth and softness of hers. "We'll be calling you judge before long."

"John will do." He smiled, and she smiled back. "I better run. Don't bother to show me out."

The two FBI agents from the Atlanta office sat in John's living room on Cherokee Road. They had found Samuel Gilmore staying at his mother's house at the edge of Atlanta and had interviewed him in depth. They showed John their written report on the interview.

The day on Hill 969 came vividly into focus. It was almost as though a videotape were being replayed in his mind. The head-splitting and deafening mortar explosions, the rattle of machine guns, the ricocheting bullets, dirt and rocks thrown up, men hit, screaming, and dying.

And, yes, he told the FBI agents, he did now remember running after a man who was bugging out. He had not known his name, and he saw no sign of any wound. He did put his pistol on him as a last desperate means of getting him back up front.

To John, the most disturbing point was Gilmore's claim that if he had not been prevented by Lieutenant Winston from getting to the medics he would not be in his fix today. By forcing him back forward, he said, Lieutenant Winston had fed him directly into a hail of enemy fire, causing him to be severely wounded and his spinal cord severed. He was paralyzed from the waist down and was confined to a wheelchair for the rest of his life.

"My heart goes out to him, but half the company was killed or wounded in that attack," he heard himself saying, "and I'm not responsible for this man's wounds anymore than for all the rest. It's only by the grace of God that I myself am sitting here today."

"We've done some checking on Gilmore," one agent said. "He's been in and out of VA hospitals for years. Apparently never held a job for long. Been on alcohol off and on, some evidence of hard drugs. It's a pathetic case."

John shook his head. "His situation is sad enough, but it's doubly upsetting when I hear that he blames me."

Several days later he was sitting in his office gazing out at Red Mountain and brooding over Gilmore when the buzzer sounded. "Mr. Winston," the receptionist said, "there's a man on the line whose name I didn't understand. He says he's a freelance writer and would like to speak to you."

"All right, I'll talk to him."

After a moment, a fast-talking, New York-sounding voice came on the line and announced a name that John couldn't catch either. It had a triple consonant Slavic ring. "I have information that the Senate Judiciary Committee has received a letter charging that when you were in the army in Korea you threatened to murder one of your own men. Could I have your comment on that?"

"Where did you get that information?"

"I'm not at liberty to reveal the source. I can say, though, that I consider it reliable."

"I have no comment. I do not think it would be appropriate for me to say anything."

"There's also information in the committee's hands that while in Korea you were charged with willfully disobeying the order of a superior officer and were tried by court-martial. Any comment?"

John's heart skipped a beat. He said nothing for a long second. Steadying his voice and trying to speak matter-of-factly, he said, "I have no comment."

"You have nothing to say at all on either of these allegations? They could be pretty damaging to your chances for confirmation, couldn't they?"

"I have no comment." Without waiting to hear more, he hung up.

Chapter 22

JOHN SAT MOTIONLESS FOR SEVERAL MINUTES, stunned by the telephone call. Here it is, he thought, at last. Probably inevitable. He'd been living in a dream world to imagine it wouldn't come out. He did the only thing he could. He got Roger Evans on the line.

"Well," John said in a resigned voice, "the fat's in the fire. What we hoped wouldn't happen has happened."

"What's that?"

John told him of the call. There was a pause at Evans's end and a long sigh.

"Damn! Must be a leak from the FBI report. It went to the committee yesterday, and I have a copy. They did uncover the court-martial. The report doesn't include the transcript. All it has is the charge and the finding of not guilty. I still hoped we could handle this in the committee without public disclosure. But that's not likely to work now. It's too good a story from a journalist's standpoint not to be run. Did he say what he planned to do?"

"No, and I didn't ask. I wanted to get him off the line as fast as possible."

"Then just sit tight. If nothing breaks in the press, we'll be OK, I think."

But hope along that line lasted only overnight. He had barely reached the office next morning when the telephone rang.

"Mr. Winston, this is Henny Waller."

"Well, how are you?"

"Have you seen what's in the paper this morning?" Her voice was frosty and formal.

He stiffened, fearing the worst. "No. What is it?"

"It's a report from an unidentified source. It says you were tried by court-martial for disobeying orders in Korea. Doesn't say how the trial came out. But then I was shocked to read that you threatened to kill one of your men in Korea and that you caused him to be permanently paralyzed. Is this true?"

"No, it's not. I . . ."

"You said you had told me everything. Is there still something else you haven't told me?"

"I told you everything concerning your father. But no, there's nothing else except my side of this new story. I want you to believe that I did nothing wrong."

"I'm beginning not to know what to believe."

"I'd like a chance to explain."

"Won't this be your third explanation? Anyway, I don't have time to hear it now. I've got to run to a staff meeting."

"May we talk later?"

"This is a busy time. I'll just have to see." And she hung up before he could say more.

He was shaken by her call, hurt by her tone of voice. Public disclosure of this damaging and embarrassing information was bad enough, but Henny's apparent anger and distrust bothered him as much, especially because he had sensed a different kind of Henny in Charleston. Somehow he had to get back in touch with her and try to explain the Gilmore thing.

In the meantime, he decided he had no choice but to tell his partners promptly. They would undoubtedly have the story through the news media before the day was out, and he had to get to them first. So with heavy heart and considerable embarrassment, he called in Joe Long and Dick Holiday and told them about his court-martial and the events leading up to it, told them about what he had striven mightily for four decades to keep from everyone, and then described the Gilmore episode.

They heard him out, expressionless. After some moments of silence, John said, "I'm sick about it all. I want to apologize if the two of you feel deceived. I honestly didn't think it should make any difference to our practice. After all, it's not as though I concealed a conviction."

"I agree," Joe said, "and speaking for myself, this news doesn't change a thing. You're the same person we've always known."

"I fully agree," Dick said. "We'll back you up."

"I appreciate that. It means a lot right now to have friends," John said, pausing and exhaling. "I think I should get away for a bit. Reporters are bound to be hounding me around here, as well as at the house, and I frankly don't want to see anyone right now, reporters or friends."

"That makes sense," Joe said. "You've pretty well turned over all your work here, so there'll be no problem. Let us know, though, if we can help."

From the mouth of Mobile Bay eastward, sugar-white sand beaches are splashed and pounded by the aqua waters of the Gulf of Mexico. For long stretches, human beings are scarcely to be seen. Here, alone with the sand dunes and swooping sea gulls, their squeaking cries barely audible above the wind and surf, John took afternoon walks. The beaches were not far from Ono Island in Perdido Bay, where Becky's cottage was. He had come here hoping to avoid contact with the world and to have time to think.

In the evenings, he sat rocking on the screened porch, listening to the night insects whir at full volume, the bay water lapping at the pier in front, watching lights twinkle on the far strip of land separating him from the Gulf of Mexico. A breeze rattled the wind chimes and brought the faint sound of pounding surf. It cooled his skin, sun-heated from the long walks on the beach.

On these lonesome nights, he found himself preoccupied with thoughts of Henny Waller. He wished there were some way he could get to her and ease her mind about the Gilmore story. He was worried that if she were sufficiently disaffected with him, she might change her mind and have her mother call a senator, or, worse, talk to a senator herself, presenting his conduct with her father in its worst light. Apart from that concern, however, he was upset over her coolness after the understanding and warmth she had shown in Charleston. He was increasingly aware that his interest in her was more than professional and was more than a concern for her simply because she was Bruce Waller's daughter. He wanted to telephone her but resisted the temptation, fearing that if he called too soon it might upset her more.

When not walking on the beach, eating, sleeping, and thinking, he spent time reading books on the Korean War. Within recent weeks, the subject had become a near obsession, as though he had to make up for all the years he had put it out of mind. Cut loose from his law practice, he had little to distract him from this pursuit. He read two books in quick succession: *The Forgotten War* and *This Kind of War*. Reading accounts of historical events in which he himself had played a part was a novel experience. He had always considered history to be about things that happened before he was born. But here was history he not only remembered but in which he had also been directly involved. He gradually came to see the event in a new light, saw it in a broader historical context than he had earlier, and gained an understanding of the many complicated nuances involved in the strategic and tactical decisions that were made. For it to be forgotten was ridiculous and shameful, he thought, in light of the war's significance in late-twentieth-century history. Something ought to be done about that. He had seen reports that a memorial was to be erected in Washington. He would have to look into that.

One morning, as he was finishing doughnuts and coffee, the phone rang with Roger Evans on the line.

"There's a little piece in the morning paper," Evans said, "obviously leaked."

"Well, let me have it," John said.

"Here are the key lines: 'Sources who asked not to be identified'— our old friends are still around—'say that the Senate Judiciary Committee is preparing to reopen hearings on the nomination of John Winston for the Eleventh Circuit Court of Appeals. Some members of the committee, according to the sources, are disturbed about the charges that have been made against the nominee and the mail they have been receiving. No date has yet been set for the hearing, but it is expected to be held in the near future.'"

"I guess that's no great surprise. Is there anything we can do?"

"I've just talked to a committee staffer. He says this news report is essentially correct, says the chairman wants to schedule a hearing in about three weeks. I think you should come back here for a strategy session."

They discussed dates, and John agreed to be there on the following Tuesday.

"In the meantime," Evans continued, "you might be thinking about the idea of retaining your own counsel. The administration, of course, is backing the nomination, and we'll do all we can to support you. But some conflict of interest might arise. It's not essential, but you ought to think about it."

Evans hung up, leaving John wondering. The idea of his own counsel had flicked through his mind earlier, but he had dismissed it. But maybe it wouldn't be a bad thing to do.

Who could it be? He wanted to avoid any entanglement with people in Alabama. Perhaps a savvy Washington lawyer? He didn't really know any very well. He mentally canvassed some possibilities. It suddenly came to him: Carter Gordon. Who could be a better choice than the lawyer who had represented him in the court-martial, who knew him back then?

But was he still alive? Still actively in law practice? He had communicated with him only twice after they had waved farewell on that airstrip in Korea. The years went by, and they lost touch.

John called his secretary and had her bring *Martindale-Hubbell* to the phone. A quick look showed that Carter Gordon was still in Richmond, now the most senior partner in his father's old law firm. The firm had an impressive list of clients and over two dozen lawyers. She gave John the phone number, and within minutes after they hung up he had Carter Gordon himself on the line.

"John Winston! Good Lord! How are you doing, old fellow? It's been a while."

"Maybe forty years. I'm fine. Spent most of my time trying cases. How about you?"

"Plowing along about the same. Easing up a little."

John would have recognized that voice anywhere, a bit hoarser, but still the same Tidewater Virginia voice he had known so long ago.

"Do you have a few minutes to talk right now?"

"Plenty of time. What's on your mind?" In the blink of an eye all those years vanished, and it was as though they had talked to each other only last month.

"Have you by any chance seen anything in the papers about my being nominated for the U.S. Court of Appeals?"

"No, but we lead a pretty provincial life here in Richmond. That's

fine news. Congratulations! Where does it stand? Have you been confirmed?"

John explained the problems facing him with the committee.

"My God," Gordon interjected, "who would have thought that old
court-martial would ever have come to light again."

"The reason I'm bending your ear about all this is to ask whether
you would consider acting as my personal counsel, if there's another
hearing."

"The Senate hearing room would be quite a change of venue from
that courtroom tent."

"You did such a good job there, I figure you can do the same kind
of job again."

"The judges are surely different—senators instead of army officers.
Politics instead of law. But if you want me to, I'd be willing to tackle it."

They agreed to meet at the Mayflower Hotel in Washington on
Monday evening to go over everything before their session with
Evans the following morning.

The conversation lifted John's spirits. Gordon had saved him
before; maybe he could do it again.

In the middle of the front lobby of the Mayflower, the two men
approached each other with dubious looks of recognition.

"Carter Gordon," John said. "It's got to be."

They smiled broadly and clasped hands. Gordon said, "It's not
the young lieutenant I knew, but it's John Winston all right. Or
maybe I should say Judge Winston." He slapped John on the shoulder. "God, it's been a long time!"

"You're pretty recognizable yourself." Gordon had flecks of gray in
his receding hair. He was a little chubbier, but the whimsical smile
behind the dark-rimmed glasses hadn't changed.

They walked the short distance to Duke Zeibert's for dinner. They
found a table for two in the nonsmoking area. A waiter immediately
appeared at their side. Gordon ordered a martini, dry and straight
up. John said, "Why not?" and ordered the same.

When the waiter returned and set the high-stemmed glasses down
in front of them, he announced that the special for the evening was
lamb chops. They nodded in acquiescence without even looking at
the menu.

They plunged into an unbroken stream of conversation, tracing their respective careers over the last three-plus decades.

Gordon described how he had come home from the army and gone back with his father's law firm, where he still was. He had a general practice, mixed litigation and office work. His parents were now deceased, but he stayed on in the house where he had grown up. He had never married.

"These days they're suspicious about that," Gordon said, "so I feel called on to say that boys are not my bag. In fact, I'm quite fond of the ladies. Twice I've been within an eyelash of getting married. Once I pulled out at the last minute. The other time my would-be bride backed off. I've just never gotten matched up with exactly the right one."

They were halfway through the meal before they took up the business that had brought them together.

"If I do say so myself," Gordon said, "I think I tried a pretty good case." John had sent him a copy of the court-martial transcript.

"It certainly got the right result," John said. "That trial had a significant influence on my career. After it was over, I got fascinated with the procedure, especially with the evidentiary questions. So you have to take a lot of credit, or blame, as the case may be, for my legal career."

"I have to keep reminding myself that the client in that case is now a veteran trial lawyer who knows as much, probably more, about litigation as I do."

"I've got you here because of that old adage that the lawyer who represents himself has a fool for a client."

"It's hard to argue with that," Gordon said. "Let's hope this time around works out as well as the last."

John nodded and smiled. "Another thing we talked about that has always fascinated me is the concept of justice according to law."

"It's important to keep in mind in our work. But you have to remember that what we face now is something different, and that is justice according to committee. All rules are off."

They rehashed the trial, recalling points that now seemed amusing, although they surely did not at the time. John described the statement from the ex-soldier Gilmore and gave his own recollection of the incident.

Gordon sat thoughtfully for a few moments, absently twirling his wine glass on the table with thumb and forefinger. Their plates were empty. "You know," he said slowly, "I think the best approach to this whole thing, the key to your case, is the same here as it was in that court-martial: namely, you. You and your record. I've always thought we prevailed in that trial because of you and your record, and my hunch is that will get us through the committee."

"I hope you're right. But this time we can't count on being saved by enemy action."

John, Carter Gordon, and Roger Evans had just sat down with coffee when a woman walked in. Except for the skirt, she might have been taken for a man. She was six feet tall, broad shouldered, with short, close-cropped hair. She wore the usual dark jacket and skirt and white blouse.

"This is Ramona Welch," Evans said. She shook hands with John and Gordon, who had risen from the sofa. She sat down in the wing chair opposite Evans. "She works with us on judicial nominations," Evans continued. "She knows more about this situation than anybody else."

Ms. Welch was all business. "The situation, as Roger calls it, is murky. The committee is split over whether to reopen the hearing. Their motives are mixed. Some are afraid of being accused of a cover-up if they don't have a hearing. Some also see a chance to embarrass the president. "

"What witnesses do they have?" Gordon asked.

"Except for Sam Gilmore," Evans said, "we don't know, and they don't say. There's no requirement that we have any notice of anything."

"When do you think the hearing will be?" Gordon asked.

"Don't know," Ms. Welch said. "As I said, there's no certainty there will be a hearing. It's all up in the air at the moment."

"Then I'm just hanging in the wind indefinitely?" John asked.

"I'm afraid that's where we are," Evans said.

"This is not unusual," Ms. Welch said. "Nominations have languished in the committee for a year or more. We have no control over it."

Evans said, with a sarcastic smirk, "That's the advise and consent role of the Senate that the Founding Fathers so wisely provided for."

They all sat in silence for some moments. Then John said, "Well, I've handed over my practice to my partners and I've nothing to do now, so I want to be sure about one thing: Are you and the administration fully backing this nomination?"

"The answer is yes," Evans said. "Of course, the White House has the final say, but I have no reason to think they're not behind you."

"If that's the case," John said, "I'm prepared to stay with it, at least for now. It seems to me that a withdrawal would be an admission that I'd done something wrong. Anyway, a lot of damage has already been done by the press stories."

"I've been hoping you'd hang in there. I hate to say it, but you've got to be prepared for weeks or even months in limbo."

"I've given up being a lawyer but am not yet a judge. It's not a good situation, to say the least."

After more discussion, he and Gordon left with assurances from Roger Evans that he would be in touch just as soon as there was something new to report. They came out at Tenth and Constitution and hailed a cab. They went back to the Mayflower Hotel and into the restaurant for lunch. As they ate, they reviewed the frustrating posture of the whole matter.

"A thought occurred to me in the cab," Gordon said. "There doesn't seem to be much for you to rush home for, so why don't you come on down to Richmond. I don't have anything pressing for the next few days. We could tour the Seven Days. You remember we used to talk about that?"

John thought for a few seconds as he chewed on an anchovy from his Caesar salad. Then, surprising himself at the rapidity of his decision, he said, "OK, I'll take you up on it. Sounds like a good idea."

It was late afternoon when they came off I-95 into Richmond. At the wheel of his BMW, Carter Gordon said, "We'll go along Monument Avenue on the way to the house."

In a few minutes John saw the first in the line of monumental figures: Lee mounted on Traveler atop a great stone pedestal bearing only that single, three-letter word. "Nothing more to say," Gordon said. Then there was the mounted Jeb Stuart, his statue capturing the flair of the dashing cavalryman, and then Stonewall Jackson on Little

Sorrel, eyes fixed determinedly ahead. Finally, there was the standing figure of the man who presided over the whole doomed effort, Jefferson Davis.

What if we were to create a monument avenue for the Korean venture, John mused to himself. Whose statues would be included? Obvious candidates were MacArthur, Ridgeway, Walker, Van Fleet, and Clark. But how should they be remembered? As victorious? Defeated? Stymied? He needn't worry: There would be no statues, no Monument Avenue to remind posterity of the Korean cause. It was not so much that the cause was lost as that it was inconclusive, unfinished. Americans still stood on the most heavily fortified line in the world, the guns quiet only because of an armistice, not a final settlement.

As Gordon pulled into the horseshoe drive in front of his two-story Georgian house in Windsor Farms, he said, "This is too much house for me, but I can't bring myself to give it up. My friends tell me there are some attractive widows who would like to join me here, so I keep thinking I should hold open that possibility."

They came into a hallway, and he led John upstairs to a guest bedroom. "Come back down to the library when the spirit moves you, and we'll plot our route for tomorrow. What would you like to drink? I have the usual stuff."

"Bourbon and water would be fine, thanks."

Ten minutes later they were in the library, a handsome wood-paneled room with bookshelves from floor to ceiling on two walls, a fireplace, several comfortable chairs, and a large desk. Gordon was seated there with a map spread out in front of him.

"Here's your drink," he said, handing John a glass surrounded by a paper cocktail napkin. "Have a seat and take a look at this map."

After a minute's scrutiny of the network of roads and place names east of Richmond, John said, "Can we do the Seven Days in order?"

"That's what I had in mind. We can at least hit the high points in a day's swing. But I want to alert you that a lot of what used to be open country and woods, more or less like it was in '62, is now full of commercial junk and housing developments."

That turned out to be an understatement. As they drove eastward out of Richmond the next morning, it seemed that they would never escape the late-twentieth-century sprawl. Where the armies of blue and gray had marched, fought, bled, and died, there were now shopping centers, trailer parks, fast-food places, filling stations, and motels. Historical markers along the highway from time to time in the middle of this clutter told them where they were and what had happened there. Beyond Mechanicsville the twentieth-century intrusions thinned, and they made their way to Gaines Mill.

"I have a soft spot in my heart for this place," Gordon said. "I had a great-grandfather badly wounded here. Took him out of the war. He lived forty more years, but they said he never got over the disappointment of missing out on the rest of it."

The day was crisp and sunny, but clouds were moving in from the west. The woods, flecked with their fall colors of bronze and red, were interrupted occasionally by fields of dead cornstalks. They drove on to White Oak Swamp, Savage's Station, and Frayser's Farm, stopping frequently to read markers, study the map, and get out and walk around. They twice crossed the Chickahominy. John was as excited as a child at Christmas at seeing these places for the first time, places he had been reading about since high school. At noon they stopped for a quick lunch at a McDonald's near an I-64 interchange.

"Both armies would have had a hell of a time crossing I-64," Gordon said in his whimsical manner. "Those eighteen-wheelers would have given them fits."

At midafternoon they approached Malvern Hill, the last of the Seven Days, where McClellan's army had fallen back and assembled a massive array of artillery. They were heading south along the Willis Church Road, beginning to ascend the long slope toward the Union batteries, the very route taken by the Fifth Alabama on the afternoon of July 1, 1862. He had read his grandfather's detailed account of this suicidal assault. An eerie feeling overcame him as he pondered the near certainty that his grandfather would have passed within a few yards on one side or the other of this very road.

The fall day had turned somber, the sky now solid gray with a portent of rain. They continued ascending the hill and reached the federal artillery positions. They got out and studied the maps and explanatory markers.

He stood among the cannon placed here by the park service to mark the line along which Union guns had been massed almost wheel to wheel. He looked down the long slopes, back down the Willis Church Road, across fields and woods stretching away into the distance, where the oncoming gray sea had broken under the murderous fire from this hill. Not one of the men in gray ever made it to the top that July afternoon.

There under the darkening sky in the quiet of the Virginia countryside, distant birdcalls the only sound, John envisioned the artillery shells pouring into the ranks of the attackers, just as he had experienced the North Korean mortars and machine-gun fire on Hill 969. He appreciated his grandfather's description of the death and dying around him as he never could have otherwise.

For a long interval they stood without speaking, looking up and down and across the once blood-soaked hill. Then John said slowly, "There's no getting around it. War is pure insanity."

"It's been around as long as we know anything about human beings," Gordon said. "But you would think that folks could figure out a better way to settle their fusses."

"It does seem so. But what do you do when Kim Il-sung moves south with tanks and 90,000 armed men? There was nothing left to do but fight or let the Communists have Korea."

As they walked in silence back toward the car, John wondered what Hill 969 was like today. It was unlikely that it was a governmentally maintained historical site. Maybe it was in the demilitarized zone, or even on the North Korean side of the line. What would it be like to climb again up its rocky side, through the stunted trees and undergrowth, to be again on the very ground where so many around him had suffered and died on that one unforgettable day in his life? It would, of course, now be deserted, he assumed, peaceful, and quiet.

Staying in Richmond a while longer would have been pleasant and interesting. Carter Gordon had taken him to dinner that night at the Country Club of Virginia and suggested other things they could do. But the seed planted in his mind at Malvern Hill—a curiosity about how those once scarred Korean hills would look today—had grown overnight into a firm conviction that he must go back and see. There was nothing pressing for him to do back in Birmingham, and the prospect of early action in the Senate committee was remote.

It was probably a crazy notion. He had seen photographs of the new Korea with its high-rise buildings and four-lane superhighways. Nothing would be as he had known it. And the idea that he could come close to finding the remote hills that he had once known was far-fetched. The country along the Chongchon was, of course, sealed off from the world by the North Korean regime, and those ridges in the east could lie anywhere north or south of the line. Yet he now found irresistible the desire to return.

So he caught a train back to Washington and spent the afternoon at a travel agency and at the office of Korean Airlines. He learned that Korea was not considered much of a tourist attraction. Most traffic back and forth was business and governmental. But this was not discouraging; it made the undertaking more of a provocative challenge, and he became determined to go.

Clutching travel brochures and airline information, he returned to the Mayflower Hotel a little after eight o'clock, having stopped for a light supper at a nondescript restaurant. As he was fumbling to get his key into the lock of his fourth floor room door, a voice from his rear said, "Lieutenant Winston."

Startled, he turned toward the sound of the voice and saw a man in a wheelchair rolling slowly toward him. "Yes?" he said hesitatingly.

"I need to talk with you," said the hoarse voice from the wheelchair.

The man had wispy gray hair and a sallow complexion. His face was thin and drawn. His eyes had a wild look, and he blinked nervously. He wore an old army field jacket.

John was uneasy. He thought the man might be on drugs. "May I ask your name and what you want?"

"My name is Sam Gilmore. You probably know what I want to talk about." His voice sounded like that of an old man. The suddenness of this encounter left John at a loss as to what to say or do.

"All right. Go ahead. What do you want to say?"

"We need a private place. In your room."

He didn't like it but what harm could there be in letting a wheelchair-bound man into his room for a few minutes? After all, he felt sorry for the man, and he might learn something that could later be useful. "All right, come in. I have some work to do, so I can't talk long."

John held open the door, and Gilmore rolled in. He stopped his chair just inside the door, which closed itself automatically. John walked past the wheelchair to seat himself across the room.

He turned around to sit and froze at what he saw. Gilmore was holding a .45 automatic pistol straight at him.

"You know what this is, don't you?" the man sneered.

The pistol swayed and shook as though Gilmore had a tremor in his hand. "I certainly do, and I think you ought to put it down."

"It's the same kind of pistol you threatened to kill me with. You remember that, don't you?"

He ignored the question and shot back, "Why are you pointing it at me and what do you want?"

"It's your fault I've spent my life in this wheelchair. I wrote letters about you, and those agents came to see me, but I know they're not going to do anything with you. They won't pay attention to anybody like me. Don't have any money, no political influence." He blinked nervously, and the pistol wavered in the trembling hand.

"Look, Gilmore," John said, making an effort to sound calm and reasonable, "we can talk all about it if you'll just put that pistol away."

Gilmore acted as if he hadn't heard John. "No, they're not going to do anything. So I'm going to have to take care of it myself."

He was standing about eight feet from Gilmore. At that close range the .45 had a powerful killing effect. It had saved his life when the Chinese were closing in.

"Gilmore, I'm sorry for you. God knows, I wish it hadn't happened. But it was the war, not me, that caused your injuries. Thousands of other men are in the same shape."

"I was on the way out of danger when you forced me back."

"My job was to keep my platoon together and carry out orders. I didn't treat you differently from any of the other men. I did what duty required."

Again, Gilmore seemed oblivious to the comment. "I've spent most of my life in VA hospitals, never married. Who would want to marry somebody like me?"

"That pistol is no way to deal with it," John said. "You'll only get yourself in worse trouble." He had decided to begin edging toward Gilmore so that he could make a lunge at the pistol and grab it. The tremor and wild rolling of the eyes gave him hope that Gilmore's reactions might be slow. He took a small step in that direction.

"Stand back," Gilmore commanded, surprising John with his alertness. "I won't be in worse trouble because I won't be around. My life is not worth living. But I don't want to end it without you. I've waited a long time to settle with you and Korea."

The sound from the .45 was deafening within the confines of the small hotel room. John felt the bullet tear at his coat sleeve and heard it smash the porcelain lamp behind him. The recoil jerked the pistol upward in Gilmore's hand. John sprang forward, knowing that he had an instant before Gilmore could level it again. His outstretched hands were going for the pistol as he saw the muzzle coming down at him.

An earsplitting report again filled the room. John felt a searingly hot and jabbing pain tear at the left side of his stomach. He gasped and went to his knees, falling against the wheelchair, grabbing the pistol with both hands and twisting its muzzle away from himself. Gilmore hung on tenaciously. Again it fired, within inches of John's face. Gilmore slumped and released his grip. The pistol fell to the floor, and all was suddenly quiet.

For long seconds John stayed on his knees, holding onto the arm of the wheelchair, his breath coming hard. He saw blood oozing from Gilmore's chest. His own coat had been ripped on the left side, and his white shirt was wet with blood. The pain was intense.

With great effort he pulled himself to his feet. He felt light-headed and unsteady. He careened toward the telephone on the desk and picked up the receiver. Black fingers closed in on his vision. The receiver fell from his hand, and he slumped to his knees. He fell forward on the floor, and all was dark and quiet.

Chapter 23

JOHN WINSTON OPENED HIS EYES. Overhead was a plain white ceiling. He heard stirrings around him, and a face appeared in his line of vision, the face of a woman wearing a white cap.

"Hello," she said in a pleasant voice. "How are you feeling?"

He said nothing, blinking his eyes. His mouth was dry, very dry, and had a chemical taste.

"Where am I?" He had a vague sense of having been here before.

She smiled and said, "In the intensive care unit of the George Washington University Hospital in Washington, D.C."

He put his elbows on the bed and sought to shift himself. Pain shot through his left side. "Ouch!" he gasped. "How long have I been here? What's going on?"

"They brought you in last night. You've undergone surgery and a massive stitching job. You had a first-class gunshot wound."

The ghastly scene in his hotel room returned. The last thing he remembered was staggering toward the telephone.

"There was another man. What about him?"

"They brought him in too, but he was dead on arrival."

A doctor appeared at his bedside. A surgical mask drooped just below his chin. His white coat looked ready for the laundry. He took John's wrist and checked his pulse. "You had a close one."

John nodded. "What's the outlook?"

"You'll be all right, but it'll take a while. Don't plan on any tennis for the next few weeks. The scar won't quite match that beauty you've got on the right, but it'll give you something to remember. Where did you pick up that other one?"

"Korea."

"Washington's getting as dangerous as a combat zone."

"This is a sort of carry-over from Korea, you might say."

The doctor described the path of the bullet through the left portion of the abdomen and how they had sewed him up. They would probably keep him here in the ICU for a day or two and then move him out to a regular hospital room. A nurse came in to give him a morphine shot, and the doctor left.

He drifted into a dreamy morphine-induced state he had not known for over forty years, not since he lay on that hard table in the confused clamor of the schoolhouse north of Pyongyang, with his right side torn open and the army nurse bending over him. For a while he was there again. It all came back: the bitter cold, the dirty, blood-caked fatigues, the moaning and screaming of wounded men lying on stretchers and makeshift tables, the evacuation south. If they could pull him through in that chaos with only a crude semblance of a hospital, it should be a breeze here in this state-of-the-art facility chock-full of high tech medical gadgetry designed to yank human beings back from the brink of death and preserve life against all the forces seeking to extinguish it.

It occurred to him that he had just suffered what could well be the last wound of the Korean War. There would, of course, be no Purple Heart, but Gilmore's demented attack inflicted a wound no less connected with the war than if it had been on Hill 969. It would indeed have been the irony of ironies if he, John Winston, having survived the Chinese and North Koreans, had been killed in the Mayflower Hotel by one of his own men.

Had he killed Gilmore? His hand had certainly been on the pistol at the moment the fatal shot was fired. His only consolation was knowing that Gilmore had wanted to end his own life. Indeed, given his condition and attitude, he might have been better off to have died on 969.

Roger Evans came by the day John got out of the ICU. "I thought I'd seen everything in this judicial nomination business, but this takes the cake. The problems we see are usually whiskey or taxes or women. This is a first."

John gave him a faint, forced smile. "The case was already complicated enough. Am I now sunk?"

"Only if it is determined that you committed murder. Do you want to tell me what happened?"

John gave him a blow-by-blow account of the bizarre encounter with Gilmore. "I think that his finger was the only one on the trigger, but I can't be absolutely certain. My reading is that he was intent on suicide after he took care of me. It's a fluke that I survived. At that close range a .45 is as deadly a weapon as you can find. From what the doctor says, an inch or two difference in the bullet's path would have done me in."

"Looks like you cheated the grim reaper again. How many times does that make?"

"More than I can count. I thought I'd faced the muzzle end of a loaded firearm for the last time when I left Korea."

"The police will investigate. I'm surprised they haven't been around to see you already."

"What effect will this have on the Senate committee?"

"No way to know at the moment. They can't very well hold a hearing until you're up and around. They've obviously lost Gilmore as a witness."

"This nomination is jinxed. Maybe I should consider withdrawing."

Evans took John's hand. "Now don't act precipitously. You have too much invested to throw it all away. I'm optimistic it'll work out well in the end, if you'll just hang in there."

John gave a long sigh. The pain was beginning to return. He needed another morphine shot. "OK. I won't do anything for the time being. As you see, I'll be in Washington for a while, so you can get hold of me here if you need to."

"We'll keep in touch. If there's anything we can do for you, let me know. And," he said as he edged toward the door, "keep up your spirits. The doctor tells me you're going to be fine."

Later that afternoon a nurse ushered into his room a black man of medium height, wearing a dark suit and tie and carrying a briefcase.

He introduced himself as Willie Reynolds, detective in the homicide department of the D.C. police.

The two shook hands, and Reynolds pulled a chair up close to the bed and sat down. He explained that he was investigating the events in the Mayflower Hotel room and that he would like to interview John to get his version of what happened.

"I'm ready to tell you all about it. You can skip the formalities. I know my rights."

Reynolds set up a tape recorder on the bedside table, and John gave his account.

"I hear you're a trial lawyer."

John nodded, and Reynolds continued.

"So you can see the main question here." He paused, and John nodded again. "Was Gilmore's death murder, suicide, a killing in self-defense, or accident? What do you say?"

He'd been giving that question a good deal of thought, and he was ready with an answer. "Either suicide or accident. The man was in a mood to end his life, but he wanted to take me with him. It's also possible that when we were struggling over the pistol it accidentally went off."

"We'll check out Gilmore's medical history. You can see the difficulty in this case. You're the only person who was there and still alive, and not without some self-interest."

"I get it, but don't jump to any conclusions."

"We get facts and then make conclusions. We'll write a report." Reynolds spoke mechanically, as though he were reciting a memorized passage. "If we conclude there's grounds to believe that an unlawful homicide was involved, we'll turn the case over to the U.S. attorney. Then it'll be up to that office to decide whether to proceed further or drop the case."

The words fell ominously on John's ears. He knew he was not guilty of anything, but the possibility that someone might think otherwise was disquieting.

Carter Gordon telephoned. "I told you that you should've stayed in Richmond."

"I thought the Korean War was over," John said, "but it looks like there was one more shoe to drop."

"Or, more precisely, one more shot to be fired."

"Actually, two shots. One for me and one for him. It's all terribly sad. But maybe he's better off. It was clear he didn't think life worth living."

Gordon suggested that John consider coming back to Richmond when he was released from the hospital and take some time there to recuperate. "You'd have this whole house to yourself, all day, every day. Peace and quiet. Good R and R."

"That's mighty good of you," John said, "but I think I'd better head back to my own turf."

Becky, who arrived after he came out of the ICU, had lifted his spirits. After three days John insisted that she return home. He assured her that he was coming along well. It was now just a matter of letting nature's healing processes work their way. She reluctantly agreed to go.

Just before she left, Becky said, "When they release you here, you can't go back by yourself to Cherokee Road. You'll be weak and need time to get your strength back. So I want you to come down and stay with us as long as necessary, until you're fully recovered."

"Thanks," he said. "I'll think about it. Look's like it'll be another week or ten days before I get out."

"I'll come back and fly home with you."

After she had gone, he brooded over the prospect. It would seem odd to pass a long series of days in Remberton, sleeping in his old room, eating three meals a day in the house where he had grown up, going about town. Since the day he left for law school he had been there only for occasional short visits. It would be coming full circle, going home again, to the place that was in his mind ultimately and forever home, albeit more than a full generation had passed away since he left. It might be pleasant, giving him time and space to recover physically and mentally and to sort things out. He would have to think more about it.

Indeed, as the hours and days passed he thought a great deal about a lot of things. He had unlimited time. He woke in the mornings, ate breakfast off the hospital tray, got washed up, put on a fresh hospital gown, read the *Washington Post*, slept some more, ate lunch, napped again, looked at magazines, ate dinner always served too early, caught the evening news on TV and a few other programs, and eventually fell asleep. In between, there were ministrations of pills and fruit juice and short visits from doctors and nurses, sticking thermometers in his mouth, changing the dressing, and wrapping his arm in a nylonlike sheath and pumping it up with a rubber ball to take his blood pressure. The daily hospital routine was unvarying. Despite its many interruptions, it left abundant time for brooding and daydreaming. Maybe his father had been right in saying that a man can have too much time to think.

In these long days and nights, the dominant thought in his mind was that this nomination for a federal judgeship had worked a radical alteration in his life, and for the worse. He was beginning to wish he had never heard of the idea, that he had never gotten that first call from Roger Evans. He wanted to throw in the towel.

He thought often of Henny Waller, wondering what she was doing and what her reaction to this latest turn of events might be. He fantasized about getting back together with her, wanting to see her again, hoping she would get over her disturbance with him. He considered trying to reach her on the phone but again resisted the temptation for fear of being rebuffed.

The pain in his side forced Korea back into his memory even more vividly. He thought especially of all those lost men of Baker Company moving on to their doom on Hill 274, the hell in the gauntlet south of Kunu-ri, that murderous day on Hill 969, and his descent into the toils of a court-martial. Why had that long-ago closed chapter risen now to smite him? It was as if the court of history was bringing some postponed judgment down upon him. He wondered what fate or divine providence might have in mind in this dismal turn of events. What would Dr. Tom Cowley say if he were here?

If God had stuck with him at Kunu-ri, he supposed that God would find it easy to be with him in this clean and tranquil hospital bed and in that lion's den of the Senate Judiciary Committee.

One day his reveries were interrupted by a nurse who stuck her head in the door and said, "There's a woman here to see you."

He assumed it was Ramona Welch. Evans had said she would be coming by to update him. He pushed himself up on the pillows and said, "OK, send her in."

But it was not Ramona Welch. Instead, coming through the door and toward his bed, to his amazement, was Henny Waller, smiling faintly but looking concerned, as though she did not know what to expect.

"Well! What a surprise!" blurted out John. "How did you find me here?" He smiled more broadly than he had in many days.

She came to the bedside and took his hand in both of hers. He was startled when she leaned over and kissed him lightly on the forehead. Her perfume was sharp and clean and slightly sweet. "It's been all over the papers. I couldn't get here any sooner because I've been down in Charleston. Look at this newspaper coverage." She pulled a sheaf of clippings from her pocket book and handed them to him.

The headlines were as bad as he had feared. One said, "Nominee for Federal Appeals Court Gunned Down in Hotel Room." Another said, "Judicial Nominee Shot, Another Man Killed, in D.C. Hotel Room." And worse, "Murder or Suicide? Candidate for Federal Judgeship in Hotel Shoot-Out; Investigation Underway." A subheadline said, "Dead man had accused Winston of causing him to be paralyzed for life."

After glancing at them, he said, "It's a wonder you'd ever want to see me again. In fact, after your last phone call I figured you wouldn't."

"I want to apologize for my rudeness. I had just seen this Gilmore claim in the paper and was upset. Now I've read the FBI report in the committee files, and I see the whole picture. But the important thing now is how you're doing. Tell me all about it." She pulled a chair up to the bed and sat down.

He gave her the whole story. Then they talked about the effect on the Senate committee.

"My staff friend says they've put it off indefinitely," she said, "but they do want to hold a hearing at some point."

"I'm ready for it now. In fact, I welcome the chance to state my case and tell the committee a few things they need to know about the war. It's funny that for so long I dreaded having all this brought out, and now I'm eager to get at it. I think my meeting with your mother changed my attitude about it." His old trial advocate's juices had begun to run again.

The conversation drifted over many things, and his spirits soared. He loved her soft Charleston accent and her slightly husky laugh. He asked about her earlier years.

She explained that when she finished at Ashley Hall, her mother
sent her off to Wellesley on the theory that she needed exposure to
another part of the country. Four years were enough, she thought, so
she came home for law school.

"While you were up there, did you ever meet any Harvard law students?"

"Yes, I certainly did. I know you went there, so I hope you don't
take offense when I say they were an arrogant and self-centered
crowd."

He laughed. "I know exactly what you mean." Then he asked,
"What were you just doing back in Charleston?"

She suddenly looked serious. "I'm afraid the situation with Mama
is getting worse. Now she has high blood pressure. Celie is getting
old and says she's got to stop working soon. The long and short of it
is that I've decided to move back and go with a law firm there."

"That's a big move," John said with surprise. "Are you sure you
want to give up the glamour of Capitol Hill?"

"There isn't much glamour there, mainly a lot of drudgery and a
bunch of people concerned about their own advancement. And endless politicking. It'll be refreshing to get away from it, back to a more
normal world. But I don't have much choice. Mama needs me
there."

"When will you make the move?"

"Right away. This is my last week on the job here."

As they talked, his eyes ran admiringly back and forth over her
thick, windblown auburn hair, blue eyes, prominent cheekbones,
full, sensuous mouth, soft creamy skin touched with pink from the
Charleston sun, ample bosom hugged by a white turtleneck blouse
beneath an unbuttoned jacket. He was aware of that same tingling
sensation he had felt on their parting at her house in Charleston. He
wanted to put his arms around her, to hug her, to squeeze her body
against his.

With some hesitation and uncertainty over whether to broach the
subject, he said, "When I'm up and around again, do you think it
might be possible for me to drop over to Charleston for a little visit?"

For a long moment she said nothing, seemingly at a loss about
what to say. Her expression became more serious. John instantly
sensed that he had made a mistake. When she finally spoke, she
sounded hesitant and uncertain.

"That would be nice, I'm sure. But all in all I think it would not be a good idea. Mama is really not in good shape, and it wouldn't be pleasant around the house. I'm facing a double challenge taking care of her and at the same time trying to move into a new career." She paused, licked her lips nervously, mustered a faint, nervous smile, and then added, "Besides, you're going to be starting a new career yourself. You'll be very busy as a new judge."

They both sat still. He closed his eyes and then opened them on the ceiling. His soaring spirits had been brought down to earth. His momentary hopes for a new and exciting relationship had been dashed. His immediate instinct was to try to talk her out of what she had just said, but his innate shyness stifled that impulse.

"Well," he said, with slow deliberation, "I can understand that. I must say, though, I'm sorry not to have the prospect of another visit. You're a fascinating person, good company. But I do wish you well, and I certainly hope your mother's condition improves."

"Yes." Silence again set in for some seconds. "Now I must go along. There's a lot to do to close out my work." She stood up and took his hand. "I know you'll make a grand judge, and I'll be following your decisions."

"Thanks." He forced a smile, trying to conceal his disappointment. "I'll always remember meeting Bruce Waller's daughter. It means a lot to me."

She lingered another moment, still holding his hand. He may have imagined it, but he thought he saw her eyes misting over. "I really must run. Good luck!" She turned and hurriedly left the room.

He was glad when the nurse told him that he could start getting up and taking showers, enabling him to escape the partial bathing he had awkwardly endured in bed. He began to sit up in a chair and to take short walks in the corridor. He spent more time answering telephone calls from friends wanting to wish him well.

Physically, he was feeling better. There was little pain left, and his strength was slowly coming back. "I'm still weak as water," he said to one of the nurses. "My mother's cook once said a chair'll rob you of your strength in a week, a bed in a day. She was right."

All of this should have brightened his days and lifted his spirits, but Henny's farewell had thrown a pall over his outlook. He could not understand it. It was clear, though, that she meant to cut off the prospect of anything developing between them. Maybe it was his age, he looking more like a father than a lover. Or there could be many other reasons why she didn't find him appealing. Indeed, as he thought about it, he could find no reason why she should. On the other hand, the explanation she gave could actually be the real reason.

In light of the apparent finality of her departure, he was surprised and puzzled when a half-dozen red roses were delivered into his room with a card reading: "Best wishes to a fine man and judge. Get well soon. Love, Henny."

Finally, the doctor said he would be discharged the next day. He called Becky and talked her out of flying back, explaining that Roger Evans would send a Justice Department car to take him to Dulles, and someone would be along to get him safely on the plane. She reluctantly agreed not to come, but only on the condition that he fly first-class for more comfortable seating and closer attention from flight attendants and that he have the airline provide a wheelchair for the change of planes in Charlotte.

When he landed in Montgomery, Becky was at the gate to meet him. She was the link between this moment and that long-ago homecoming when, as a bubbly, pregnant young wife, she had been there then to meet the young lieutenant on the railroad station platform. Now, as a middle-aged woman, she was here in the airport terminal to meet the would-be U.S. circuit judge. These two men, though inhabiting the same body, were not the same. Decades had transformed one into the other, but the shadow of Korea lay over them both.

Within an hour they pulled into the driveway of the house on Taylor Street in Remberton, the house to which they had driven together from the railroad station all those years ago. Once again, he was home.

For the first few days he slept late and came down for breakfast with Becky after Frank had left for work. He had to reaccustom himself to having the big meal in the middle of the day. Becky had a cook who came and prepared it, then cleaned up and left at midafternoon, Monday through Friday. He found it unexpectedly pleasant to be living in a normally functioning household for the first time since Sally's death.

These were fine autumn days, mild and often sunny, sometimes cool but never cold. The camellias were beginning to bloom, promising a glorious profusion of color through the coming winter. Squirrels scampered among fallen acorns, in and out of the trees. Hunting season was in full swing, but he had long ago lost interest in it.

His strength grew, and he lengthened his walks, extending his outings through streets he had known all his life. He was seeing Remberton more closely than he had since leaving for law school, as he had not since then had such an extended time here. He knew every house along his route. What he knew, though, was who lived there forty years ago. Many had changed hands, and he was unfamiliar with the new inhabitants. Some were strangers who had moved into town from elsewhere. Others were children, or even grandchildren, of his contemporaries. More and more he became aware of the passage of time, of the passing of the generation ahead of him and of his own generation too. The business and professional people, the people who ran the place, were now a new and younger crop.

When he walked the full length of Center Street from the courthouse to the railroad station, where weeds now grew in the cracks of the deserted and unused platform, he passed hardly a store that was what he had known. Either the building was shut up and empty, victim of the shopping center out on the interstate highway, or was occupied by something entirely different. The merchants he had known so well were no longer there, and the parents of his friends were gone. The only evidence of their having lived was in the cemetery.

He felt he was in their midst when he stood there at the Winston plot. He could have hit the graves of nearly all with the strong heave of a baseball. Over there was Dr. Lucius Craighill, and just here was Noble Shepperson. Two lots beyond was his law partner, Edward Kirkman. Off to the left was the druggist, and in the next plot was the family that had run the leading clothing store. A little way toward the gate was Jeanie's father, Ben Harris, one of his favorite men around town. Near him was Dr. Tom Cowley, gone to his sure and certain reward. In the other direction, a few plots away, were Sally's parents.

John found a curious kind of solace in the cemetery. He felt at home there, with all those familiar names on the gravestones, names of those he had known so well and among whom he had grown up.

There were now more here than in the town. He wandered along the lanes under the shiny dark leaves of the magnolia trees and beside the venerable camellia bushes, now filled with buds beginning to open, moving from one grave to another, flooded with memories, mostly happy, running back to the time before which he could not remember.

The passage of time was brought home to him even more forcefully by the graves of his own crowd. There was Baby Sister Carpenter, ten years dead from cancer. Here was Craig Anderson, who had become a college English teacher and died five years ago under mysterious circumstances that suggested suicide. And there was Skip Johnson, who dropped dead of a heart attack only a couple of years ago out in a pasture checking on his cows. Near the gate was Berta Rollins, taken by a stroke three years ago, lying beside her father, the late probate judge.

He stayed for long intervals at the Winston plot. Contemplating the identical dates of death on the graves of his father and mother, he wondered whether his life would have been different if they had not gone to Montgomery that night. And with still-lingering pain, not yet turned altogether into warm memory, he sat down by Sally's grave. Sally, Sally, why did she go? He wanted her now, needed her now.

Bartow Simmons was the closest old friend who was still around. He dropped by the house late one afternoon, and they talked about old times as well as the current Remberton scene.

"It's hard to believe I'm the most senior doctor in town," Bartow said at one point. "Did you know we have five other doctors at the hospital now?"

"No, and, what's more, I don't know any of them."

"One is a Pakistani."

"How in the world did he get to Remberton? Is he American trained?"

"Yep. Cornell. Got here through some medical placement service. Did you know that the new motel is run by Indians?"

"Indians from India?"

"Right. They claim to speak English, but you can't prove it by me."

"This place is really getting cosmopolitan. But you won't have arrived until you have a Korean community. They're everywhere now, huge clumps of them, with churches, stores, the works. I'll bet that before 1950 you'd have been hard put to round up more than several dozen Koreans in the entire United States."

They discussed the whereabouts of some of their crowd. "Jeanie Harris and her husband come back every now and then," Bartow said. "They live in Louisville. Have you ever met him?"

"No."

"There's a funny thing going on here," Bartow said. "You look at all those empty stores downtown, you think the place is drying up. But in fact, we're growing. A new shirt factory just opened up last year. There are blocks of new houses out there off Jeff Davis." There was a hint of pride in his voice. "I think it's happening because of the interstate. Look at all that stuff out there."

"I have." He didn't bother to conceal his disgust.

After days of talking with Becky and Frank in the evenings and at dinner—Frank came home every day from the *Progress* for dinner at noon—John felt he had a fairly complete picture of Remberton today. "It's still a good place to live," Becky said. "Of course, I think more of my crowd is here than yours. Your group seems to have scattered."

"Or died."

In his talks with Becky he never mentioned Henny Waller, but he thought of her often. He argued to himself that he should be thankful for having met Bruce Waller's daughter and let it go with that, treating it as a short, closed chapter. Anyway, he would only make a fool of himself in going after a woman that age. But he did feel hurt by her rebuff. He remembered now a similar feeling long ago when Jeanie Harris announced her defection; that had hurt more than he had been willing to admit. He could now see clearly that if Sally had not pursued him, they would never have been married. The fact was, he concluded, that he was not good with women. It was not that he was uninterested; it was just that somehow he lacked the right courting instincts. Of one thing he now felt sure: He would not risk the pain of more rejections.

After one of those moments of reflection, he said to Becky, "You know, I've had one marriage, a pretty good marriage as they go, so I think I'll stay away from women hereafter."

"That's ridiculous," she said. "You've got a lot of good years ahead, and I can imagine you might be surrounded by a flock of interested widows, grass and sod, as Daddy used to say. Don't make any drastic statements like that." She paused and smiled impishly. "You might end up eating words again."

One night at supper, Frank announced, "I just had a great idea today." He still had the appearance of a ruffled bookworm, albeit a graying one. Looking at John, he said, "Do you remember you had started a project to collect and publish the Major's recollections of the war?"

"I surely do. And I've always regretted I wasn't able to carry through on it."

"Why not now?"

John said he would think about it, but he found himself in no mood for the project. He was preoccupied with his Senate hearing and remembrances of his own war. His secretary had sent him several books on the subject that he had not seen, and he spent time with them each day. He was constantly learning facts of which he had been unaware when in the midst of it all, and his perspective on the war was gradually shifting.

On one of his walks he did drop by the *Progress* offices. Time and Frank's ideas had wrought many changes. The large room fronting Center Street, where he had sat with his father and Effie McCune and where the Major before them had sat, was now devoted to the sale of office supplies. Frank had taken over the adjoining building occupied by Ratcher's Grocery when it went out of business with the coming of the supermarkets out on the interstate. The editorial and business offices were now located there. Frank had a comfortable private office. Effie McCune was long gone, and John didn't know any of the staff except his nephew, Win Brandon.

As hoped, Win had studied journalism at the university. He had then taken a job on the *Atlanta Constitution*, but after several years Becky and Frank prevailed on him to return. He was now Frank's assistant, although he had done most of the work for several years and was soon to become editor in name also, thus carrying on the family tradition.

John was pleased to see that all the pictures accumulated by his father and grandfather still hung on the walls in these new quarters.

He was especially happy to see the sharp visage of Woodrow Wilson staring out across the front office, still waiting to be vindicated by the uncertain U.N. John wanted to say to him, "Mr. President, we rose to the occasion in Korea. At least we tried."

Looking over the reconfigured *Progress* offices, he thought about what his life might have been. He could have been right here all these years as editor. Frank, he assumed, would have been happy to handle the business side of things. It was hard for him now to imagine passing those decades in Remberton, to grasp what he would be like without the experiences he had had in the legal world—law school, the drama of the trial bar, the president's nomination to the court, all exciting. But then, too, he would not have been exposed to the embarrassing resurrection of his court-martial, he would never have heard of Sam Gilmore, and he would not have been shot in a Washington hotel. Moreover, for better or worse, he would never have met Henny Waller. Yes, life would certainly have been quieter and safer in the Remberton editorial chair. But he was not ready to say that he should have taken that route. Nor was he ready to say that he could come home now, as some had suggested, if his nomination should fail. Thomas Wolfe was probably right. He had to live with an inexplicable paradox: Remberton was a grand place to come from, a great place to grow up in and to visit, the place he had always considered home, but it was not a place to come back to, at least not for him.

Becky finally got him to go to church one Sunday morning. He hadn't been for months, a backslider, as she put it. With Sally gone, it had been easy to fall into a pattern of lounging around the house on Sunday mornings, drinking coffee and reading the paper, especially because he found the minister at their church to be uninspiring.

Now he was back in the church of his childhood and youth. Yet he looked around the congregation and saw few people he knew. The preacher was a young man, probably in his mid-thirties. He lacked the commanding presence of Tom Cowley, but John assessed him as being above average in relation to what could be expected these days. It was refreshing not to be subjected to the kind of lecture on economics or sociology he had encountered at church in recent years.

The sermon was built on the parable of the prodigal son. It was a familiar story. John had heard it numerous times, but it never grew old. Here was a grown son who had left home and ultimately fell into a degraded existence, living among swine. After hitting rock bottom in his life, he returned home. There his father greeted him with open arms, ordered that the fatted calf be killed, and put on a feast in his honor. This demonstrates, the preacher said, the forgiving power of God. No matter how low one sinks, how sinful his ways, he can always come back and be forgiven.

At the conclusion of the sermon, the congregation rose and sang "Amazing Grace." John hadn't heard it for years. They didn't sing it in the Episcopal church Sally had gotten him into. The third stanza caught his attention: "Through many dangers, toils, and snares I have already come. 'Tis Grace that brought me safe thus far, and grace will lead me home."

Yes, he had known them all too well—dangers, toils, and snares— and saw them again looming ahead in the Senate Judiciary Committee. If grace or whatever it was had brought him safe thus far, would it do the job again?

Two days later Roger Evans called. "We've got the police report. You came out all right. They say Gilmore's gunshot wound was likely self-inflicted, although it could have been accidental. The evidence provides no basis, the report says, for concluding you were guilty of unlawful homicide."

"It's reassuring to know they arrived at the truth. Do you think the committee will want to go into that episode at all?"

"I wouldn't be surprised to hear some questions about it."

"Where do we go from here?"

"The committee wants to hold a hearing early next month, assuming you're recovered and up to it."

"I'm ready to go. What's the word on their witnesses?"

"Do you know a Lt. Col. Kenneth Turner?"

"Can't say that I do. Who is he?"

"He sat on your court-martial. They apparently want to hear from him about how the members of the court assessed your conduct."

"They found me not guilty."

"I know, but the committee wants to go behind that and find out what the members really thought about what you did and maybe how they voted."

"Here we go again with no res judicata. Have they ever located Richard Alton, my platoon sergeant?"

"Army records show him missing in action."

John was silent for a moment, shaken by this long-delayed word that one of his favorite enlisted men didn't make it back. "Missing in action," he murmured. "Still missing after forty years. Have you heard of any campaigns, any clamoring by congressmen, for an accounting of the missing in Korea?"

"Can't say that I have. Plenty, though, about those in Vietnam."

"That's the point. Why all the fuss about MIAs there, but silence on more than three times as many in Korea?"

"I'm afraid it's part of the forgotten nature of the whole thing."

"Except the Senate Judiciary Committee is going to have to do some remembering. I'll see to that. Are there other witnesses?"

"Yes," Evans said. "Arthur Zander. You remember him, don't you?"

"The battalion adjutant. The only witness for the prosecution. Not a very attractive fellow, I might add. They have the transcript of the trial with his testimony. Why are they calling him?"

"The staffers say that at the trial the rules of evidence kept him from revealing what Colonel Burkman told him. The hearsay rule excluded it. They want to hear what that was."

"So they're trying to get at something that was not, and could not have been, introduced at trial?"

"Right. No hearsay rule in the committee. No rules of evidence at all. Everything's wide open."

"Any other witnesses?"

"An officer of the D.C. bar association and a representative from an organization called the Committee for Judicial Integrity. They monitor all our appointments."

"What are they going to say?"

"That however all the facts turn out, these charges cast a shadow over you and would besmirch the image of the federal courts. I should add that the staff has collected editorials from a dozen or so newspapers around the country saying pretty much the same thing and calling for your withdrawal. They'll be put in the record."

After a long moment John said, "Will that cut any ice with the committee?"

"Hard to say. We still think you can get confirmed."

"Look's like I'm my only witness."

"It does. But we think you can present a strong case. It's going to be an unusual proceeding. The real target, politically speaking, is the administration. But, of course, that won't be mentioned. What may emerge instead is a trial of the Korean War and you."

After a moment's silence, John said slowly and deliberately, "I've had a lot of time to think about it. Now I want to get it all out—Hill 1080, Burkman, the court-martial, Gilmore, and the war to boot. The lid's off."

In his room, packing to leave for Washington, he reflected once more on this house in Remberton, the house he considered his ultimate, earthly home, a refuge from the storms of life, a place to come to in the darkest hours, the house of his fathers, the house where he himself had lived from birth onward, until that fateful departure for Korea. It had always been there, and he could not imagine it not being there, a haven and a refuge but curiously not a place he could bring himself to remain in. Now he was leaving again, leaving on another fateful journey, a journey toward a reckoning with himself, his past, and his future.

Chapter 24

THE SPECTATORS' SEATS WERE FILLING UP in the Judiciary Committee's spacious and ornately furnished hearing room—its decor hinting of imperial Rome—when John and Roger Evans arrived. They sat down in the front row just behind the witness table. As the opening hour of ten approached, senators began drifting in to the high-backed chairs behind the long, curved table on an elevated platform at the front.

Carter Gordon arrived breathlessly and plopped down by John. "Had to walk up from Union Station." They shook hands warmly. "You're a little on the thin side," Gordon said, "but otherwise you look in good shape."

"I'll be in better shape after this is over."

When the chairman banged the gavel and called the hearing to order, only four senators were present.

"I thought this was a hearing before the full committee," John whispered to Evans.

"It's rare for all of them to be here at once," Evans whispered back. "They'll come and go."

The chairman, whose boyish looks belied his age, announced that the purpose of this reopened hearing was to examine two matters brought to the committee's attention since the previous hearing. He assured the listeners that the committee's sole concern was to ascertain the facts insofar as they bore on the nominee's qualifications to be a judge. He described the charge on which the court-martial had been based and the allegation made by Sam Gilmore.

John clenched his teeth. He had come prepared to meet the
charges against him and to vindicate himself, but he had not anticipated the stunning impact of hearing himself publicly charged with
willfully disobeying an order and causing a man's paralysis—charges
now being stated openly by a United States senator before the news
media and the whole world. Intense embarrassment and mild nausea
swept over him.

The chairman whispered to the senator on his right and to the
one on his left, both of whom nodded. He then intoned, "The committee calls as the first witness, Mr. Arthur Zander."

A short, overweight man came from somewhere in the rear and
moved around the front row of spectators' seats to the witness table.
His dark eyes were set deeply in a round, fleshy face, surmounting a
double chin and topped by a bald dome. John recognized him
despite the added weight and years.

The sight of Zander in the flesh only a few feet away flipped John's
mind back to that courtroom tent, with Zander on the stand, in
fatigues, overweight then as now, telling the court that he, John Winston, in the face of the enemy had refused to do his duty as an officer.
It forcefully hit him that he was again on trial, not in a forlorn tent in
Korea, but in the most public forum possible, at the center of the
national government, in a proceeding that everyone in the country
could read about in the paper. Was he now, forty years after the fact,
to be found guilty? Guilty by what standard? Not by any rules of law—
this was not a court. No, the judgment would be political, perhaps
moral.

Lost in thought, he was only dimly aware of Zander's identifying
himself as a retired automobile dealer from Worcester, Massachusetts, and reciting facts about his Korean service. Refocusing his
attention, he heard the committee's chief counsel—the chairman
had designated him to conduct the questioning—saying, "Now, Mr.
Zander, were there facts about this case that you did not testify to at
the trial?"

"Yes, sir."

"Why did you not offer this testimony then?"

"I was told it was not admissible under the rules of evidence."

"Please tell the committee what those facts were."

Zander cleared his throat and coughed. He nervously fingered the neck of the microphone facing him on the table. "Colonel Burkman, who was killed on the very morning of the trial, told me that he was convinced that Lieutenant Winston would not participate in the attack on Hill 1080, which was planned for two days later."

"Did he say what the basis for his opinion was?"

"He said Lieutenant Winston told him that he could not in good conscience take part in a futile operation, that men would be killed needlessly. Colonel Burkman said flat out that Lieutenant Winston was refusing to obey an order and that could not be tolerated. He also said—and I mention this only in the interest of full disclosure— that he thought Lieutenant Winston had gone yellow."

The word struck John like a blow in the stomach. Yellow . . . yellow. It reverberated through his mind. His knuckles went white as he gripped the arms of the chair. Carter Gordon touched his hand and whispered, "Take it easy. You'll have your chance."

When John was able to bring his mind back to the proceedings, he heard a senator asking, "Do you remember everything told to you forty years ago?"

"No, sir. But this was no ordinary event. It stands out in my mind, partly because of what happened later."

"What was that?"

"The attack on Hill 1080. We suffered heavy casualties."

"Does that mean that Lieutenant Winston was right in the way he assessed the situation?"

"I suppose you'd have to say partly so."

"Why just partly?"

"He was not right in thinking that it was up to him to decide whether a particular operation was justified or not."

The chairman, seeing no more questions from his colleagues, thanked Mr. Zander, who rose with obvious relief and left.

One of the senators also left, and two others arrived. Seated behind them were six staffers, none over thirty years old. They and the senators exchanged notes intermittently.

The chairman then announced, "The committee's next witness is Lt. Col. Kenneth Turner."

A short wiry figure with a steel gray crew cut and the weathered look of an outdoorsman came from the rear, took the oath, and seated himself at the witness table.

"By Jove, I recognize him" Gordon whispered. "He sat on several of my cases. This is spooky, like resurrecting the dead. Do you remember him?"

"Only vaguely."

Preliminaries out of the way, counsel asked the colonel—long retired from the army and now in the insurance business in Boise, Idaho—"The court found the accused not guilty. It had eight members. What was the vote on the finding?"

"With all respect, I have to say that I'm doubtful whether it's proper for me to reveal the actual vote. The deliberations of a court-martial are considered confidential."

"Colonel Turner," the chairman said, "we appreciate your concern. Before this hearing, the committee anticipated and considered the question you've raised. It's the opinion of the committee that you may properly reveal this information in response to a request made in the course of a formal inquiry of this sort. Therefore, we ask that you answer the question."

"To the best of my recollection—and this has been a long time—the vote was five to three."

"Five to three for acquittal?"

"No, sir. Five guilty and three not guilty."

"A majority found Lieutenant Winston guilty and yet he was acquitted?"

"Yes, sir. The military code requires a two-thirds vote of the court for conviction, and it does not consider five to be two-thirds of eight."

"Would you tell us how you voted?"

"I voted guilty."

Guilty . . . guilty by a vote of five to three. He sat rigid, a viselike grip on the chair arms, that one fatal word throbbing in his mind and bouncing around the room, into the ears of the spectators and on to the pages of newspapers everywhere. No one would ever understand how he could be anything but guilty when five out of eight had so decided.

For a minute or so he heard nothing except that one word playing over and over. Then the voice of a senator broke through, addressing the witness. "Did you hear what Mr. Arthur Zander just told this committee?"

"Yes, sir."

"If he had been allowed to say at trial what he just told us, do you think that would have changed the result?"

"I think it probably would have. It would have taken only one more vote to convict. The three who voted for acquittal were a little shaky."

The chairman thanked the witness and announced that a vote was being taken in the Senate and the committee would be in recess for about twenty minutes. He added, "When the committee returns, we'll consider the matter brought to our attention by Mr. Sam Gilmore." He banged the gavel, and the senators disappeared through the door to their rear. The room erupted into a hubbub as the crowd began milling around.

Evans excused himself, and John and Carter Gordon remained in place. "At least we finally got one of our questions answered," Gordon said.

"What's that?" John said in a voice full of resignation.

"How the members of the court-martial voted."

John sighed. His eyes were dark and deep-set, his expression looking as though the weight of the world had been laid upon him. "It's an answer I could have done without. We knew that vote was theoretically possible, but it's pretty bad to hear it announced in a packed room filled with reporters. With that vote there's no doubt in anybody's mind I'm guilty. And then that business about being yellow. It was all I could do to keep from jumping up and collaring Zander."

"When you get at the table, you'll pull it all out in good style. So right now try to relax. Would you like to step out in the hall?"

"No, thanks. I'll just sit here and collect my thoughts. You go ahead."

Gordon left, and John was alone in the front row. He had to get hold of himself. His years of trial work had conditioned him to be unflappable in the courtroom, to maintain a calm, even-tempered composure, no matter how emotional the issues. As an advocate he was always dealing with other people's problems, their lives, money, and well-being. He could be detached. But this was different. This was his own life, his reputation, his future. His normally tight control had left him. Yellow and guilty—the words hung in the air as though they were tangible objects, vultures hovering over him. That was all he could think of—yellow and guilty—the two most devastating charges he could imagine. He was sick at the stomach. What could he now do to rebut them, to dispel the impression they had left? He would have to reconsider the written statement he had spent days drafting for submission to the committee.

The crowd gradually filled the hearing room again. Senators returned, one by one. The chairman appeared and gaveled the room to order. Three senators were seated with him.

"Let me state again for the record," he said, "that after the witnesses have all testified, the nominee will have an opportunity to say whatever he wants to say, and committee members may have further questions to ask him." He whispered to the senators sitting on his right and left. Heads nodded. The chairman then called on the chief staff counsel to proceed.

The counsel recited the complaint filed with the committee by Sam Gilmore. He said that a written statement had been obtained from Mr. Gilmore and had been made part of the record, that the committee had desired Mr. Gilmore's presence, but that unfortunately Mr. Gilmore had died. He summarized Gilmore's sworn statement. John squirmed uncomfortably, again sickened at hearing himself accused of preventing one of his men from getting medical attention and of thrusting him back into a line of fire, causing him to be paralyzed for life.

"A strange coincidence with these witnesses," John whispered to Gordon. "First Burkman and now Gilmore." Gordon nodded knowingly but said nothing.

The chairman took over. "It has been brought to the committee's attention for the first time this morning that there is a witness who can provide information about this matter and who is available only today. By unanimous consent, the witness will be invited to testify." Pausing and looking out over the audience, he continued, "Dr. Kim Yung Suk, if you are in the room, will you please come forward."

John shot bolt upright in his chair. He jerked his head to the right and saw a small Korean man coming around the end of the chairs and walking to the witness table. He recognized him instantly, despite the wire-rim glasses and the dark, Western-style clothes—a suit and tie. No dirty, bloody fatigues, but still the full head of black hair and high cheekbones.

"I can't believe it," John gasped to Carter Gordon. "How in the world . . . ?"

Kim raised his right hand, took the oath, and sat down.

In response to the counsel's questions, Kim explained that he was a doctor at the Presbyterian Medical Center in Chonju, Korea, but in 1951 was a lieutenant in the ROK Army, acting as an interpreter and liaison officer with American units. He came to know Lieutenant Winston well, he said, having slept in the same bunker with him for several weeks.

"Were you with Lieutenant Winston during the attack by his company on Hill 969?" the counsel asked.

"Yes, sir. I was close by him at all times." Kim's English was still excellent, but it was spoken with an unmistakable Korean accent. The sound of that well-remembered voice transported John back to that dim and damp bunker scratched into the side of that shell-scarred Korean hill.

"At any time during the attack did you see Lieutenant Winston tackle one of his men and put a pistol in his chest?"

"There was a problem—please excuse me for saying so—that some of the soldiers would break and run toward the rear when heavy enemy fire was encountered. If I may add, many of my own country-men were guilty of this also. The Americans called it "bugging out." I had seen some of the noncommissioned officers tackle men who were bugging out. It was viewed as a serious offense, an abandon-ment of their comrades and a weakening of the unit strength. I had heard Lieutenant Winston complain about it and say it had to be stopped. That day, when we were on the hill under very heavy fire, I saw this man near us—we were all crouching down on the ground—jump up and throw down his rifle and start to run. Lieutenant Win-ston leaped up and went after the man and pulled him to the ground. I could not see clearly what happened then. Mortar shells were bursting around us and throwing up clouds of dust and rocks. In a moment I saw the man coming back toward his rifle. Lieutenant Winston was running back to where I was when he was knocked off his feet by a mortar round. I thought he had been killed, but he had only been dazed."

"Did you see Lieutenant Winston point a weapon of any kind at this man on the ground?"

"No, I did not."

"Is it possible that he did so, even though you couldn't see?"

"That is, of course, possible. There was much dust and confusion. I want to say that if he had done so, it would have been entirely justifiable under the circumstances. A combat situation of that sort is something that no one can understand who has not been there."

"Do you know the name of the man Lieutenant Winston tackled?"

"No, I do not."

"Do you know what happened to him?"

"No. I never saw him again."

"Dr. Kim, is there anything else you would like to say to the committee that might be helpful to it?"

"Yes, sir. And it is the most important thing I have to say. To put it briefly, Lieutenant Winston saved my life." He then described the patrol led by Winston and how he was wounded and fainted on the way back and was left behind, unknown to the patrol in the darkness. "They found that I was missing only after they had returned to our lines. Lieutenant Winston then voluntarily came back to look for me. Fortunately he found me and carried me in his arms back to our lines, a distance of more than a mile, in the dark through a valley where enemy patrols were known to be. If Lieutenant Winston had not come back and found me, I would have died of the wound or been killed by the North Koreans. I owe my entire life to him. He should have been awarded a medal."

"Do you know what happened to Lieutenant Winston after that night?"

"Only what I have read in the newspapers. But I would like to say that I cannot believe that he would disobey an order from a superior. He was one of the most conscientious and dedicated officers that I met in the entire war."

The hearing room was quiet. John felt tears brimming in his eyes and struggled to keep his emotions under control.

After a few moments of silence, Kim continued. "It is indeed regrettable that the U.N. was not able to defeat the Communists and give us a unified country. To leave Kim Il-sung's dictatorship in power over half our territory is tragic. However, the saving of the South Koreans was a major accomplishment. I am happy to have this opportunity—one I never dreamed I would have—to thank the United States for what it did. All of us in South Korea today would be like the

North Koreans, under Communist control, if it had not been for the United States, and I want to say that I think your sacrifices were worthwhile, and we are grateful to the American people. The war was not in vain."

"We appreciate your statement," the chairman said. Looking up and down the table, he continued: "There apparently being no more questions, we will excuse you, Dr. Kim. We are grateful to you for giving us the benefit of your testimony, and we wish you well."

A staffer had pushed a note in front of the chairman as he was talking, and now he added quickly, "Several votes are scheduled on the floor shortly. We think it necessary to adjourn the hearing until tomorrow morning. We will hear any additional witnesses at that time, and we will hear from the nominee. So, the committee is in recess until ten o'clock tomorrow." He banged the gavel, and everyone rose.

John leaped up and bounded toward Kim, who was rising from his chair at the witness table. As Kim turned, their eyes met, and for an instant they stood apart looking at each other with mild incredulity. Then without saying a word, they spontaneously embraced. Tears suddenly filled John's eyes. He feared he might break down. Then he backed away, clasping Kim's arms with his hands, looking at him as if to be sure it really was the Kim he remembered.

"A ghost out of the past," John said. "I didn't know whether you were even alive. How did you . . .? Why . . .?"

Smiling broadly, Kim said, "My daughter works at the Korean embassy. I'm in Washington visiting her. Your name was, of course, well known to her. She has heard it from me many times. She saw articles in the newspaper about accusations made against you. When I arrived yesterday, she told me all about it. So I telephoned up here this morning. I wanted to tell these people what I know about you."

"This is all unbelievable. I can't tell you how grateful I am. That was a moving statement, and I'll always remember it."

Reporters crowded in around them. They peppered Kim with questions about his connection with John and how he happened to appear as a witness. Several flashbulbs popped. In response to their questions as to how he thought the hearing was going, John said he would present his statement tomorrow and would have no comment now.

"I hope very much you can have lunch with me," John said to Kim.

"Yes, that would be nice."

"And can your daughter join us?"

"That is not possible. She is involved in an important conference at the embassy."

Roger Evans had picked up his brief case preparing to leave. John introduced him to Kim and said, "Will you join us for lunch?"

"No, thanks. I've got to get back to the office. That testimony this morning was a little rough. Are you all set for tomorrow?"

"I will be."

After John introduced Carter Gordon to Kim, Gordon said, "I need to get back to my room and phone the office. Do you want to get together later on your statement?"

"No, I need to work it out myself. I'll call you if necessary."

John and Kim left the Senate office building and walked together down Capitol Hill, talking as they went. The day was cool and overcast, with the feel of late fall in the air. Brown leaves still clung here and there to bare tree branches, fluttering to the ground with a casual irregularity.

Kim's astonishing appearance had lifted John out of the despondency into which he had been thrown by the earlier proceedings. Seeing the man he never expected to see again and hearing his surprising tribute had left him with the reassuring feeling that whatever he might have done with Colonel Burkman and Sam Gilmore, he had—in at least one instance—acted as a decent human being. His spirits rising, he talked animatedly, wanting to know all about Kim's life since the war.

As they walked along the busy street, Kim recounted the whole story. After recovering from his wound, he served for the rest of the war as an interpreter with a Staff Judge Advocate's office in Seoul. Then he studied medicine and began his career as a surgeon in Chonju, where he had been ever since. He had married and had two children—the daughter who worked here in the embassy and a son who worked at a bank in Seoul. His wife was well and working part-time as a nurse.

"Why are the senators so interested in these happenings from the war, all so long ago?" Kim asked.

John explained how the appointment process can get tangled up in politics, but that his case had been uneventful until Sam Gilmore had surfaced and then his court-martial had come to light. "It's been an ordeal, and I've considered withdrawing my name. But somehow I don't want to. And the Justice Department people keep telling me I'll be confirmed."

They passed Union Station and turned up New Jersey Avenue and went into the Hyatt Regency. They found a table in the restaurant just off the atrium and began perusing the menus handed them by the waitress.

"Two years ago," Kim said, "when I was in the States for the first time to visit Soon Hee, I discovered something called chef's salad, and I see it here again. I never saw so many different things in one dish."

"What about kimchi?"

"Not quite so much, and it is hot and much stronger."

"Would you like to try the chef's salad again?"

"I think so. Here I see at the next table another American invention—iced tea. So, being in America, I go American and have that too."

"Do you remember those talks we had in the bunker about religion?" John asked after they gave their orders.

"Yes, I do. We had some interesting discussions."

"What do you think now? You've done and seen a lot since then."

"After all the suffering I have seen—and even though Kim Il-sung is still in Pyongyang—my faith is not shaken. All these earthly things are transient. You have a hymn that says, 'A thousand ages in thy sight are like an evening gone.'"

"Taken by Isaac Watts from the 90th Psalm."

"Correct." Kim smiled in evident appreciation of John's biblical knowledge. "Have you thought about the happenstance that I should arrive in Washington just in time to speak to your committee? And have you thought about the fact that if you had not been removed from your company, you might have died on Hill 1080?"

"I've thought about Hill 1080 a thousand times. Sometimes I even wished I had died there. Why should I have been saved when others were not?"

"A similar question: Why did you go back and find me that night on patrol?"

"Something inside me said go. I didn't really think about it. I just knew I had to go."

Kim smiled and nodded. "That is the way it works sometimes."

Their salads arrived, and they plunged forks into the jumbled mixture. As they ate, they reminisced about life in the bunker, some of the men in the platoon, and that day on Hill 969.

"It's curious," John said after a pause, "but recently I got a sudden desire to go to Korea, and I went to a travel agency to see about it. Then this shooting put an end to that idea."

"You should now revive the idea. I can show you the modern Korea, something you could not imagine in comparison to what you saw. It's a different country."

"Is it possible to visit that area where we were?" John asked.

"Those positions are now in the DMZ. Nobody can go there."

"So all those men who died taking those hills died in vain."

"No. They died to preserve the Republic of Korea. Also, they showed that communism would not be allowed to expand."

As they ate in silence for a bit, John reflected over the unhappy fact that no American, high or low, could visit the sites of some of the war's bloodiest actions. After other wars, veterans often came back years later to revisit scenes of unspeakable horrors, scenes of heroism, death, and destruction. But not in Korea, not north of the DMZ. Sealed off from the world, a massive, unmarked American graveyard stretched across those interlacing hills and valleys along the Chongchon and on the desolate ridges around the Chosin Reservoir. There were no long neat rows of white crosses honoring the dead. Instead, in that forlorn territory approaching the Yalu, the bleached bones of unidentified thousands had weathered baking summer sun and freezing winter for forty years.

They resumed talking, and Kim explained more about his hospital. He was going from here to Louisville to visit some officials at the Presbyterian headquarters. "That church founded my hospital and many others long before the war. It is good to know that Americans have made contributions to Korea other than military."

They exchanged addresses and telephone numbers. John urged Kim to return and visit him in Birmingham with Soon Hee. He would show him the great medical center there.

"Incidentally," John asked, "do you still sing?"

Kim smiled. "Ah so. You do have a good memory. I sang in the church choir every Sunday for years, but I gave it up recently."

They rose from the table and walked out to the street. As a taxi pulled over for Kim, the two shook hands warmly and renewed invitations to visit each other.

John looked affectionately into this Korean face from the past, the face of a man he never expected to see again—didn't even know was alive—and was struck with the miraculous circumstance that had brought them together. Sadly, though, his instinct told him it was unlikely they would see each other again. He clasped him on the arm. "Take care, old friend, and again, many thanks."

"God bless you," Kim said and stepped into the cab.

Chapter 25

UP IN HIS ROOM AT THE HYATT REGENCY—he couldn't go back to the Mayflower—John took off his coat and tie and shoes and got comfortable. For a while he sat at the desk reading and reconsidering the draft of his carefully prepared statement. But he found it hard to concentrate. He got up and paced the room. Then he lay down on the bed.

He savored his reunion with Kim, thinking back about what Kim had said to the committee and their long luncheon talk. It had lessened the despondency he had been thrown into by the first two witnesses. But as he lay here reliving the morning's proceeding, he felt again the sting of those two words: yellow and guilty. Hearing them said publicly and hearing for the first time that the court-martial members had voted guilty five to three had cut him to the quick. Then Kim had appeared like a burst of sunshine breaking through the gloom. How extraordinary it was that he should be here in Washington just at this moment. He was deeply touched by Kim's statement that he had saved his life. Could it be that Kim had now done the same for him? If not his life, at least his good name and confirmation?

Uncertainty as to what he should do and say boiled up afresh. He wanted the appointment to the bench. At the same time, he wanted to lay his past to rest, to have some final reckoning with his Korean War experience. Could he have both?

He went back to the desk and took out his legal pad and a pencil.

But after nearly an hour of writing, scratching out, and rewriting, he gave up and lay back down to think some more. He knew all the facts, all the considerations and arguments. More talk with others would not help. In his own solitary brooding, alone and far from home, he must make a decision, a decision that, whichever way it went, would alter his life for all time.

He dozed off. When he awoke, it was a little after six. It was dusk, and a light rain had begun to splash against the window. He got up, threw some cold water in his face, and turned on the evening TV news. The world was going on as usual. He ordered a bowl of tomato soup, a grilled-cheese sandwich, and a beer from room service. When his order came, he ate while watching a panel discussion about new ideas for combating crime.

He spent a restless night, as bits of the hearing and his talk with Kim, along with images from the deeper past, came to the surface of his mind and broke through his light sleep, waking him intermittently. Dreams and conscious imagination mingled. He saw himself being sworn in as a judge, standing in a black robe, right hand raised, in the high-ceilinged, wood-paneled courtroom, flanked by the other judges. "I, John H. Winston, do solemnly swear . . ." He tried to imagine how the newspapers would cover the occasion, how they would recite the testimony at this hearing. Toward morning he found himself wide-awake in the dark, thinking. The luminous dial on his watch showed 5:30 A.M.

He got up and took a long, hot shower. When he emerged in a terry-cloth robe, day was breaking outside his window. The passage of the night, restless though it had been, the shower, and the coming of the new day had cleared his mind wonderfully. As though by sudden revelation, he now saw with perfect clarity what he should do.

He sat down at the desk, took the pen, and began to write on the yellow pad. The words flowed quickly and easily. Within half an hour he had completed the statement he would deliver to the committee.

He waited until seven to telephone Roger Evans at home and Carter Gordon at the Sheraton-Carlton and tell them what he intended to say. Then he shaved and dressed and went down to a hearty breakfast.

The Judiciary Committee hearing room filled gradually with spectators as the hour of ten approached. Reporters were standing around the entrance as John arrived.

"Mr. Winston, do you have a copy of your statement available?"

"No, I'm afraid not. I have only my own copy, and I'll read it to the committee."

"Can you tell us what you plan to say?"

"I think the senators ought to hear it first."

Roger Evans joined him inside the room. "Are you sure this is what you want to do?"

"Yes. I've thought about it a lot."

Evans and John and Carter Gordon sat down in the front row. Senators drifted in to their high-back chairs. Staffers were milling around and sitting down behind them.

The chairman appeared through the door, spoke to one of the staff, and took his seat in the center chair. After saying a few words to the senators on either side, he banged his gavel and announced that the committee would come to order and that the hearing would be resumed on the president's nomination of John H. Winston to be a judge on the United States Court of Appeals for the Eleventh Circuit. He then said, "The committee grants the request of the nominee, Mr. Winston, that he be allowed to make a statement before the other witnesses are heard. Accordingly, Mr. Winston, you may proceed."

John rose and moved to the witness table. He took the oath and sat down, arranging his typed sheets and handwritten yellow pages on the table, pulling the microphone closer. Carter Gordon poured a glass of water from the pitcher and pushed it toward him.

"Welcome back, Mr. Winston," the chairman said. "We had not expected to see you again, but, as you know, new information has come to light, compelling the committee to reconvene. We are ready to hear from you."

"Thank you, Mr. Chairman. I appreciate the committee's consideration of my nomination. With the committee's indulgence, I would like to submit a statement on this entire matter, and I ask the committee's patience in hearing me out."

"We welcome whatever you have to say," the chairman said, leaning back as though settling in for a long ordeal. Eight senators were present, the most at any one time. Every seat in the room was taken, and spectators stood along the back and sidewalls.

His long-awaited moment was at hand. The weeks of mental tur-moil and uncertainty were about to end. He felt strangely calm and confident, almost serene.

"Mr. Chairman and members of the committee," he began, "I appreciate the opportunity to present my views about the matters that have caused this hearing to be convened. In a sense, this hearing brings before the committee the Korean War itself, in all its historic dimensions, as what I did there cannot be well understood otherwise. I take great satisfaction in having had a very modest role as a member of the first army in history to fight under the banner of a world organization to put down illegal aggression and maintain international peace. Although only a lieutenant in the infantry, I believe I did my duty and behaved in accordance with the best standards of the American military service.

"As to the sad case of Sam Gilmore, whatever I did I did because at that moment it had to be done. As unfortunate and regrettable as his lifelong disability was, he was in no different position from that of thousands of other soldiers. Who lives and who dies, who is wounded and who is left untouched, are all matters over which those in combat have little or no control. We were all in the midst of death, and it is only by the mysterious hand of providence or some quirk of fate that I myself sit here today. Sam Gilmore had a duty not to desert but to stay and fight, along with everybody else. I was seeing to it that he fulfilled that duty. I asked no more of him than I demanded of myself.

"As to the charge brought against me and for which I was tried by court-martial, the committee has the entire transcript of the trial and the members can see for themselves what the evidence was. Although we have now heard that the vote within the court was five to three in favor of guilt, the fact remains that I was tried according to law, judged according to law, and as a matter of law was acquitted. I want to reiterate that I did not say that I would not obey orders. I would have carried out whatever orders were given me if I had been allowed to remain with my unit. My battalion commander was obviously agitated over what I said, and, in my view, he misinterpreted what I did say.

"While I believe that the court-martial properly found me not guilty, I want to say I have a profound sense of regret and guilt over the fact that my conduct caused my removal and prevented my participation in the operation on Hill 1080. In saying this, I realize that if Colonel Burkman had not sent me to the rear, I might not be here today. The casualties were extremely heavy. Although my remorse has been repressed for many years, this confirmation proceeding has brought the sense of guilt back to the surface. Countless times I have wished that I had shared the fate of my company on Hill 1080 and taken my chances on living or dying."

John stopped and shuffled his papers. Not a sound was to be heard from anywhere in the room. He took a deep breath and exhaled.

"In looking back across all these years, I see my actions as those of a rather brash young lieutenant, full of idealistic notions about this crusade against the forces of darkness. Having now read several histories of the war and the international situation at the time, I can better understand why the war from the U.N. side was conducted as it was.

"Now, Mr. Chairman and members of the committee, I come to my main point. The dignity and authority of the courts of this country and the public respect for the judiciary are crucial, though intangible, factors in the preservation of a regime of law. We must preserve effectively functioning courts, and the public perception of the persons who are judges has a significant bearing on their effectiveness and on the acceptability of their decisions. More than any other human beings in our legal order, judges must be of impeccable character, free of all questions or doubts. Although I have not the slightest doubt that I behaved lawfully and honorably in Korea, reasonable minds could think otherwise—and some apparently do—in light of the accusations that have been made. Any substantial doubt about me in this regard, even unfounded, in my view, is enough to counsel against my accepting appointment as a United States judge. Accordingly, after much thought and with great regret, I have concluded that I should request the president to withdraw my nomination, and I have done so by letter this morning."

A low hubbub of voices swelled from the spectators. The chairman brought down his gavel. "Order. The room will be in order." The crowd immediately quieted.

"Mr. Winston," the chairman said, leaning forward toward his microphone, "I must say that this announcement comes as a complete surprise. It's a very serious decision. Have you discussed it with anyone in the administration?"

"Yes, sir. I discussed it with Associate Attorney General Evans."

"Do you mind telling us what his reaction was?"

"He tried to talk me out of it. Let me say that I take this action in the public interest, not in my self-interest. If my own interest were controlling, I would not withdraw, but I think the uncompromised administration of justice calls for this step. My giving up the opportunity to serve as a judge may be viewed, and I so view it, as at least a partial atonement for my not being on Hill 1080 with my platoon, where I should have been."

The chairman said, "Those are admirable sentiments, and we respect you for them. Do you have anything else you wish to say to the committee?"

"Yes, sir. With your permission I would like to say something about this war that I think important. With the question of my confirmation out of the way so that I no longer have any stake in this proceeding, I can present these points in an objective, disinterested manner, thinking only of what this war should mean to us and future generations."

He pushed aside his handwritten notes and focused on the typed statement he had prepared in advance. Here he considered himself to be speaking on behalf of all those who did not come back, as well as for all those who served and suffered but survived the war. He was for the moment their advocate, taking this onetime opportunity, in the highest and most public forum he would ever have, to make the case for the significance of their service and to try to bring them to their rightful place in the history books.

Reading in a clear, strong voice, he began. "Our failure to remember the Korean War dishonors the men and women who served and died there, and it has left us without an understanding of its significance and the lessons it teaches. The war is significant in several ways. The Korean War was the first time the nations of the world united under a common flag to repel armed aggression and to implement the principle of collective security. It was the first time that Western powers directly confronted communism in active, armed conflict. It checked the spread of communism, putting teeth in the policy of containment. It introduced the world to the brainwashing of prisoners of war and the use of POWs as pawns. It revealed the Communist techniques of negotiation. It was the real beginning of the Cold

War, which then escalated to new heights, removing all hope that it was a short-run phenomenon. It introduced the world to the concept, novel in the twentieth century, of limited war. It presented more dramatically than ever before the question of civilian control of the armed forces under the United States Constitution."

He paused, took a swallow of water, and then continued.

"The war raised questions about deterrence that remain to be analyzed. There was a failure of deterrence on both sides. On the Communist side, there was the failure of North Korea and its allies, the Soviet Union and China, to be deterred from initially launching the war. On the U.N. side, there was the failure of the U.N. Command to be deterred by the clear warnings from China that it would enter the conflict if U.N. forces crossed the 38th parallel.

"Moreover, one lesson looms large: The United States must never again let itself become as militarily unprepared as it was in June 1950. Our army then was understrength, undertrained, underequipped, and overweight. We practically invited Uncle Joe to make a move. Now with the Cold War ending, we face a similar threat: the assumption that we no longer need a strong armed force. Korea tells us that that line of thinking must be resisted."

He was pleased to note that he had the senators' attention. They were not leaning back with detached looks or whispering back and forth with staffers. All were now sitting upright with their eyes on him.

"Korea was the U.N.'s first real test. Kim Il-sung launched his attack just five years after it was created. To its everlasting credit, it rose to the challenge. The U.N. did what it was founded to do, did what the League of Nations failed to do. To fulfill this vital role in international affairs, the U.N. must be strengthened and be ready to prevent or roll back aggression wherever and whenever it occurs. Korea stands as the critical precedent.

"The memorial now being planned will fail in its teaching mission for future generations if it does not make clear the role of the U.N. At the memorial, the U.N. flag should fly alongside the U.S. flag, as it always did in Korea. This forgotten chapter in world history must be unforgotten."

John leaned back in the chair. He had finished, had delivered his sermon, had gotten his pent-up thoughts about the war off his chest.

After a moment, the chairman said, "Mr. Winston, thank you for your statement."

The chairman looked to his right and left. There was no sign that the senators wished to say anything. They sat motionless, as though mentally wrestling with what they had heard. He said, "Mr. Winston, I think it appropriate on behalf of the committee to thank you for your service to the country. Your discussion of the Korean War will help all of us understand it better and help it gain the place in our historical memory that it deserves."

After whispering to the senator on his right, he said, "In light of the nominee's decision to have his nomination withdrawn, it will be unnecessary to hear from other witnesses. There being nothing remaining for the committee to act upon, I declare the hearing concluded and the proceedings adjourned."

The gavel banged down loudly, the senators rose, and the room immediately erupted into a loud buzz of talk.

Carter Gordon was at John's side, putting an arm on his shoulder. "Great statement! You pulled it off in grand style. Something they never expected. But I'm sorry you won't be a judge."

"This case will go down as unique," said Roger Evans, shaking John's hand. "You could have had it, if you'd hung in there, but we admire this gutsy move. I myself regret that we've lost a fine judge, but maybe now you can get your life together again."

"Let's hope so," John said, smiling with an immense sense of relief.

"If you hadn't withdrawn," Evans added, "I understand that a couple of senators were going to give you a pretty rough time with questions, but you pulled the rug out from under them. They looked disappointed. Anyway, it's been grand getting to know you. Good luck."

Reporters swarmed in on all sides and began peppering him with questions.

"Was pressure put on you by the administration to withdraw?"

"No. I made the decision myself."

"Did you decide to withdraw because you thought you would not be confirmed?"

"No. My understanding was that I would probably have been confirmed."

"What will you do now?"

"I'm not sure. I'll have to give it some thought."

The questions kept up for another ten minutes as the hearing room gradually emptied. He answered them all jovially, realizing that for the first time in months he had nothing to worry about. He had come to terms with it all and laid it to rest forever. The last reporter left finally, and John turned to pick up his papers and his briefcase. Only Carter Gordon remained.

"Well," Gordon said slowly, with his familiar owlish look of amusement, "this is the second time you and I have been out to the brink together."

"Let's hope it's the last. Three strikes and I'll surely be out."

They walked together to the elevator and pushed their way in with constituents from the provinces there to call upon and seek favors from their senators. When the elevator door opened on the main floor, they moved through the crowded corridor out onto Constitution Avenue. They stood there for a few minutes chatting, expressing the hope they would see each other again under happier circumstances.

A cab pulled over to the curb. "Thanks again," John said as the rear door opened.

"Keep in touch," Gordon said, grasping John by the hand. And then he was gone.

Yesterday's overcast had cleared, and the sun had broken through the morning haze. Across the way, the Capitol dome loomed high above the trees, now bereft of their leaves. John stood on the sidewalk, oblivious to passing traffic and people streaming in and out of the Senate office building. He felt a peculiar sense of detachment, as though he were on some other plane, his burden lifted, the dark secret of forty years exorcised. It had all come out for the world to know. He had said his piece about himself and the war. Renouncing the judgeship had curiously released him from all sense of confusion, turmoil, and apprehension. The war, he thought, with the long-hidden shame and grisly memories it had inflicted on him, had finally been put into perspective, laid to rest, his system purged of its bedeviling effects. He was free, free at last to pick up with his life and go on.

Picking up with his life was not hard to do. His partners had told him repeatedly that they would welcome him back, so back he went, but in an "of counsel" status, with a lighter routine: He would stay out

of the courtroom, take depositions, and write briefs. He accepted a
long-standing offer to teach a seminar in trial ethics at the law school
in Tuscaloosa, commuting an hour each way on the interstate. He
did not lack for invitations to dinners and cocktail parties, but, as he
had resolved, he resisted overtures from widows on the Birmingham
social scene, some quite attractive and persistent.

He thought occasionally of Henny and her mother, wondered how
they were doing. He again felt a desire to see her, but he did not
dwell on the thought, reminding himself that he must treat that as a
closed chapter, something to be put behind, like the Korean War.

And so the months passed. From time to time there were second
thoughts. Had he made a mistake in withdrawing? Would his
appointment as a judge really have had any adverse effect on the
judiciary? But such thoughts did not linger. He was satisfied he had
done the right thing, both for the courts and for his own peace of
mind.

Then one day the mail brought a notice of the dedication of the
Korean War Memorial in Washington. How his name got on some
mailing list for this event he did not know. At first he laid it aside.
Having relived the war during the agonizing months in the nomination process and having finally come to terms with it on his day of
reckoning in the Senate Judiciary Committee, he had no desire to
relive it. Old wounds might be reopened, painful memories
renewed.

He later reread the literature about the dedication ceremonies
and began to have doubts. Maybe he should be there, out of respect
for those who did not come back. He began to feel ambivalent about
it. He didn't want to go, but something kept tugging him in that
direction.

Chapter 26

AT MIDMORNING JOHN GOT OUT OF THE TAXI near the intersection of 17th Street and Independence Avenue. The sun beat down from a blue and cloudless sky.

"Gonna be another scorcher," the driver said, a heavy black woman whose T-shirt was already wet under the arms. "Hottest summer I ever seen."

He struck out across a long grassy expanse of the Mall toward the tent city, beyond which was the memorial and the site of the dedication ceremony.

He hadn't planned to come. He was unhappy that the U.N. flag had not been included in the memorial. And he didn't want to risk the revival of disturbing memories. But then he was notified of a deposition to be taken in Baltimore two days beforehand in a case in which he was involved. So with some misgivings he had changed his mind at the last minute and decided to stop over and attend. It was the 27th of July, 1995, the forty-second anniversary of the signing of the armistice at Panmunjom.

He saw unending lines of people streaming toward the tent city from Independence Avenue and across the Mall from Constitution Avenue. He could easily spot the veterans. They had to be at least sixty, and most were older-looking. Some were accompanied by family members—women who appeared to be their wives, along with sons and daughters, now grown and approaching middle age, and grandchildren. Some of the men, wearing the special pins issued for the day, were being pushed in wheelchairs. Here and there was a blind man with white cane or guide dog.

In the suit and tie he had worn from Baltimore, he was not dressed for the steadily mounting heat and humidity, and not in sync with the style of the crowd. Minimal clothing was the order of the day; shorts, T-shirts, and sundresses abounded among all ages. Comfort obviously overrode concerns about appearance.

As he came in among the tents, band music filled the air. John Philip Sousa's stirring pieces alternated with the sad and haunting music of Korea, music he had not heard for over forty years. In his mind's eye he saw rice paddies, thatch-roofed houses clustered in small villages against high hills, women in flowing white dresses, old men in billowy trousers with black birdcage hats; he smelled the night soil of the countryside.

Past him moved a gaggle of Korean children, herded along by a Korean woman, like a mother hen with a brood of chicks. This new generation of Koreans, whether here in the United States or in Korea, would know nothing of the country that lived in his memory. That country was gone, and in its place was a land of high-tech industry, high-rise buildings, multi-lane highways, jet airports, and global trade.

Laughter, shouts, and general crowd noises mingled with the band music. He did not understand the festive air. He saw nothing joyous about the war. All of his dark memories of death and suffering began to well up, memories he thought he had put behind. But from the shouts around him he sensed long pent-up emotions being released, a collective expression of joy over the nation's long deferred show of gratitude.

"About time," a man passing him said, "thirteen years after the Vietnam boys had theirs."

He scanned the faces of the men in their sixties, hoping to find one he might recognize, despite the ravages of time. But he saw none. He passed along the line of huge tents, some containing exhibits sponsored by the participating countries—Turkey, the Netherlands, the United Kingdom, and others.

"Water! Anybody want water?" called out a man standing by a mountain of crates, freely handing out the six-ounce plastic bottles. John eagerly took one. He was already perspiring heavily, and the threat of dehydration was serious. He had taken off his coat and loosened his tie.

He came to a tent filled with computers. In one group, data were available on everyone killed in action. In another group were data on all those missing in action. His eyes brightened. Maybe now he could clarify the fate of those he had often wondered about in bygone years.

He went first to the KIA section. The procedure was simple. All he had to do was type in the last name of the individual and press the return key. There then flashed on the screen the individual's full name, service number, hometown, rank and branch of service, and date killed. By pressing another key, he could obtain a printed copy of the information.

One by one he entered the names of his fellow lieutenants in Baker Company, no word of whom he had ever received after that catastrophic night on Hill 274: Malcolm Mason of Terre Haute, Indiana, the company exec; Alex Puccini of Milwaukee, commanding First Platoon; Chris Ridley of San Jose, California, commanding Third Platoon; Mike Forney, the forward observer, from Bowling Green, Kentucky. The machine reported no information on any of them.

He then moved over to the computers containing the MIAs. He entered each of the names again. Mason, Pucinsky, and Ridley were all reported to be missing in action, as of 25 November 1950. He saw no way they could still be alive. He could think of only two possibilities: Either they died on 274 or they were taken prisoner by the Chinese and died in their hands.

Mike Forney's absence from both the KIA and MIA data meant that he must have survived the war. John wondered how he got out of that hellish night. Where was he now? He could well have died of natural causes since then, as had a host of men who'd returned from the war. Indeed, as he reflected on the crowd here today, he realized that the ranks of the veterans were inevitably thinning. Time, like an ever-rolling stream, bears all its sons away.

He typed in the name of Capt. Howell Grimes, the Baker Company commander from Amarillo, Texas, whom he had last seen on the chaotic withdrawal south of Kunu-ri. Not finding him among the missing, he went back to the KIA computers and typed in the name. It was immediately projected on the screen, showing him to have been killed in action on 21 March 1951. He shook his head over the irony of Grimes' having survived the collapse of the army along the Chongchon only to die in the victorious advance back north. He was left with the depressing thought that he alone of the officers in Baker Company was still alive, with the possible exception of Forney.

He wandered along the lines of tents, threading his way through the heavily perspiring crowd, steadily growing in size. He had now removed his tie completely and rolled up his sleeves, hoping not to become a customer of the first-aid tent he was passing, already busy with cases of heat exhaustion. He took another bottle of water and continued sipping.

He passed the food tents, emitting a variety of aromas, including the unmistakable smell of kimchi. He went into a tent that seemed to be serving a mixture of Korean and Chinese food. He ordered an egg roll and an oversized cup of lemonade. It was too hot to be hungry.

Among the sea of crowded tables he found an empty chair away from the sunniest area and sat down. The tent's sides were rolled up, permitting a hint of a breeze to pass through, or at least to reduce the stifling atmosphere generated by the throng of over-heated humans. Band music wafted in over the crowd noises, alternating between American and melancholy Korean pieces. He finished the egg roll and sat sipping the lemonade, cooling down slightly. With the oppressive heat and the absence of anyone he knew—indeed, all those he remembered well were gone—he wished he had stuck by his inclination and not come.

Four men all well over sixty and two women sat at the next table, laughing and occasionally calling to others at nearby tables. From what he overheard, he surmised they were all from Arizona. One of the men rose, signaling a passerby.

"Come over and meet these folks," he called out loudly.

John paid little attention until he heard the introducer say, "This is Gene Tompkins from Phoenix."

It took a few seconds for the name to register. Could this be Capt. Eugene Tompkins? He studied the man carefully. He was bald, with deep-set dark eyes and a gaunt face. He looked ten years older than

Tompkins should have been. John would swear he had never seen the man before, but he had to find out.

He got up and edged over to their table. "Excuse me," he said, looking at the gaunt face, "I couldn't help overhearing the name Gene Tompkins."

"That's right."

"Were you by any chance the supply officer of the Second Battalion at Kunu-ri in November '50?"

"I sure was. Who are you?"

"John Winston, second lieutenant, commanding Second Platoon, Baker Company."

Tompkins stared at him. "Winston? Yeah, Winston! I remember you!" Without getting up, he shot out his hand, and they shook.

"You and I and my company commander, Capt. Howell Grimes, were together for a little while there just before we started south," John said.

"Right. I was the acting battalion commander. There wasn't anybody else left." Turning to the woman sitting beside him, he said, "Agnes, this is Lieutenant—er, what's your first name?"

"John. John Winston."

"This is John Winston from my old outfit." Then looking at John, he said, "This is my wife, Agnes. She's kept me going all these years." John and Agnes shook hands. She was a plain, stocky woman, looking tired and uninterested.

The man sitting next to him rose and said, "Gene, I'm going to look around. I'll catch up with you later."

"Sit down here and tell me what happened to you," Tompkins said to John.

"Well, to make a long story short, I got out but not in the best shape. I was hit and passed out on the back of a tank. The next thing I knew, I woke up in an evac hospital somewhere south and was operated on and shipped to Japan. What about you?"

"Took me a lot longer to get back. The Chinks got me."

John's interest picked up. He had never talked to anyone who had been captured by the Chinese. "How did that happen?"

"You might recall that this withdrawal was a stop-and-go thing, with enemy fire coming in from one side or another. A lieutenant colonel comes along and says he wants me to collect some men and clear a ridge off to our left where Chinks were putting down fire on us. We rounded up twenty or thirty men from the trucks in our vicinity and started across the paddies. We thought we could come up on the ridge from the rear. We got down in a ravine when all of a sudden we hit a whole bunch of the enemy ahead. Then they came in from behind us. They rushed us. We must have been outnumbered three to one. It would have been suicidal to try to fight them off. Anyway, they marched us north. We picked up a couple of other groups of Americans. Must have been a hundred of us in all. We walked for four days north. You may remember our battalion's objective was the Yalu. Well, I made it. They finally herded us into a camp overlooking the river."

"Did you spend the rest of the war there?"

"No. We were there about a year, and then they moved us to another camp somewhere to the west."

"I've read about those camps."

"Let me tell you this. Whatever you've read can't begin to give you the picture. Food was barely enough to keep a human alive, and it wasn't enough for many. They died around us all the time. In the winter we buried twenty or thirty every morning in the frozen ground. I don't know how I made it."

"Did you ever see any of our men?"

"I thought I saw a handful of the enlisted men, but I'm not sure. Otherwise, there wasn't anybody I knew."

He went on to say that he came out in the general POW exchange after the armistice and went back home to Phoenix. He resumed work for his family's construction business, but his health was never the same. He worked only part-time and retired after a few years.

Agnes interrupted and said, "Gene, if you want to see some of the exhibits before the ceremony, we'd better get started."

"OK," Tompkins said, struggling to his feet. "Winston, this is something, isn't it? You and I may well be the only survivors of all the Second Battalion officers."

"You're the only man from Kunu-ri I've ever run into in all these forty-four years, maybe the only one I'll ever see. It's almost weird, unreal. We're dealing with ghosts."

"It's got to be a small and diminishing club. Getting downright exclusive."

They exchanged addresses and said they would try to keep in touch. As they shook hands and parted, John had the odd sensation of being for a moment connected with his distant past, of touching a living link to another time and place, to another John Winston, to an experience he did not expect to have again on this earth.

The crowd had now swelled still more, and it was pushing toward the site of the ceremony. John fell in with them and moved along. He was struck with the contrast between this crowd and gatherings of Vietnam veterans he had often seen on television. Here no one was in old army uniforms. There was no sullenness, no looks of put-upon victims, no air of protest, no signs of drugs, no deliberately unwashed types, and few beards. He still couldn't appreciate the air of high celebration. For him, the pathos of the occasion was overwhelming.

He stretched out on the grass along with the vast throng to listen over loudspeakers and watch the proceedings on giant screens erected behind the seats for dignitaries and special guests. The sun beat down relentlessly. He took another bottle of water from a strolling distributor, his fourth so far. It was approaching 3 P.M., and the temperature was now in the high nineties with humidity to match. If someone had dumped several buckets of water on him, he would not have been wetter. Near him he saw two limp men being carried out horizontally to the first-aid tent.

The band was playing the moving strains of the Korean national anthem. "Until the East Sea's waves are dry, and Paek-Tu-San worn away, God watch o'er our land forever, our Korea set free . . ." Then came the "Star-Spangled Banner," followed by a chaplain's invocation: "Almighty God . . . grant to them who served an abiding peace, a holy hope, and a blessed remembrance."

The chaplain's words caused John's mind to drift far away, back into the long line of men moving northward on foot through the chopped-up hills and valleys on the clear cold day after Thanksgiving, men grousing and complaining yet optimistic over reaching the Yalu and ending the war by Christmas, men marching unknowingly into the Chinese maw and to their doom. He thought of all the mothers and fathers and wives and children of those lost men. Were any of them here today?

Vice President Gore had spoken, and now the president of the Republic of Korea was delivering a message in Korean. When he finished, another Korean stood and gave an English translation. "The sacrifices of the Korean War veterans to defend freedom and peace were not in vain. . . . The free world's participation in the Korean War, its first resolute and effective action to stem the expansion of communism, changed the course of history. In this sense I would say that the Korean War was the war that heralded the collapse of the Berlin Wall and the demise of communism." Loud applause.

Now President Clinton was speaking. "They set a standard of courage that may be equaled but will never be surpassed in the annals of American combat. . . . Thousands of Americans who were lost in Korea to this day have never been accounted for. Today I urge the leaders of North Korea to work with us to resolve those cases." Prolonged applause and shouts. The president asked for a moment of silence to honor all those who lost their lives in the war.

John's thoughts were filled with images of his platoon sergeants: Sergeant Sewinski, ripped open by a burp gun on Hill 274, and Sergeant Alton, lost on Hill 1080. There was Corp. Robert Donovan, who had escaped from the Chinese with him only to be killed in the half-track. And then he saw himself with Capt. Bruce Waller, both of them grimy and torn at the end of that unforgettable day on top of Hill 969, half their men left below, either dead or wounded. Lifted into some higher emotional realm, he was now oblivious to the heat and perspiration.

From this distance all those lost men in Baker and Fox companies seemed so young. How much time had passed over his generation! Lines of his favorite First World War poem ran through his thoughts:

> They shall not grow old,
> as we that are left
> grow old:
> Age shall not weary them, nor the years
> condemn.
> At the going down of the sun and in the
> morning,
> We will remember them.

The president's voice came back into his hearing. "The larger conflict of the Cold War had only begun. It would take four decades more to win. In a struggle so long and consuming, perhaps it is not surprising that too many lost sight of the importance of Korea. But now we know, with the benefit of history, that those of you that served, and the families who stood behind you, laid the foundations for one of the greatest triumphs in the history of human freedom. By sending the clear message that America had not defeated fascism to see communism prevail, you put the free world on the road to victory in the Cold War. That is your enduring contribution. . . ."

When the president concluded, a female soloist with a powerful voice gave forth with "America, America, God shed his Grace on thee. And crown thy good with brotherhood from sea to shining sea," movingly stringing out the last half-dozen words. She followed with a maximum-volume rendition of "God Bless America."

Immediately, a formation of helicopters flew low overhead, setting up a din of chopping sounds. They were followed by waves of jet fighters. They thundered in from the east along the Mall, one after the other, coming in low, their unearthly roar drowning out all else. It was like an air strike, and John half-expected to see tracers streaking out ahead and orange plumes of napalm billowing up in their wake as they shot across the Potomac and over Arlington Cemetery.

It was all over. He was physically and emotionally drained. He wanted to see the memorial itself, but the crush of the crowds was overwhelming, and he was hot and sopping wet. He would come back in the morning. For now, he wanted nothing but a cool hotel room and a good shower. Except in Korea, he had never looked forward more to a shower.

The eastern sky was lightening behind the Capitol dome as John walked across the dewy grass stretching from the Lincoln Memorial toward Independence Avenue. An overnight thunderstorm had broken the heat, and the morning was fresh and almost cool. He had the world nearly to himself. Traffic on the streets was light, and he saw only a few distant human beings as he approached the newly dedicated memorial.

Then in the half-light he saw them—the nineteen figures, sculptured in steel, soldiers advancing up a slope. He moved closer.

The realism was overpowering. They could be real men, like

dozens of men he had known and commanded, carrying rifles and carbines—there was a radioman too, with antennae—wearing steel helmets and ponchos, spread out irregularly in combat formation, moving out at dawn for the attack. He almost called out to them. "Keep moving. Follow me!" Under their helmets he saw faces he remembered, faces etched with fatigue and determination.

As he stood in the quiet dawn, thinking of those men who would never be coming back, tears began to flow freely.

He pulled a handkerchief from his pocket, dried his cheeks, and dabbed his eyes, thankful that the place was deserted. He knew then that he would never forget Korea, that indeed he didn't want to forget, that he had an obligation not to forget.

Suddenly, he thought he heard his name being called, distantly and softly. He stood still. No, he must have imagined it. But then he heard it again, quiet but unmistakable. "John." It came from behind in a low, tentative-sounding female voice. "John Winston."

He turned around. There, standing a dozen feet away, in the dawning light, was a woman in a sleeveless summer dress. It took him only a second or two to recognize the swept-back auburn hair and well-remembered face.

For several silent moments, he stared at her. Then in a hushed voice he asked, "Henny?"

"Yes. It's Henny." There was that slightly husky Charleston accent he had found so appealing.

He moved toward her, and she came forward to meet him. He took both her hands in his. He saw her eyes searching his, eyes filled with sadness. Without thinking, he threw his arms around her waist and pulled her against him. Her arms went around his neck, and they hung together for a long moment.

He released her, and she backed up a step. A tear rolled down her cheek, and he brushed it away. "I was here all day yesterday but never saw you. I knew you must be here somewhere, so I came back."

"I almost didn't come at all."

Her lips parted as though to speak, but she hesitated, searching for words. "Do you remember when I saw you last in the hospital?"

"I could hardly forget it."

"Well, telling you not to come to Charleston was very painful. I wish I'd never done it. I did it to make Mama happy and out of a sense of duty. She was so sick. She died last year. I've wanted to see you ever since, but . . ." She broke off and looked away.

He took her hands again. "I'm sorry to hear about your mother." He paused and smiled faintly. "I can't believe this. It's only by chance that I'm here. And here you are! It's got to be a miracle."

She laughed softly. "I've heard that miracles actually do happen."

After a momentary silence, and feeling a bit awkward, he said, "I was just studying the memorial. Come over and look at these statues."

They strolled around the nineteen figures and walked the length of the long black granite wall with its etchings of men and women and equipment.

"Those statues look so real, and the way they're spread out gives a sense of movement," she said. "The wind seems to be whipping around them."

"That's the way it really was."

They strolled up to the apex, toward the single flagpole, where on a low wall appeared the inscription "Freedom is not free." On an opposite wall was inscribed the price:

> Killed in Action
> U.S.A. 54,246
> U.N. 627,246
>
> Missing
> U.S.A. 8,177
> U.N. 469,267
>
> Prisoners of War
> U.S.A. 7,140
> U.N. 92,770
>
> Wounded
> U.S.A. 103,284
> U.N. 1,060,453

They studied these numbers for a full minute before either spoke. Then she said, very quietly, "I feel like I'm at my father's grave."

On the granite terrace a little farther on they came to the inscription carved into the flat stone:

> Our nation honors her sons and daughters
> who answered the call to defend a land they never knew
> and a people they never met
> 1950 Korea 1953

"You know," John said slowly as he reread the words, "I feel as though I did come to know those people and their land. What it means to say is that we didn't know them before the war."

They walked slowly around the pool of remembrance without talking, taking in the whole setting from different angles.

"I think it's time for a good breakfast," John said. "What do you say?"

She smiled. "Sounds mighty good."

They walked back toward the tent city. Ahead, the tall, peaked shaft of the Washington Monument reflected the first sunlight of the day. As they neared the tents, they caught the music from a memorial service. A female soloist with a voice as powerful as the one at the dedication ceremony was singing "Amazing Grace." They paused to listen. She came to the line he best remembered, belting it out with maximum volume: "Through many dangers, toils, and snares I have already come. . . ." They stood, hearing the rest of the words: "'Tis grace that brought me safe thus far, and grace will lead me home."

They went into the computer tent, to the bank of computers with the KIA data. John punched in the name of Bruce Waller, and when his name and information flashed up on the screen he printed it out. He gave the sheet to Henny and stood by quietly while she read it.

They came out and listened again to the memorial service, still under way. Now a choral group was singing the piece composed especially for the occasion. The massed voices climaxed in the key line, drawing out the words with heightened volume: "Freedom is not! . . . freedom is not! . . . free!"

Henny folded the computer printout and put it in her pocket book. "Time for breakfast," John said. She nodded, and they turned and walked on toward Constitution Avenue.

Epilogue

THE AUTUMN AFTERNOON WAS SUNNY AND MILD. Henny called it a day of wine and roses—one of Charleston's best, she said.

Guests were arriving by twos and threes at the main front of the Citadel chapel. Far across the parade ground, the long line of barracks, topped by their battlements, stood out under the clear blue sky. At the chapel entrance, two cadets in full dress were on duty to serve as ushers. In their high-necked gray blouses, white gloves, red sashes, and standing appropriately erect, they presented a rather dashing appearance.

They had planned a small, simple wedding. Only sixty guests had been invited, family and close friends. They would have no attendants. The rector of St. Michael's Church would perform the ceremony. The reception would be at her house on Meeting Street. For their honeymoon, they would spend a week on Barbados.

As the guests were ushered down the aisle to the front pews, the organ played a mixture of classical and modern pieces selected by Henny. There was to be no procession. When the appointed hour of five arrived, the organ broke into the "Trumpet Voluntary."

From the side of the chapel, near the front, the rector of St. Michael's emerged, resplendent in clerical raiment, followed by John and Henny, walking side by side. He wore a three-button navy blue suit with vest. She wore an orchid corsage on an emerald green dress that set off her dramatically swept-back auburn hair.

The organ stopped, and the rector began intoning the marriage

ritual, proclaiming that they were gathered in the sight of God and
this company to unite this man and this woman in holy matrimony.

John was surprised to find himself nervous. This is ridiculous, he
thought, for a man of my age. Nervousness is for young first-timers.
He had trouble paying attention to the rector's words and prayers.
His mind wandered.

He was in the dim light of a bunker, seated on an ammunition
crate. Bruce Waller was splashing I.W. Harper into their canteen cups
and then they were clicking them together and he was saying,
"Here's to Henrietta Montrose Waller." Forty-four years ago—could
it be?

The rector's voice broke through, asking John to face Henny and
repeat the vow. He rallied and spoke in his best courtroom voice. "I,
John, take you, Henrietta, to be my wife, to have and to hold from
this day forward, for better or for worse, for richer, for poorer, in sickness and in health, to love and to cherish, until we are parted by
death."

Then it was Henny's turn. "I, Henrietta, take you, John, to be my
husband. . . ." She spoke in her soft, slightly husky voice that he
found so entrancing. He looked deep into her eyes, and as her words
rolled on he felt chill bumps sweep over him, and he knew that he
truly loved this woman.

High above, the colors of the great stained-glass window glowed in
the late afternoon light. "To the Glory of God and in memory of
The Citadel's patriot dead . . ." He was transfixed by the thought
that they were standing at the exact spot where Nancy and Bruce
Waller had stood and said these same words, made the same vows,
looked at the same stained-glass window a year before Henny was
born.

They exchanged rings, and there were more prayers and words. In
stentorian tones, the rector finally pronounced them husband and
wife. "Those whom God hath joined together, let no one put asun-
der."

Then, as though speaking to the uttermost parts of the earth, he
intoned: "God the Father, God the Son, God the Holy Spirit, bless,
preserve, and keep you. The Lord mercifully with his favor look
upon you and fill you with all spiritual benediction and grace, that
you may faithfully live together in this life and in the age to come

have life everlasting. Amen."

The organ burst forth with "Joyful, Joyful, We Adore Thee," and the soaring notes of Beethoven's Ninth Symphony filled the vastness of the chapel. John and Henny turned and walked forward to greet the guests, who spilled out of the pews, congratulating and hugging them, all now aglow with smiles.

Becky took him by the arm. "I see you're enjoying eating words again."

He laughed and said, "I must be getting used to it."

Carter Gordon, down from Richmond, jostled against John and mumbled whimsically in his ear, "This is your best proceeding yet. Beats a court-martial and committee hearing."

"And I handled it myself! Didn't have to call on you for help."

Laughing and raising her voice above the organ, Henny said, "Why are we all standing around here? Let's move on to Meeting Street."

Yes, move on indeed, thought John Winston, slipping Henny's soft, warm hand into his, move on with life renewed, move on into the long evening of life. Not for years had he felt such a sense of love and joy and peace.